THE CIRCUS OF THE DAMNED

DEAL WITH A DEVIL SERIES

CORNELIA GREY

RIPTIDE
PUBLISHING

Riptide Publishing
PO Box 6652
Hillsborough, NJ 08844
www.riptidepublishing.com

The Circus of the Damned

Cover Art by Kanaxa, www.kanaxa.com
Editor: Danielle Poiesz
Layout: L.C. Chase, www.lcchase.com/design.htm

ISBN: 978-1-62649-166-3

First edition
November, 2014

Also available in ebook:
ISBN: 978-1-62649-165-6

THE CIRCUS OF THE DAMNED

OF THE DAMNED

DEAL WITH A DEVIL SERIES

CORNELIA GREY

RIPTIDE
PUBLISHING

To my grandmothers, Annita and Palmina,
for their constant, loving support
and for setting an amazing example.

TABLE OF
CONTENTS

CHAPTER 1

For the best part of three days, Gilbert Blake sat inside the dark, dank pub. The thin, dirty rain that drenched the dark brick walls of the city, its bowels of iron pipes and cramped alleys, and the pub's wooden sign hadn't stopped in all that time. The sign was purple—or it looked like it had been once upon a time—and missing so many letters it was impossible to guess what the pub's name had been. Gilbert hadn't cared; he'd just entered and stuck around.

The pub was a crammed underground hole without a single window, the atmosphere rank and suffocating. A narrow wooden door opened on steep iron stairs, encrusted with years' worth of mud and grease. Drunken patrons yelled and drank and lay passed out in corners, after wasting entire paychecks on dice and cards. In the sawdust-covered pit, bloodstained by a hundred fistfights, a fellow was turning the handle of a potbellied instrument that sounded like a choir of skinned cats.

"So, ready to pick a card, mate? My balls are shriveling up over here," Gilbert scoffed.

His blond hair and beard were a wild mess, and a tumbler of savage homemade vodka sat by his elbow. He was beyond drunk and about to land the hit that would keep him and Emilia fed for a month. He couldn't remember the last time he'd slept or eaten, or even gotten up to take a piss, but he was sprawled like a king on his chair, cards in hand and a smirk firmly planted on his lips. A small crowd surrounded him, watching his every move. His opponent was sweating in a ripped shirt and vest, combing his fingers over and over through his long, brown beard.

Gilbert couldn't remember exactly when they had started that particular game. Could have been a couple of glasses ago, could have been five bottles. Emilia was asleep, nestled in his scarf, dead to the world, her little body curled in a warm, furry ball against his neck, and there was a considerable pile of cash stacked in the middle of the table. Bills and coins, a golden ring, some brightly colored currency from some country he didn't know, a lone ruby earring, and what looked suspiciously like a gold tooth that had been ripped out of somebody's jaw.

Gilbert waved a deck of fanned-out cards under the man's nose. He'd forgotten the fellow's name, or maybe hadn't even bothered to ask it. He chugged back the last of his vodka and decided to call him Bristlesprout.

With a suspicious glance and a grunt, Bristlesprout carefully selected a card and yanked it out, slapped it against the table, and covered it with a ham-sized hand while shooting threatening looks all around, as if daring the others to steal it from him.

"Anyone tries to help this wanker, I'm gonna break your fingers," he warned, looking at the ragtag crowd through bloodshot eyes. The faint of heart took a step back. Everyone else pushed even closer. "I know somebody's working with him."

Gilbert smiled and waved his hand over his glass, which swiftly filled back up. Everyone's eyes were on the glittering pile of coins, though, so only a skinny drunkard rubbed his eyes in disbelief, then went in search of a stiffer drink. He knew better than to call out the tall, muscular man with the seemingly magic powers.

Bristle had his reasons to be suspicious. Gilbert had already materialized in his own hand the cards that the man had hidden in his pocket, his beard, and most notably, the crack of his ass. Oh, he'd given the fellow some breathing room too. No gambler would bet against someone who always won. Winning every time wasn't the goal, and neither was impressing the bystanders. The goal was coaxing more and more cash out of the pockets of his adversaries, letting them win occasionally to push them to raise the stakes, then making them slowly drop out one by one with swift moves, apparently strokes of blind luck—until he was left with one poor bastard drunk enough and gullible enough to empty his pockets on the table. In this case, his new friend Bristlesprout.

Gilbert had purposefully botched the last two tricks, failing to guess the card that Bristle had creatively hidden in his underpants—it had been the three of spades, and Gilbert would do without that card from now on, thank you very much—and spectacularly embarrassing himself when trying to make a coin disappear in his palm and instead causing a deluge of quarters to fall from his cuff. That one had brought a roar of laughter from the crowd, convincing everyone that the failed magician was by now too drunk for his own good and was just about ready to be plucked like a chicken.

Bristlesprout had fallen for it like a charm. Seeing his chance, he'd pushed all his winnings forward, even producing that golden tooth to add to the considerable pile. Gilbert had made a big scene of rummaging in the pockets of his black leather jacket, sighing and complaining and commiserating his bad luck, looking like he could barely scrape together the amount.

Oh, he could look like a miserable loser when he wanted to. It was a remarkable talent.

"Now, take this." Gilbert snapped his fingers under the table, and a black crayon materialized out of thin air. Then he handed it to Bristlesprout. "Write something on the card. Or draw, I don't care. You can turn it over, 'tis not a guessing game this time."

Shooting him a dark glance, Bristle turned the card over—it was the queen of hearts—and snatched the crayon from Gilbert's hand. "The fuck you playing at, crook?" He grunted. "I wanna know exactly what stupid trick you're gonna botch this time. I don't want no fucking cheating at my table, understand?"

A loud screech came from the pit, attracting everyone's attention. The disheveled musician was being carried away by the neck by an impressively large man wearing an expensive-looking black suit with a bright-purple band around one arm. The musician's wooden instrument lay abandoned on the ground. As everyone watched in silence, four other giant men crossed the room, shooting threatening glances at the patrons while surrounding a much shorter, older fellow. This one wore a bright-purple suit and top hat that were rather insulting to the eye.

God damn it. Gilbert followed the man with his gaze, a heavy feeling sinking in his stomach. This was the last thing he needed: Count Reuben himself, owner of the dump and pretty much every other shithole in town. The man controlled a good half of Shadowsea's less-than-legal activities and was never seen without his personal guard, a cohort of murderers and henchmen whose favorite activity was stomping people to a pulp and tossing them in the river.

Gilbert examined them in mild apprehension as the pub's staff stumbled over themselves, running around to set out a fancy dining table for Reuben in the bloodstained pit. His guards' expensive suits were ill fit to their bodies, bulging with muscles, and telltale lumps revealed a knife here, a baton there. Their purple armbands and hatbands now dotted the room.

Gilbert downed his vodka. *Damn.* He hadn't planned on having to deal with so many guards. They were already gravitating toward the table—the amount of money strewn over it wouldn't escape them even in the dark. Hell, they could probably *smell* it. Oh, Reuben would be *pissed* that someone was gambling in his den without giving him a cut.

But Gilbert couldn't leave; he couldn't give up now. Not after he'd worked so hard, not when he was *this close* . . .

No. He had to finish this and then just get out. Fast.

He straightened his broad, muscular shoulders and leaned back into the chair with a sharp smile. "Where were we? Oh, right, my friend, our pleasant game. Now, you're going to mark that card. Anything you want. Then you're going to hide it, destroy it, dispatch it overseas via carrier pigeon, I don't fucking care. And I—" He brought his hand to his chest in a theatrical gesture. "—I, the great Gilbert Blake, will bring it back and materialize it in front of your very eyes."

The crowd murmured with comments and a few derisive snorts here and there. Gilbert had discovered that his boasting speeches made folks see him as an even bigger loser, rather than impressing them. That was fine by him. He wasn't there to preserve dignity or gain respect; it was cold, hard cash he was after.

Bristlesprout thought it over for a moment. "All right. But on one condition," he finally said, his eyes gleaming with glee. "I want your hands flat on the table the entire time. For everyone to see. Just wanna make sure you're not copying my stuff on another of your shitty cards."

Gilbert swallowed a mocking grin and carefully schooled his features to give off a hint of fear and nervousness, as if his trick had been spoiled. "But—"

"I'm not finished," Bristle interrupted. "I want everyone on your side of the table to take a step back. Or three. I don't want anyone near you, nobody who can slip you a card or write on it for you or some shit. I want the fucking desert around you, you got it?"

"B-but I . . ." Gilbert stammered, looking around to gather sympathy from the spectators, eyes skimming over a dozen purple spots at least. *Really*, he thought smugly, *I should have taken to the stage, wooed crowds in theaters all over the country*. It was sheer talent, that's what it was. "I didn't say that. Surely, a magician can't be asked to . . ."

"Well, if you want to back out . . ." Bristlesprout spread his arms to embrace the pile of bills and coins on the table. "Of course, that means the jackpot goes to me. But if that's what you want . . . I'm going to have to take all this money, then."

Oh, hell *yes*. He'd fallen for it so hard that Gilbert could have gotten him to bet his fucking balls, too. Time to make his final move and *crush* him.

Gilbert swallowed, then looked longingly at the money. Emilia stirred against his neck, sniffling, and her long whiskers tickled his skin. "I guess that's fine." Reluctantly, he brought his hands down on the table. "The hands thing, I mean. And the people. Looks like I don't have a choice, do I?"

Under Bristlesprout's severe gaze, everyone on Gilbert's side shuffled back, whispering and pushing and elbowing each other. Only the men in purple didn't budge, but they didn't come closer, either. Bristle smiled then, like a cat that'd found an unattended bird's nest and was sharpening his claws for the buffet of the year. He didn't deign to respond, and he bent his head and started drawing something on the card with great care, the tip of his tongue poking out from his mouth. When he was done, he proudly lifted the card and turned it left and right to show everyone a crude rendition of a cock and a pair of oversized balls pointed at the mouth of the poor queen of hearts.

"That's . . . quite the piece of art." Gilbert was about to slap his own forehead in utter despair for the human race, then remembered himself and left his hands lying on the table. "Now make the card disappear."

"Oh, I intend to," Bristlesprout assured him, smug smile still firmly in place.

And he really made an effort. He ripped the card in two, then four. He dug in his pockets and produced a gnarled box of matches and lit one after a couple of attempts. As the stench of sulfur hovered over the table, Bristle carefully selected two card pieces and held them over the flame, watching as they blackened and curled up and finally turned to ash, slowly consumed by the fire. He let the border go with a muffled curse as the flame brushed his fingertips, and the final bits turned to ash on the table. Once that was done, he brushed away the ashes, satisfied, and turned his attention to the other two pieces.

Gilbert saw the moment the idea struck the man. Looking, if possible, even smugger than before, Bristlesprout ripped what was left of the card to minute shreds, then shoved the pieces in his mouth. He grabbed his glass, an inch of cheap rum at the bottom, and tossed it all back, swallowing in one gulp. He made a big show of smacking his lips, then burped loudly and settled back in his chair.

"Can't wait to see how you're gonna get *that* back, magician." He curled his lips to tongue at his not-very-clean teeth. He dug a thick, dirty knife out of his belt and picked his teeth with it, removing one single shred of spit-soaked card. "There, I'm gonna help you out. You can have this," he said, flicking the sodden piece at Gilbert.

The wet bit of card stuck to his cheek. People laughed, Bristlesprout louder than anyone.

Something went dark in Gilbert's mind, as though a shutter was abruptly slammed down. Oh, he was a jolly fellow for the most part, but his temper was a little . . . volatile. People who had known him for a while learned that soon enough, learned to recognize when the thunderstorm was rumbling in and flee. But it had been a long, long time since he'd stuck around long enough for someone to get to know him.

So nobody noticed the dark clouds gathering behind his brow, nobody saw how his shoulders stiffened and his strong arms tensed, how his hands turned to claws where they rested on the table. Only Emilia stirred against his neck, not quite waking up, but her light mouse sleep disturbed nonetheless. That little brown mouse had been his only faithful companion for years and had saved his life more than a few times. *She* knew him. Even asleep, she could tell he was getting worked up.

"You seem determined to make my life difficult," Gilbert said, not quite able to contain the cruel curl of his lip. Bristle didn't even notice. He was already celebrating, busy trying to calculate how much he'd just won and eyeing ladies in the crowd that might have been impressed by his wit. "You had a couple of pretty good ideas there."

And they really had been good ideas. Any third-rate illusionist would be utterly screwed. Without an accomplice to slip him a card with a copy of the dick Bristlesprout had so artistically drawn, no sleight of hand would bring back the original card, so utterly and disgustingly destroyed.

Of course, things were a hell of a lot different when you were playing against an *actual* magician.

Very slowly, Gilbert lifted his hand, turning it left and right to show everyone it was empty, fingers spread and sleeve pulled back to reveal his wrist, his forearm. Then he slapped the hand down on the tabletop.

He stared at it and focused. His palm grew warm and, under it, he started to feel a hard, smooth surface, very different from the rough, splintery wooden table. Gilbert felt the surface grow and stretch and, as his eyes bore into the back of his hand, he could almost *see* it—the queen of hearts growing under his palm, just as he pictured it in his mind, down to the last detail, to the hastily scrawled penis.

Then he abruptly lifted his hand, and everyone around the table shouted.

He leaned peacefully back into his chair, letting the smug grin return to his lips, and nonchalantly lifted his hand to pick away the bit of chewed card stuck to his cheek. With his fingertip, he placed it on the lower-right corner of the newly formed card, where he'd left a tiny bit missing. He liked things done well.

People were leaning close and squabbling over the card, ripping it from one another's hands, talking and yelling. A toothless man tried to gnaw on the card with his bare gums. The men in purple were exchanging meaningful glances across the room, and Gilbert knew his time was running out. He had to wrap things up and take his leave.

"How'd he do it? Man, how the fuck did he do it?"

"No, I can't believe it. Lemme touch it. Hey, stop hogging—"

"The fucking devil's helping him. No other way. The devil himself, I tell you . . ."

The only person perfectly quiet in the midst of all the excitement was Bristlesprout himself. He had gone very pale and was sitting very still, hands limp on the table, looking at the smears of ash with a somewhat-dazed air. He lifted his gaze to the card and, as a tattooed lady waved it around, snatched it from her hand and peered at it closely.

Gilbert leaned forward and sunk both hands into the pile of money. He'd been waiting long enough to tuck in. Let Bristle think about it all he pleased.

Oh, that felt good, holding the cold coins and crumpled bills between his fingers. It would keep them fed for a while, him and Emilia. Might even be enough to splurge and buy passage on one of the underground trains toward the coast, to someplace warmer. He would travel in style for once instead of screwing up his spine hobbling along on a goat cart. And it was time to blow this dump of a town. It was burned, now, anyway. Rumors spread fast, and no one else would play against him after tonight.

That was the only downside of the job, really, of working the pubs and gambling holes like he did—one trick and the whole city was useless to him. These folks had very long memories when it came to losing money. That was why his one trick had to be a damn good one: it was the only shot he got, and it had to be worth it.

Truth be told, it usually was, he mused, sweeping coins and rings in his deep pockets, then folding a handful of bills and tucking it in the inside pocket of his leather jacket. He brushed his fingers above the seam and it vanished—the pocket was no more, just a smooth patch of lining. A life of sleepless nights on the streets had given him a lot of time and motivation to cultivate his natural talents, especially when his particular gift could earn him a bed and a warm meal. But with this one, he'd really aced it. And now that he'd been spotted by Reuben and his watchdogs, in addition to the big scene he'd made, he wouldn't be back here for a long, long while. Provided he didn't end up in the river instead, courtesy of the count's men. They didn't appreciate people causing trouble or failing to pay up a cut, let alone at the same time.

As he tucked in for the last handful of coins, a large, burly hand clamped down on his wrist, pinning it to the table.

"How the fuck'd you do it?" Bristlesprout growled, staring at him with bloodshot and vaguely crazed eyes. They had obviously been playing for longer than Gilbert had thought, and most importantly, had been drinking longer than he'd thought, and the man was suffering from the blow.

Gilbert, not so much, not after that last trick. Using magic was like a peaceful daze floating through his veins, which made him happy and sedated. Or in short, high as hell. When using magic for extended periods of time, he tended to forget a lot of things. Once he'd been at it for a week nonstop, until he'd been shaking and nearly incoherent and had passed out on the floor of a brothel. He'd woken up stripped of all his possessions and feeling as though he'd been chewed up and spat out by an elephant. He was no fool; he knew he'd nearly killed himself. He'd been careful, after that.

Or as careful as he could muster, anyway.

"Told you, man. I'm a magician," he replied, with what could have been a smile but was really just him baring his teeth. He closed his fist and let his wrist grow warmer until it burned so hot that Bristle had to yank his hand back. Gilbert picked up the ruby ring and twirled it in his palm, then made it disappear. He snapped his fingers. (Yeah, maybe he was slightly high on it still. But man, it felt so fucking *good*.) "And I never reveal my secrets."

"The fuck you are. The *fuck*." The large, disheveled man in front of him was growing agitated, his pallor quickly turning to a violent flush, his eyes glassy with alcohol and anger. Gilbert saw the tension in Bristle's muscles, saw the way he was puffing out his chest and squaring his shoulders, rearing up for a fight, and he knew how this was going to end. If the sudden quiet and the watchful eyes surrounding them were any indicator, everyone knew. "You're a cheat, that's what you are. A fucking, filthy cheat."

Gilbert cast a quick glance around. Reuben's men were closing in, faster now that they risked never getting their hands on part of the money if he got away. His chances of getting out of this with minimal fuss were dwindling fast. And Gilbert was fucking angry. He was tired and intoxicated; he'd been working his ass off for three days, and now it would all be ruined because of this big, drunken moron. And damn his bad luck that Shadowsea's most infamous slumlord just *had* to be there.

Gilbert was pissed that he couldn't even remember the last time he'd slept in an actual bed, let alone had clean sheets. Pissed at the fucking rain that never stopped, at the endless stream of suffocating cities that made up his entire life. Pissed that this was all he had to look forward to: cheap tricks and scams in filthy pubs. Pissed because if Reuben's men beat him to a bloody pulp out back, there would be no one to mourn him save for a little brown mouse—not a friend, not a lover, not even a mother because nobody wanted a cursed son. And he was pissed, most of all, at Bristlesprout's livid, sweaty face.

Gilbert narrowed his eyes. "If I were you, I'd shut up now."

The man was too far gone; he probably hadn't even heard. "A fucking, filthy cheat, that's it. I'm not falling for that. You fucking wanker. I'm not gonna let you take my money, you goddamn cocksucker, you *freak*—"

He fell silent with a strangled sound. He brought his hand to his throat, choking loudly as he began to shake. Growing frantic, he clawed at his skin and heaved, lurching forward as if he was going to puke his guts out. Men and women yelled, shoving and climbing over one another to get out of the way. Bristle's face was nothing short of purple now. He was sweating buckets, rolling his wide, frantic eyes as he stumbled, toppling the table over with a loud crash, coins spilling all over the floor. The confusion increased as people dove in to get their hands on what little money was left, elbowing the livid Bristle as he fell to his knees, hands around his neck. The men in purple hesitated, taken aback, looking at their boss for orders. Out of the corner of his eye, Gilbert glimpsed Reuben standing up, observing the situation.

Through it all, Gilbert remained seated, legs spread and arms folded—straight-backed and perfectly still, like a merciless king—his gray, ice-cold eyes fixed on the man crawling on the floor at his feet. He was clenching his fist, slowly, inch after agonizing inch, observing the effect it was having. Oh, Bristle would be just fine . . . more or less. But he would think twice about insulting a magician in the future.

Something moved against his neck. Emilia was now poking out from his scarf, her delicate nose quivering as she sniffed the air. She caught on to what was happening soon enough and scuttled up to bite

Gilbert's ear, not too hard but sending him a clear message. *Just stop, you moron.* He should follow her advice, he really should—that mouse was smarter than he was by a long shot; she'd proved it time and time again. But it was too late now. The show was on.

Bristlesprout was on his hands and knees, his purple face turning blue, drooling, heaving, choking as if he was fucking dying, and a couple of people had mustered enough interest to be worried. Others were skirting around the man, still busy collecting money but trying to be a tad more discreet about it. Not that anyone was doing anything about it; they were just hanging around looking at Bristle and poking him in the side with the tip of their boots.

"D'you think he's dying?"

"His ticker's given out, I tell you."

"Bet he drops dead within the minute."

"Two minutes! Five quids down."

Old habits die hard. Gilbert understood, but nobody was going to win the bet, he could promise that.

It was time for the grand finale, before folks started losing interest. Gilbert spread his fingers out in a fluid movement and Bristlesprout heaved with a horrifying hurling noise. His neck swelled monstrously, and something way too big and covered in brown feathers emerged from his unnaturally wide mouth with a sickening, sucking noise. The man tensed, every muscle shaking, his neck and face bright red as, with a final push and a gagging sound, a decent-sized hen tumbled from his mouth and onto the floor, covered in drool. The bird shook herself, looking confused and more than a little offended, then ruffled her feathers with disdain and set off to investigate the crumbs under a table.

The silence was nothing short of deafening.

It was only broken by the hen's disdainful clucking and the sound of Bristlesprout throwing up on the floor, spreading the stench of alcohol and bile in the already-stinking pub. Yet, people were too shocked to even back off. They no longer know where to look between the man, the hen, and the magician still calmly sitting on his cheap throne.

Bristlesprout lay gasping on the floor, glancing up at Gilbert with a dazed, haunted look on his face, suddenly stone-cold sober, like he'd never been so terrified in his life. Which he probably hadn't. He wasn't going to cause any more trouble, Gilbert knew. In fact, he was probably going to spend the next month holed up in a room somewhere, consuming vast amounts of alcohol while trying to convince himself none of it had ever happened. Having a chicken crawl out of your throat would do that to a fellow.

Before Gilbert could even think about backing off and possibly out, a burly hand clasped his arm. One of the men in the black suits meaningfully tilted his head, the purple silk on his hat catching the light. He had a mouth of foul, rotten teeth and breath that could knock a donkey over from a mile away, at least. Gilbert would think of him as Skunktongue. And Skunktongue was pointing at a narrow open door near the fighting pit, leading to a dark back room that promised nothing good.

"Count Reuben was very . . . *impressed* by your show," the man said, doing nothing to conceal the threat in his voice. "He would like to speak to you in private. *Now*."

The hand on Gilbert's arm may as well have been an iron grip. There was no way to flee, Gilbert realized with a detached calm as he contemplated his options. He had the feeling that once he got back there . . . he wouldn't be coming out anytime soon.

So he stood up and broke Skunktongue's nose with a punch.

The room blew up in a matter of instants. Among crashes, shouts, and curses, punches flew, the pent-up energy of the place finally breaking free like a dynamite explosion. Gilbert didn't waste time thinking and promptly ducked to avoid a chair somebody swung at him, which crashed into the stomach of a gray-haired fellow, sending him diving into the shouting crowd. Underground gambling dens were volatile at the best of times, let alone after a guy had just thrown up a live chicken. This night, the place was nothing short of a fucking barrel of black powder, and Gilbert had lit the match and tossed it right in.

Gilbert couldn't tell who was lurching at whom or why, so he dove into the crowd, trying to elbow his way toward the exit. *Out. Out. Out.* It was his only chance to get away from there.

He blocked a blow with his elbow then proceeded to smash the nose of a redheaded, spidery man, who fell back on a table, sending all the drinks piled on it crashing to the ground. Two large, very unhappy Chinese men lifted the redhead with a growl and tossed him into the crowd, bringing down three random fellows, then lurched toward Gilbert.

He ducked fast, and the two men crashed against two women who sported aviator helmets and were busy choking the daylights out of each other. The four toppled with assorted curses, getting in the way of two Purple Men trying to shove their way through the crowd—and just in time to make way for a flying chair that caught Gilbert on the shoulder, throwing him off balance.

Something small and sharp sank into his other shoulder—teeth. Emilia was very much unhappy about the situation and determined to let him know.

"Sorry," he muttered, landing on his knees and rolling forward to avoid a kick. He sprang up to grab the purple-circled arm already reaching for him. Gilbert held the man in place as he landed three rapid punches to the stomach, then kicked him away to be promptly swallowed by the roaring crowd. In the brief instant when the tangle of bodies parted to absorb the fellow, Gilbert glimpsed Bristlesprout crawling toward a corner of the pub, muttering to himself. For a split second, Gilbert almost felt sorry for him. Then someone punched Gilbert in the face.

Pain exploded in his nose, shooting through his skull. He cupped his hand over it, groaning as his fingers were coated in warm blood. A familiar screech came from the pit. Somebody had lifted up the musician's discarded instrument and was swinging it around like an oversized club. The tattooed lady, Gilbert saw before she leaped from the pit with a gleeful war cry and smashed the thing on somebody's head . . .

A giant hand closed around Gilbert's neck and yanked him around. He found himself face-to-bleeding-face with Skunktongue, who sported even fewer teeth than before, and whose mouth and chin were covered in spit and blood. "Gotcha, magician," he growled, spraying blood on Gilbert's face and lifting a fist big enough to crush Gilbert's skull like an eggshell. "You're coming with me, now. But first, I'm going to smash all of your— *Ow!*"

The man dropped him and staggered back, screeching, arms waving frantically. Emilia had leaped right onto Skunktongue's face, sinking her teeth into his cheek. By the time he understood what was happening and threw a wild punch at his own face, Emilia had gracefully jumped off, swiftly disappearing into the crowd. Skunk destroyed his own nose and collapsed to the ground like a wet rag.

Oh, Emilia was pissed off all right. She'd be fine; it wasn't her first brawl—she was just annoyed because she'd been woken from her nap. She hated that. She would find him outside. If he made it out at all, he considered darkly, trying to elbow his way toward the steep stairs. The men in purple were being held back by the brawling crowd, but it was also making it hard for him to reach the—

When the bottle smashed over his head, he heard the crash before he even registered the pain. He stumbled, glass shards cascading down his face and gin soaking his hair, stinging like a motherfucker where his scalp must have been cut open. His knees gave out, and he hit the ground, being shoved and jostled as the fight went on around him. The sea of legs and kicking boots swam before his eyes as he was seized by a sudden bout of nausea that spread from his pounding head all the way to his stomach. The glimpses of purple were getting steadily closer—he couldn't stop now. He dragged himself upright, vaguely aware that passing out on the floor would mean all his ribs would be shattered and quite possibly his skull kicked in, as well.

Man, that wanker had gotten him good. His head was spinning so badly, he could barely keep his balance, let alone use his magic to push his attackers back or cause stuff to drop on their heads, stopping them so he could escape. He wiped his hands over his bloodied eyes to try to see where he was going, wobbling in the general direction of the stairs. But before he could make any progress, a shout rose above the crashing and cursing and yelling: "The magician! Get him! Count Reuben's orders!"

As if a wave had ripped through the room, the crowd surged up and crashed toward him, carrying unwilling participants in its wake. Gilbert cursed, stuffed his hands in his pockets to grab two handfuls of coins and tossed them in the air, a glittering rain falling over the crowd. It was enough to distract them for the few moments he needed to dive toward the narrow metal stairs.

Skunk's now very nasal voice shouted, "He's getting out! Grab him, *grab the bastard*!"

There was a burly guard at the door, except instead of keeping people out, he was now looking down at Gilbert with the definite intention of keeping him *in*—standing tall and broad and ridiculously muscular on the top step. *Fuck it.* Gilbert charged headlong and, as Guardman leaned in to grab him, Gilbert abruptly bent forward, headbutting him right in the groin. The guy folded over on Gilbert's back, so he wrapped his arms around the guard's thighs and simply straightened, heaving him up and over his shoulder, dropping him down the stairs. Guardman toppled down the steps with a sequence of curses and meaty thuds, taking down all of Gilbert's pursuers in the process. That ought to earn him a few moments.

He burst out of the door, boots skidding on slippery cobblestones, and dove into the maze of alleyways before him.

CHAPTER 2

Cold rain streamed down his face, falling from the gray sky as dawn approached. Gilbert stumbled on the uneven cobblestones, the trash scattered on the ground, and his own feet, following the pools of gaslights from the scattered streetlamps. His only chance was to hide somewhere in the maze of bricks—anywhere would do since after half a dozen blind turns he couldn't even tell where the fuck he was. He mostly knew his way around this bloody city, but not when this drunk and running this fast, and certainly not when he was too busy listening for his pursuers to look where the hell he was going.

Skunktongue shouted from somewhere behind him, leading the chase. Forget about the back room, they would clobber him to death right here on the street. He had to keep running, as far as his legs would take him. Which, if the darkness creeping at the corner of his vision was any indicator, was probably not very far.

Skidding around a corner and into another alley, Gilbert barely avoided crashing into bins that stank of dead things and found Emilia running up his leg and around his chest and back to cling once again to his scarf. A sting of relief crossed his aching chest—breathing was growing more painful by the minute—but really, he should have known better than to worry. She had always been smarter than him. Her body was cold and soaking wet against his neck, and she was surely going to sulk at him for a week at least. He'd apologize later, provided he survived, which he was cautiously optimistic about. If only he could find a manhole or some stairs to the roofs; if only his head would stop pounding; if only he could focus, use his magic.

He burst out of the alley and almost ran face-first into roaring fire.

Gilbert couldn't even scream as he felt his eyebrows and beard singe. He threw himself to the side and crashed headlong into someone. They fell together, entwined, landing with a splash in a puddle as someone gurgled a filthy curse and a rain of hard, round objects pelted Gilbert's head and shoulders. It was . . . They were . . . *skulls*, he realized with a start. There were bloody skulls falling from the sky. "What the . . .?"

The scorching fire faded suddenly, as if it had been moved away from him, and somebody spoke. "Humphreys, are you all right?"

"I'm jussst fine. If only this bloody *moron* would get off my arms . . ." another voice replied, coming from somewhere below Gilbert's nose. A strange hissing sound, like a *whoosh* of wind twisted and garbled until it resembled words.

Scrabbling blindly, Gilbert leaned against something thick, smooth, and elastic that twitched and shuddered under his hand. He jerked back, blinking as his vision cleared. He felt more . . . *things* moving beside him, *around* him, like rubber snakes slithering away.

The person rose up before him, and Gilbert stared dumbly, still sprawled in the mud. It wasn't a man. It was . . . God, that bottle to the head must have screwed him up worse than he'd thought because he could *swear* there was a bloody octopus towering above him, wearing a three-piece suit, rumpled and wet but complete with the polished golden chain of a pocket watch. The jacket had four sleeves, a tentacle in each, and two tentacles poked out from each trouser leg, tips pooling elegantly on the ground to keep it—him?—upright. His skin was dark purple, and he looked agitated—if Gilbert correctly read the expression in those big, black slanted eyes. His tentacles twitched nervously as he straightened his suit. Truth be told, had Gilbert been more coherent, he would be pretty agitated too right about now.

"Don't you have a tongue, sssir? You could at leassst apologize."

Dear God, that thing can speak. "Yes. I— You're right. I'm sorry." He shook his head, and the wave of pulsing pain kind of helped him stop thinking about Squidlet over there and focus on more pressing matters. "Right. I . . . need help. Please. If you could . . ."

He couldn't speak clearly. His head was spinning. There was rain and blood in his eyes, and Emilia was squeaking too loudly in his ear. A splash of color caught his attention—a bright-red sign painted on a black, wooden wagon parked just behind the creature. It read, *Circus of the Damned.*

Oh. *Oh.* It was starting to make a little more sense now.

A man stepped forward, getting down on one knee before him. He wore a red jacket with polished brass buttons, and a tall stovepipe hat sat on his long red hair. He had an air of authority about him. *He might be the ringmaster.* And maybe the source of the fire that had nearly burned his face off, given that the man was placing three torches in the ground. He was also quite spectacularly handsome.

Gilbert was stunned for a moment as the man leaned forward to peer at him intently. He had sharp features, a smattering of freckles on his nose and cheeks, and he was staring at Gilbert with the most stunning green eyes he'd ever seen. The vodka and the gin bottle might have something to do with it, as well, because he couldn't recall getting quite so stupid from staring at someone's face before. Ever. Something felt all fluttery in his chest, and he lost his breath for a moment.

The man's brow furrowed as he reached forward, and Gilbert was somehow spellbound at the thought of being touched by him, but then Redhead grabbed him by the collar and gave him a good, hard shake, and the moment crumbled, shattered by the violent hammering in his head.

"Ow, *ow*, fuck. Stop that, my fucking *head*—"

"Clear up, mate. Are you sick? Do you need assistance?" Redhead asked, not rude, but not so kind, either. The illusion crumbled further. For his enchanting face, this fellow was not so charming after all.

"Just leave him," said an annoyed female voice as someone came up behind the ringmaster, leaning forward to look at Gilbert.

He tore his eyes away from the handsome man that currently had his hands on Gilbert and saw a tall woman, her striped, sleeveless shirt revealing the most muscular arms he'd ever laid eyes on. She could have snapped his spine like a twig if she fancied it, and probably without breaking a sweat. Reflexively, Gilbert shot her a bright smile. She had a lovely, rounded face, with carefully arranged black curls and a bright-red flower pinned to her hair. And she most definitely did not seem impressed.

She answered his smile with an eye roll. "He's a drunk, and a sleazy one at that. We have no time to waste with the likes of him. Just leave him on the bloody pavement, and let's move on."

"Drunk or not, we're not about to let a man drown in a puddle in the middle of the street, or"—the ringmaster leaned closer and sniffed, then drew back with a grimace—"in his own vomit, more likely. Mate, how much have you had to drink? You reek like a goddamn distillery."

No, that's the gin bottle that was smashed on my head, Gilbert wanted to protest, but his tongue was tangled in his mouth.

"And look. He's bleeding." The supposed ringmaster grabbed Gilbert's nape and unceremoniously tilted his head down. Redhead's fingers were steady and warm on his skin, which was damp and chill from the rain, and his body reacted to the man's touch, a heated thrill sizzling in his veins.

A yell and a crash came from far too close, abruptly waking him from his stupor. "That goddamn magician, I swear! *Find him!*"

Fuck, they were *still* after him, the relentless bastards. Gilbert had to snap out of it and sort himself out if he didn't want to end up beaten to a bloody pulp in front of Redhead's beautiful green eyes.

"Leave it, that's not going to kill me," Gilbert muttered, grabbing the stranger's arm to push his hand off. He nodded toward the alley behind him. "But the gang of angry drunks that's chasing after me might. Please—" he looked around, then pointed at the black wagon "—hide me in there. I didn't do anything *bad*, all right? It's just a stupid brawl, I swear. Help me, take me with you. I can pay, I . . ."

He trailed off, realizing that the ragtag gang had closed in around him, and everybody was staring. The ringmaster, still kneeling; the lady with her strong, tattooed arms folded and a disapproving frown on her face; the octopus man, worrying his pocket watch with a tentacle; and a willow-thin young woman with black hair and a red-sequin costume. Gilbert shot a frantic glance at the wagon. There was no horse, so Gilbert had no idea how the hell they were moving it, but he didn't have time to care. The only thing he cared about was getting inside it, one way or another.

And it looked like he would have to convince them all if he wanted that to happen.

"Well, that isss quite convenient," Squidlet said, snapping the watch shut and slipping it into his pocket. "Jussst what we needed. Let's grab him and tosss him in the back of the wagon, and we'll be on our merry way."

"Yeah, right. We can't pick up any moron that comes along." Muscles shot him a reproachful look. The flower in her hair trembled as she shook her head. "This is a circus, Humphreys, not a public hospice."

"At this point, I would take a bloody murderer along," Squidlet—or, well, Humphreys—hissed in return, his purple color seeming to darken. Gilbert couldn't quite distinguish the expressions on his face, but he could detect his temper well enough nonetheless. "We've got lesss than half an hour left! I'm this close to breaking into a house and kidnapping sssomeone from their bloody bed if . . ."

Gilbert stared at them. What was the octopus talking about? Who the hell were these people? Kidnapping? Were they murderers? Lunatics? They certainly looked the part. Were they wandering around with their wagon searching for victims?

Oh, whatever. It couldn't be any worse than being beaten to death by an angry mob. He'd take his chances with the circus. He was a magician, an *actual* one, not a sideshow freak. He'd get rid of them in a heartbeat. As soon as his goddamn head stopped *pounding*.

"I'm no murderer," he protested, interrupting Humphreys. It wasn't much to be proud of, especially since he wasn't exactly certain it was true—he may well have killed somebody at some point in his life and hadn't stuck around long enough to find out—but never mind that.

He tried to get up, but his knees refused to comply so he settled for pushing himself to a seat, bracing a hand in the puddle. The shouting was growing louder—they must be on the right track—and there he was, sitting in the pissing rain conversing with a bunch of . . . rather *unusual* individuals who were, apparently, deranged criminals, as well.

Good Lord.

Gilbert was growing more frantic by the minute and so was Emilia, wet and pissed off, gnawing at his earlobe. "And I can help, I promise you that. I'm a magician! Just take me with you to the circus. I can work for you, to pay you back, I swear, help me out. *Please.*"

"A magician?" Muscles sounded rather doubtful. She clenched her fists, giving Gilbert a glance that promised he would pay dearly if he tried to fool her. "Why, of course. You sure look like one."

All right, so he looked more like a thug, dirty and half-drunk, on the verge of passing out on the pavement and drowning in his own vomit, but Humphreys, for one, didn't seem to care. "See, he's a magician. That is marvelousss. All ssset. Just *grab the man*, for heaven's sssake."

"Let's not do anything hasty," the ringmaster interrupted, glaring at his companions, then turned back to Gilbert. "You. Can you prove what you're saying, or are you too damn drunk to do that?"

Pinned down by the man's piercing eyes, Gilbert was breathless for a moment. *Prove it?* How in the hell was he supposed to do that? Did it look like the time to be playing magic tricks when there was a fucking *horde* of... *Oh, for God's sake.* He didn't have enough time nor functioning brain cells to talk Redhead out of this; it would be easier to show him. The sheer panic might be enough to kick-start his magic into action. The shouting seemed dimmer now, maybe they had taken a wrong turn somewhere, but he could tell they were still in the maze of alleyways, searching for him. He wasn't ready to bet his life on the off chance that they might give up looking now.

He was pretty sure he'd lost his cards and dice, and his head was pounding and stuffed with spider threads. He couldn't remember any of his usual tricks. They had all vanished, trickled out of his brain as soon as the ringmaster had asked him. *Isn't that perfect...* He grunted to himself, looking around in the rain for something, anything, he could—

Struck by inspiration, Gilbert scooped up a handful of water from the puddle he was sitting in. He held up his hand, the gray water trembling in his cupped palm. He focused on it, felt the familiar pinpricks burn behind his eyes, and the trembling intensified. The trembling turned into minute ripples, as if a wave was shifting across the minuscule lake in his palm, never breaking ashore. Then the water swelled, rising upward in a rounded, gentle shape.

"*That* is definitely not natural," Gilbert heard someone murmur, but he didn't break his gaze or his concentration. The water trembled, fluttered, and finally tore itself free from his palm, molding into a definite shape: a butterfly. Its wings spread as it came to life. It fluttered above his hand before the ringmaster's captivated eyes, its translucent, gleaming wings unperturbed by the falling raindrops. It flew in a graceful circle, hovering near the ringmaster's handsome face, and Gilbert couldn't help a pang of satisfaction at the small smile that hovered on the man's lips, the way his green eyes had warmed up.

The water butterfly flapped its wings and flew upward toward a sky of bruised clouds and thin, gray rain, vanishing.

There was a moment of silence as the four strangers stood with their heads tilted back, staring at the sky in something like wonderment. Gilbert smiled.

"So, you meant an *actual* magician." At last, the ringmaster brought his gaze back to Gilbert. Something had changed. He was staring at Gilbert as if he actually mattered, a spark of recognition, if not benevolence, in his eyes.

Gilbert just nodded, looking him in the eye. It was an odd sort of connection, there on the wet pavement. For an instant, he almost forgot about the others watching, and the *other* others, still out to get him. The moment was broken, though, when Humphreys snapped one of his tentacles with a loud, wet smack.

"That's sssplendid. Now can we *please* take him and go?" He was twitching nervously, his flushed purple tentacles snapping and whipping the air. He opened his pocket watch again and cursed. "Jesse, *come on*. You're going to damn us all even more than we already are. The hour is upon us, we're not going to get another chance."

"You know the rules," the ringmaster replied sternly, without a single glance backward. "We only take the willing, and that's not up for debate. It never has been." His eyes had gone cold and severe, the lines of his face hardening. "He deserves the same respect you all were granted."

Very solemnly, he grasped Gilbert's face with both hands, looking him in the eye. Gilbert's heart fluttered in his chest, and he was kind of worried Emilia would bite the man, but she had stilled, seeming equally dazed. There was something about him. Something utterly spellbinding. "What—"

"Look at me, magician. And listen closely to what I'm about to say because it is important. This is the most important decision you'll ever make in your life."

Gilbert was woozy and scared, and the world was swimming slightly in front of him, fluttering like the water butterfly's wings. His body was bristling and itching with the need to run, if he could only make his goddamned legs work. But the ringmaster's touch seemed to placate him, somehow. Or maybe it was something in his eyes. They had become impossibly bright and green, drawing him in, piercing his thoughts like a blade. The man's words echoed deep in his chest, final like a pact etched in stone, sealed in blood, and he couldn't have stopped listening even if he'd wanted to.

"You can join the circus. You can hide in our wagon and come with us, if that's what you would like. The circus is short one performer, and we must fill that position at once." There was a loud *click*, and a hissing sound, probably Humphreys with his watch. But it was so difficult to focus on anything other than the ringmaster's voice. *Jesse, his name is Jesse* . . . "But— Hey. Listen. This is the important part. If you come with us, if you decide to join the circus, the deal is forever. You understand? *Forever*. Once you're in, you can never get out. Ever. For the rest of your life." He paused, letting his words sink in. "I need to know that you understand and accept this. If you never believe anything again in your life, believe this: if you join, you will remain with the circus until the day you die, and beyond that . . . Your soul will be damned for all eternity. There is no way out. None at all. Think about that, and give me your answer."

"Oh, for God's sssake." Humphreys griped from somewhere nearby.

Gilbert was still confused, fuzzy, and between the head wound, Jesse's captivating green eyes, just how close his mouth was, and that strange scent of fuel and smoke and fire, he didn't know what to blame. But that stuff Jesse had said . . . It had to be gibberish. It didn't make any sense. *But hey, so the man is a little weird.* None of them looked very normal, after all. Jesse was also handsome and charming. And if worse came to worst, if they really did try to lock him up in that creepy wagon of theirs, Gilbert could escape in any way he pleased. As if a scraggy circus could hold him prisoner until his dying day, of all things.

And even so, he thought hurriedly as something was smashed to pieces in what sounded like the next alley over. *Fuck.* Yeah, he'd be more than willing to spend the rest of his life with tentacled creatures juggling whole damn skeletons if it meant not dying *right now*.

"I'll take the tentacles," he blurted, clutching the ringmaster's hand, the contact enough to ignite his blood. Jesse's eyebrows shot up, and Gilbert realized that it might not have made as much sense out loud as it had inside his head. Somewhere dangerously nearby, there was a gunshot. "*Yes.* I'm saying yes, it's a deal. I'm all yours, for life, whatever you want. Just get me the hell outta here."

Jesse exchanged meaningful glances with Humphreys, Muscles, and Sparkles. Humphreys hissed, seeming quite relieved, and his tentacles flailed around a bit. Gilbert couldn't disagree. The pressure in Gilbert's chest eased, and he sighed. He wasn't even perturbed when his hands met one of the skulls before a quick tentacle yanked the thing away from him.

"Oh, fine," Muscles sighed, and Gilbert was grabbed by two strong arms and slung over her shoulder as if he weighed nothing. He was still too drunk on relief, alcohol, and magic to feel embarrassed as he was carried, head dangling and arse in the air, to the back of the wagon. The ringmaster opened the black wooden doors just as the voices and footsteps got frighteningly close. The crowd must have turned down the right alley at last. They were no longer running or shouting, but they seemed angry nonetheless.

His train of thought was lost when the woman tossed him none too gently into the wagon, and he landed on the wooden floor with an undignified *oomph* and an indignant squeak from Emilia. That was most definitely not going to help his poor head. The door was slammed shut as he tried to get up, but he only managed to drag himself to the wall and slump against it. It was pitch-black in there, except for the lines and pinpricks of faint light seeping between the uneven, ruined planks. He pressed his cheek to them, splinters scraping his face, and instinctively lifted his hand to pet Emilia, who was vibrating nervously on his shoulder, quickly sniffing around the new environment. She was wet and cold, but she leaned into his touch, turning her tiny head under his fingers.

"Sorry, Emi," he murmured, scratching behind her ears. It was kind of ridiculous how many times he'd refrained from plunging headlong into outright suicidal endeavors, how many days he'd kept on living merely so he wouldn't leave Emilia alone in this hostile world. Her sharp teeth had made him wise up more times than he could count, and her reproachful black gaze had often been more eloquent than any in-depth conversation about the meaning of life. He surely owed her better than a romp in the pouring rain. He couldn't really provide her with a warm and comfortable home or an endless supply of cheese, but there were a few things he could have granted her, if he'd made a bit more of an effort. Such as avoiding pub brawls, for instance.

He silently promised himself he would do better next time, even as his vision began to blur. He pressed his eye to a small hole in the wall, trying to see what was going on outside. He was hoping this wasn't just an elaborate prank before the circus fellows handed him over to the murderous mob.

He glimpsed dozens of moving legs as too many people streamed into the alley. The first words he heard, in a deep, nasal now-familiar voice were, "Hey, you stupid freaks. You seen some guy with a rat on his shoulder?"

"Why, good sssir, I can't ssseem to remember ssseeing . . ."

"I'm not talking to you, you slimy . . . whatever the fuck you are," Skunk replied, without even bothering to hide his disgust. "You, with the hat and ridiculous coat. You look like you're the boss around here. You better tell me where the rat man went right this fucking second or you won't like what happens to your . . . pet and your whores."

Gilbert sighed with relief. That was a good enough guarantee that the circus people might not feel so inclined to do the man any favors.

There was a moment of icy-cold silence, then a sharp, smacking sound followed by a yowl. It could have been, say, a cane hitting someone in the face.

"Constance, if you please," the ringmaster said, perfectly polite, as if he were sitting around in a gentlemen's club smoking cigars and discussing the weather. "Would you be so kind as to handle these sorry fellows, if it's not inconvenient?"

"Why, it would be a pleasure." Muscles—Constance—seemed entirely too gleeful as she stepped forward. Her broad back obstructed the view from Gilbert's peephole. He was too tired to move to another, so he just leaned his forehead against the wood and closed his eyes.

The screaming began, accompanied by crashes and smacks and loud thuds, as the wagon wobbled slightly, as if someone had hopped on board.

"That ought to teach them something about manners," Jesse said, his voice coming from somewhere above Gilbert's head now. "Let's move along, shall we?"

Something splintered and cracked, quite possibly against a human body, and one of the men outside shrieked like a strangled chicken.

"What, passing out already, my dove?" Constance commented. "So soon?"

With a rumble and a loud hiss, the wagon started hobbling along, slowly, creaking and jumping on the cobblestones, shaking Gilbert around like a rag doll. Gilbert exhaled as the tightness in his chest fully eased, and he let himself be lulled by the sharp jolts of the wagon and the terrified screams they were leaving behind. It looked like he'd survive, after all.

Then he slumped further against the rough wooden wall, sliding down into darkness.

CHAPTER 3

W hen Gilbert woke up, the world was still and quiet. He blinked, trying to get his bearings. The dim light sliced through his head like a hacksaw, and he shut his eyes, groaning. He pressed the heel of his hand to his forehead, in the exact spot where he could feel his blood pulsing under the skin. But the worst pain was at the back of his head, a dull, constant thumping, like a very large hammer hitting again and again. Gilbert rolled to the side, curling in on himself, and whispered a stream of curses that would have been enough to damn him to Hell, if that ship hadn't sailed quite a few years before. Too late he realized that he had no idea if he was alone in . . . wherever he was and waited for someone to reproach him.

But no voice spoke up. As the hammering in his skull faded slightly and he started considering a second attempt at opening his eyes, he tried to focus on why he had no idea where he was—or how he'd ended up there, for that matter.

He was fairly sure he should have known that, even with how out of sorts he had been the night before.

With a deep breath, he hauled himself to a seat on the edge of the bed and opened his eyes. His head protested vigorously, but it wasn't that bad—he'd woken up in far worse conditions. Nothing would ever beat the brutal homemade chili grappa an old Italian had offered him once. That had nearly blinded him, he was sure of it.

Blinking, he distracted himself from his memories of excesses past by examining his surroundings. He was in a small room, long and narrow, with reddish wooden walls and an arched wooden roof. The furniture was sparse—cabinets and a table and the narrow bed he sat on, all pushed up against the walls. They seemed bolted in place. Emilia sat on the table, busying herself with something he couldn't quite see. She seemed perfectly fine and at ease, and that truly did wonders to calm his nerves. She would know if he'd stuck himself in some ridiculously dangerous situation. If she was untroubled, then he could relax too.

The walls were almost entirely covered in faded quilts and mirrors and assorted paraphernalia. It was all covered in dust. A bright-red glittered cape hung in the corner, along with an absurdly tall, black stovepipe hat. Gilbert snorted, shaking his head at the garment. It looked as if its owner had been in a circus or some—

Oh, right.

So, his current situation was not so much ridiculously dangerous as just plain *ridiculous.*

He groaned, fighting the instinct to flop back down on the bed, and rubbed his face with both hands. He was beginning to remember. He'd joined the bloody circus, of all things, to escape from a . . . What was it? Right. From the bloodthirsty mob that had been chasing him. And he'd signed on for the rest of his life.

Yeah, right. I am so *out of here.*

Gilbert glanced around, spotted his boots neatly placed by the foot of the bed, and got to work putting them on and lacing them tightly. He got up, patting his knees, and grabbed his jacket, which was hanging from a hook between the glittery red cape and what looked like an ancient morning coat.

He brushed his fingers against his jacket's inner lining, which slit open under his touch, and rummaged in the secret pocket. Cards, crumbs, a—was that a *tooth?*—and a good amount of money. They hadn't even robbed him. He thought about it for a moment, then left a few crumpled bills on the dresser. Since he wasn't going to honor his promise and work for them, this was better than nothing. His fingers left traces in the dust coating the dresser, and he wiped his hand on his trousers.

He leaned over and patted his shoulder, and Emilia obediently scuttled on, carrying a piece of cookie with her and settling comfortably in his scarf. Gilbert tried the door. It was unlocked, so he slowly pushed it open, squinting as he walked down three creaking wooden steps.

There wasn't much sunlight to speak of. The day was hopelessly gray, the dull sky cloaked with clouds, turning what little light that filtered through cold and heavy like lead. He guessed it was probably around midday—luckily everyone seemed to be still asleep. He'd be able to slip out unnoticed.

He hopped off the steps and started walking, looking around for the way out as he buttoned his coat against the chilly, murky air. His wagon was at the edge of a small encampment. A handful of wooden wagons, their once-bright colors faded, were scattered on a field of dry grass. There were gnarled, dead trees all around, and lanterns hanging from a messy net of cables like a sagging spiderweb. A black iron fence ran a few yards to his right, so Gilbert started following it. It was too high and too sharp to climb over, but it would lead him to a gate, sooner or later. He could see a forest of skeletal trees on the other side and wondered how far they could have possibly gotten from civilization the night before. Couldn't be *that* far. Or at least he hoped so, since he'd have to make it back there on foot. He had to find a city, find a station, hop on the first train, and get the hell away.

A shiver crawled down his back, and Gilbert cringed, tugging on his scarf. Emilia's warm little body pressed against his neck was comforting, but he would be much happier once he was away from this place. There was something odd in the air—a dead chill that seeped into his bones and made him an unbearable kind of cold, made him want to leg it as far as possible, as quick as possible. He wasn't sure what he expected from a circus, but it wasn't this silent parade of ruined, faded wagons. He'd expected color, lights, music, and dancing performers. This was eerie.

He'd just glimpsed the gate—a hole in the iron fence with a crude wooden sign hanging over it—when he heard the whispers. He glanced around quickly, trying to determine where the voices were coming from so he could run in the opposite direction. But there was no one there, certainly not anyone close enough for him to hear them whisper. There was only a small, black, windowless wagon at the very edge of the encampment. *Strange.* He had come from there, and he swore he hadn't seen any—

His eyes burned. He blinked. It was getting hard to see; his vision growing blurry. The grass, the fence—it all grew unfocused. There was just the black wagon, clear and bright like a gas lamp in the night, a fixed spot as the world began to melt around it.

"What the . . .?"

He rubbed his eyes, squinting. The whispering was growing louder, murmurs echoing in his ears. Three, four, too many voices to count and that were now louder than screams. He brought his hands to his ears, but the sound wasn't fading. It was coming from somewhere inside his head. When he blinked again, he thought he saw someone—a tall, dark figure, fluttering, on the verge of melting into the mist itself. Gilbert's eyes watered when he tried to focus. He couldn't see, but it seemed like it was smiling.

And then it all was gone. The voices, the water in his eyes, the person. Gilbert blinked, slowly bringing his hands down. It all looked perfectly normal now: no mist, no swirling. Just a rickety black wagon that looked about to crumble at the first gust of wind.

There were other sounds, though—rustling, creaking. A door being shut. *Damn.* The circus was beginning to wake up after a late night, and his chances of getting out of there unseen were dwindling fast. *Time to stop with the sightseeing.*

He jogged to the exit and turned to cast a glance at the sign once he was on the other side. It was black, old, and scraped, and it read in flourished red letters: *Circus of the Damned.*

How lovely. Well, at least he wouldn't have to stick around to find out exactly why the troupe had picked such a cheerful name. By the time they went looking for him, he would be long gone.

What a shame, though. He wouldn't have minded seeing the handsome ringmaster again. He may have been a raving lunatic, but he was an attractive one, nonetheless. When he'd knelt before Gilbert in the rain, looking at him with those green eyes, so, so close . . . close enough that, for a moment, Gilbert had foolishly thought the man would kiss him.

Ah, it was too late to do anything about it, anyway. He had to forget about it. He jogged down the dirt road, in the damp mist past the dead trees, heading as far from that damned circus as he could get.

CHAPTER 4

As it turned out, the closest city was Shadowsea.

The circus hadn't traveled far at all—merely camped on the outskirts of town. Gilbert considered his options, then decided to dive in. He would make his way to the station as quickly and discreetly as possible, and soon he would be on a train headed to the other side of the country. He could hide well in crowds; he'd been doing it all his life. He would be fine.

He made his way toward Grand Saudade Station, keeping to the side streets and rat-infested alleys. All sorts of street foods were for sale around the market, which supported a large population of animals and more than a few people who fought the rats and foxes for leftovers, and there were cramped stalls at every corner, minuscule stores packed into holes in the walls, squashed in the intricate maze of alleys between too-tall brick buildings that were painted black from years of coal smoke. Dark clouds crowded above. There were *always* clouds and mist, a heavy soup of burned coal, fires, chimneys, and ovens vomiting a constant stream of black smoke. It was raining again, too, an almost impalpable drizzle, just enough to make him damp, chilly, and uncomfortable.

Emilia made a displeased noise and burrowed deeper in his scarf, hiding from sight. He patted her comfortingly on the back. He wasn't very happy, either.

"Don't worry. We'll be somewhere dry soon enough." He still had plenty of cash. For once, he'd be traveling in style.

The scent of roasted vegetables spread from a shop that served broth and noodles. The bench in front of it was crammed with people, and for a moment, he was tempted to elbow his way in but he'd rather keep moving. He bought a cup of fried oysters for himself and an apple for Emilia from a thin woman who sported a visibly cracked glass eye. He munched quickly, shoulders hunched under the rain as he walked through the crowd, bumping into this guy or that, until he reached an enlargement where the crowd was even thicker. A wide metal stairwell sank underground, into the very bowels of the city, with its rusty iron sign that read, "Great Saudade Station."

He swallowed the last oyster and balled up the greasy wrapping paper, tossing it carelessly aside before joining the crowd headed down below. Something prickled at the back of his head, then—a familiar itch telling him that there were eyes on him, a dark shape at the edge of his vision that should not be there. He dug into his pockets for a squashed cigarette, then looked around under the pretense of asking for a match. But the shadow vanished, replaced by a short man with ginger hair carrying a platter of pigs' feet on his head.

Could it be one of Reuben's watchdogs? He tensed his muscles, ready to bolt at the merest glimpse of purple silk as he scanned the crowd. It would make sense for them to patrol the stations—they surely expected for him to leave town—but there was no one on his trail, even with his heart still thumping loudly in his chest. He was just on edge. Count Reuben was not to be underestimated. Time to stop waffling about; he had to get out of that city and not come back for a long, long time.

People crowded on the stairs like a dark wave, going down toward the gloomy tunnels where the air was heavy, an almost unbreathable cloud, or rising up into the soupy fog above. The iron steps were plastered with scrap tickets and food leftovers, and Gilbert hurried down into the underground air that tasted like copper and soil and old piss. Standing on iron steps always made him queasy, made something inside him tight and sore. And not just because of the stench. Iron had a way of sucking out his magic, draining it, leaving him powerless, almost gasping for breath if he remained in contact with the metal too long, and he hated that naked, defenseless feeling. He'd figured that one out after iron manacles had made him collapse, nearly delirious from the gaping void left in his chest where his magic should have been.

The station's main hall had a low, arched ceiling, a dirty tiled floor, and brick walls the color of soot. Rounded tunnels opened like yawning mouths all around, surmounted by tarnished plaques bearing numbers and letters. It made Gilbert slightly uneasy. As a rule, he tried to stay as far away from the trains as he could, but this time he didn't have a choice. The place was bustling with people—street thieves leaning against the walls, eyeing passersby with less than honorable intentions, tradesmen hurrying by with their goods, and the occasional chaperoned lady.

Gilbert brushed up against a gentleman in a mint-green suit and hat, watching him wince in absolute horror at the contamination, at the terrible breach of etiquette. Their two worlds were supposed to be hermetically separated, even in those few places where they were actually forced to coexist in narrow quarters, such as the underground.

He made his way to a secluded alcove he knew well, where one of the invisibles had carved his dwelling place in a city that pretended he was already dead, if he had ever existed at all.

"Hello there, Filmore," Gilbert said, leaning against the corner.

"Why, hello yourself, Boss," a raspy voice replied. Filmore was an old man with a bushy, ginger beard and mustache covering most of his gnarled face. He was comfortably seated among a pile of papers, blankets, and pillows on a wooden plank furnished with small wheels. He had no legs, and that was his means of transport—not that he needed to move much. He was smoking, peacefully, and busy shuffling scraps of dirty paper as he took notes in his black booklet.

Filmore knew everything about the station. He'd been there longer than the people who actually worked in it. He knew its layout, its secret tunnels, its ventilation system, and the pumps that kept it from flooding. Somehow, he heard everything too, even what was said in sealed offices, far from any prying ears. Word on the street was that he had domesticated roaches and rats to make up a little army of spies that told him everything he needed. He knew by heart the whole rail network and its timetables; he was the first to know if there were diversions or a blocked track and, it was murmured, could predict accidents.

That was why people wanted to stay on Filmore's good side: so he'd warn them if their train was going to crash. The station authorities let him be, and people brought him all the food he could eat. *How* he knew what he did, nobody was really sure. People told of a time when he'd saved some guy who regularly brought him stolen cigars but let another man, one who'd never given him a penny, get on the doomed train. Gilbert had never been able to confirm the tale, though, not that he'd tried very hard. Sometimes he suspected that Filmore had manufactured the stories so everyone would make sure to give him a penny or a cigarette or half an apple to remain in his good graces. At any rate, his prices were small, and a guy had to live somehow, so Gilbert was more than happy to give his contribution.

And besides, you never knew. There might just have been some truth to it all.

"So, Boss, where you headed on this fine day?" Filmore puffed out a cloud of smoke, never lifting his eyes from the notebook in which he was still scribbling furiously.

"I'm not sure," Gilbert answered honestly, hands in his pockets. "I've got to get out of town, far and fast. Somewhere that not too many people might think to look for me would be best." He didn't bother lying. Filmore was trustworthy, if you were his friend, and Gilbert had spent many a hangover slumped in Filmore's corner, confiding his drunken thoughts to the man. He didn't even know what, but Gilbert had always been generous, and Filmore had taken a liking to him and Emilia. Emilia more than him, probably. True enough, Emilia's twitching nose emerged from his scarf, and she scuttled down his sleeve to hop onto Filmore's shoulder. He tossed her half a chestnut, and Emilia happily munched on it.

"The weekly steamer for the mines leaves in twenty minutes. 'S cold and wet and pretty lonely up there, but nobody will be able to follow until next week. And before that, you could always catch the cargo transport to the refineries, and from there, hell, sky's the limit. They have daily shipments to every corner of this damned country," Filmore rattled out without a pause. Gilbert imagined the little trains and locomotives and interchanges, a constantly moving net spreading all over the land, precise and exact. An unpleasant feeling crawled up his neck as he pictured them, and he shook his head, banishing the image.

"That's wonderful, just what I need. Thank you, man." He dug in his pockets and grabbed a handful of bills—way more than what he usually gave, but what the hell. Having the bills thrust under his nose gave Filmore pause, though, and he stopped writing to look up at Gilbert.

"Now, Boss, you know that's not how this works." He carefully selected one small bill and pushed the rest back. "Filmore doesn't take more than he needs."

"I know, I . . . I didn't mean to—" Gilbert protested, although Filmore hadn't taken any offense. He held the cash out for a moment longer, then gave up and folded it away. "We've known each other for a while and, well—"

"And it looks like you won't be around for a while, eh?" Filmore scratched Emilia's head with a gnarled, soot-stained finger. "You in trouble?"

"Yeah. You could say that." Gilbert scratched his head. "I may have pulled one scam too many in Reuben's territory. Got his watchdogs on my tail wanting to bash my head in. And there's a weird circus that . . . Never mind. I just gotta give it a few months' time, you know? Vanish for a while."

"Mighty good idea, if Filmore may say." Filmore nodded, then moved on to scratch under Emilia's chin as she sat contentedly, done with her chestnut. "Little one, keep an eye on Boss here, all right? Don't let him get in any more trouble." He was silent for a moment as Emilia squeaked emphatically. "Well, that's because he's a dumbass, darling. Next time, just get out of there and let him deal with it on his own. I always tell you, you're way smarter than he is."

Gilbert should have been insulted, he supposed, but really, the fellow was conversing with his mouse. He wasn't going to take anything personally.

"Platform Thirteen Below. The one deep down. It's not like a lot of folks take that train. Fifteen minutes." Filmore lifted his arm so that Emilia could run up to his hand and jump back on Gilbert's shoulder. "See you around, Boss."

"See you around, Filmore. Take care." But Filmore was already back to his booklet, waving him away.

Gilbert smiled to himself and left, making his way to the tight, claustrophobic tunnel marked 3-C. It was a long one, sloped down, dark and damp. Condensation ran in rivulets down the sooty tiles. Nobody went to the mines, except a new shift of workers every couple of months, so the train had been relegated to the deepest, dirtiest platform.

Every platform had a turnstile with a mechanical box to collect the fares, and this one was tarnished and creaking and missing pieces, unlike the polished, fancy ones on the most popular lines—the ones used by the rich folks, the city lines, and the luxury trains headed to the coastal resorts. Gilbert inserted the coins for the fare. He'd tried jumping the barrier exactly once, upon which the machine's scrawny-looking mechanical arm had grabbed him, quick as lightning, and vigorously shaken him upside down before tossing him several feet back behind the turnstile. So he patiently waited as the machine clicked and gurgled, counting the coins, and the mechanical hand, missing a couple of fingers, handed him some change. The iron gate opened, and Gilbert stepped onto the platform.

It was a narrow strip of mostly broken tiles, which ended abruptly where the black hollow that housed the tracks opened. It wouldn't be a long fall by any means, but Gilbert averted his gaze and kept resolutely away from it. There was always this little nightmare crawling at the back of his head: He was pulled and dragged toward the edge, as if by a powerful magnetic force, and no matter how hard he tried to back away, every step led him closer to the edge as the piercing whistle of a train came. And as he fell onto the tracks, he was blinded by the large, bright-yellow light at the front of the train, and he knew it was too late.

He shook himself out of it. It was so stupid—just a nightmare—and yet it made him sweaty and uneasy anytime he set foot on a damned platform. The one close encounter he'd had as a child was just that—a close call. Nothing had truly happened. But he still kept as close as possible to the tiled wall, decorated in garish colors, and walked to the dingy beerhouse halfway down the platform. He half expected to find it closed. There were fancy ones upstairs, with expensive liquors and maids in pretty ribbons, and tearooms with cake and china cups and damask upholstery, of all things. This one, on the other hand, was a proper dive—a sooty counter, three mismatched stools, a few cracked shelves of bottles. The kind of place where Gilbert felt much more at home.

He took a seat, the stool creaking pitifully, and a gray-dressed, pale-faced girl emerged from the back room. She had taupe hair and a tired face, and she didn't even bother pretending to smile at him.

She just kept wiping at a glass with a rag, smearing the soot rather than removing it, waiting for him to speak. He ordered a pint of, well, whatever piss they called beer down here, which she poured without comment. Gilbert was partial to stouts and dark beers while this was a watery, pale yellow, and tepid at that. Still, it was better than nothing.

He paid and left her a good tip—he always felt generous when he had a little spare cash—and the waitress lingered, looking at him with a spark of interest in her eyes. Maybe she was just bored and hoping for a little diversion, enough to crook her lips in something like a smile and say, "Where are you off to, handsome?" She tucked a strand of hair behind her ear and tilted her head to the side to reveal her milky neck.

Her smile was coquettish, and normally Gilbert would return the flirtation in kind, if only to fill the empty minutes as he waited for the steamer to arrive. She wasn't bad to look at, with that pasty complexion typical of the inhabitants of the lower levels of the city, the ones who didn't see the sun often. Surely working in the underground made it even worse. And behind a stained, half-parted curtain, Gilbert glimpsed a small room and the corner of a bed. She was one of those who lived down here as well, and in all likelihood, she didn't see many people on that platform, mostly mine workers who were not the prettiest-looking bunch.

The girl was staring at him, waiting for an answer, so he stretched his mouth into a smile and mumbled some trite platitude in response, a joke of sorts, judging by the way she dutifully pretended to laugh. It was a halfhearted dance, done out of tired habit more than anything else, but still—there was nobody else on the platform, and there was no sign of the train yet. And maybe, on another day, he would actually be interested in pursuing the idea. Hell, he might even sweet-talk her into bed. But today, there was nothing even remotely appealing in it for him. Instead, his mind conjured up, unbidden, a picture of piercing green eyes, a cascade of red hair on broad shoulders, the scent of smoke and fuel close to him as strong hands yanked him forward.

Damn it. There was no point in dwelling on that guy. He was never going to see him again, end of story.

Gilbert downed what was left of his beer and was about to order another when a low vibration started shaking his stool, the mismatched glasses precariously piled on the shelves, and the platform itself, before a shrill whistle announced the imminent arrival of the train. Relieved, Gilbert placed an extra coin on the counter and thanked the girl with a nod. She didn't return it, she didn't even see it, already back to wiping her glasses, so Gilbert tucked his hands in his pockets and went to press his back against the wall of the solitary platform, waiting for the train to appear.

Despite his best judgment, he wondered whether he had made a mistake, running away like he had that morning. Maybe he should have given it a try, hung around the circus and its strange people and its handsome ringmaster, just for a little while. What could it hurt? It might not be so bad to have a roof over his head and guaranteed meals for a change. He might even get to bang the hot ringmaster if he played his cards right. He hadn't even seriously considered it, he'd packed up and left because . . . well, because that was what he did. What he had always done. The thought of something different hadn't even crossed his mind. He had no home, no mates, no family, and he tried not to think about that. Nothing to be done about it, anyway, and he'd gotten used to being alone a long time ago.

He had no obligations to anyone; he was free to roam the big, wide world. But for what? To find himself alone in a dirty underground station headed to Crapville, off to contract tuberculosis holed up with the miners and their destroyed lungs. *It might not be that bad*, he tried to cheer himself up. Miners got bored, there was nowhere to spend their wages, and bored people liked gambling. He'd just be careful not to make any live birds crawl out of anyone because there would be no getting away if someone wanted to kill him up there. And the mines had plenty of corners where to stash a body.

Emilia poked out from the scarf and headbutted his chin ever so gently, then remained there, a warm ball of fur pressed against his neck. Poor darling. She did her best to console him. But sometimes that warmth wasn't really enough. It was kind of sad, and a little bit terrifying, to think he depended on this little, fragile animal for affection, that she could be taken away from him so easily in so many ways. So he didn't think about it. *And besides*, commented the corner of his brain that was obstinately thinking about it, *the same could be said for people*. There wasn't really much difference at all.

At least she would never leave him on the tracks, frightened and helpless, to be run over by a screeching train. Which was more than he could say for his own mother.

Announced by the familiar, threatening yellow light, the steamer emerged from the tunnel, wheels screeching as they clung to the rails, a monster of brass and iron plunging forward, vomiting black smoke. A cloud of dust enveloped Gilbert, filling his mouth, making his eyes burn, and he squashed himself against the wall until the locomotive passed him and the train slid to a stop farther down, huffing. Another piercing whistle echoed in the cramped tunnel. *Is that really necessary?* He doubted that any passengers were waiting for the signal, so it must just be the bored driver trying to entertain himself. Nobody got off the train, not even the conductor. Gilbert looked around for a moment, waiting for someone to appear, then shrugged and opened one of the doors.

The interior was even more cramped and suffocating than the station, all dark wood and heavy damask wallpaper, any trace of color long swallowed by years of soot. When he'd decided to travel in style, this wasn't exactly what he had in mind. He would get out smeared black and half-choked to death, but he supposed it was better than traveling the whole way on a rickety goat cart.

Gilbert had his pick of seats in the empty carriage, so he sprawled on a random bench just as the train shook and trembled and huffed loudly, pulling out of the station. Gilbert parted the window curtain with his fingertips to peer outside, but there was nothing except the darkness of the tunnel. The air was heavy, the seat uncomfortable, the pillow a nest for moths, and the gas lamps were eating up what little oxygen was left. *Wonderful.*

He sighed in relief, the pressure around his chest easing. Once he was on board, he was fine. It was being near the goddamn tracks, seeing the train barreling full speed toward him. He shuddered, closing his eyes. It was kind of a joke that the only memory he conserved of his family was the stuff of his one gut-wrenching nightmare that he would give everything in his power to just tear it out of his brain. But his traitorous dreams kept playing it over and over again in his head, never allowing him to forget.

It was the face of his mother—he didn't remember anything else about her, not even her name, but that, that he *knew*—looking at him with something like horror on her oval face, her gray eyes so similar to his own. She had watched him from above, her hand clutching a dark shawl around her shoulders, before she'd turned around and left. Left him, cold and terrified and crying, bundled up on the rail tracks. Because who would want such an unholy creature for a child?

Damn. Gilbert shook his head and blinked, trying to wipe the blinding light of the incoming train from his mind. It was ridiculous. It had been years, and he was safe now. He had survived. Some kids had dragged him off the tracks in time, and they'd taught him to beg and pickpocket, and his life on the streets had begun. And unlike most of them, he'd made it through that wretched childhood. He had his magic, after all. And while it had pushed his mother to abandon him in the first place, it had also kept him alive afterward.

Gilbert tucked his hand in his pocket and pulled out two red dice, faded and chipped. He toyed with them, twirling them around in his fingers with dexterity and a little bit of magic, mindlessly conjuring up the results he wanted. Eight. Three. Five. Snake eyes. It seemed incredible that at one point in his life, this had actually been a difficult task, that it had taken all his concentration to make one single die tip over. But hunger had a way of making you a fast learner, and he'd soon figured out that his tricks could keep him fed and clothed. Keep him alive. He'd learned to manipulate them without even thinking about it. Not just his dice, anyone's—and once he was standing a yard away from the table, with his hands raised and still winning, nobody could accuse him of cheating.

Under normal circumstances, he took care not to overdo it, though. He didn't want to make it look supernatural, didn't want people to tell others about him. He couldn't work if people knew about him, so he had to be careful and stay hidden or his thieving career would be over. And besides, if his own mother had reacted that way upon finding out about the unnatural things her child could do, he had no illusions about how the rest of the world would take it.

He'd probably tossed everything down the drain with the stunt he'd pulled the night before, though. *God damn it.* There was no way those people would forget about him now. He was usually smarter than that; he knew to not get carried away. What the hell had he been thinking?

"Is this seat taken?"

Gilbert was yanked out of his reverie by a deep, gravelly voice. His gaze snapped onto the only other occupant of the carriage, who seemed to have materialized out of thin air. He'd swear the man hadn't been there a moment ago. But now there was a tall, handsome man in front of him, his skin the warm color of mahogany. He wore an immaculate pinstripe suit, and a bowler hat on his perfectly shaved head. He was leaning on a silver-topped walking cane, staring at Gilbert with impossibly captivating, slanted black eyes, patiently waiting for an answer.

"Oh, sure. I mean, no, it's not. Have a seat." Even as he blurted it out, Gilbert chastised himself, wondering why on Earth he'd said that. He didn't want company on this trip. The entire carriage was empty, quite possibly the entire train, and the stranger had to sit by him? Surely he wanted to chat to while away the time. Gilbert most definitely did not want that, though, and it wasn't like he ever had any issues saying no. It was as if the words had tumbled from his mouth of their own accord, like dice controlled by someone else's magic.

The man sat down in silence, and Gilbert tried to mind his own business, studiously looking anywhere but at his travel companion. But it wasn't easy when there was nothing to stare at except the gray, smoky carriage interior and the solid wall of darkness outside. Besides, he was painfully aware that the dark eyes of the man were unabashedly fixed on him. He wasn't even trying to hide it, openly staring. He didn't seem threatening, nor challenging, just interested in a detached way. He had his head tilted to the side, and he reminded Gilbert of a bird.

Gilbert contemplated the several hours of travel still ahead and deeply regretted not taking the cart. Goats would have been preferable, all in all. He slumped further in his seat and started playing with the dice again.

"So, you planning on staring for the whole trip?" he asked. "Because let me tell you, I know I'm handsome and all, but you're damn creepy."

The man made a thoughtful noise. It looked like he was thinking really hard, weighing Gilbert's words and posture. "Interesting."

Gilbert pretended to be *un*interested—it wasn't his first creeper, nor would it be his last—but the truth was, there was something deeply disturbing about the way this man was looking at him. Something inside Gilbert was twisting, and if he hadn't known it was impossible, he would think the guy was poking around inside him, as though he were day-old soup and the man was sifting through the bits to check if he was tasty. He had the odd, sudden feeling that those eyes were seeing way beyond his skin, seeing him torn open, every inch of him. That thought made his mouth go dry, his stomach twist in a knot. It was ridiculous. There was no way. It was just the claustrophobic train and the smoke going to his head. That and the man's unflinching, impossibly deep black eyes.

Gilbert looked away, supremely uneasy, and when he spoke, his voice came out shaky. "Well, knock yourself out, then."

The man didn't even blink.

By the time the stranger finally stopped staring and leaned back against his seat for a bit, Gilbert was sweating and feeling as if an army of spiders were crawling all over his skin. Once those black eyes were off him, the probing intrusion stopped, and he had to suppress a sigh of relief. When had he become so sensitive?

"So, Mr. Blake, I have to say I'm not too happy to find you here." The man stretched his back, glancing around the carriage. "If memory serves, you made a deal. And already you're failing to hold up your end of it."

Gilbert's gaze snapped to the man.

"How do you—" His body was already reacting to the danger; his reflexes honed by a lifetime on the streets. His pulse was speeding up as he tensed, eyeing the carriage door, readying himself to run or fight, whatever would be necessary. "Who . . . who are you? Who sent you?"

If this fellow was one of Reuben's spies, he might not be alone. And if others came in from both carriage doors, there would be no leaving, not with the train hurtling at full speed through the dark tunnel. *Damn it.* He should have trusted his instincts back at the station, shouldn't have underestimated Reuben. He'd gotten himself trapped like a fool.

"Well, I know a lot of things about you, Mr. Blake, so I suppose it's only fair I share something in return," the stranger replied with an affable smile, twirling his cane. "I'm Farfarello, from the Malebolge, in the eighth circle of Hell. And I wasn't sent by your friend in purple, so you can stop freaking out and focus on our little chat."

Gilbert shook his head. *What on Earth . . . ?* This conversation had taken a turn he most definitely was not expecting.

"From Hell, are you now?" Gilbert snorted. "So you're telling me, what, that you're the *devil*?"

"*A* devil. Hell is pretty big and with a thriving population, I should add," the man specified.

All right, then. Gilbert was almost sure that the fellow posed no threat. He was a lunatic, and a stark-raving one, at that. Damn, Gilbert sure seemed to be attracting plenty of those lately. He relaxed again in his seat, slumping comfortably, and resumed playing with his dice. Farfarello—if that was even the lunatic's real name—knew who Gilbert was and about the men in purple. Gilbert racked his brain, trying to remember if the guy had been there that night in the pub. He didn't think so—someone like that would most definitely stand out—but then, he had been drinking buckets, and a lot of people had come and gone during those three days. The madman must have seen him there, later recognized him in the street, and followed him onto the train . . . for whatever reason he might have.

Oh well. At the very least, it would be a diversion from a trip that promised to be very long and just as boring. He might as well humor the fellow a little.

"All right, devil from the Malebolge. So what is it you want from me? I wasn't aware your kind made courtesy calls. Heading up to the mines for a little vacation?"

Farfarello's smile was delighted, in an unsettling, sharp, poisonous kind of way. "Why, Mr. Blake, something tells me you're not quite taking this seriously. Allow me to remedy that."

Gilbert still had a mildly amused smile on his face when he felt it. He was twirling the dice around his fingers, spreading his palm to roll a five, when it surged up out of nowhere, a foreign power that took over and crushed Gilbert's magic like a fruit fly, effortlessly tipping the dice over. Snake eyes.

The shock left Gilbert breathless. He didn't . . . This had never happened to him. His magic had never been interfered with. The man had recognized him for what he was, and he had magic too, much stronger than Gilbert's. The power he'd glimpsed was endless, like a mountain, a whale ready to smash Gilbert's pathetic rowing boat. He had never seen anyone that powerful. Hell, he wouldn't have been able to imagine it before, and it left him nothing short of terrified.

Oh God. No, it's impossible. Could he really *be . . . ?*

Wide-eyed, he looked up to find the stranger staring at him again, with the smallest, knowing smile on his lips. "Ah, I see I have your attention now," he said, nonchalantly crossing one leg over the other.

God damn did he have it. He couldn't have had more of his attention if he'd pulled out a revolver and held it to Gilbert's temple. Cold sweat beaded on Gilbert's forehead, and he let his magic poke a little, trying to investigate that power, size it up if at all possible. But he couldn't *see*, or feel, anything—the stranger had shut him out. He couldn't perceive a thing. Besides, he had no real idea of what the hell he was doing. But the stranger most certainly did. He arched an eyebrow, looking at Gilbert as if he were a child trying to hide the shattered china under a handkerchief and utterly failing. Oh, the man knew. He knew everything.

It dawned on Gilbert then, cold and numbing, that this was a hostage situation. He was alone on a train headed to the middle of nowhere, locked there for hours with this predator, so much bigger and infinitely stronger than he was. For an instant, Gilbert considered fighting back with his magic, but even as he thought it, he knew it was a terrible idea. Emilia up against a lion would have had better odds. A hundred escape plans flew through his head, and he discarded them, one after the other, at the speed of light, until he was left with nothing, just the clear understanding that if this guy wished Gilbert dead, he was well and truly fucked.

So he straightened up, swallowing, because at this point he should probably try being more polite, to see if he could weasel his way out of it.

The gaslights around the train car flickered. The smoke turned to mist, the fire into a dancing will-o'-the-wisp, making Gilbert's vision blur, his eyes burn and water as he tried to hold the stranger's gaze, which was gleaming red. Gilbert turned his eyes to the black spider inked on the man's throat, which moved every time he swallowed as though it was tapping its eight little legs in impatience.

No. Not a *man*. Gilbert was ready to give him the benefit of the doubt on that devil thing.

"Don't be so scared, Mr. Blake. I'm not here to harm you." The spider danced as the man spoke. "I just wished to take a look. You've joined an old friend of mine lately, and by extension, myself. Your soul is connected to me now. And while I'm always interested in our new acquisitions, there is something about you, Mr. Blake, that makes you especially intriguing. You might bring about more change than anyone expects."

"Our new acquisitions?" Gilbert repeated, dazed, mouth hanging half-open. That was when it finally clicked, and the surprise pushed him to forget himself for a moment. He snorted a laugh. "You're with the *circus*? Did you *follow* me all the way here? You set up this whole farce, all because of those goddamn *freaks*—"

The man's gaze flashed red, hard and unflinching, and something clenched in Gilbert's throat, cutting his voice off with a painful squeak. He fought against it, but he was choking, an unbearable pressure pushing his voice back down his throat. Then, the fire in the stranger's eyes dimmed back to the deepest black as he relaxed in his seat, and the pressure eased. Gilbert gasped, breathing in, clutching his throat. The man no longer seemed angry, but there was something dark and dangerous in his gaze that warned Gilbert very clearly about what would happen should he dare say it again.

"That is not a very nice word, Mr. Blake, and I strongly suggest you refrain from using it again. Especially among the very fine members of the circus." His voice was steel, making Gilbert's skin crawl like it would from the sound of nails scraping against a mirror. "But to answer your question, no, I'm not part of the circus. I hear, however, that *you* are now. A deal's a deal, and you should avoid trying to weasel your way out. You're just going to make a fool of yourself."

Gilbert was pissed now. Being scared out of his mind made him angry, it always had. His throat was sore when he replied. "I don't care for your opinion, or who the hell you are, but I'm telling you right now, I am not going back there. I've paid them for the favor, and that's it, we're done. I've got nothing to do with a bunch of—" He cut himself off abruptly, the muscles of his throat already tensing. "With those people. And unless you're planning on turning this train around and dragging me all the way back there . . ."

"As if I would need to do such a thing. I think you're in for a big surprise. But you will see soon enough. And from what I've just witnessed, I believe it will do you good. You're an arrogant man, Gilbert Blake, and I will be delighted to watch you learn a little humility." The man stood up and fixed his coat and hat, as if getting ready to leave, with a smirk on his face. "Oh, and if I may suggest, you might want to take a little nap now. To make the boring trip seem shorter."

"I'm not tired," Gilbert petulantly replied, because he didn't know what else to say. Good Lord, he was such a pathetic idiot. Had he been in the stranger's shoes, he would have crushed himself with a flick of that immense power.

The stranger just smiled, without showing his teeth, and tipped his head down. Quick little pinpricks began running up Gilbert's leg, and he lowered his gaze to see that the silver spider from the silver cane knob was now crawling over him, sticking its metallic legs into the fabric of his clothes hard enough to bite into his flesh.

"Fuck! What the—" He swatted at himself, trying to kill the thing, to slap it away, but it was too fast. It jumped on his hand and ran up his arm. "What the hell are you—"

That was when it bit, sending a searing pain piercing through Gilbert's biceps, leaving him breathless. Dizziness spread fast, a thick, gray curtain falling on his mind, pinning him down, shrouding him in darkness. He was falling, falling toward unconsciousness, as the poison spread in his veins too fast to fight, the carriage floating and wobbling, its chilly lights dancing.

"Oh, and when you see the ringmaster," the gravelly voice added, the last thing Gilbert heard before plunging headfirst into darkness, "tell him that Farfarello sends his regards."

CHAPTER 5

The first thing he heard was a grunt.

More grunts followed, and slow puffs of air hit his face. Hot, moist. Stinking, like rotten meat and onions. A low, rumbling noise sounded and then a quicker set of puffs. Something wet touched his cheek and sniffed him loudly.

Someone was *sniffing* him.

Gilbert groaned, clawing his way out of slumber. Good Lord, how much had he been drinking? It seemed like all he did of late was wake up in strange places without a clue how he'd ended up there. But he would get out of that habit, he swore solemnly. Truly, it was a miracle he'd survived this long.

He shifted around, grunting, on a soft padded surface. He was in a bed, which was a success considering some of the places he'd woken up in the past. And there was someone warm next to him; he could feel the heat radiating from the body. So, at the very least, he'd gotten lucky. One could do worse.

Lazily, he stretched out a hand, not even bothering to open his eyes, to grope around and investigate. Something wasn't quite right, though. All he could find was thick, warm pelts.

A loud warning growl suddenly made him very much awake.

Gilbert's eyes shot open, and he found his hand wrist-deep in fur. On the belly of the *giant brown bear* standing by his bed.

His scream actually sent the animal stumbling back, paws over its ears, as Gilbert launched himself over a table and out the door. In his haste, he tripped down the steps outside and ended up sprawled on the damp grass below. When he lifted his head, moaning, heart still pounding wildly in his chest, there was a little crowd of very still people staring at him in shocked silence. There was a familiar-looking girl clad in red glitter perched on top of bright-red stilts. Beside her was an impressively muscular lady, a daring red costume revealing her strong arms and legs. Then a strange, purplish creature, reminiscent of an octopus tucked in a pinstripe suit—

He knew those faces all right. Humphreys. Constance. He had to be— God, he was at the goddamn circus.

He stood up with as much dignity as he could muster, wincing. His shoulder and his knees hurt, not to mention his pounding head and his shattered pride. Emilia was squeaking loudly in his scarf, woken abruptly by the fall and sounding like she was in a foul mood, like him. He took a moment to make sure she was all right. She was; she just looked supremely pissed. He couldn't really blame her.

As the awkward silence continued, Gilbert inspected the meager crowd staring at him. There were a few new faces. A pudgy clown was wrapped like candy in a striped black-and-red costume that was faded and stained and vaguely disturbing. Not as disturbing as his face, though, which was smeared in white greasepaint with bruised black eyes, blood-red lips, and too-pointy teeth. A deathly pale girl stood near a ginger-bearded dwarf, her white hair almost glowing in the weak sunlight. Two younger girls were huddled side by side near a caravan, sporting identical black dresses and brown hair, and identical faces too.

"So this is the new fellow." A squeaky, uneven voice came from somewhere below Gilbert's line of sight. He glanced down, still massaging his aching head, and jumped back, barely holding back a scream when he saw a two-foot-tall wooden mannequin standing right before him. Its jaw hung open, unhinged; big red eyes were painted sloppily on its face; and there was a black hat carved directly into its head. God, he'd had that . . . that *thing* bollocks-level until now and he hadn't even *noticed* it.

As Gilbert stared, aghast, the mannequin lifted a wooden, fingerless hand and croaked out the most disturbing, dead laughter he'd ever heard in his life. "*Ha-ha-ha. Ha-ha-ha.* He is funny. Can we keep him?"

What the *devil* was this place? Wooden toys moved and spoke openly, for heaven's sake! Sure, the existence of magic didn't shock him, but to be so public about it? And how did he get here anyway? He woke up in a bed of his own and—

Struck by the sudden remembrance of his sleeping partner, Gilbert whirled around. And there it was, slowly climbing down the steps on all fours, the massive brown bear. God, it looked even *bigger* in the light of day, barely able to squeeze through the doorway. Something glistened around its neck, but Gilbert didn't linger to find out what. Instead, he leaped forward over the satanic mannequin and found himself smack in the middle of the ragtag group of performers. Who were all still staring silently at *him*.

What the hell? At least maybe the bear would start eating one of them *first*.

The octopus man, Humphreys, took a step forward, lifting a tentacle in what might have been a friendly gesture or the opening gambit of a deadly attack, for all Gilbert knew.

"Please, don't be ssscared, sssir. I promise you, Mildred means you no harm. She's also absolutely mortified for waking you up in sssuch an abrupt manner. She was merely curious, that is all." He waved his tentacle in a conciliatory gesture. "I assure you she hasn't eaten anyone in . . . Oh, I can't remember how long *exactly*, but it's been a few years for sssure."

Was that supposed to be comforting? Because it wasn't. *Damn. Keep your priorities straight, Blake.* He shook his head, trying to force his brain to stop pounding and start working properly.

"Fair enough. Listen—this has been lovely, and I'm sure you're all wonderful people, and bears and, um, octopuses, but I must take my leave, now and—" Gilbert stopped. Something wasn't right. He shook his head, looking around. It was nearly dusk, and he had already woken up in that same place. That *morning*. He'd already seen those wagons, the black iron fence, the hanging lamps. He shoved his hand in his pocket and pulled out a little stub of paper: the underground ticket. In case he needed any more damning evidence. "Wait, just wait a moment. I can't . . . I can't be here, I-I left. I *already* left."

Humphreys spoke slowly, soothingly, as if addressing an unpredictable, frightened animal. "Perfectly normal to feel a little, how to put it, a little *confounded*, sssir, but believe me when I say it will all become clear in due—"

Fury mounted in Gilbert's skull like a boiling, frothy wave. "You followed me all the way to the city?" He very nearly yelled, not even caring that he was vastly outnumbered. "I cannot believe this! What did you— Did you lunatics have me kidnapped?"

"Hey, watch your mouth, mate," the stout dwarf replied, his voice deep and gravelly as he puffed out his broad chest. "No, we didn't kidnap you. We're not that eager to have you around, delightful as you're being right now, you little arrogant—"

"Be nice, Hugo. He's going through a rough moment, you know that. It was a tough adjustment for us all," the graceful albino lady interrupted him.

"That's no excuse to insult," Constance replied, sniffling disdainfully, the red flower in her hair vibrating. There was a general murmur of approval.

"That's just what I'm saying." The dwarf sounded more conciliatory now, looking at the albino lady with something like adoration on his features. But Gilbert was only half-listening, feverishly going over what he could remember of his day. Damn it, being angry always made it so hard to focus, and their stupid *chattering* sure wasn't helping, and his head wouldn't stop spinning . . .

"Be quiet!" he snapped, his voice shrill and squeaky in a way that under any other circumstance would have embarrassed him. He felt the urge to pace back and forth but didn't want to get a single step closer to any one of them, and they were *everywhere*. They'd bloody surrounded him, so he settled for trembling with nervous energy. "No, I-I remember I went to the city, and I was on the train, and then . . . and then that guy, he said— God, he knocked me out and dragged me all the way back here, didn't he? You sent him after me?" He was approaching a meltdown and fast. His brain sizzled with anger, the need to fight rising, since fleeing hadn't worked so well. "Oh, I'm going to show him. How *dare he*! I'm—I'm going to kick his ass, I'm . . . I'm . . ."

"Here we go," the girl on stilts said, rolling her eyes, waving a cigarette in a cloud of smoke. "He's gonna blow."

"Somebody get the ringmaster," Humphreys called out, and the two girls vanished behind the caravan, the patter of feet quickly fading.

"That's right. That's right! You go get him. You bring him to me, and I'll—" In a flash, Gilbert was swept by the memory of the immense power he'd felt in the train carriage earlier, crushing and breathtaking, and a sliver of clarity sliced through the fog of anger. Maybe it was actually for the best if they *did not* meet, and he should get the hell out of Dodge before the fellow—oh, right, the *devil*, good *Lord*—arrived again. "You know what? Never mind. I'll be on my merry way, and don't you even think of trying to stop me."

"We're not going to ssstop you, sssir," Humphreys said, fiddling with his inseparable pocket watch. His purplish complexion seemed darker, and Gilbert spared a moment to wonder if that was embarrassment he could read on the creature's face. "This is such an unfortunate sssituation. Because you see, sssir, I'm afraid you . . . you can't leave."

"You just watch me," Gilbert yelled stomping away. He shot fiery glances all around, daring them to step in and try to stop him. He still had a few aces up his sleeve. Ha! See how they liked throwing up a live hen. "Because I say I can, and I am leaving right now!"

"Yes, but . . ." Humphreys exchanged glances with the other performers. Their expressions were compassionate and a tad condescending, as if Gilbert was a little thick in the head and there was something he just wasn't getting, something simple and elementary. Oh, that infuriated him. "You can go, sir. Nobody's going to ssstop you. It's, well . . . you *can't* leave. You simply can't."

Gilbert thought he would burst into flames out of sheer frustration, veins pulsing in his temples as he turned back and yelled. "I can't leave, I can't leave. You keep saying that! But what the hell does it mean?"

"It means just that." The calm, deep voice sounded like a gong in the little clearing, drawing everyone's attention to the speaker. It was him: the red-haired ringmaster, as handsome as Gilbert remembered, looking at him with those sharp green eyes. The ringmaster—Jesse, his name was Jesse—had his hands in his pockets and a cold expression on his face. "That you are free to run as far as you please, as many times as you want, but you will never be able to leave here."

"I won't? And pray tell, who's going to stop me?" Gilbert snarled, even as something knotted in the pit of his stomach. "You?"

The man shrugged, the golden fringes on his red-and-black jacket shimmering in the fading light. "No. The circus will."

That was so utterly ludicrous it actually shut Gilbert up for a moment. He should walk out—the man was obviously crazy, everyone around there was. But he couldn't stop staring at the ringmaster as he calmly walked over to Gilbert, coming to a stop a few paces ahead of him.

"The circus?" Gilbert repeated.

"Yes, the *circus*." Jesse rolled his eyes. "Look, I warned you before you decided to join. I told you it was forever."

Inside his head, Gilbert was swearing very creatively. "Don't be ridiculous. I'm leaving right now, and I'm warning you: don't you send that guy chasing after me again. I swear, if it's the last thing I do, I'm going to take him down."

That gave Jesse pause. He looked at Gilbert with an actual spark of interest in his eyes, head tilted to the side. "What guy?"

"Don't mock me. The guy you sent after me on the train, with his fancy suit and his cane. Oh, for fuck's sake," Gilbert scoffed. "Deny it all you want, but he wouldn't stop yapping about this bloody circus. I don't know how the hell he carried me all the way back here, but let me tell you, devil or no devil, it's not going to happen again. If I see him again, he's a dead man."

Or more likely, I am. Really, there had never been an emptier threat in the history of the world.

He was torn from his thoughts by Jesse, who was suddenly close enough to take his breath away. He fisted his hand in Gilbert's lapel. His green eyes gleamed, hard and cold, peering at Gilbert from mere inches away with heart-stopping intensity.

"What devil?" he asked slowly.

So the ringmaster cared about this. *Interesting*, Gilbert thought in the corner of his mind that wasn't bewitched by Jesse's sudden closeness. His scent—smoke, and fuel, and fire—was nothing short of intoxicating, and Gilbert's body responded to it, his blood heating up inside his veins. His eyes were irresistibly drawn to the sharp lines of Jesse's face, framed by unruly red hair. His lips, so close, begging to be tasted.

"You, *magician*, I said, what devil?" Jesse's grip tightened, yanking Gilbert forward so their chests were brushing.

"Oh, just *some* devil," Gilbert replied deliberately, a smirk curling his lips upward as he held Jesse's cold gaze. He could see the anger brewing there, feel it sizzling in Jesse's body so tantalizing close to his.

Oh, Gilbert was literally playing with fire, and he was loving it. "And now that I think of it, he had a message for you too."

Jesse tilted his head up, his face near enough to Gilbert's that he would only have to lean over to kiss those lips. "Tell me. Now."

Gilbert reacted then, grasping the wrist of Jesse's free hand and twisting it down, hard enough to be painful. They were locked in a silent battle of wills, holding on to each other, defiantly staring into each other's eyes—Jesse's hard and simmering with anger, and Gilbert with a mocking smirk on his lips, which he knew would make the ringmaster even more furious. He'd made an art of pissing people off, and he was thoroughly enjoying pushing Jesse's buttons.

"And what if I don't?" he rasped, holding Jesse's gaze. They were so goddamn close. Gilbert's body was burning up, consumed with a yearning so delightful it almost made him forget how angry and scared he was, forget about the troupe surrounding them in threatening silence.

Damn, he bet Jesse would be an amazing fuck—fiery and aggressive, demanding. He wondered whether Jesse would bite him, pin him to the bed, grab him in the throes of pleasure hard enough to leave bruises. The thought sent a heated frisson down Gilbert's spine, all the way to his cock, and he had to bite his lip to hold back from leaning down and devouring Jesse's mouth.

Jesse was trying his damnedest to keep up his cold facade, but Gilbert could see him burning underneath too—consumed with the need to know, to ask, maybe to knock Gilbert to the ground and pound into him until he got his answer. Oh, this devil had to be someone important then, and Gilbert was almost tempted to pony up, just so he could know more about what it was that made Jesse's blood run so hot. But Jesse made his decision first, his expression shutting down into one of cold determination as he released his iron grip on Gilbert's jacket, taking a step back. Looked like he wouldn't give Gilbert the satisfaction.

"I don't have time to waste with you and your stupid games," Jesse scoffed. "We didn't send anyone after you. But you are free to believe whatever you want." He made an annoyed gesture toward the gate. "Knock yourself out. Run away as many times as you like. When you're ready to listen, then we'll talk."

And with that, he turned his back on him, and Gilbert could practically *feel* his attention completely shutting off. It was as though the air had grown a few degrees colder. As he left, the ringmaster addressed the rest of the troupe. "Keep an eye on him, make sure he doesn't hurt anyone or try to set stuff on fire like he did." He pointed his thumb toward the dwarf, who looked very much embarrassed. "Don't bother me with him again until he's ready to listen. Until then, it's useless. You've all been there, you should know."

If there was something that grated on Gilbert's nerves more than, well, the many things that usually did, it was being ignored, having people talk about him like he wasn't even there. And Jesse doing it . . . Somehow the burn was so much worse. Gilbert craved the man's attention, those green eyes on him. Not that he would admit that out loud anytime soon.

"Well . . . well, fine. I'm leaving then. See if you can keep up this time!" he called out to Jesse's retreating back. Everyone looked at him with the patiently exasperated expression usually reserved for petulant children throwing tantrums, which did nothing to ease his irritation.

Everyone but the ringmaster, of course, who just shrugged, not even bothering to look back. "See if I care. Have a nice trip."

Gilbert was so furious, he didn't have any words left, so he turned on his heel and stormed out of the encampment before he well and truly lost it and people started vomiting chickens.

CHAPTER 6

T hat was the start of a lengthy string of failures.

The second time, Gilbert changed his strategy. Instead of heading out of town, he headed deep into it. Down into the most infamous slums, deep in the heart of a rookery—a cluster of buildings and chimneys and dismissed factories that had been turned into a beehive of crime, a den of thieves, murderers, prostitutes, beggars, and assorted lunatics. Anyone with half a brain knew that, unless you were one of *them*, the Devil's Acre was to be avoided at all costs. Even the constables wouldn't dare set foot in it.

The penalty for trespassing was death.

So, obviously, Gilbert was familiar with the place. Once upon a time, he'd done a favor for Andrea, the Lady of the Acre—a determined, muscular woman who was missing half her face and covered it with extravagantly decorated masks—who ran the main lodging house and watering hole down there. The entire slum, at that, in her perennial war against Reuben for dominance of Shadowsea's underworld.

If there was one place where Reuben's men wouldn't follow him, it was within the borders of Andrea's bloody kingdom.

Gilbert walked in through a cramped side street while smoke and noise came from the railway bridges crisscrossed above it. His hands rested at his sides and his scarf was pushed down to leave his face clearly visible. Somewhere above his head, among the many chimneys on the roofs, he heard an exchange of whistles in different tones and pitches. Somebody was deciding whether he was allowed to go in or if a gang would take the drop on him at the next corner. It felt like walking with a bull's-eye painted on his back in the blood of all those whose lives had been claimed by the Acre.

Despite being reasonably sure that he was welcome, that scrutiny never failed to make his stomach knot. It was why he didn't come often, if he could help it.

Andrea's inn, the Rotten Duck, was a ramshackle building propped up by beams and ropes, and was the beating heart of the Devil's Acre. When Gilbert pushed the door open, he was enveloped by the warmth of the stove, the crowd, and the shouting that filled the inn at every hour of the day and night. The thick smoke of gas lamps and a hundred pipes hovered over mismatched tables and chairs but under the low ceiling. In a corner, a handful of drunks were throwing darts and knives at a board, trying to avoid killing the poor sod standing in front of it.

Andrea stood behind the bar, wearing a mask of expensive-looking cream leather with silver inlays and peacock feathers arching over her head. She was working on something like a bundle of dynamite sticks tied together, and she didn't even raise her gaze when Gilbert took a seat in front of her.

"Why, Blake, I haven't seen you around in a while. Something to drink?"

"Always." Gilbert took out some money as Andrea set aside the explosive and bent to grab an unmarked bottle from beneath the bar. She poured a pint of it, and Gilbert didn't even bother asking what it was. He sniffed the drink when it was placed right under his nose, and the pure alcohol burned a trail up his nostrils. *Wonderful. Just what I needed.* He shrugged and tossed down a mouthful, which burned like live coals down his throat.

"How have you been, Miss Andrea?" he croaked, his vocal chords singed.

"Good. Keeping busy." She was back to tinkering with her explosive, and pointed her screwdriver toward the dartboard. "Have you met Richard, my new husband?"

Gilbert glanced over as the man standing by the board took a knife to the shoulder and went down screaming. Far from being concerned, the others burst into roaring laughter. "Which one is he?"

"The one rolling around on the floor."

"I see. Seems like a good fellow." Gilbert turned back as Richard was kicked away and someone else promptly took his place. "Which husband is that, the fourth?"

"Fifth, actually."

"Oh, sorry. What happened to Willard?" That was the last one Gilbert remembered, at any rate. He was so short and his bald head so carefully polished that people sometimes used it as a mirror.

Andrea shrugged. "Thought he could rob the mail coach alone with an empty bottle of gin."

Gilbert cringed and raised his glass in a toast to poor old Willard. "Ouch. Big mistake."

"And his last," Andrea added coolly. Not that Gilbert expected too much emotion from a woman who had once removed an ear from a man's head, then fed it to him after he'd called her some less-than-pleasant epithets. She'd been as calm and composed as if she'd been having tea with the queen. "So, I hear you're in trouble, young man. Not that I'm surprised. I know it takes dire circumstances to bring you to the Acre."

Gilbert downed the rest of the infernal drink. Well, he couldn't say he was surprised, either. There was little going on in Shadowsea that Andrea didn't know about. "You know me so well. And yes, I suppose I am. I may have pissed some folks off, you know. I did something stupid in one of Reuben's gambling holes, and ended up trashing the place and taking with me a big chunk of cash."

"'S what I heard. His dogs have been tearing up the streets looking for some blond magician with a rat. I had an inkling it might be you they were after. You really should be more discreet, Blake." Andrea's eyes were glimmering in delight. She loved it when Gilbert worked his scams in Reuben's pubs and left a little collateral damage on his way out. It was the best way to remain in her good graces. She considered it a personal favor whenever someone took money out of the count's pockets.

"Yeah, well. Can't really disagree with you there." So they *were* still looking for him. *Fuck.* He had really screwed up this time. He could only hope someone else would do something even more stupid soon, so that Reuben might forget about him and move on. "So, if it's all right with you, I was maybe hoping to hole up in here for a—"

"Say no more," Andrea interrupted him. "Feel free to stay for as long as you like. I'm always glad to hear you're making life difficult for that pile of worms in a suit."

Gilbert waited, but she didn't add anything else, just finished tinkering with her screwdriver and leaned down to take a closer look at the explosive. So, it was a done deal. Excellent. He slouched more comfortably on his seat, glancing back as someone else screamed by the dartboard.

Something familiar caught his eye, something that didn't belong there. A gleam of silver . . . A tall, elegant shape, standing very still in a corner . . . Fleeting piercing black eyes . . . Before realizing it, Gilbert was already standing, vibrating with tension, eyes frantically scanning the room. But he saw nothing. Whatever he'd glimpsed was gone.

If it had ever been there in the first place.

He turned back around, shaken and pissed, to find Andrea standing at attention, alarmed by his sudden reaction, hand hovering near her belt.

"What is it?" Her voice was low, like dull thunder before an avalanche. Gilbert knew that, with a word, she could unleash her troops on anyone who dared trespass in her dominion.

Gilbert raised his hands, shaking his head, and took another quick look around the room just to make *sure*, because the echo of that crushing power was all too vivid in his mind. "No. It's nothing. I'm sorry. I thought I—" He wiped an unsteady hand over his mouth. "I should retire for the night. Look, it's not just Reuben; I-I've got some, some weird people after me. Like, *really* weird. Trust me, if you see them, you'll know. They've already kidnapped me once. So do you think— Could you have a couple of your guys watching the door?"

"Absolutely, darling, Diana, Bartholomew. Accompany Mr. Blake to the Dandelion Room and stay on guard until morning."

"Thank you, Miss Andrea. I . . ." Gilbert wanted to say more, but she was already waving him off.

A tall woman with olive skin and a red cloth wrapped around her head stepped forward, and if Gilbert hadn't been looking for them, he would never have noticed the knives artfully concealed on her person. Behind her was a stocky man with a shaved head and a bushy brown beard, his bare arms covered in scars and smudged tattoos. They all but swept him out of the room and up the stairs and shoved him inside a room at the far end of the corridor.

Diana stood in the doorway, hands on her hips. "I want you to lock this door and keep your weapons near you at all times. This is one of the safe rooms—reinforced walls. You'll notice there's no window in there, no entrance but this door. And nobody gets past Barts and me. If a whole damn army comes, we'll wake you up, and you can join the fight. Until then, you can sleep like a baby."

"Thank you, I—" Gilbert barely had the time to see Bartholomew arriving with two stools and a rifle slung over his shoulder before Diana slammed the door in his face.

There was a rather impressive selection of bolts on the inside, so Gilbert halfheartedly locked a bunch of them because, really, if something could get past his keepers, he seriously doubted that a couple of bolts would stop it. But this was all precaution, anyway. He was fairly sure the circus freaks didn't want him *that* badly. They wouldn't risk a bloodbath to get him back. They'd just been trying to scare him, to mess with his head.

As for Reuben's men, he wasn't the least bit concerned about them. They wouldn't get within a mile of the Acre, and certainly not for him.

The room was sparsely decorated, with a rickety bed crammed in a corner, a table, and a tin basin. The main feature was the extravagant yellow wallpaper with its dandelion motif. That was Andrea's quirk: all her rooms were wallpapered and named after a different flower, no matter that the guests were usually too drunk to appreciate it.

There wasn't much he could do, so Gilbert sprawled on the bed with a sigh, arms folded behind his head, and stared at the dandelions. But when he closed his eyes, what he saw was icy-cold green. *Damn it.* The memory of Jesse's body, thrumming with anger, with such passion, pressed close to his still made Gilbert's blood run hot, when he thought about it. And those mesmerizing eyes, they just wouldn't leave him alone.

Fuck. He rolled onto his side, squeezed his eyes shut, and focused on Diana and Bartholomew's voices as the two bickered outside his door. All of a sudden, he felt tired to the bone, and gratefully let himself sink into sleep, trying to avoid the damned green eyes wide-open in a corner of his mind.

He woke up what seemed like an instant later, being tossed off the bed.

The floor was shaking, jumping. The clattering and loud whistling noises pierced Gilbert's eardrums like needles. He blinked rapidly, grasping for purchase on the unstable floor, trying to adjust to the bright light coming in from the window, which was . . .

Impossible. Wait a minute . . .

He lifted himself to all fours and whipped his head left and right. Sure enough, he saw the cramped interior of a caravan, the now-familiar dusty furniture and patched curtains. Under him, the floor jumped abruptly, nearly sending him sprawling once more. The goddamn wagon was *moving*!

"Goddamned wankers, this time I'll . . ." He trailed off, taking the time to check that Emilia was safe in his scarf, then stumbled to the door. He yanked it open, determined to give them all a good piece of his mind. "What the fuck—"

And nearly tripped on his own feet as he backed away, stumbling and clutching the doorway to hold himself upright and not kill himself by falling off the rolling wagon. There was a *thing*, a giant, bronze polished *thing* right before his eyes—bigger than the goddamn caravan, bigger than a *house*, all plates and gears, clicking and turning and huffing and—

"Look who's back! Hey, our new friend's met Herbert."

Two bright-purple poles came swinging toward him, clicking loudly on the road. Gilbert stared up, too stunned to even think, to see the slender woman in her red costume waving at him from above, easily keeping the wagon's pace on her stilts. On top of the moving mountain of gears rested the biggest stovepipe hat he'd ever laid eyes on, big enough for a grown man to crawl into.

"Who the hell is Herbert?" he blurted. Then promptly mentally kicked himself. God, of all the things he needed to ask. "And can we please all stop? I need a moment to . . . I said stop the bloody wagon!"

"Our elephant. He's right in front of you."

Gilbert opened and closed his mouth, looking for something sensible to say. That thing was supposed to be an elephant? Upon closer inspection, it did seem to have ears—broad, rounded brass plates bolted to the sides of what might possibly be a head. And as

Gilbert clung to the door, frozen, the elephant—Herbert—lifted its long trunk of gears and wires and trumpeted loudly in his face.

"See, he likes him already," the lady on stilts yelled over the hissing steam.

"I told you he seemed nice," another woman replied. "Elephants are great judges of character, you know."

A second wagon rolled on toward Gilbert's, propelled forward by a bulky contraption at the front, huffing and whistling and churning out a thick plume of white smoke. In fact, Gilbert could see a few more similar plumes scattered down the road, the wagons themselves hidden by Herbert's bulk. Constance was looking out from the wagon's window, and the ringmaster himself was perched in the driver's seat above the contraption.

"You . . . you!" Gilbert cursed as his wagon hit a bump and nearly tossed him off the steps. "Where the hell are you taking me?"

The ringmaster didn't bother replying, so Constance called out, "We're moving to another city. We have to work for a living, you know."

Gilbert slammed his hand on the doorway. "I'm not going anywhere with you! You hear me? How did you take me *again*? What did you do to Diana and . . . and the other guy? Did you—"

"Whoa. Whoa! Stop squawking, would you?" Jesse interrupted. "We didn't do anything to anybody. We have a show coming up, and we're going there, end of story. We're just doing our goddamn job."

"What game are you playing at?" Gilbert growled, holding on to the doorframe to lean out toward Jesse. If he fell, Herbert would probably trample all over him, but he was too pissed off to care. "You let me go, then chase after me to bring me back?"

"For the love of God," Jesse snapped, rolling his eyes to high heavens. "I told you I don't give a rat's ass about having you here. In fact, I'm beginning to sorely regret it. And I'm *still* not talking to you. Go on, run away. We'll talk when you're actually willing to listen."

"Oh, bugger off." Gilbert jumped from the still-moving wagon— who the hell was driving that thing?—landing with as much dignity as he could muster. "Try to catch me this time, asshole. I dare you!"

Jesse flipped him the bird and sped on, vanishing from sight in a cloud of smoke.

Gilbert stomped off along the trail of wagons, suppressing a long streak of colorful curses. He had no idea where he was or how far from the city, but what the hell. He had to leave Shadowsea anyway, since obviously staying at Andrea's wouldn't work. He kept his head down as more faces poked out of windows to watch him go.

"Leaving so soon?" someone called out, and Gilbert *of course* didn't dignify that with an answer.

Some of the wagons were chained together, moving along like a miniature train, led by Humphreys, who was wearing a very dapper travel coat and a fancy plumed hat. "Mr. Blake, what a pleasure to sssee you again! Are you leaving?"

"Yeah." Gilbert grunted. All right, he was determined to ignore them, but Humphreys was so polite and cordial, he just couldn't *avoid* it.

"Well, sssir, you are of course most welcome to do so, but I'm afraid that the circus . . ."

"I know, I know, the stupid circus won't let me leave, I simply *can't* leave—I know the drill," Gilbert interrupted, still marching on. Then he added, under his breath, "We'll see about that."

It was only after a few miles, when the noise and whistling of the traveling circus had vanished in the distance, that he came across the last wagon. It was the ancient black one, and it had no driver nor any contraption propelling it forward. It left no trail of smoke as it rolled in eerie silence along the road, apparently of its own volition.

As he passed it, keeping his distance, a silent chill descended upon him, seeping into his bones, the sudden freeze cold enough to take his breath away. There was something damned about that circus all right, and he had no intention of sticking around to find out exactly what.

This time, he didn't sleep for almost three days.

He hitched a ride on a commercial transport and sulked among the sacks of wool all the way to the coast. To the docks. He boarded the first ship that would have him, setting sail for the icy Northern Sea. He struggled to keep awake as long as his body would allow, losing game after game of cards in the canteen—no tricks this time, he didn't want to be tossed overboard, thank you—until he was almost hallucinating from sleep deprivation. He finally fell asleep facedown on a table, lulled by a dirty sailors' song about prosperous mermaids.

When he woke up, the circus troupe was busy around a giant striped tent in the middle of the encampment. Gilbert didn't even look at them as he ran out, steadfastly ignoring their calls.

The fourth time, he got himself thrown in prison, locked in solitary confinement for attempting to urinate on a constable's leg, and woke up in the goddamn wagon as the troupe was gathering for dinner.

The fifth time, he hid out in the luggage area of a zeppelin headed across the ocean. When he awoke in the wagon with a hen perched on his pillow, he started screaming.

After that, Gilbert lost count. He went without sleep for longer than he thought was humanly possible. His brain was mush, he didn't know what day it was, or what city he'd woken up near. He didn't even bother asking anymore, just mechanically walked away from the circus, traveling as far as his legs would take him before he passed out from sheer exhaustion and it started all over again. He was furious and scared and drained. He yelled and raged on until he was more or less delirious and rambled to everyone who would listen about the evil cursed circus that was out to get him.

People treated him like a poor lunatic, and maybe they weren't very wrong in that assessment. He probably looked like one too. He couldn't remember when he'd last shaved; his beard was long and unkempt. His eyes were bloodshot, the bags under them so deep that Emilia could have slept in them.

Until, one day, he decided to stop.

He opened his eyes and found himself right where he expected to be: in the dusty caravan, with its colorful throws and old circus props, Emilia chewing on a cookie on the table, next to the little bowl of nuts that someone always left for her. Suddenly, he wasn't disappointed anymore. The place looked familiar. Comforting, even. Like he'd come to rely on the one constant in his life, that he would always wake up here.

And now, he had to be rational about it. As rational as the situation would allow, anyway. He'd been so busy running around like a headless chicken that he hadn't stopped to think about it even for a moment, too scared and furious. Well, he was done running.

He had to face it. He'd been brought back from places the troupe couldn't have possibly reached. No human could have kept track of him, could have found him, much less dragged him back against his will. He'd been watching his back every instant, and he was certain that no one had been following him. Not even the spider guy. Gilbert hadn't caught a glimpse of him again, nor felt the presence of his power.

Lying there on his back, in what had somehow become the closest thing to a home he had, Gilbert was strangely calm, full of a detached clarity. The force that brought him back every time was not human. Maybe it truly was the circus that refused to allow him to leave.

Maybe it was time to try another approach: Listen. Figure out what it was, how it worked. Why it wanted him. And then figure a way out of it. It might not be so bad hanging around for a while, he reasoned. Would give him an excellent place to hide from Reuben's men too, on the off chance they were still after him.

He covered his face with his hands and took a deep breath.

No more running.

After washing his face and cleaning up as best as he could, Gilbert grabbed Emilia, pushed the door open, and walked out. He hesitated on the steps, looking around, a chill wind ruffling his hair. It was almost dusk, and the encampment was quiet. The bear was rolling and wriggling in the grass, scratching its back. The pale lady appeared from behind a wagon, wobbling under a large sack of potatoes.

Without thinking too much about it, Gilbert jogged down the steps and over to her, stopping at a respectful distance, uncertain.

"Um. Here, let me. I mean, if I may?" He held out his hands. She looked at him for a moment, then smiled and nodded.

"Why, thank you." She let Gilbert take the sack, then led the way. "This goes to the canteen. I'm Ramona. I take care of the cooking."

"Oh. That's . . . lovely. It's a pleasure to meet you, Miss Ramona."

She was so nice. So polite. He felt a little out of his depth, like he did with Humphreys. He supposed it just wasn't the company he was used to.

"I didn't quite catch your name, Mr. . . . ?"

"Blake. Uh, I mean, Gilbert. Gilbert is fine."

They reached a wagon painted a faded green, with large, low windows and a crooked pipe at the top pouring out thin gray smoke. A few folks sat at a long table set up outside—Gilbert recognized the twin girls and the dwarf—and Humphreys was inside the open door with a rag wrapped around his head and a knife, pot, or vegetable in every tentacle. Whatever conversation had been going on stopped abruptly as everyone turned to stare at him. Gilbert swallowed.

"You can put it down here, Gilbert, thank you. Mr. Humphreys is the fastest potato peeler in the country."

Gilbert offered the girl an awkward smile and obeyed, propping the sack up by the wagon's steps. When he raised his head, the ringmaster was in front of him, casually leaning against the doorframe, wearing a shirt with the sleeves rolled up and a vest, hands casually in his pockets. His forearms were covered in tattoos, including a rattlesnake wrapped around his elbow whose tail disappeared up his sleeve. His red locks were tied back in a loose ponytail, and Gilbert wondered whether that was the hint of a smile on his lips.

"So. You done?"

Gilbert harrumphed, looking with sudden interest at the tips of his boots, while the conversation picked back up at the table. Something smelled delicious over there, and Humphreys was back to chopping energetically. Gilbert's stomach grumbled. He heard voices chattering at the table:

"It's about time."

"What are you complaining about? You stayed locked in your wagon for two solid months. We had to feed you through the window."

"You're one to talk, you tried to set the circus on fire. *Twice.*"

"*Hey.* Magician." Jesse snapped his fingers. "So, are you ready to shut up and listen now?"

Gilbert took a deep breath and shrugged, stealing a last glance at the table. He couldn't even muster up a little hostility. "Yeah. I guess so."

The ringmaster's face softened. Now that definitely was a smile—perhaps the first one Gilbert had seen on his lips. "Why don't we grab a cup of tea and a bite to eat, then go have a quiet chat in my caravan?"

Grateful, Gilbert returned the smile. "Yes. I'd like that."

CHAPTER 7

"So, how many times did you run?" The ringmaster turned his back to Gilbert, fiddling with a teapot over the stove.

Gilbert sat at the table where Emilia was helping herself to a cookie. He rubbed his hand over his face. "Honestly? I lost count."

"That's too bad." Jesse chuckled to himself. "We had a little bet going on. The guys will be disappointed."

Gilbert offered an uncertain smile to the man's back. He didn't quite know how to reply, so he busied himself with looking around the wagon. Bundles of herbs were hanging from the ceiling, and every nook and cranny was piled with ancient tomes, papers, wooden trinkets, a few mechanical toys—a miniature hot-air balloon, a wind-up elephant. A trunk shoved in the corner was spilling over with torches, thin sticks with one end wrapped in blackened fabric.

"So. Gilbert, is it?" Jesse said, placing two steaming mugs on the table before taking a seat. "You weren't listening when I told you this was forever."

"No, I was listening." He really had been, even though he'd been panicked, half–passed out, and reeling from a head wound. How could he be expected to display sound judgment given the situation? "I just didn't— I didn't take it literally, that's all."

"So you didn't believe me." Before Gilbert could grumble something in his own defense, the ringmaster waved him off. "Never you mind. You're certainly not the first one. Sugar?"

"No, nothing. Thank you." They sat in silence for a moment as Gilbert pressed his fingertips to the scalding-hot enamel cup. "So you *really* weren't chasing after me? None of you?"

"So it would seem."

"Then how does this work? Why do I keep waking up here?"

Jesse shrugged, warming his hands around his mug. "You're the magician. I figured you'd have plenty of theories about that."

Gilbert didn't find it amusing. "Well, it's your goddamn circus," he snapped.

The ringmaster brushed it off, busy buttering a dry-looking slice of bread. "I can't tell you exactly *how* it happens because I don't really know myself. I am no magician. I can only tell you the rules, and they're quite simple. You've seen it yourself. You can run as far as you like, and it doesn't matter. You could flee to the end of the world. But you'll have to fall asleep sometime, and when you do, you will wake up here. We are the Circus of the Damned, after all. Did that not make you wonder?"

"I have noticed that, thank you." Gilbert pinched the bridge of his nose. "Does it happen to everyone?"

"Yes."

"Even you?"

"Yes. It comes in quite handy at times, I have to say." Jesse shoved what was left of the bread in his mouth. "If I have to take a long trip, I don't need to bother arranging for the return. I can just take a nap."

Was he trying to be funny? Because the whole situation didn't seem like a laughing matter. It was, in fact, quite tragic. "So you travel often? Far away from the circus?"

Jesse swallowed and smacked his lips. "Actually, no."

Oh, for the love of God. Gilbert could feel a migraine coming. "Fine. Fine, so if you can't tell me how it happens, can you at least tell me why?"

"That's how the deal works. When you agree to it, you sign over your life to the circus, and your soul, as well. And the circus—and all within—belongs to the devil." Jesse pushed another cookie toward Emilia, who happily accepted it. "No one can ever leave this circus, Gilbert. Not while living, and not after death. The spirits of the old performers, they are all still here. They will remain here for as long as the circus lives on. Which, if I have any say in it, will be forever."

Jesse's face had darkened, a grim determination hardening his features. Gilbert rubbed his chin with his hand. The fellow on the train had spoken of a deal too. "So, this *deal* you're referring to. I get the impression you don't mean the one I made with you that night."

Jesse scrunched up his nose. "No. Yes. It's . . . complicated. I'm the one who struck the deal, in the beginning. I'm the one responsible for upholding it, and the other performers join in, one by one. Including you. You made the deal with me, but truth is, I'm just a . . . middleman. Through me, you've joined in the original, ongoing deal. Does that make sense?"

As much as any of this makes any sense, I guess. "More or less. And it's a deal you made with *whom*?"

Jesse stared straight at him, seeming actually mildly surprised. "Oh. With the devil, of course."

Why, of course. How silly of me to even ask!

Gilbert rubbed at his eyes, holding back a groan. His first instinct was to call bullshit, but he couldn't deny that there was something unnatural at work in this place. Hell, *something* had yanked him back to the circus from all over the country as though it was nothing.

He should be more upset about it, but it was really difficult to *believe*. Jesse spoke of it with such calm, as if it were the most mundane of occurrences, instead of a tale better suited for the halls of a madhouse. But after all, not that long ago, he'd made a hen crawl out of somebody's throat. He wasn't exactly in the best position to call anything *weird*, now was he?

"And this devil . . ." He sighed, leaning back in the chair. He hesitated for a moment. *Oh, what the hell.* "Does he happen to run around with a silver spider as a pet?"

"How do you . . .?" Jesse's eyes widened, his cup frozen in midair. "So you weren't lying to me when you said—"

"Ha. So you're the one who didn't believe me," Gilbert teased. Jesse had the decency to look embarrassed, a light flush appearing on his cheeks. "And no, I wasn't. He caught up to me on the train, the first time I ran. Dark skin, shaved head, expensive clothes. He had a spider tattoo on his neck, right here." He placed two fingers on the spot. "And he had a strange name. Far— Frar—"

"Farfarello." Jesse's expression had shut down again.

"That's the one. Does he come around often? No offense, but I'm not in a hurry to meet your friend again."

"He's not a friend. And he hasn't been around in years. I'm in no hurry to meet him again either." Jesse almost slammed the mug down, his words clipped. "You had said he had a message? What does he want now?"

Gilbert was almost taken aback by the sudden change in Jesse's mood. Bringing up that devil seemed to be enough to stir up a whole damn storm inside him. So, maybe this deal wasn't so mundane to him after all. "Nothing that I know of, except to have some fun at my expense, apparently. He just wanted to send you his regards."

"His regards, my ass," Jesse muttered, shoving the mug away. "That son of a bitch has no regards for anyone but his own damn self."

Gilbert recognized that kind of anger. There was something more to it, something personal—that much was clear. He could practically see the emotions battling under Jesse's skin. He was trying to look cold and composed, but there was no hiding whatever turmoil just mentioning this Farfarello guy had awoken in him.

Gilbert didn't like that one bit. It stirred something dark and angry in the pit of his stomach, jealousy as heavy as a stone.

"And you're telling me this *devil* owns my soul, now? Thanks to you," he spat, harsher than he intended.

Jesse lowered his eyes for a moment. "Yes. I'm afraid so."

Fantastic. Gilbert wanted to smash something. "This is bullshit. There's got to be a way out of this. Look, I will repay my debt—hang around for a while, work for you, pay you back helping to sell some tickets or whatever—but come on. I'm not about to spend the rest of my life hiding away with a bunch of—"

He snapped his mouth shut before he could say it, but Jesse's eyes grew cold in an instant, hard and sharp like gemstones.

"No, go ahead. Say it." His voice was just as icy. "A bunch of freaks. And you're too good for us, am I right?"

Gilbert raised his hands. "I didn't mean—"

"Yes, you *did* mean. That's *exactly* what you meant." Jesse leaned forward. "I don't know who the hell you think you are, but you better listen carefully and make your peace with it right now: you *are* a freak. You're one of us, whether you like it or not."

"I'm not a goddamn—" Gilbert almost yelled, then caught himself and lowered his voice, trying to keep calm. "I am *not* a freak."

"Right, because any average guy on the street has magical powers that they try to keep secret, doing a piss-poor job of it at that. And if people found out what you really are, they would crown you and call you prince regent, is that right, *magician*?"

That shut Gilbert up. He didn't know how to reply, how to explain, but it was *different*. So he could do magic, so what? It wasn't like he couldn't appear perfectly normal if he wanted to. Live a perfectly ordinary life. Walk on the street without anyone looking at him twice. People didn't stare at him in horror, didn't recoil from him, didn't laugh. He could stop doing magic and forget about it and be just like everybody else, if he'd so choose.

"It's different," he managed to say, his throat closing up. That word, it had been thrown at him, hurled like a stone, more times than he could count. Screamed at him, spat at him with such venom, such utter disgust. "That doesn't make me a . . ."

"Well, it sure seemed like your buddies that night didn't think so, now did they?" Jesse was still staring straight at him, and the sharpness of his gaze almost physically hurt. "Had they caught you, they would have bludgeoned you to death, then burned your pitiful remains to the cry of witchcraft."

"Maybe so." Gilbert swallowed, his voice hoarse. "Mighty convenient for you, wasn't it?"

Jesse's eyes narrowed. "What's that supposed to mean?"

"Is that what you do? Whenever you need fresh blood for your goddamn deal, you hang around waiting for someone to be in mortal danger so you can rope them into joining this fucking—"

"Don't you *dare* act like we've forced you into anything!" Jesse's hand slammed on the table. "I was perfectly clear with you about what it would mean, and I seem to remember you *begging* us to let you join."

"Yeah, because the alternative was being *beaten to death*! I would have agreed to anything you'd said. Don't pretend you don't know that!" Gilbert fought to calm himself down and pointed a finger toward Jesse. "You needed someone to join for whatever goddamn reason, and you took advantage of the situation. How mighty generous of you."

"You can keep arguing all you want. It doesn't change the fact that you're stuck here now."

"What, you saved my life, so now it's yours? Is that how it works?"

"Apparently, *yes*." Jesse snapped his mouth shut and took a deep breath, eyes closed, visibly trying to keep his head. "You want a reason? I will give you a reason. If I don't replace a dead performer within a *day*, then I violate the deal. And all the souls are lost. You hear that? The living die, and all the souls suspended in the circus get dragged down to Hell. That's the devil's prize, and trust me, he can't wait to get his hands on it. So you'll forgive me if my first concern is making damn sure that doesn't happen. And stop pretending you didn't get anything out of it: you saved our lives, we saved yours. Fair deal."

Silence stretched as Gilbert felt his animosity fade. Now he just felt tired. There wasn't much he could reply with to that. It was the truth, after all. They had both been in desperate need; they had saved each other. He supposed it really was fair enough. Jesse looked worn out too. Clearly Gilbert's accusations had hit a sore spot.

"Listen . . . I'm sorry. You all seem decent folks, and I'm not saying—"

"No, you're right. You have a reason to be pissed. That was no way to make this deal." Jesse sighed. "But time was running out, and I wanted to protect my troupe, no matter what I had to do, and you got caught in the middle of it. It wasn't fair to you." He lifted his gaze, meeting Gilbert's eyes. "Look, I can apologize for the way we . . . the way *I* went about doing it, but it's a done deal now. Even if I wanted to, there's nothing I can do to change it."

"Well," Gilbert said, eventually. "You did save my life, so I guess being here is better than being dead. It's my fault, really, I got carried away and got that mob chasing after me. I screwed up."

They were silent for a moment, quietly making a truce. Then Jesse offered him a small smile. "So what did you do?"

Gilbert cleared his throat, sheepishly. "I may have caused a live hen to crawl out of someone's mouth," he admitted, and saw that Jesse was genuinely amused, surprise lighting up his face. The smile looked good on his face, and Gilbert wanted to make him laugh too.

"Hey, it wasn't my fault! He was being a sore loser, and I got pissed off."

"So you made a chicken come out of somebody's mouth?" The ringmaster chuckled. "Do you make a habit of being so marvelously subtle with your abilities?"

"It was a hen, not a chicken," Gilbert retorted, piqued.

"Well, that actually explains a lot. One of the guys that Constance beat up that night had been holding a hen hostage." Jesse shook his head to himself, still smiling. "I'm happy to report that we rescued her and that she's settled in quite well. Her eggs are a welcome addition to our breakfast, when Mildred doesn't steal them first."

Gilbert rubbed his forehead. Too many names—he was already losing track. Constance, she was the strong one with the tattoos, but . . . "Which one is Mildred again?"

Jesse grinned. "She's the furry one. You met her up close. How ungentlemanly of you, you didn't even ask her name?"

It took Gilbert a good few seconds to understand. "The bear? Oh, right. I, uh, I forgot."

"She's a real prima donna, let me tell you. Wait till you see her on show nights."

Gilbert had to laugh, shaking his head. It was hard not to when Jesse was looking at him with that smile. "So this is it," he said, mostly resigned, staring at his hands where they lay on the table. "I belong to the devil now. There really isn't a way out."

"I'm afraid so. Sorry." Jesse reached out, briefly covering Gilbert's hand with his tattooed one. His skin was warm and dry. "Why don't you give it a try? Give us a chance? I promise you, it's not that bad. You might even come to like it here."

Gilbert sighed. It wasn't as if he had much choice, and the one thing he'd learned was to take what life threw his way and run with it—until he ended up in a ditch somewhere, that was. Besides, he didn't quite believe the ringmaster's words. There had to be a way out of here—there was always a way out—and he'd be damned if he didn't find it. Literally. He would ask around, keep working on it. As they started to trust him, something was bound to slip out, and he'd be ready to bolt. But in the meantime, he might as well make the best of it.

"All right," he said, meeting Jesse's beautiful green eyes and smiling. "Consider me on board."

CHAPTER 8

He'd thought he would toss and turn the night away, but Gilbert apparently had some sleep to catch up on. He woke up to a soft light streaming in the narrow window, and his stomach grumbled like a bear. He actually couldn't remember the last time he'd eaten a proper meal.

Still, he caught a glimpse of his face in the elaborate mirror hanging on the wall and stopped to wipe the dust off the glass with his sleeve. Then, he spared some time to wash up properly and trim his beard with a pair of ridiculously tiny silver scissors he'd found tucked in a drawer. If he had to start socializing with the troupe, he didn't want to scare them off because he looked like a lunatic vagrant. Once he was somewhat presentable, he opened the door and ventured out, taking a deep breath of cool morning air.

He followed the scent of hot coffee and freshly baked bread, which made his stomach grumble even louder. When he rounded the corner, he saw, well, everyone, sitting around the table in front of the pale-green wagon. Conversation stopped as they all turned to look at him, and Gilbert froze in place, wondering whether he should just retreat and hide out in his wagon until the end of his days. His stomach, though, propelled him forward, toward the delicious-smelling food he could see piled on the table. And besides, after a moment, they all went back to their plates and to munching and chattering among themselves.

Jesse came out of the canteen wagon, carrying a pot of coffee. "Good morning, Gilbert. Come on over. I promise we're not going to eat you."

So he shuffled along and sat down at the far end of the bench, and Constance, sitting in front of him, shoved a platter of bread buns, jam, and butter toward him. "Help yourself. You must be famished."

Gilbert took his time buttering a piece of bread as he looked around the table, inspecting the faces. There was the slender woman with the black hair. The octopus man was in the wagon again, fussing over the stove. As he peered around, the twins arrived, rubbing the sleep from their eyes, still tightly pressed against one another. They had to maneuver a bit to climb on the bench, and Gilbert finally noticed that they were joined at the hip.

Took me long enough. So much for being observant.

The creepy clown sat at the end of the table, not eating, and the red-eyed mannequin was perched beside him. *That* thing definitely didn't eat. Unless it sucked people's souls, maybe, or something equally disturbing.

"So, this is...almost everyone," Jesse said, passing Gilbert a mug of steaming coffee. "You've already met Constance, and Mr. Humphreys over there, and Ramona in the kitchen. And you saw Miriam that first night," he said, pointing at the black-haired girl. "The twins over here are Ethel and Bobbie, and sitting beside Ramona is Hugo." The dwarf lifted his hand, waving hello. "And over there, Todd on the table and Clown."

Gilbert opened his mouth to ask, then thought better of it. But Jesse smirked. "Yes. His name is actually Clown. And don't worry. He doesn't like anyone; it's not just you."

Gilbert looked around and nodded at everyone. Then, realizing that Jesse was staring at him, he cleared his throat. "Um . . . My, uh, my name is Gilbert. Gilbert Blake. It's, um, it's nice to meet you all."

"Liar," Constance teased, good-naturedly, and everyone around the table chuckled. "You'd rather be a thousand miles from here. But don't worry, it's not as bad as it looks. I promise it will feel like home in no time."

From the other side of the table, Hugo inquired, "So, what is it you do?"

"I'm, uh, a magician. Of sorts. Illusions, lifting stuff with my mind. I mostly . . . well, I mostly do card tricks and dice stuff," Gilbert said. He didn't exactly know how to put it, but Clown obviously did, snorting out loud from the other end of the table.

"You mean you cheat people out of their money. No wonder they wanted to beat you up."

"Clown, now be nice. We talked about this." Constance lifted a finger in warning. Clown grumbled something but obediently shut up.

Gilbert laughed, feeling some strange relief. It was actually refreshing to have someone around who spat out the truth as it was. Someone with an attitude that Gilbert actually recognized. Everyone else was too . . . too nice? He wasn't used to that. It didn't happen much on the street. It freaked him out a little.

"No, that's fine. He's right. That's precisely what I do. I just didn't want you to think I was . . ."

"A thief and a miscreant?"

"*Clown!*"

"Yeah, that, pretty much." Gilbert sipped his coffee. He did feel more at ease now, as if the ice had been broken a little.

He was about to say something else when a loud squawk came from below the table. Constance cursed and bent to retrieve a hen from underneath, placing her on the surface. "Heavens, Gertrude, be careful. You'll get squashed one of these days if you don't pay attention." Then she seemed to remember something and turned to Gilbert. "By the way, is this chicken yours? One of the guys chasing after you was waving her around, saying it belonged to you. He tried to hit me on the head with her."

"Oh. Yes, I suppose she is. Sort of." Gilbert shrugged. Then he caught up with what she'd said. "He tried to what? And what did you do?"

Constance gracefully pushed the last bit of bread in her mouth with one elegant finger. "I hammered him into the ground like a nail, that's what I did. And took the poor thing home with us."

"We named her Gertrude," one of the twins pointed out. Gilbert nodded, reaching for another bun, because he didn't really know what else to say.

"So anyway, a magician, huh? I can't remember ever having one of those around. It's going to be an interesting addition. And right on time for the Carnival of Hallows, too," Hugo commented.

"What's that?" Gilbert asked, his mouth full.

"Just about the biggest, most important show of the year," Constance replied. "On All Hallows' Eve, the spirits in the circus grow stronger. The boundaries between their world and this one are at their weakest. There are people out there, people who *know*, who want to get close, close enough almost to touch the other world. So they come to us."

"And bring plenty of money," Hugo added, much more pragmatic. "Which we sorely need. It will be a miracle if we make it there at all, this year."

"We will. We don't have a choice." Jesse shrugged.

"And when would this carnival be? Anytime soon?" He was actually quite curious to see the troupe in action. He'd never been to the circus before.

"I should say so! It's less than a week away, in fact. We'll just about make it on time," Constance said. "Now that you decided to stop running."

"What excellent timing. It will be quite fassssscinating, I'm sssure." Humphreys emerged from the kitchen carrying a platter of ham and cheese. "It's ssso pleasant to have sssomeone new around, isn't it? We don't have many occasions to interact with strangers, you know, Mr. Blake. I would wager the only time is whenever we welcome a replacement."

Speaking of which . . . There was something Gilbert had been meaning to ask, something he'd thought of during the night, as he replayed his conversation with Jesse over and over in his head, trying to digest all the information. "If I can, uh, if you don't mind me asking, who did I replace?" Gilbert felt a little uncomfortable about that question. Yes, some time had passed, what with all his running around like a headless chicken, but still, a member of the troupe had recently died. It had to be tough on all of them.

There was a moment of silence as the performers became very much interested in their plates. Gilbert tried to backtrack. "I'm sorry. If you don't want to —"

"No. It's fine. It's only fair you should know," Jesse interrupted with a faint smile. "His name was Antoine. He was a brilliant musician."

"He had a really big mustache, and he played a lot of instruments all at the same time," one of the twins explained. "A big drum on his back, a trumpet, a harmonica, cymbals. Some bells, and a guitar sometimes, or an accordion."

Gilbert whistled in appreciation. "That's a lot of instruments for just two hands."

Hugo chuckled, gruff but affectionate. "Yeah, well. He kind of had a third one. That was a big help."

"Well, he sounds like a talented fellow. I-I'm very sorry for your loss."

"Don't worry about it. He lived a long life. He was so old, he could barely hold up his instruments. He would have hated it if he hadn't been able to play anymore," Constance said. "I think he chose to go before that could happen."

They all smiled affectionately at the thought. It was clear that this man had been very loved. Gilbert felt as if he was intruding on the private matters of a family, and he didn't feel comfortable at all. Another thing he wasn't really used to. "So . . . I'm living in Antoine's wagon now?"

"No, that one has been empty for a while. We have a spare, see, and the circus takes care to never place the new member in the wagon of someone who just died," Miriam explained, puffing out a cloud of smoke from her cigarette. "We don't really know why. It's how it works."

Why, this circus sure has a lot of very specific rules. That, or the devil who had set it up did, at any rate. But Gilbert was glad for this particular rule, nonetheless. It would be quite disturbing to wake up in a bed and know that twenty-four hours earlier, somebody had been sleeping in it and now was dead.

"Mrs. Frances used to live there. She was an amazing puppeteer," Jesse said. "She had the most incredible collection of marionettes. Built them all herself. She was incredibly talented."

"And she could still drink anyone under the table at the ripe age of eighty-four," Hugo added with a chuckle.

"Well, she certainly drank *you* under the table, and not a few times, if memory serves," Jesse ribbed him gently. Then he sighed. "She passed away a few years ago, when Ethel and Bobbie joined us."

That explained all the dust in his wagon, then. He should ask for a rag so he could clean up a little. Since he was going to spend some time in there . . .

"We were little, back then. But we're eleven, now," one of the twins chimed in.

Gilbert nodded, discreetly helping himself to another bun.

"So, you're going to have to sort out an act for the big show, eh, magician? Got anything in mind yet?"

Caught by surprise, Gilbert almost choked on his bread. As he coughed, Jesse patted him on the back. "Jeez. Try not to kill the guy on his very first day, would you, Hugo?"

When he was finally able to breathe again, Gilbert leaned forward, eyes wide. "I-I'm sorry, what?"

"This is a circus. I believe you picked up on that?" Hugo spelled it out for him. "Well, we perform for a living, and you'll have to be a part of the show too. We can't afford to be short one performer at the Carnival of Hallows, of all times. Got to earn your keep, you know."

Gilbert opened and closed his mouth. Oh, he had *not* seen that coming—really, he probably should have. "But can't I do that, I don't know, working around the camp? Taking care of, uh, something..."

He didn't even *know* what went into living in a semistable camp, what the needs of a group of people living together on a regular basis might be. Surely they had to, um, cook. Which he couldn't do. And buy food. And pump water? Chop firewood? God, he was *clueless*. Could he be any more damn useless? He was a *drifter*. Everything was already set up and running when he arrived at lodging houses and pubs and chophouses; he just paid to use them and moved on. It had been so long since he'd lived in some sort of solid community that he didn't even remember what sedentary life entailed. Oh, this was going to be a serious adjustment, and he was already sorely regretting getting caught up in this whole thing.

"Don't worry. There will be plenty of stuff to take care of *in addition* to the performances. What do you think we spend our days doing? It takes a lot of work to keep the camp going, you know."

Actually, he really, really did not know. But he nodded anyway. He didn't want to look like any more of an idiot. "Yes, I'm sure it does. I'm... Well, it's all kind of new to me."

"We've all been there," Hugo said. "So why don't we start easy, huh? Ethel and Bobbie here will take you for a tour of the camp while the rest of us pack up, show you around a bit. And then you can go clean out the chamber pots in all the wagons, all right?"

Gilbert's mouth fell open. The folks around the table looked at each other, trying to hold back, then burst out laughing.

"He's joking, don't worry." Jesse chuckled. "Hugo, you've got to stop doing that. Someday you'll make someone truly choke on their breakfast, and then we'll have to find someone new all over again!"

"I'm sorry, boss, but really, look at his face! It's priceless."

"I swear he cannot wait for one of us to croak just so he can pull that one on the poor new sod that joins." Constance rolled her eyes, but she was smiling. It seemed Hugo wasn't the only one amused by that particular prank.

"No, but seriously, after you're done with the tour, come find me. I've got a couple of errands to take care of before we hit the road. The roof of Clown's caravan is leaking again, and if I hear Todd complaining about his joints getting moldy one more time, I'm going to chop him up and use him as kindling." Hugo buttered another bun. "I trust you know how to use a hammer, yes?"

Well, the last time Gilbert had used one, it had been to hit some guy on the head during a particularly heated dispute. But he figured the principle was more or less the same. "Uh, yes. Sure."

"Excellent. And Mildred's foot is bothering her again, so she'll need a massage. You can take care of that while I do the repairs on Herbert. Get you started on something easy, eh?"

Hugo shoved the entire bun in his mouth and got up, off to do whatever it was he needed to do. That seemed like some kind of signal because everyone else followed suit, including the ringmaster, conversing amicably and apparently having already forgotten about Gilbert's presence.

"I— Yes, but— Excuse me? What do I— Hello?" He raised his hand, desperately looking at the retreating backs of the troupe, but his attempts at attracting attention were futile. Surely Hugo wasn't actually suggesting Gilbert give a foot massage to a five hundred–pound brown bear, right?

When he looked back down, he found himself alone except for the twins, who were both staring at him in silence, hands folded on the table. One of them wrinkled her nose at him, sniffing loudly. "Has anyone ever told you that you smell kind of funny?"

Great. He was starting to reconsider his position. Maybe the bear thing wasn't so bad after all.

"So is that a real mouse you have in your scarf?" one of the girls asked.

"Why, it is indeed. Her name is Emilia, and she's been traveling with me for a while. Would you like to touch her, um . . ." Let's see. Identical faces, identical dresses, identical voices, but the one on the left was the friendlier one, and from the way she spoke, she even seemed younger somehow. What the heck. He had a fifty-fifty shot, so he just went for it. "Bobbie?"

"Nope. Wrong." She giggled.

"Damn. I mean, blimey!" *Gah!* Gilbert fought the urge to punch himself on the forehead. First he couldn't get their names right, and now he was cursing in front of little girls? *Could this be more of a train wreck?* "I'm *so* sorry. I promise you I'll get it right. At some point."

Both twins burst out laughing. Then Bobbie—the actual Bobbie, this time—patted him on the arm. "Don't worry. We're used to it. And I'm sure Ethel would love to hold Emilia, if she doesn't mind."

"Mind? She'll be delighted." Gilbert carefully pulled Emilia out of her nest in his scarf and handed her over into Ethel's waiting hands. "She's a real cuddler, this little one, and she keeps complaining that I don't spoil her nearly enough."

The twins cooed and fussed over Emilia, who closed her eyes with a blissed expression on her tiny face and basked in the attention as Gilbert followed the girls around the encampment. He'd pretty much seen everything that needed to be seen in his first exploration. There wasn't much beyond the handful of wagons, the big striped tent, the canteen with the table and benches laid out outside, and the gate with its arched entrance. Gilbert wondered why they even bothered to put up the fence at all. It looked like a lot of work for no good reason whatsoever. And several hundred pounds of iron to carry.

"How long do you stay in the same place?" he asked as they strolled past the big tent.

Bobbie shrugged. "Depends. Sometimes just a night at a time while we travel. Like now. Maybe a week when we have a show. And in the winter, we stay put much longer. There isn't much to do, and it gets kind of boring. It's harder to travel when it's cold, and people don't come to the shows as much."

"And do you always take the time to set up the big tent and the fence? Even when you stay for one night?" Gilbert asked. It really made no sense. "It seems like really hard work. Why do you need it? Who does it?"

"But we don't put it up. The circus does."

Gilbert scratched his stubble. Again with the "circus" doing things. "And how does that work?"

Bobbie shrugged again, busy rubbing Emilia's head with a fingertip. "I don't know. It just does. It's like, we look away for a moment and then the tent and the fence are there. They like following us, I think."

Gilbert pulled a face. Well, he supposed that made about as much sense as anything else in this mad circus. Although, the devil must have his reasons for doing all this, right? An iron fence, of all things, surrounding an encampment of people who, he supposed, all possessed magic to some degree. He wondered whether it was really to protect the performers from the outside world, or to protect the world from whatever lurked within the circus.

Maybe it wasn't a shield at all, but a *cage*.

"That's where we sleep. Miriam too," Ethel said, pointing at a small, graceful wagon that was painted red with little paper flowers and lanterns hanging along the roof. Then she pointed at a nearby gray caravan. "And that one is for Constance and Ramona. The other red one is Jesse's, and the ugly gray one, that's for Clown and Todd."

Well, no surprise there. At least they didn't live in coffins or something. It was already a step up from Gilbert's usual arrangement. "You've already seen the canteen, and behind that is the food storage. Let's go see the animals," Bobbie said, leading him toward the back of the tent. As Gilbert followed obediently, the black wagon caught his eye. It seemed to have materialized at the very edge of his vision. He was almost sure it hadn't been there a moment ago. But now that he'd seen it, he couldn't tear his gaze away, as if the wagon was drawing his eyes to it with a secret power.

"What about that wagon there? Can you show it to me?"

The twins looked at each other, frowning. "No," they said in unison, then Bobbie spoke. "We don't like to go near that. There are spirits in there. Only Jesse goes inside."

Now *that* was an interesting piece of information. He would have to find out more about it. "That's fine. Don't worry. Let's just go to the tent, all right?" Gilbert smiled kindly, relieved when the frowns disappeared from the girls' faces, like a cloud lifting.

Behind the big tent was a broad, empty area where the mechanical elephant—kind of hard to miss, that one—was busy cleaning his stovepipe hat, holding the brush in its trunk. Nearby was another wagon that was more like a cage on wheels, really, and decorated in red and green. It took Gilbert a long moment to realize that the door was wide-open and that the bear was outside, sprawled on her back and contentedly rolling around among a few bales of hay. A cold dread fell on him.

"Stay very still," he said, instinctively stepping in front of the twins. "Somebody must have left the door unlocked. Now back away slowly. Let's go get the ringmaster, or someone—"

"Oh, don't be silly! We never keep Mildred locked up." Bobbie scoffed, walking around him. "The cage is where she travels, that's all. She can't walk all the time, not like Herbert. She gets tired. And people would get scared otherwise, just like you did."

"I wasn't *scared*," Gilbert protested, as Ethel carefully handed Emilia back to him. The twins nonchalantly strolled next to the bear, bending to scratch her belly. She made a delighted grumbling sound and, without even waking up, lifted her paws to give them better access. A string of perfectly polished pearls gleamed around her neck. "I was being . . . cautious, that's all."

"Then why don't you come closer? You'll have to rub her feet soon anyway, and we need to wake her up awhile before we leave. She gets grouchy otherwise," Bobbie said. Gilbert, still standing ten feet away, considered the issue and decided that he was going to cross that bridge when he got to it. Which, if he had it his way, would be *never*.

"Oh, I wouldn't want to disturb her. A lady needs her beauty sleep. How about this big guy over here?" He forced a smile on his face, pointing at the elephant. The twins looked at each other, then decided to take pity on him and led the way.

"You've met Herbert before, I think. Herbert, say hello," Ethel said. Herbert, obediently, waved his brush-holding trunk and trumpeted a greeting.

"It's nice to meet you too, mate." Gilbert put his hands on his hips and tilted his head back, squinting up at the creature. He really did not understand how it was possible. The elephant was all polished sheets of metal—carefully hammered and bolted and welded in place—and pipes and gears and what looked like hundreds and hundreds of pieces. It must have taken years to build something so complex. And he couldn't see any sort of furnace or engine or anything to keep the thing going. "So what is it, exactly?"

"Why, an elephant," Ethel replied, patiently.

Gilbert pinched his nose. "Yes. No, I can see that. I mean, how does it work? Did someone from the troupe build it? Or is it another thing the circus did?"

"He was already here when we arrived. Hugo built him a long time ago," Bobbie explained. "Hugo is good at building things and fixing them. And he makes them alive too, that's what he does. He's the one who made Todd move and talk."

Oh. That was a new one. Gilbert, still fascinated by the elephant's complex mechanism, shouldn't have been so surprised. There was no reason to believe his magic was the only possible kind. He wondered what the other performers could do. Good thing that Hallows Carnival thing was coming up; he would have front-row seats for a very interesting show, indeed.

"Wow. That's, well, that's pretty impressive."

"You can bet your arse it is." Hugo's voice came suddenly out of nowhere. No, actually, it seemed to be coming from *inside* the elephant's belly. Gilbert jumped, caught unawares, and Hugo popped out, smeared with oil and holding a wrench, a belt full of tools around his waist. "Don't look so surprised, fellow. Do you think this machine takes care of itself? Hours and hours of dedication, that's what it takes.

And if you're done with your tour, magician, you could start making yourself useful, eh? This isn't a charity hospice."

"But Hugo!" Bobbie complained. "We haven't showed him the tent yet!"

"Want to see the tent? There. It's the big thing with the stripes." Hugo pointed above their heads with the wrench. It would be hard to miss, seeing as how it towered over the entire encampment. "Now, off you go, girls. Help Ramona pack up the canteen. The man needs to work."

The girls exchanged a displeased glance and ran off as Gilbert clumsily waved after them. "Bye, uh, thanks for the tour!" Then he turned to Hugo. "So what do you need me to do?"

Hugo threw the belt at him, and Gilbert gave an *umph* when it hit him in the stomach. "Stand there and pass me things when I ask you to. Or just stand there, if there's nothing I need."

He lay under the elephant and went back to tinkering, humming to himself. Gilbert awkwardly held up the belt and glanced around. Having the bear so close was making nervous beads of sweat roll down his back, and he needed to think about something else. So, he started talking. "So, I wanted to apologize. You know, for the way I've been acting for the past . . ." He wasn't even sure how long it had been. Oh well. "Since I joined. I mean, you guys have been nothing but perfectly nice to me, and I haven't really been that friendly, I guess. Very rude of me." He paused, waiting perhaps for an answer, but none came. He wasn't even sure if Hugo was listening to him. "It's just . . . It's tough to get used to the idea. I've always been traveling on my own; I'm a city man, I— Being stuck in a place like this, far from everything and everyone, it's hard for me to accept, you know?"

He was sort of getting carried away with his rambling when Hugo slid out from under the elephant again with a long-suffering sigh. "You talk too much, magician. And you're not even original. I'm about to take my own life with this wrench from the sheer boredom."

Gilbert was at a loss for a moment. "I . . . beg your pardon?"

"I've been here a long time, fellow. I've heard it all before." Hugo pointed the wrench at him. "I've seen plenty of folks like you. Just because you look pretty, because you don't look like Humphreys or like me, you think the world out there will be ready to welcome you with open arms. You think you can be *normal*."

Gilbert tried to speak, even though he didn't precisely know what he wanted to say. "But I—"

"And how has that worked for you so far, hmm? Not too great, I'd wager? You can't escape what you are, magician. You will never be one of *them*, and you can only pretend for so long." Hugo shrugged. "Trust me. Soon you'll be grateful to be in a place where you don't need to hide who you are. And at the end of the day, other freaks are the only ones who will ever look out for you. Don't you forget that."

That word again, *freaks*, grating on his skin like a rusty nail. Gilbert wanted to retort—what was it with everyone giving him lectures lately, trying to teach him how to live his life?—but he kept quiet and nodded. They didn't understand that it was different for him. He just had some extra abilities, that was all. That didn't make him a freak.

Right?

"Now. If you're done with the confession, we can pack up and go fix that roof. Herbert's as good as he's going to get anyway. That should keep him going till we stop for the night, but it's a temporary fix. He needs a new piece; there's no way around it. I'll get it after the Carnival, when we have some spare cash." He patted Gilbert's arm. "Just take it easy. As I said, you're not the first, you won't be the last. You'll understand sooner than you think."

"I . . . All right. Thank you. I'll try to keep an open mind." Gilbert waited while Hugo bent under the elephant to pick up the last instruments. He felt a little better already. For all his gruff exterior, Hugo was a good guy. Maybe he'd made his first friend in the Circus of the Damned.

"So," he began, with a bright smile, intent on cementing that camaraderie with some convivial talk. "You and Miss Ramona, eh? You two make a lovely couple."

A loud clang came from under the elephant, and Hugo pulled out, flushed, massaging the back of his head where he'd cracked it against the brass. "We are not— Miss Ramona is a perfectly modest lady, how dare you *insinuate* that she might—" He was sputtering with indignation, waving his wrench around. "I'm warning you, magician.

I better not hear you talk smack about Miss Ramona or I'll . . . I'll be forced to defend her *honor* from—"

Uh-oh. Wrong topic. Gilbert raised his hands in surrender as Hugo jerked that wrench around like a rapier. Gilbert worried the man was going to challenge him to a duel right then and there. "I'm sorry! I apologize. I meant no disrespect. I just noticed, well, that you two seem very close, and I thought you were . . . married, you know, all *perfectly* respectable and—"

Hugo stopped like a man struck by lightning. "M-me? And Miss Ramona . . . married?" He stammered, blushing, an expression of such beatitude on his face that one would think Gilbert was an angel sent from the heavens bringing the sweetest revelation. Then Hugo caught himself and frowned, harrumphing, and very nearly growled at Gilbert. "You shut up and mind your own business. And go change the hay in Mildred's wagon before we leave! She's had an upset stomach these days, and it's going to stink to high heavens. And then give her that foot massage and . . . just shut up!"

He planted a shovel in Gilbert's hands and stomped off, deaf to Gilbert's pitiful protests. "No, but . . . I thought we were having a moment, here. Hugo, wait!"

Nothing. Gilbert, dejected, watched him leave, then turned to glance at the cage and sighed.

He really shouldn't talk to anyone ever again.

After he was done cleaning the wagon, Gilbert really did end up massaging Mildred's feet until the twins came to summon him. *Time to leave.* As they pulled away from their temporary camp, Gilbert turned back to watch the big red-and-white tent disappear in the distance, and wondered whether it would really magically appear wherever they happened to settle next.

He spent the afternoon perched on his wagon with Humphreys, who taught him how to maneuver the contraption for the first half hour and spent the remaining several hours debating the advantages of plaid versus tweed vests, since he was considering purchasing a new one after the Carnival of Hallows.

By the time they came across a suitable clearing to stop for the evening and he was finally free to stumble off the wagon, Gilbert swore he would rather travel locked in the cage with Mildred and her upset stomach rather than spend another afternoon like that. And he could no longer feel his butt.

The troupe set to work at once, unlocking the canteen wagon and setting out the table and chairs, while Ramona and Humphreys busied themselves at the stove. Gilbert was hovering around, hands in his pockets, feeling rather useless and wondering exactly at what point the fence and tent would materialize out of thin air—oh, he was going to keep an eye on that, all right—when the black wagon rolled in slowly, bringing with it a whoosh of cold air.

Gilbert shivered, pulling a face at it, and turned his back to it only to find the twins staring at him with their arms folded.

"Hello there, ladies. Don't worry. I wasn't planning on getting anywhere near it. Just looking, I promise."

The two exchanged glances. "That's not it," Bobbie said, then pointed at a midnight-blue caravan Gilbert hadn't noticed before, chained to Jesse's red one. "We think Miss Dora wants to meet you."

Wonderful, another name to add to the list. Gilbert doubted he'd ever remember them all. As it turned out, this name belonged to an elderly lady standing at the door, wearing a broad, dark-green gown, looking solemn and austere. Her ebony skin was etched with deep wrinkles, her gray hair pulled in a tight bun. Her eyes were shut, and yet Gilbert couldn't shake the feeling that the woman was staring straight at him.

"That's . . . that's nice. I hadn't realized there was anyone else still to meet." Gilbert pasted an unconvincing smile on his face. His stomach was grumbling, and the delicious smell of roasted vegetables was already spreading from the canteen. "Maybe she can join us at dinner, yes? I will see her there."

He was already moving on when the twins grabbed his jacket to stop him. "Miss Dora almost never comes out anymore. Jesse brings her food and takes care of her. She gets tired easily, you know. She's been here for a long, long time, and she's very old," Ethel said. "But when she calls, you have to go."

Gilbert took a deep breath, pushing against his rising frustration. "Can't this wait until after dinner? I'm famished."

The twins just gave him a *look*. "When she calls, you have to go," they repeated in unison.

Gilbert was really too old to get into a quarrel with two little girls, but he couldn't stop himself. "Well, I haven't heard her *call* anyone—"

"*Magician*," the woman bellowed then, in a tone that made him feel like a scolded, petulant child. "Yes, you, with the rat on your shoulder. Is this enough of a call, or do you require a written invitation? Don't you keep me waiting, lad. I might just die of old age before you get your lazy arse in here."

Gilbert stood for a moment with his mouth hanging open. Then he shut it and, ignoring the know-it-all gazes of the girls, headed toward the blue wagon with his tail between his legs. He'd had a grandma once. He barely remembered her, but he *did* remember one thing: you didn't say no to that tone.

CHAPTER 9

The wagon's interior was absolutely spotless, tidy and elegant with dark polished furniture, green velvet drapes, and an arrangement of dried flowers on the counter. *Way* nicer than his own wagon was, or would ever be, for that matter. Gilbert stood, hands awkwardly tucked in his pockets, as the woman sat on a plump velvet armchair beside a small, round table covered in a black doily. She gestured for him to take a seat, as well. She poured him a cup of tea from a gleaming silver teapot and then one for herself, and he took the chance to study her. The high neck of her green gown was held closed by a cameo brooch portraying a little skull. Her eyes were still closed—she was blind, he supposed—and yet she moved with complete confidence, as if she could see better than he could.

"For God's sake, boy, have a seat. I'm not going to bite you."

He obeyed, accepted the offered cup, and sniffed it cautiously before taking a sip. It was sweet and pleasant—rose, maybe.

"So, you're the new magician." Dora tilted her head to the side, her closed eyes seeming to look straight at him. He had the curious feeling that she could see him all too clearly, as if his every hidden thought, his every misdemeanor, were in plain sight for her. And yet he wasn't as bothered by it as he'd expect to be. It wasn't an unsettling prodding or a bothersome intrusion, not like it had been on the train with the devil. More like a gentle, light poking here and there.

"Yes. My name is Gilbert, and the mouse on my shoulder is Emilia." *How* the woman had seen the mouse earlier, and from so far away, at that, he didn't ask.

Belatedly, he realized he should have shaken her hand or something. He awkwardly juggled the saucer and cup in one hand, wincing at the loud clicking noise, then balanced them on one knee to offer his hand, only to realize she couldn't see it. But before he could slap himself for his irredeemable ineptitude and pull the hand back, she reached out and gave it a strong, firm shake.

"I'm Dora. I have been a fortune-teller here for . . . quite some time, to say the least." She settled back in her chair, taking a slow sip from her cup.

"Oh." He fidgeted, suddenly uneasy. A fortune-teller? She didn't look like any of the fortune-tellers he'd met over the years. They all had tents filled with cheap incense that made him sneeze. They had snakes and skulls and candles and jars of dead things that stared at him and gave him the creeps. They had velvet shawls and jingling fake jewels and long, lacquered nails and faces encrusted with makeup. They yelled and rolled their eyes a lot and sometimes drooled a little, too.

Dora wasn't anything like that, and her wagon was just about the tidiest room he'd seen in his entire life. It actually made him a little uncomfortable, like he was going to break something or stain something or bring in mud with his shoes. He was used to rowdy pubs and dirty alleys, and he didn't quite know how to handle himself in such an elegant place.

"The twins were saying you've been with the circus a long time. Longer than anyone else?" he asked, eventually, fiddling with his cup. He might as well try to get something out of this meeting. If she'd been there for so long, maybe she would know something about the original deal that Jesse had made. Something that, with a little luck, might hold the key to Gilbert's freedom.

"Not everyone else," she tutted, shaking her head. "But quite a long time, yes. I joined the Circus of the Damned when I was but a child."

Ah. So, the circus was much older than he'd imagined. He'd assumed Jesse had founded it, but he must have taken over when the previous ringmaster had died or something. Dora must surely have been there when the deal was made then. And so had somebody else, apparently . . . Was there really someone older than her around? He sure as hell hadn't seen them.

"Oh. I see. So you've been here for a really long time," he said, then nearly bit his tongue. *Oh, bollocks.* He was quite adept at stuffing his foot in his mouth today. "No, I-I'm sorry, I didn't mean to imply . . . You're such a radiant, youthful—"

Dora burst out laughing, and for a few moments, she looked just like a young girl. "That's all right, magician, don't blow a gasket. I am indeed very old. And yes, I have been here for many years. I joined when I was a little girl, brought here by my mother. She was a seer too, but much more powerful than me. The dead stirred below the earth when she walked upon it, and the spirits followed her around. They stormed her body and her mind, hunting for passage into this world." She twirled her fingers slowly around the rim of the cup. "It killed her shortly after we arrived. And I spent the rest of my life here."

He swallowed. Nearly her whole life in the circus. It was unimaginable to him. "So you inherited her power? I mean, do the spirits follow you around too?" he asked, holding his breath.

"Not really, no. Or perhaps, it is the circus that protects me, barring access to the entities who would hurt me. What was a curse for my mother has become a blessing for me. As you so observingly remarked, I did indeed live to a ripe old age."

Dora bent to rummage in a nearby bag and produced a spider-thin web of black thread. Upon closer inspection, Gilbert saw that the thread was gracefully woven in circles of smiling skulls, surrounded by graceful patterns. She pulled out a ball of yarn and a metal hook and started deftly crocheting, spinning the doily between her fingers.

"But I do keep in touch with the spirits that inhabit the circus," she continued. "The ones of the dead performers. They sleep most of the time, but they are awake and much stronger now, as Hallows' Eve approaches. They are old friends and often visit me in here. As I get closer to death, it's easier for me to spend time with the souls I will share eternity with rather than with the living. And besides, it's nice to know I'll be in good company on the other side."

Gilbert nervously cleared his throat, wondering whether any of the ghosts were in there at the moment, spying on him, talking about him while he couldn't hear. He didn't particularly like that thought, so he tried to steer the discussion back to his topic of interest. "So, when you joined, you could have left if you'd wanted to, right? I mean, people could still leave the circus, back then?"

"Oh, no, I am not *that* old. The deal was made long before my mother and I joined. And I know that you aren't happy about the prospect of remaining here for the rest of your life—I struggled with that myself, even though the circus was my family, my safe haven. But we've all learned to live with it, and so will you. It's just how things are. There's nobody left who remembers what it was like before, when people could leave." Her fingers moved at impressive speed, swift and nimble. She wasn't even looking at her work and yet another perfect skull had already materialized in the doily. "Except the ringmaster, of course."

Ha. Finally, he was beginning to get somewhere. So, the ringmaster back in the day had already done something, meddled with something he shouldn't have? And Jesse must have taken over the deal when he'd stepped in as ringmaster. Gilbert needed to find out more about the other guy, what rules he'd laid out exactly in this deal with that devil. "The ringmaster, yes. Obviously, very important. I assume he took care of you, much like the ringmaster does now with the twins, right? Did you know him well?"

"Oh, the whole troupe took care of me. They all became my family. And while I sometimes struggled to accept it, living in the circus was the best thing that could have happened to me. I certainly wouldn't have lived this long if my mother hadn't brought me here, nor as happily. Freaks don't have an easy life on the outside. But then, you already know that."

Gilbert was most definitely not going to answer that, not going to get distracted thinking of a family he didn't even remember. He must have had a father, a home, maybe siblings, and yet, all he carried with him was that one ragged memory of his mother's horrified face as she left him to die. If he hadn't possessed his magic, if he had been a regular child, maybe he would have gotten to grow up in a home. To be loved. But he'd been left on the train tracks, instead.

Gilbert tightened his jaw. He'd grown up just *fine* without a family, carving a home for himself on the streets. First with the children who had rescued him and their den of thieves, then later by himself, when they too had caught a whiff of the things he could do and had started whispering, frightened at first, then hateful. He didn't need a family, nor did he want one. He was good on his own, the way he'd always been.

At least, that way, nobody could ever abandon him again.

"Well, I guess I do," he said vaguely, ignoring the shadow that fluttered over Dora's features. If she could see what was going on in his mind, then she could also see that he had no intention of discussing it, and apparently she chose to respect that. "So, the ringmaster. Did he ever tell anyone why it became impossible to leave the circus? It is a fairly big deal."

"Of course. It's not a secret, Gilbert. It's how the deal works— we all know it. Once you become a member of the circus, your soul belongs to it, and is forfeited to the devil. And if the deal expires, he gets to collect your soul and everybody else's and carry them to Hell. In the meantime, you're stuck here to do his bidding, finding new performers—new souls—to replace the deceased ones. It's fairly straightforward, really." Dora rattled this off with utter nonchalance, as if she were discussing her favorite crocheting techniques.

Gilbert frowned. "Yes, I know that. Jesse explained it to me. But why? Let's say I found someone to replace me. Then the number of performers would still be the same, and I could be free to go. Right?"

Dora tutted. "No, dear, I'm afraid it doesn't work that way. You have made a deal. You can't just get out of it when you feel like it."

Gilbert grumbled something unrepeatable under his breath. "So you're telling me that no one has ever been able to leave the circus in— When was the deal made?"

"Why, you ask difficult questions, magician. I may be able to see the future, but my memory of the past is that of an old lady." Dora chuckled. Her voice was pleasant, rough, and smoky. "Jesse and Farfarello must have made the deal, oh, I can't remember . . . one hundred and eighty years ago, maybe two hundred? But you should ask him directly. He'll be happy to tell you, I'm sure."

What? Gilbert raised his hands. "I— Wait a moment. Jesse? But you said two hundred years."

Dora's fingers stopped dancing on the doily as she parted her mouth, apparently surprised. She put her crocheting down on her legs and lifted her head, seeming to peer intently at Gilbert through her shut eyelids. "Oh, Gilbert, has nobody told you? Jesse has *always* been here. He's been the ringmaster of the Circus of the Damned for almost two centuries."

Gilbert tried to open his mouth, but he seemed to have forgotten how to speak.

With a concerned expression, Dora leaned forward and patted his knee. "You look awfully pale, dear. Would you like another cup of tea?"

Too shocked to reply, Gilbert found himself with a second steaming cup of rose tea shoved in his hands, and he looked down at it in a daze. His fingers felt numb where they held the china saucer, and his thoughts were heavy and slow like molasses.

Two hundred years? Jesse is two hundred years old? It seemed impossible. Of all the unbelievable things he'd been forced to swallow and accept as real in the last few weeks, this was one thing too much. One thing he didn't want to believe.

When he managed to tune back in to the conversation, Dora had already moved on, as if it wasn't that big of a deal, as if Gilbert's brain wasn't very nearly melting trying to accept that, too, on top of everything else.

"But there's a reason I called you in here, and believe it or not, it wasn't to traumatize you with revelations about our ringmaster. I have wanted to speak with you for quite some time. I felt the spirits stir when you arrived. I know that there is something in you I need to see. I was almost running out of patience waiting for you to stop trying to escape," Dora said, a gentle smile on her lips. Instinctively, Gilbert returned the smile, a little dazed. "I would like to read your fortune, if you will let me."

He didn't really believe in that sort of thing, but he was still reeling, and besides, what the hell. What he did or didn't believe wasn't worth shit, apparently, since reality seemed determined to go its own way without consulting him.

"Sure. What do you need to do?" He rubbed a hand over his eyes. "Like, do you have a crystal ball or tarot cards or . . . or you will gut open a trout or something?"

The last person who'd read his fortune had done that. It had been rather gory and disturbing, and completely inaccurate, at that.

Dora laughed. "Oh dear, no, nothing of the sort. Just give me your hand, please. That is all I need."

She clasped his hand in her dry, warm ones, her grip surprisingly strong. He was fairly sure that if he tried to pull back, he wouldn't be able to unless she let him go. Dora brushed her fingertips across his palm, following the lines on his skin. Her touch sent little tingling pinpricks up his wrist, all the way to his elbow, and he felt strangely peaceful, almost hypnotized by the gentle movements of those ebony fingers.

"A cloud of the deepest purple is closing in, and fast," Dora said, startling him. Her voice had completely changed; it was distant, echoing as if it were coming from across a vast hollow. "It is low and heavy. A grave danger follows you closely, chases us all, and you must keep ahead of it. You must keep hiding or you will be lost. Because its purple eyes are many, and they are everywhere. You are not as safe as you believe. None of us are."

Gilbert swallowed. He fidgeted nervously, hand caught in Dora's iron grip. Her eyes were open now, filled with opaque white smoke, storming like the clouds she spoke of. Her face was drawn and ghastly, and she looked a thousand years old, those milky white eyes drawing him in like bottomless pools in her ebony face.

A cold wind was blowing through the wagon, tearing at the curtains, toppling Dora's flowers, even though the door and windows remained shut. His heart was pounding, frightened yet endlessly fascinated at the same time.

"A silver dancing spider. The devil wants something that you want. You want something that belongs to the devil. You want what the devil owns, and he will come, soon, to try to take it away. The devil in love. And you— Are you willing to fight for what your own heart desires?"

He was still stunned in place when she abruptly shut her eyes. The wind fell at once, her grip softened, and she relaxed back in her chair, her hands going limp. After a moment of perfect stillness, she shifted, taking a deep breath, as if she was waking up.

"What did I say?" she asked. She looked exhausted, and small, almost swallowed up by the massive velvet chair.

"Something about a purple cloud coming. And the devil with the silver spider." He frowned. "You don't remember? You just said it."

"The *spirits* said it. I am not ... entirely here when they take over." Dora massaged her temples, scrunching up her nose. "Yes, I— The cloud, I do not recognize."

"I do." He groaned. "And I also recognize the spider guy. I've had the dubious pleasure of meeting him in person not too long ago. He's Farfarello, right? The devil who owns the circus."

Dora stilled at once, then perked up in surprise. "You *saw* him? Oh, that cannot be a good sign. He hasn't been around in so many years. I was a child the last time I saw him."

He dug his hand in his pocket, looking for his dice to play with. It always helped him release some restless tension. "So you've met him too, then? And did he— Do you remember if he ever told you anything about the deal or ...?"

"I was a child, magician. He never said anything important in my presence, not that I can remember." Dora took a deep breath. "But I remember that he was always nice to me. Once, he made the silver spider dance for me. But my mother wouldn't let me anywhere near him, and then he left, and he never came back again. I thought I wouldn't see him again in this lifetime. And yet you saw him."

"He was the one who first came to find me. Spoke to me, said he wanted to meet me. I have no idea why, though. He just told me to give his regards to Jesse." He paused, fidgeting with his dice. "You said I want something that belongs to him, but that's not true. I don't want anything of his."

Dora tilted her head to the side. She didn't look convinced.

"It's true!" Gilbert insisted. "I really don't. What does he even own, the circus? Well, I sure don't want to take over *the circus*. That's ridiculous. It's the opposite of what I want."

"You could say that he owns the circus, yes," Dora said slowly, mulling it over. "But that isn't quite correct, is it? There is only one thing that became his the moment the deal was made ... and that is Jesse's soul."

Gilbert shifted uncomfortably on his seat, a sinking feeling in the pit of his stomach. The thought of Jesse belonging to that devil bothered him in ways he didn't want to think about.

"But . . ." He cleared his throat. "Not just Jesse's. All of our souls belong to him, right? So maybe I want my own soul back. My freedom. That would answer your riddle."

"It sure would. But you are wrong on one thing: our souls don't belong to Farfarello, not yet. Not until the deal is broken, not while the Circus of the Damned still lives. We belong nowhere, really, suspended in limbo. We are not his for the taking yet. Only Jesse is."

So all those souls in wait . . . Something clicked in his head. "The black wagon."

"Yes. That's our cemetery. Even the dead have to abide by the deal and remain with the circus. That's where their spirits reside, and the rest of us are seldom admitted. As I said, they visit me sometimes, but I am close to joining them."

He rolled his dice around in his palm. A sinister thought was taking shape inside his head, one he was loath even to consider. But if all this hinged on Jesse, if he was the keeper of the deal and the only one whose soul already belonged to the devil . . . What if Jesse were to die? Would the deal be extinguished then, leaving the performers free to go on their way, setting all the accumulated souls free? Or would the circus die with him, the only irreplaceable piece on the game board, whose death would cast them all down to Hell?

The sinking feeling in his stomach turned to nausea at the thought. The only way to get his freedom back might be . . . killing Jesse.

"You might want to ask Jesse why the devil stayed for so long after the deal was made. And why he eventually left," Dora said, leaning heavily on the armrest. She seemed exhausted, her hands resting limply in her lap. "It might help you understand why he came back to see you. Now, off with you, magician. I'm very tired. I need some rest."

Gilbert didn't protest, even though there were a hundred questions bubbling up in his throat. The trance had thoroughly worn her out, and she looked like she was about to fall asleep on him any second.

"Yes, of course. Thank you, Miss Dora. Have a nice, uh, nap. Shall we, um, bring you some dinner later on?"

But she just waved him off, her head tilted back against the headrest. So he took a moment to gather himself and grabbed Emilia from the table, where she had attacked the tea cakes, and they quietly headed out. As he was about to shut the door, Dora called one last warning after him, her voice once again sounding as if it were coming from a great distance.

"Beware the purple cloud," she said. "It's close. And it's coming for you."

A last ripple of icy-cold wind slammed the door in Gilbert's face.

CHAPTER 10

T hat night, Gilbert truly couldn't sleep.

He'd gone through dinner mechanically—under the looming circus tent that had promptly materialized while he was occupied—his mind reeling from what Dora had said, then he'd retreated to his wagon right away. Almost everyone had already gone, anyway. Only Ramona and Humphreys had been left, sorting out the canteen, and he hadn't really felt like asking them for any details. If anything, he should ask Jesse, but he hadn't felt like doing that, either. Not yet.

My God. Jesse was two hundred years old, for fuck's sake. Gilbert couldn't wrap his mind around it. That was almost seven times the span of Gilbert's life. It was absolute madness. Not that he *cared* or anything, of course, despite what Dora seemed to think. She'd all but outright stated that Gilbert wanted Jesse, and that was silliness, that's what it was. Why, just because he was pissed off at the idea of some devil *owning* Jesse's soul? His was a perfectly rational reaction. Anyone with a scrap of a conscience would do the same. It wasn't as though a bitter, biting jealousy was currently eating through his insides like acid. Or as if the mere thought of Farfarello's hands on Jesse—of *anyone's* hands on Jesse—was enough to make him want to punch the wall until his knuckles started bleeding.

All right, so maybe he had a *thing* for Jesse. So what? The ringmaster was an eminently likeable man. Not only was he handsome, but he had a charisma that drew Gilbert in like a damn magnet. He was just *nice*, all right? When he wasn't being completely insufferable, that was. He was obviously a good man who cared for his troupe, and he took care of orphaned little girls and gave a home to those who were spat out and rejected by the rest of the world.

And went around making deals with devils too, the ever-present nagging voice in his brain reminded him. Not that Gilbert hadn't made a number of, um, judgment errors in his life, as well. It was just that . . .

Good Lord. Two hundred years?

Ah, God damn it.

Gilbert raked his hands through his hair. He was all over the fucking place, freaked out because of what Dora had said about that damn purple cloud, that was all. Was it really possible that Reuben's men were *still* chasing after him? It made no sense. He'd only stolen a bit of money and caused a ruckus in a pub that had already been a fucking mess. The count had much bigger issues to handle in the city; there was no reason to still be after him.

What the hell does Reuben want from me?

Who cared. They could keep looking for him until the end of time. As long as he remained hidden in the circus, they would never find him. *And besides*, he halfheartedly tried to reason with himself, *this might not even be real.* Dora's words were so vague. Maybe he was just being paranoid, jumping to conclusions. Who knew what that purple cloud stood for? That was why he loathed fortune-tellers. They got you worked up with skilled words and fancy tricks, and then you got all freaked and read all sorts of things into it.

God. He thumped his fist on his forehead, squeezing his eyes shut. His head felt about ready to explode, too full of swirling, loud thoughts. They were driving him insane. This was precisely the time when he would get out and lose himself among the shouting crowd in some rowdy pub, drown out the voices in his head with all the alcohol he could stomach until he no longer remembered his own fucking name. And here he was, instead, stuck in the middle of nowhere, surrounded by that goddamn, too-loud *silence.* He couldn't live in a place like this, couldn't survive far from the mayhem of the cities. Here he had no other choice but to hear himself think.

Struck by a sudden intuition, he marched to the cabinets and started yanking them open. Hugo had said something about the puppeteer lady being a drinker, hadn't he? With a little luck, she'd have stashed something in there. His sanity hung in the balance. He needed the fucking voices to stop, just for a while. *Come on, Frances. Help a guy out here.*

He rummaged through enamel tea ware, loudly knocking cups off the shelves, and he was on the verge of hyperventilating before he dropped to a crouch and tore into the lower cabinets. Black clothes, shoes, and trinkets, all neatly stored with lavender sachets. Gilbert's movements slowed down as he realized that he was rummaging through Frances's personal possessions, and from the look of things, he was the first to touch them since she'd passed away. His hands stilled completely when he encountered an open velvet box brimming with folded papers, and he took a deep breath.

What the hell am I even doing?

He forced himself to calm down, pushing back the fluttering panic in his chest, as if shoving a frightened bird back into its cage. He struggled to focus on what was in his hands, turning resolutely away from the storm of thoughts still raging in his head. With a vague sense of shame, he realized that he'd messed up Frances's clothes that had been impeccably folded on their shelves, and he clumsily tried to smooth down the wrinkles in the velvet and lace.

No. He couldn't keep living in that wagon, not like this. There was something disturbing and just so *sad* about the thought of settling in among somebody else's possessions. If this wagon had to become his home, temporary as it might be, he couldn't be an intruder in it, squatting among the ruins of someone's life. But he wouldn't be the one to clear out her belongings, either. He had never even met the woman.

His gaze fell on the open box, neatly placed on the floor in front of him. He could see envelopes, postcards, a little leather booklet that might have been a diary. And on top of everything, a faded daguerreotype, portraying a tall, serious-looking woman with her hair cropped short in a boyish cut. She wore white gloves and was holding a wooden cross, from which a puppet dangled, attached to a number of strings. The puppet's beady eyes, set in a little wrinkled face under a spray of straw hair, seemed to be peering right at Gilbert with undiluted hatred, reproaching him for nosing around its owner's belongings.

All right, that was it. He was going to get Jesse, right now. Gilbert may be a remorseless thief, but this? This was something different entirely. He wasn't that much of a bastard. And hell, if Jesse had really been around for two centuries, then he must have known this woman longer than anyone else, must be the closest thing she had to a family. He should be the one to take care of this.

He was about to stand up when he noticed the tiny handles on the side of the bed.

He hadn't given it much thought; the mattress was resting on a wooden frame, that was all. He hadn't considered that it might be hollow. Carefully, he pulled at the handles, and after a little gentle tugging, a large drawer slid forward. And there, safely sheltered from dust and light, was a collection of the most disturbing puppets he had ever seen.

He noticed the one from the picture right away with its big head of faded straw hair and eyes crudely painted black on its deathly pale face. Then there was a devil face carved in red leather, with bared fangs and horns, its cold eyes conveying such cruelty that Gilbert felt a shiver crawl down his back. He cautiously picked up another puppet. This one wore a black tunic and hat and a strange mask with a long beak—like some sort of bird—and hollow black eyes. It gave him the creeps. All of them did. Little girls, dog-faced demons, witches, and monsters. They all had the same small, cruel eyes, and every single smile was a grimace. And all of their strings had been cut, the ropes lying in tatters in the drawer.

Gilbert cautiously put down the bird-faced puppet, his throat suddenly dry. He couldn't stop staring at them, as uneasy as they made him feel. They seemed to be looking back at him, examining him with their beady eyes. He had the feeling they might be quietly talking about him, in silent voices he didn't hear but perceived, confused murmurs at the very edge of his consciousness. Dora had said that spirits hung around the circus, and maybe Frances's own was hovering around right about now.

The more he looked at the puppets, the more drawn to them he felt, as a voice almost too low to hear seemed to whisper in his ear, perhaps planting the seeds for the thought that suddenly sprang, unbidden, at the forefront of his brain: *Why, those puppets would truly look great in a performance, wouldn't they?*

He had no clue how to use them, especially since their strings were all snipped. But perhaps, if he could make them move with his *magic*, he might be able to come up with something truly impressive. And a little disturbing, too, which might not be bad. Not bad at all.

Yes, the more he thought about it, the more he convinced himself. He was almost certain that Mrs. Frances also wanted him to use them. And as for the puppets themselves, maybe they wouldn't mind being under the limelight again rather than going back to spending years locked in a secret drawer. Maybe they had been patiently waiting for someone to dust them off and bring them back to life. Maybe they had been waiting for him.

Whatever the case, he needed to clear some space for them, right now. There was no way he was sleeping in that bed again knowing their beady little eyes were hiding underneath him. He cautiously pushed the drawer shut, shrugged on his jacket, took the box of papers, and left, jogging to Jesse's caravan.

The light was still on inside, and as soon as he knocked, Jesse answered the door, wearing his jacket and scarf, as if he'd been ready to go out himself.

"Oh," he exclaimed, raising his eyebrows. "Gilbert. I was . . . I was just about to come talk to you. Is there something you need?"

"Yes. Hello. I . . ." Gilbert didn't quite know where to start, actually. *Hi, can you come help me move the puppets from Hell waiting to murder me in my sleep?* didn't sound quite right. But he did know that he was *not* going to mention his conversation with Dora. Not yet, at least. He wasn't ready. "May I come in a moment?"

"Oh. Sure. Please." Jesse stepped aside, letting him past. Gilbert waited awkwardly, not quite knowing what to do with himself, until Jesse gestured for him to take a seat. "What is it?"

Gilbert placed the box on the table. "I found these in a cabinet in Frances's . . . in my wagon. I thought, I don't know, I thought you should handle them. Keep them, burn them, whatever. I didn't think it was my place."

Jesse quietly leafed through the contents, and his fingers hesitated on the picture, his expression unreadable. Gilbert wondered whether that was what Frances had looked like when they'd first met. "Thanks. It was nice of you. Where did you find this?"

"In one of the cabinets, tucked between her clothes." He didn't like how that sounded, so he hurried to add, "I wasn't— I didn't mean to pry, going through her things. I meant no disrespect. I was just looking for—"

"No, you don't have to apologize," Jesse interrupted him. "In fact, I should— I mean, we could have at least cleared the caravan for you. I didn't even think of it. You need room for your own things."

"Yes. Thank you, I was coming to ask you about that, too. If you, I mean, if you'd help me with her other things, and stuff." Gilbert smiled, grateful, then pulled at his jacket. "But as for my things, well . . . this is pretty much all I have. I travel light."

"Well, that will have to change." Jesse smirked, wrinkling his nose. "You definitely need a new wardrobe. And since you're stuck in that caravan for the rest of your life, you might as well make a home for yourself out of it. You can start collecting things you like. You have a place to keep them now."

That left Gilbert speechless for a moment. He hadn't thought about it that way. It made it all seem so real—he was stuck there *forever*, for the rest of his life. The finality of it almost took his breath away. Oh, he could feel the panic lingering at the edge of his brain, ready to take over. But on the other hand, having a home, for the first time since before he could remember, didn't sound so bad. Having a place that was truly his, for himself and for Emilia, something no one could take away. A slow, tentative smile bloomed on Gilbert's lips. Yes. He might like that.

"And besides, you're going to need a costume too. I can't have you on stage in your ratty shirt and old trousers, now can I? This circus has a reputation to uphold."

Gilbert self-consciously pulled at his clothes. A costume? He wasn't sure he liked that idea. "Yes, but come on, we don't have money to spend on fashionable clothes. Right?"

"We won't need to. We've got trunks of old costumes and clothing that we've accumulated over the decades. I'm sure I could find something suitable for you." Jesse got up and patted his legs. "I'll help you clear out the wagon, then we can go take a look. What do you say?"

"Well, I . . ." Gilbert would rather say no because he really wasn't too happy about the idea, but Jesse looked so eager that he really couldn't bring himself to disappoint. "Sure. I would love to."

It didn't take very long to clean out the wagon. Mrs. Frances hadn't had much beyond the strictly necessary, and what she'd had was impeccably folded and stored. They'd placed her possessions in a wooden box—small enough to be carried by one man—together with her only indulgence, a collection of painted porcelain thimbles. They'd left the cutlery and cups, and then moved the puppets to the newly freed cabinets, as far away from the bed as possible.

"Do you think it would be all right if I used them in my performance?" Gilbert asked, a little uncertain, holding the puppet with the straw hair. It didn't feel quite as limp in his hand as he'd expected. "Do you think she would mind?"

Jesse picked up another puppet, a red-and-black jester with a jingling hat and a sharp-toothed smile. "Not at all. In fact, I think she'd be happy to know that her darlings will not be forgotten in a corner but will be taken care of. I know it, in fact." He took one last look around and shut the lid of the box with a sigh. "And so am I, really. It's hard to think that all that's left of her presence on this Earth can be stuffed in this little box. I'm glad that something of her might live on. She built them herself, you know, one by one. She dedicated her life to these puppets. It will be nice to still have them around."

Gilbert weighed the puppet in his hand as a prickling, tingling sensation spread through his fingers. Maybe something of her really did live on in her creatures. And he had a feeling that something was more than happy not to be shut away in a trunk.

"So, shall we go rummage through some old, moth-eaten clothes?"

"Well, if you put it so charmingly, I don't see how I can ever refuse." Gilbert cracked a smile. As Jesse picked up the box and headed to the door, Gilbert put away the last puppet, sitting him down beside the others, and closed the cabinet door. Even so, as he left, he thought he could feel their little black eyes boring into his back, following him all the way to the door. Not threatening, not friendly, just . . . disturbingly *alive*.

Jesse led him to a small wagon parked behind the striped tent, in easy reach from backstage and not far from where Herbert and Mildred were snoring loudly. It turned out to have crammed into it not only a most impressive wardrobe but also a colorful selection of props and instruments, stacked up to the ceiling. There was a rack piled high with costumes, and Gilbert brushed his hand over the fabrics—sequins and lace and velvet and ribbons and feathers—before something on the floor attracted his attention.

"Do I want to know what you guys do with these?" Gilbert asked, lifting a heavy set of chains with four manacles attached. They seemed just long enough to lock a grown man in a very unnatural and uncomfortable position.

"We haven't used those in a while. Some wannabe illusionist got himself chained up in a tank of water and was supposed to magically escape before he drowned. He wasn't around long," Jesse replied, his words muffled as he bent to rummage in a trunk at the far end of the wagon.

"So the tank is here somewhere?" Gilbert glanced around with renewed interest. He hadn't figured out a routine yet, and you never knew what might come in handy.

"'Fraid not. Goliath, that was our strongman at the time, smashed it with a hammer to get the poor sod out when he couldn't get free from the chains. Too late, though."

Never mind. Gilbert tossed the shackles away and rubbed his fingertips as if he'd been burned. *The damn things are probably haunted too.*

"Here. I think these should be all right to begin with." Jesse stood up with an armful of clothes, and Gilbert was relieved to see that there wasn't any glitter or feathers involved. A few ruffled shirts, black-and-white striped trousers, a couple of vests. Gilbert watched, rather bewildered, as his arms were filled with clothes, until Jesse lifted up the final garment, looking extremely proud.

"This will be perfect for your stage costume. It needs to be dusted a bit, but it's in excellent condition. You will look absolutely dashing."

It was an elaborate black jacket with double rows of silver buttons at the front, not too dissimilar from the red one Jesse wore. Gilbert accepted it hesitantly, rubbing his fingers on the expensive fabric. He was fairly sure he'd never even touched such a valuable item of clothing before. "Listen, this is great, and I'm very grateful. But it's too much. I'm not really the kind of person who—"

"Don't tell me you were thinking of going on stage wearing some old ratty suit? We're a circus, Gilbert. People expect a show, weirdness and wonder, and that's precisely what we aim to deliver." Jesse punctuated his sentence by shoving a tall top hat with a silver buckle on Gilbert's head. "Their lives are plain and dull enough. There's no reason to depress them further with your lackluster taste in outfits."

Gilbert was ready to give in, but when Jesse pulled out a *cape* as well, he had to put his foot down. "No. I appreciate it, and I'll do my best to patch together a decent costume. But I really don't think I'll be needing that. *Ever*."

"Oh, this isn't for the show. This is for tomorrow."

Gilbert must have missed something here. "Why? What's happening tomorrow?"

"Oh. Oh, sorry. I was— That's what I was coming to tell you. I got so worked up about moving Frances's stuff that I— God." Jesse grimaced, rubbing his forehead. "The circus is kind of in deep trouble, and I need your help. Fast. Hugo came to find me while you were seeing Dora. Herbert broke down . . . for good. There's no way Hugo can make him walk tomorrow, or any day after that, without some expensive replacement piece whose name I can't even pronounce."

"Oh," Gilbert replied, failing to see his involvement in all of this or why this was such an urgent issue. He also noticed that Jesse didn't seem the least bit curious about how his meeting with the fortune-teller had gone. He hadn't even asked about it, and— "*Oh*! That carnival thing! It's in a few days, isn't it?"

Jesse seemed pained. "It's in less than a week, and we have still got *miles* to go. It will be a miracle if we make it there on time, and that's assuming Hugo finds that goddamn piece right away and Herbert doesn't break down again. It's a fucking mess, God *damn* it."

Gilbert adjusted his grip on the mound of clothes in his arms. "Yes, but, I mean, I get that it's a big show and all. But it's not the end of the world if you . . . if *we* miss it, right? I mean, there are other shows, and we can always go back there next year."

"No, there aren't." Jesse shook his head, looking irritated. "The cold season is coming, Gilbert, and we won't be able to get a scrap of a show until the spring, except perhaps a couple in the December festivities—that's if we're lucky. And we haven't been able to set aside a single penny this last year. It has been miserable. People don't have money to eat, let alone to spend on a trip to the circus. We *need* to make this show, Gilbert, because it's what will keep us fed this winter. The only other option is *starve*."

Gilbert's mouth hung open. Yes, they'd mentioned something along those lines, but he hadn't understood. The situation was much more dire than he'd imagined. And there he was, just scrounging along willy-nilly, being fed and carried around—and now clothed, too—without doing a thing in return.

"Of course, I'm sorry. I understand. So, what, we're having a show tomorrow, to put together some cash? I don't have a routine planned yet, I'm afraid, but maybe tonight I could . . ."

Jesse shook his head. "No. This town is too small. And too poor. Nobody around here can afford to shell out money for circus tickets, and besides, we have no time to advertise. No, we need to be a little more . . . creative this time. That is why I need your help."

Gilbert was not following. What did this have to do with a cape? "Look, Jesse, you're going to have to just come out and say it because I don't understand. *What* exactly do you need me for?"

Jesse folded his arms, shifting uncomfortably. "Well, from what I understand, you're quite capable in the area of cheating people out of their money, am I correct?"

Oh. "Why, yes, I am indeed. Glad to hear my reputation precedes me."

"So tomorrow, you and I will take a little trip together to gather some cash for Herbert's repairs." There was definitely a blush on Jesse's cheeks. "It's been a long while since I've had to do this, but we have no other choice. I guess I'm, well, a little rusty. So . . ."

"So you're coming to the expert for assistance." Gilbert winked. "Happy to help. I wouldn't want to get out of practice. And besides, I'll be glad to actually make myself useful around here."

Jesse nodded, then proffered the cloak once again. "I have a couple of ideas, and it might help to dress up a little. I'll tell you on the way there. We'll have quite a few hours to kill anyway."

Gilbert frowned. "Why wait until tomorrow when we're so short of time? Let's go right now. I'm sure we can still find something open, and—"

"No, no." A look of horror crossed Jesse's features. "We can't go to *this* town. Are you mad? How long do you think it would take them to connect the two strangers who just robbed them with the freak camp nearby and come looking for revenge? Haven't you had enough angry villagers chasing you to know that?"

Gilbert could have smacked himself. He was so used to stealing and running that he hadn't even stopped to consider that the circus couldn't disappear as easily as a lone thief.

"We'll catch an early train in the morning and go. As far as possible. Just the two of us. We'll move faster that way. We'll switch trains, travel until nightfall, stop in whatever big city we come across. We'll be far enough for the circus to be safe."

Gilbert hummed. "It's going to be challenging to make our way back, though. If the trains aren't timed right, it could take us days."

Jesse's smirk made him look like a mischievous kid. "Oh, Gilbert, but we won't need to travel back at all. All we have to do is fall asleep."

As the realization hit him, Gilbert's lips parted in a slow smile. "Fancy that. So it really does come in handy sometimes."

He accepted the cloak from Jesse, and they started walking back to the wagon, slinging his "new" clothes over his shoulder. So, he had a wardrobe now. He'd never really thought he'd end up with one of those. He hadn't needed one before, and well, he'd always assumed he'd die before he was old enough to settle down.

Dora's warning suddenly rang out in his mind. About the purple cloud closing in on him, about his needing to stay hidden. He almost stopped in his tracks. Could this be what she was talking about? She had told him to keep a low profile, and there he was, about to put on a show in yet another pub, in plain sight. What if Dora was right, and Reuben's men were still looking for him? What if they recognized him? What if they followed him back to the circus? He could put everybody in danger.

"Hey, Gilbert? You all right?" Jesse was looking at him, concern darkening his green eyes. He reached out to place his hand on Gilbert's arm but seemed to catch himself at the last moment.

Gilbert debated whether to say something. Jesse already had so many things to worry about: making sure Herbert got fixed, that they made it to the Carnival of Hallows, and that they didn't all starve to death during the winter. There was no point in adding to that weight with Gilbert's paranoid thoughts. He doubted Reuben even remembered who the hell he was, and the only "evidence" he had was some spirit talking of purple clouds. Reuben's authority didn't even reach out of Shadowsea. Gilbert was just letting Dora's words get to him, working himself up for nothing.

He twisted his mouth into what he hoped was a reassuring smile. "Sure. Um, thinking about my performance. I don't have much time to come up with it." Jesse didn't seem convinced, still looking at him in a funny way. Gilbert decided to forcefully change the topic. "So, what will you do? With Frances's papers?"

Jesse shook his head, walking beside him. "I probably should burn them. I mean, it's not like anyone should read them, right? But I have a hard time destroying things that people wrote. Those were her thoughts, her feelings. She took the time to commit them to paper. Now that she's gone . . ." He sighed. "I have a little box full of scribbles from a few friends I've lost over the years. I never read them, and yet I can't bring myself to dispose of them. Ridiculous, isn't it?"

Two hundred years of losing people? That cast a whole different light on Jesse's words, and Gilbert almost felt sorry for him. On top of everything else Jesse had to worry about, he had to deal with that . . . Gilbert couldn't imagine spending several lifetimes watching friends die. Just one more reason he'd rather be on his own all along. "No. No, it's not ridiculous at all."

Gilbert stepped closer, so they were walking shoulder by shoulder. He'd have liked to touch Jesse, but he had his hands full of old clothes. Jesse smiled at him, and they walked together in silence through the sleeping circus.

CHAPTER 11

"**C**ome on, fine gentlemen, is there no one who dares defy the Incredible Fire Wizard? The greatest performance you've ever seen in your life, guaranteed!"

Gilbert chuckled, leaning comfortably back against the bar, as he watched Jesse strut around like a peacock on top of a table at the other end of the pub, boasting to the crowd with a loud, pompous voice. God, he could look truly ridiculous when he wanted to. Gilbert was actually quite impressed.

The pub was dirty, crowded, and loud, just the way Gilbert liked them. Damp stone boxed them in, with a ceiling low and arched—like a former prison, with rusty chains still bolted to the walls—and most importantly, it was aboveground. Gilbert had been adamant about that; he'd learned his lesson back in Shadowsea.

When they'd disembarked the train in the city—a city of miners, if the smeared-black faces that filled the streets were any indicator—it hadn't been hard to find the local gambling den for the usual drunkards, thieves, murderers, and lecherous noblemen. Really, Gilbert was so familiar with them, all he had to do was follow his nose. Jesse had insisted that they shouldn't rob honest workers, which only went to show how little experience he had at this. Honest workers didn't *have* spare cash to gamble away. At least, not the amount Gilbert was aiming to earn that night.

He took a deep breath. He was back where he belonged, doing what he was best at, and it felt so goddamn *good*.

They had walked in separately; they needed to pretend they didn't know each other for the little sham they'd come up with during the endless train trip. They'd brainstormed a number of ideas, though, partly to kill time and partly because Gilbert wanted to distract Jesse from asking too many questions about his dislike of trains. As usual, he'd wanted to stand with his back against the wall as the trains approached the platforms, and Jesse had latched onto that like a worried parent. "You could have said something. We could have come some other way, taken the wagon perhaps, found a coach or—"

"Look, I just don't like being *near* them while they're moving. It's no big deal. Let's get on, shall we?" Gilbert had replied, huffing, and had spent the next half hour trying to dodge more questions and more concerned offers of alternate transportation. It was sweet of Jesse to worry, but he'd been driving Gilbert nuts—the part of him that wasn't worriedly checking every person he saw in search of a telltale glimpse of purple.

He'd been in sore need of a diversion from both topics. And Jesse wasn't the only one with questions. Dora's words echoed in Gilbert's head, leaving questions all but burning on the tip of his tongue. The need to talk about it was growing, steadily, from an itch of curiosity to an almost unbearable ache. He wanted to know what had happened between Jesse and Farfarello, wanted to know exactly what the deal entailed. And why the devil had been so keen to remain with Jesse, afterward, as Dora had told Gilbert. But it wasn't the time or the place. And he wasn't entirely sure he was ready to hear the answers, anyway.

Jesse's booming voice brought Gilbert back to the here and now. "I will now dazzle you all with a show of the most unbelievable power! Prepare to behold such wonders that you will never see again in your lifetime."

Gilbert looked around at the people packed into the pub, who seemed largely unimpressed with Jesse's ramblings, barely sparing a couple of derisive snorts and insults for the fool parading around on a table shouting nonsense. Gilbert, discreetly wrapped in his new black cloak, turned to pick up a pint from the counter, keeping an eye on the handsome ringmaster, and sipped his dark beer. Nothing stronger for him tonight. He didn't want a repeat of last time's hen fiasco. His job was to mingle with the drunkards until his moment came, but in the meantime, he could chuckle as he watched Jesse fool around on that table, botching even the simplest tricks: spilling a whole deck of cards from his sleeve, falling on his ass as he attempted a somersault, setting the purple feathers on his hat on fire as he juggled three torches.

He should advise Jesse to perform a comical number in the circus, if he wasn't already. He was absolutely priceless. As Jesse stomped on his hat, flailing around and trying to put out the flames, Gilbert decided it was time to step in. He lifted his arm, pointing at Jesse in righteous accusation, and bellowed, "You, sir, are the worst charlatan I have ever encountered in my life! Why don't you spare us all your dreadful incompetence?"

Jesse straightened up, looking supremely offended. "How dare you! I should like to see you do better, you puny boar-pig!"

Gilbert had to bite his tongue to keep from laughing. He puffed out his chest in outrage. "Is that a dare, you . . . you useless codpiece?"

"Why, it is indeed, you impertinent maggot!"

"Ha-ha!" Gilbert exclaimed, spreading his cape with a dramatic gesture. Most of the customers were now looking curiously at the two bickering idiots. "Your arrogance will be the end of you! Because I am none other than the Amazing Blake, the greatest magician to ever walk the Earth! You dare challenge me? Think again and beg my forgiveness, before I crush you with my magnificence!"

Gilbert had no idea how he was coming up with that crap, but man, he was having the time of his life. For a moment, he worried that he may have gone too far, but everyone around seemed to be getting into it, a couple of people already yelling "Yeah!" and "Right you are!" to spur him on.

Jesse's lip trembled, but he didn't laugh in Gilbert's face. He called back in an equally outraged tone, "Never! I'd sooner die than defer to a cheap country-fair charlatan such as yourself. Come up here and face defeat like a man, if you dare!"

Gilbert spread his arms dramatically as he strode through the room, the crowd parting like the Red Sea to let him reach the long table that would witness their epic duel. "You all hear this fool?" he addressed their rapt audience. "I shall not be responsible for the terrible fate that awaits him. Who among you gentlemen would *bet* a single penny on this miscreant?"

He'd said the magic word. Instantly the pub was all abuzz as people called back and forth for odds and figures, and soon money started emerging from pockets and pouches and being handed around. A broad man with a scar on his face collected it. He wore a top hat with a *purple* . . .

Gilbert froze in place. The man had a purple band on his hat and on his arm too. A queasiness filled Gilbert's stomach, his heart speeding up in his chest. What *the hell* was one of Reuben's men doing so far away from Shadowsea? He had no reason to be there, and collecting bets, of all things. Gilbert was *sure* that Reuben's influence did not reach that far.

As he slowly marched to Jesse's table, he took his time glancing around under the pretense of waving to the yelling and cursing crowd. He caught a few more gleams of purple. The men seemed to have materialized out of thin air and were now scattered around the pub, trying to feign indifference. But to Gilbert's expert eye, it was obvious that they were occupying the vantage points from where they could keep an eye on the whole room.

They had most definitely *not* been there a few minutes ago. *What the hell . . .*

A drop of cold sweat rolled down his spine. He didn't believe in coincidences under the best circumstances, and after Dora's words . . . *Fuck.* If they were truly still after him, for whatever reason, he'd been warned and he'd walked right into it like a complete fool. But there was no backing out, not now, not when the circus desperately needed that money.

When he climbed on the long, narrow table, turning up the cape's collar to partially hide his face, Jesse gave him a quick questioning look. Gilbert shook his head and tried to stay in character. He wanted to warn Jesse of the danger, but how could he, when all eyes in the room were on them? All he could do was focus on not blowing this. And hope to God Reuben was just branching out his business and had actually forgotten all about him.

"It is time. Prepare for defeat and humiliation," Jesse boasted, theatrically. "*En garde!*"

His opening gambit was bringing the torch to his mouth and spitting out a long streak of fire. It reached far enough for Gilbert to feel the warmth through his clothes. That got everyone's attention, and a chorus of shouts rose from the other patrons. Somebody behind the bar was trying to protest, clearly unhappy about it, but he was quickly silenced by the roaring crowd when Gilbert retaliated with a broad sweep of his arm, lifting a stool with his magic and sending it crashing into the wall above Jesse's head, showering him with splinters. Insults and curses were hurled at him for his lousy aim as the crowd shouted some more.

"Come on! We want blood!"

"Set that wanker on fire, mate. I've got my money on you!"

Gilbert saw even more bills being passed the scarred man's way, disappearing into a large purple pouch. He looked back just in time to avoid a burning stick flying right by his head, very nearly singing his ear. "Hey, are you *crazy*?" he yelled before he could catch himself. "You could have burned my bloody ear off!"

Jesse gave him a wicked smile, standing perfectly straight on the table, like a dancer. "Oh, I'm sorry, *Amazing Blake*. I didn't realize you cannot keep up with a real fight!"

Something in Jesse's smirk made the same defying spirit awaken inside him. Men in purple be damned, Gilbert Blake didn't back down from a challenge. Sure, it might get them even more money, but there was more to it than that. A matching predatory smile bloomed on his lips. If Jesse wanted war, then by God, he'd have it.

Without another word, Gilbert wrapped himself in the cloak, then tossed it open wide, revealing a blood-red lining that hadn't been there before, and a cloud of bats flew screeching out toward Jesse. The crowd exploded in screams and cheers as Jesse deflected the furry bullets, and the bats went flapping madly around the pub, bumping into walls and people alike. Jesse responded, enveloping his fists in live, burning flames and flicking his hands forward, throwing twin fireballs at Gilbert. He turned to his side, and the flames passed beside him, hitting the wall behind him and fizzling out on the damp stones. But the people were shouting and pointing, and something was way too hot behind his head . . . Damn, his cloak was on fire!

Before taking care of that, he had to return the attack. Jesse was already swinging around a burning baton, and with a flick of Gilbert's hand, it turned into a hissing, writhing black snake, which wrapped around Jesse's wrist in an instant. That actually caught Jesse by surprise. He appeared stunned for a moment, then with a fluid motion, he flung the snake into the crowd. The people were going wild, the pub now absolutely packed as more interested parties came from outside, attracted by the commotion. More cash kept ending up in the purple silk pouch.

Jesse looked up at him, impressed, something predatory in his eyes as he licked his lips, then launched himself at Gilbert, hands leaving streaks of fire in the air. Gilbert was distracted, trying to yank off his burning cloak, and lost his balance when Jesse slammed into him. They both crashed onto the rickety table, which gave up and shattered under Gilbert's back in an explosion of shards.

They fell to the floor with an *umph*, buried under the broken planks. Gilbert groaned, touching his nape, then opened his eyes and realized that not only was he buried in rubble that was starting to catch on fire but Jesse was straddling him, body pressed flush to his, face mere inches away. His green eyes burned with the excitement of the fight, that wicked grin still on his lips. His chest heaved, and his mouth was parted as he gasped, his body tense and thrumming with energy, his scent of fire and sweat going straight to Gilbert's head. Jesse shifted, and suddenly Gilbert became very much aware that he was *between Jesse's thighs*. He took in a sharp breath as a very inconvenient area of his body awoke, right then and there, with a hundred shouting people just waiting for them to crawl out of the rubble.

He looked up at Jesse and saw his eyes go wide and his expression change—God, he felt it too, not that he could miss it since he was *riding* Gilbert's crotch, for heaven's sake—and for a split second Gilbert wondered if Jesse would set his trousers on fire and neuter him on the spot. But Jesse's smirk turned hungry, his eyes greedy, and he ground down slowly and deliberately. Gilbert had to hold back a moan because *fuck*, the friction on his hardening cock was delicious, and Jesse was so fucking gorgeous, and Gilbert was fairly sure he was growing hard too.

"We need to get out of here," Gilbert gasped, urgent, trying desperately to bring his thoughts back on track. "The men in purple . . . might be after me. We have to leave, *now*."

Jesse nodded, quickly. "Get the money and go. I'll distract them."

He stood up and spread his arms, loudly declaring himself the victor among the cheers and curses of the gamblers. As all eyes were on Jesse, Gilbert crawled in the rubble, keeping out of sight and looking for Reuben's man, the one with the pouch. *There.* He was standing by the counter with people already crowding him, demanding their winnings. The fat purple pouch peeked out from under his jacket.

Gilbert narrowed his eyes and focused, his brain sizzling, until the contents of the pouch crumbled, vanished, and materialized again inside the lining of Gilbert's jacket, the coins spread all around the bottom. He got up, still hunched, trying to hide his face as he edged toward the rear exit while Jesse stumbled toward the main entrance, loudly lamenting his fatigue after his supreme effort and would anyone kindly provide him a glass of gin as he took a breath of fresh air outside.

They hadn't reached the exits yet when an angry shout came from the counter. "It's gone! The money's gone! What sorcery—" There was an instant of gelid, utter silence where Gilbert could practically hear everyone's brains leap to the same conclusion.

"The magician! Get him!"

The roar was deafening as the crowd surged forward like a wave, going after both of them, just to be on the safe side. With a sharp gesture, Gilbert sent a chair crashing through the window, and he leaped out, turning in time to see a ball of fire erupt from Jesse, shattering the glass right after him and fizzling off by the time he landed on the cobblestones. In a second, they were up and running, a bunch of would-be pursuers stuck in the window frame as they tried to all get out at once. Jesse and Gilbert turned 'round the first corner as the door burst open and a cascade of angry gamblers poured out.

"God, and you make a habit of this?" Jesse yelled, with what breath he could spare. Gilbert couldn't even muster up the energy to retort.

They ran, picking random alleys, shoving and yanking each other when they almost went separate ways, until they emerged in a blind alley. There was nothing there but impervious walls of black bricks and a moldy wooden barrel in a corner. Gilbert pushed Jesse back against the wall, crowding him, and whispered, "Just trust me, all right?"

He was aware of Jesse nodding, of Jesse's warm body pressed flush against his, and then he forgot about it all. He squeezed his eyes shut, breathed deep, and felt the air morph around them, the sounds and lights growing dimmer, as if a translucent cloak had fallen over them. This time he was sober, nobody had shattered bottles on his head, and he could rely on his magic to get them out of trouble. It was the one trick that had saved his ass more times than he could count: a flimsy veil of invisibility, falling between him and the world.

Through the impalpable barrier, he saw their pursuers burst into the alley and heard them arguing about which way to go. Damn, he should stay away from cities *forever* because getting chased by a blood-hungry mob was really getting old.

Gilbert's head was beginning to ache from the effort, and he prayed fervently that they would leave soon. It wasn't easy keeping the barrier in place, and he'd never managed it for more than a few minutes.

"It's working. You did it!" Jesse whispered, warm breath brushing Gilbert's cheek. Jesse shifted, craning his neck to look down the alley, and . . . *Oh.* Gilbert was suddenly very much aware of the hot body pressed against his in all sorts of inappropriate ways. The friction on his cock was getting all too pleasant, and he felt his body respond. Apparently he had a thing for risky, public sex, and damn if it wasn't the worst possible moment to figure that one out.

Gilbert shifted now, trying to pull his hips back, but he just ended up rubbing against Jesse instead. It sent a frisson down his spine, all the way to his cock, and *fuck*, every hope he'd had that Jesse might not have felt that was shot to hell when he heard Jesse's surprised gasp. He looked into those wide, green eyes, completely stunned for a second. Jesse was flustered and beautiful, and there were a dozen men behind them ready to bash their skulls in. So Gilbert did what he did best— that was, something unbelievably rash and stupid—and bent his head to capture Jesse's parted lips in a ravenous kiss.

Jesse's hot mouth tasted of dark beer and smoke. They kissed between gasps and moans, grasping at each other's clothes as their bodies heated up, moving together as if they'd done this a hundred times. Gilbert broke the kiss and lunged for Jesse's throat, moving aside the rigid collar of his ringmaster's jacket to suckle on his soft skin, and *oh*, that was definitely a spot to remember because it made Jesse's hips shudder against his as he clenched his hand in Gilbert's hair and moaned loud. Not too loud, Gilbert hoped, but he couldn't be bothered to turn and check. He nibbled at Jesse's neck and whispered hoarsely, "This doesn't hide sounds, you know."

Jesse's head thumped back against the wall, and he let out a shaky chuckle. "They're gone, Gilbert."

He cast a glance back and realized that they were indeed alone in the alley. With a sigh, he let the magic vanish, the barrier disappearing as the pressure on his head eased, replaced by an elated, almost giddy, feeling. When he looked back, Jesse was sagging against the wall, a matching slightly dazed smile on his lips.

"We did it." He chuckled, pushing away tousled red hair from his face.

Gilbert groaned his approval. "Which thing are you talking about exactly?"

Jesse laughed and swatted him on the shoulder before they slowly disentangled, Gilbert listening for any signs of their pursuers. He was still catching his breath as the last of the excitement drained from his veins. God. The high of the magic, their fight, screwing Reuben's men over once again, the chase. And then . . . To think he'd been worried that life in the circus would be boring. He couldn't remember the last time he'd had such a thrilling night.

And yet, as he watched Jesse straighten his jacket—still rumpled and flushed, breathing hard—Gilbert knew that one kiss was nowhere near enough. He wanted more, to kiss him again and again. Wanted to see Jesse naked, to take his time, learn his body by heart, the pattern of his tattoos. He wanted to know what it was like to sink in Jesse's hot, tight body and see his green eyes full of pleasure, over and over again.

But he wasn't any good with words under the best circumstances, and he seriously doubted any of the desires grappling in his mind could be voiced out loud, so all he did was stare at Jesse with a foolish smile on his face. Jesse returned the smile with his bitten-red lips.

"Let's find us somewhere to sleep, shall we?"

And as Gilbert's heart did a funny jump in his chest, he realized that right now he would have said yes even if Jesse had asked for his liver in a jar.

Oh, dear God. I am in so much trouble.

CHAPTER 12

Gilbert was woken abruptly by somebody banging on the door. He nearly toppled off the bed, blinking like an owl in the bright light streaming through the windows. Where was he? What time was it? And what the ever-loving hell was going—

"Magician! Goddamn you, get your arse out of that bed, now!"

Barely awake enough to confirm that yes, he was indeed clothed and therefore yes, he could answer, Gilbert rolled out of bed, stumbled to the door, and yanked it open before the pounding made his head explode.

"What?" he mumbled. He was so not a morning person.

A very annoyed Hugo was on his doorstep, hands planted on his hips. "So, have you got it? I have to go to town right away if I want to find the good stuff at the scrap market, you know."

Gilbert stared at him blankly. *So* many things he didn't understand in that sentence.

"The money, magician. From last night," Hugo explained, pinching his nose. "Good Lord, what have I done wrong in my life to deserve this? Hello? Are you *awake*?"

"Oh. Oh, yes, sure. Sorry." Gilbert shook his head, trying to clear it, as he patted down his jacket. There, he could feel all the coins, weighing down the lining. He pressed his hand to his eyes and tried to focus. He was never any good at magic when he'd just woken up, though, and all he managed to do was make the lining split open, sending a cascade of coins and bills raining all around him, to the floor. "Oh, shit. Sorry. Here, let me—"

But Hugo shoved him out of the way, muttering, and gruffly collected it himself. When he stood up with a considerable mound of coins and notes in his arms, his frown actually turned into something like admiration. "Why, well done, you two." He whistled, then patted

Gilbert's arm. "I'm off to the market. Try to be awake when I get back, I might need some help with Herbert."

He shut the door in Gilbert's face, leaving him blinking at the ruined wood, a little dazed.

He looked down at himself. He was still dressed, down to his boots, and he was starving, his rumbling stomach informed him. With a sigh, he decided he might as well go grab something to eat. There was no way he'd be able to get back to sleep, especially not as the memories from the night before flooded his brain, demanding his attention. He glanced around for Emilia and found her snuggled on a quilted pillow. He poked her gently, but all she did was turn over and go back to sleep, resolutely ignoring him.

He stepped out in the gray, early-morning light, huddling in his jacket against the biting cold, and headed to the canteen. It was locked up, and the camp was deserted. He poked around until he found a few crackers and a piece of cheese, and he sat somewhat dejectedly at the large, empty table, munching slowly.

He couldn't stop replaying what had happened in that alley the night before. It seemed impossible. If he hadn't just dropped several pounds of coins on the floor, he would probably dismiss it all as some pathetic, wishful dream. Jesse's lips had been so warm under his, his body thrumming with energy as he pressed against Gilbert, responding so eagerly, kissing him back with just as much hunger.

Maybe it had been the excitement of the moment, the adrenaline running high from the fight, the chase. The magic, making them crazy. This was a spectacularly bad idea. Neither of them should get involved, not when they were stuck together in the circus for the rest of their lives. Things would get complicated. Messy. And it wasn't as if Gilbert could pack up and go if things went sour, and they wouldn't be able to avoid each other. But he wanted Jesse so goddamn much, it seemed a fair price to pay if only he could be with him, even just for a little while.

Maybe he should go to Jesse now. They could talk about this, figure it out. *Oh, who am I kidding.* Jesse was two hundred years old, for fuck's sake. That was already reason enough to drop the whole thing like a nest of poisonous spiders. And besides, Jesse was not his for the taking. His life, his very soul, already belonged to another—to a devil, and an infuriatingly handsome one, at that. It would drive Gilbert insane to be with Jesse and know he wasn't—would never be—his.

With a groan, he buried his face in his hands, as the still morning air was broken by a pitiful, trumpeting lament. Herbert was probably awake, alone, and stuck in place, unable to move until Hugo fixed him. Shoving the last piece of cheese in his mouth, Gilbert hauled himself up from the bench and headed toward the back of the tent. He might as well keep the poor thing company until the dwarf returned. If nothing else, they could be miserable together.

He was surprised to find Jesse already there, comforting and patting Herbert's side, murmuring at him in a consoling tone. Gilbert stopped in his tracks. He should probably say hello or something, but he was speechless for a moment. Jesse was so beautiful, even standing there in his worn-out clothes, red hair tied in a ponytail, and a sweet expression on his tired face. Gilbert's heart hiccuped in his chest, and all he wanted to do was to kiss him, right there, right now.

"Oh. Gilbert, good morning. I see Hugo dragged you out of bed." Jesse smiled at him, snapping him out of his reverie. Gilbert returned it with one that felt too wide and goofy on his face.

"Hi. Good morning. I . . ." An endless stream of platitudes flowed in his head: *did you sleep well, would you like breakfast, or would you maybe like to come back to bed with me because I, for one, sure wouldn't mind.* Instead he stepped closer, the damp grass squishy under his boots, and placed his hand on Herbert's tusk. "Do you think Hugo will be able to fix him? Will we make it on time?"

Jesse's lips trembled with uncertainty. "I sure hope so."

Gilbert desperately wanted him to smile again. "Hey, you saw how well we did yesterday. If all else fails, we can turn to a life of crime."

Jesse politely chuckled, but he didn't seem convinced.

"I'm serious, Jesse. I've been feeding myself that way for my entire life. If push comes to shove, I can figure out a way to feed us all." He craned his head to the side, forcing Jesse to look him in the eye. "Stop worrying, all right? Even if we don't make it to the carnival, we will not go hungry. I won't let it happen."

Jesse nodded, his lips tight. His eyes were glistening, and he looked absolutely exhausted—not just from lack of sleep, either. It had to be the pressure. Feeling responsible for everyone in the circus, making sure nobody went hungry, without a single day of rest in almost two centuries? Jesse had been burning the candle at both ends for so long, it was a miracle he was still standing. Although it was hard to believe he had really been alive for centuries now; he seemed too young and scared.

"We'll sort something out. Trust me," Gilbert said. "You don't have to take care of everything by yourself, all right? I'm going to help. It's not only your responsibility."

"Except it is," Jesse replied, as two heavy tears rolled down his face. He wiped at them angrily with his hand. "*I'm* the one who got everyone trapped in this circus. *I'm* the one who made this goddamn deal to begin with. And I—" He stopped, swallowing hard as another tear followed. "And if I fail, if I break the deal, *I'll* be the one condemning everyone to Hell. And I . . . I can't let that happen, Gilbert. I've already screwed up so bad, I just can't."

"Oh, Jesse. Come here." He moved closer and wrapped his arms around Jesse, who leaned into the hug, resting his head on Gilbert's shoulder. Gilbert stroked his hair, murmuring, trying to offer some measure of comfort.

"I told you you're not alone in this. I'm here. I'm not going anywhere. We'll figure it out, I promise," he said. And he realized, with a heavy feeling in his stomach, that he meant it. A week ago, he would've fled to the other side of the world to escape the circus, and now there he was, on the front line fighting for it, if only to lighten the unbearable load that weighed on Jesse's shoulders. He never wanted to see that desolate expression on Jesse's face again.

They remained in silence for some time, as Herbert nudged them with his tusk, trying to comfort them in his own way. Gilbert held Jesse, fingers deep in his soft, red hair as he rested against Gilbert, breathing deeply.

"Hey," he said when he thought Jesse had regained control and looked as though he was beginning to be embarrassed about his moment of weakness. Gilbert pulled back and offered him a carefree smile. "Listen, so, if I'm going to be a part of this Hallows' show, I need to have a routine figured out, right? I've thought about it, but I have no idea what I'm doing here, man. Think you could help me out with that?"

Jesse swallowed, wiping at his now-dry cheeks and nodded, a little shaky smile on his lips. "I, uh, sure. Want to see about it now? We're stuck here waiting, anyway."

Gilbert hugged him one last time. "Why, sure. I can't wait."

It was the first time Gilbert went inside the tent, and he looked around as he followed Jesse between the rows of tiered seats toward the circular, sandy ring at the bottom. It was more or less as he'd imagined it: draped in white-and-red fabric, cables and poles holding up the structure, an assortment of lamps and lanterns. His steps echoed under the high fabric dome, and he wondered how different this place would be filled to the brim with adoring spectators.

"So, I've never really seen a circus show before, and I guess I don't quite know what I'm expected to do. How to, you know . . ." Gilbert waved his hand around. He was determined to keep Jesse occupied, distract him at least for a little while. "I thought that maybe you could show me how you do it?"

"Sure. I'd be happy to, but . . ." Jesse seemed perplexed. "You already work with the public, right? Like the night we found you."

"Well, yes, but it's different. I can cheat at cards and do a hundred other tricks, but I don't really put on much of a show. It's not like I make hens crawl out of people's mouths every day. As a rule, my magic is supposed to be as discreet and invisible as possible. I can't let people know that I'm scamming them." People didn't take very kindly to that; there were usually death threats involved. "And now, the thought of having to show it off in front of a crowd, of letting everyone see it, *on purpose*? It's weird for me. I feel, I don't know . . . uneasy."

Gilbert shuffled his feet in the sand. That had come out a little more jumbled than he'd intended, but Jesse just smiled, seeming a little nostalgic.

"I understand. I think we all went through it. We all had to learn to stop hiding. It's a bit of a shock, but you'll get used to it soon enough. It feels pretty good, you know." As he spoke, Jesse opened a trunk and dug out two charred fabric balls attached to long strings.

"Look, it's all a matter of timing and being able to read people. You're a con artist, aren't you? Hell, that's your job. You're probably better at it than most of us. And we don't risk getting our head bashed in if we mess up. We just get booed."

Gilbert didn't reply. It was a matter of habit, he supposed. He was used to getting roughed up. That was ordinary business. Being booed? Well, he was about to experience a whole new brand of humiliation. How wonderful.

Jesse held the balls in his hands, and the fuel-soaked fabric caught fire in an instant, burning bright and merry. He hung the strings from his fingers, one for each hand, letting the spheres dangle almost down to the ground. "Remember, Gilbert, your goal is to amaze."

He started swinging them in ample circles at his sides, the flames trailing behind the spheres in brilliant reds and oranges, the light lingering long enough to give the illusion of two bright, flaming wheels spinning at Jesse's sides. Gilbert barely had the time to think, *This looks simple enough,* when Jesse tilted his head down and really *started*.

He swung his arms in an intricate dance, and the spheres spun too fast for Gilbert's eyes to follow, painting beautiful, complex streaks of fire in the half darkness of the tent. Above him, behind him—the spheres swung all around Jesse's body without ever brushing him, encasing him in an ever-changing cage of light that lasted but an instant. Jesse moved, quick and steady, not missing a beat of the tune only he could hear, but Gilbert could glimpse its echo in the fading swirls of light like a heartbeat painted in fire and air.

He was watching, utterly spellbound, as Jesse's perfect dance slowed down. One of the spheres fizzled out, and with the flick of his wrist, Jesse flung the other one up in the air. It rose straight up above him, leaving a vertical trail of fire before it stopped, suspended for an instant, a single bright light under the tent dome. And when it fell, Jesse caught it with his bare hands.

Before Gilbert could react, Jesse cradled the flaming sphere to his chest, and he started to burn.

Gilbert gasped as the first flames caught on Jesse's shirt, growing brighter and stronger by the second. Every instinct screamed at him to *do* something, put the fire out, but there wasn't a trace of pain on Jesse's features. In fact, he was smiling.

The fire spread slowly at first, climbing up the fabric of his shirt, not blackened nor charred, and Gilbert gasped when it enveloped Jesse's skin, when it caught on his red hair. His hand and wrist were now burning vividly, completely covered in orange flames as Jesse calmly spread his arms. The fire was speeding along the canvas that was Jesse's skin, spreading faster, and before Gilbert could even gasp in astonishment, the flames roared up, wrapping around Jesse's whole body.

Fuck. Jesse was . . . frightening, and unbearably beautiful, standing there, calm and silent, arms spread, his entire body enveloped in flames that danced and flickered high above his head. It took Gilbert's breath away. Jesse was like some otherworldly, magical creature. Hell, he could have been a god, the god of fire, standing before Gilbert in the empty circus tent. He could see the flames dancing on Jesse's skin, his face. His eyes were piercing behind the wall of fire, his clothes and red hair fluttering.

"Is it an illusion?" He barely dared whisper, for fear of shattering the magic.

Jesse smirked. "Why don't you come see for yourself?"

Gilbert hesitantly stepped forward. God, it had to be *some* illusion. But he could feel the wafts of hot air, the dry heat of the flames, so strong it burned the exposed skin of his face and neck.

Illusion, my ass.

Jesse was no illusionist: he was the master of fire.

Gilbert didn't need any more proof, but he tried reaching for the flames anyway. Then he snatched his hand back quickly, blowing on his scalded fingertips. Jesse smiled—a smile that outshone even the dancing flames. *God.* Part of Gilbert wanted the seats to be full of people worshiping Jesse as he deserved, and yet part of him wanted to keep Jesse's magnificence all to himself. He was so beautiful and *dangerous* right now that it made Gilbert's blood sizzle.

Abruptly, Jesse lowered his arms and the flames went out with a *whoosh*, all that fire sucked away, leaving nothing but faint smoke rising from Jesse's skin and still-intact clothes. Gilbert wondered if he would be scalding hot to the touch, too, wondered what Jesse's skin would taste like if he put his mouth to it right now.

The ringmaster looked at him then, a smile on his lips. "So that expression on your face? That's exactly what you want to make your audience feel."

Gilbert opened his mouth, but he couldn't even fucking *speak*.

Was there a way to explain, to make Jesse understand just how beautiful he looked, how enchanting his performance was? There was so much boiling inside Gilbert, but the words were getting stuck somewhere in his throat. And maybe it was for the best.

He tamped down a sigh at the thought. Things were so complicated already. They were racing to reach the carnival, trying to make sure the troupe wouldn't starve to death, and he had a whole routine to figure out. Oh, and there was a devil owning Jesse's soul and Reuben's men were still after Gilbert. But even so, all he could think about was how desperately *crazy* he was about Jesse. It had been a matter of days, and yet it felt like a lifetime.

Gilbert couldn't say that to Jesse. Any of it. So he swallowed it down, tucking his shaky hands in his pockets, and offered Jesse an unsteady smile. "I don't know what to say. You are . . . wonderful."

"Thank you. That's very sweet of you." Jesse blushed. The sincerity in the pinkness of his cheeks felt nice, and Gilbert wanted to see that blush over and over again. He loved that he was the one who put that expression on Jesse's face. "So you get the idea? After this, sometimes I do a fire-breathing trick, guiding the flame like a dragon around the ring. And maybe a brief number with an assistant. That's more or less it."

Gilbert opened his mouth to reply, but his stomach preceded him with an embarrassingly loud grumble. *Oh God,* and right after Jesse's breathtaking performance. Was the universe punishing him for something?

Jesse snickered. "My, sounds like somebody's hungry."

Gilbert pulled a face, shoving his hands in his pockets. "Give me a break. I've only eaten a bit of cheese since yesterday."

"Don't worry. I'm the ringmaster. I can't let my magician starve, now can I?" Jesse teased. "Let's go to the canteen and see if we can't rustle something up."

"Careful! You're going to burn it."

"Nonsense. It's absolutely perfect. Here, taste for yourself," Jesse said, handing the knife to Gilbert. Speared on the blade was a big, red apple that Jesse had just finished coating in freshly made, delicious-smelling caramel. "Wave it around a little before you— *Careful*, Gilbert, wait a moment, it's piping!"

"*Ow*! Mother of—" Gilbert spat out the food, but the scorching caramel was clinging to his lip and felt like it was *melting* him. He wiped at it with his fingers, only managing to burn those, as well.

And Jesse was laughing at him.

"What the hell! That's like pouring fire in my mouth."

"You're the one who insisted on having the apples. I wanted to make an omelet!" Jesse pointed his own caramel apple at Gilbert. "And I told you to wait. It needs to cool down."

"Yeah, well. I like living dangerously." Gilbert carefully blew on the apple before attempting another bite. It was delicious: the fresh taste of the apple combined with the warm, sugary caramel. It was the best thing he'd eaten in his life. *Ever*. And most importantly, fussing around looking for the apples, the sugar, and the bowl; using his fire to melt the caramel; and reprimanding Gilbert for being such a spoiled little brat was all working wonders on taking Jesse's mind off everything as they waited anxiously for Hugo's return.

They munched on their apples in comfortable silence. Jesse took studious little nibbles, neatly working his way around the fruit, pausing to wipe away the strings of semisolid caramel that clung to his mouth. It looked like he'd had a lot of practice. Gilbert, on the other hand, was biting chunks off at random, his apple threatening to fall to the ground at any moment. And he was fairly sure he had caramel in his beard. He would never be able to get that out.

And then, with his mouth full of apple, he decided now was as good a time as any to get the answers he needed.

"So, I understand that you are a little older than you look?"

Jesse paused, apple halfway to his open mouth. He slowly brought it down and gave Gilbert a somewhat sheepish smile. "I was wondering how long it would take you to ask. Dora mentioned she'd told you." He toyed with his apple. "Does it— Does it bother you?"

"Nah. I don't even think about it." Gilbert winked at him. He actually did think about it, but that wasn't Jesse's problem, nor should it be. He had no intention of adding his own issues to Jesse's burdens. "And besides, I've always had a thing for older men."

Jesse elbowed him in the ribs, but the relieved smile on his face spoke volumes. He must have been worrying about that.

"Oh, and thank you. You know, for the whole demonstration before," Gilbert said around a bite of apple. "I am almost convinced I can do it now. Although please don't expect it to be as good as your act."

Jesse reached over to pat Gilbert's knee. "Don't worry, you'll be just fine. It might be scary as hell at first, but you'll love it. I promise you. It's the best thing in the world."

"So you keep telling me," Gilbert quipped. "It must be nice. To still feel so passionate about something after almost . . . a couple of centuries, is that right? You must really love what you do."

"Yes. I really, really do. It's the one thing I am certain of. And sometimes . . . sometimes, it's all that keeps me going. Even when I hate everything else." Jesse glanced up, his eyes crinkled as he smiled and murmured, "Look at that. You got caramel in your beard."

He reached to rub his thumb over Gilbert's beard, and without thinking, Gilbert snatched his hand, holding it in his midair. It felt nice, having Jesse close, his scent of smoke and fire mixing with the sweet caramel.

Belatedly, he realized that he had to do something now. He couldn't keep holding Jesse's hand like that. So, he did what he did best: acted without thinking. He brought Jesse's hand to his lips and placed a gentle kiss on his knuckles, then, with a last squeeze, let it go.

Jesse pulled his hand back slowly, looking a little stunned. He seemed to be blushing, just a little.

"Would you like another apple?" Gilbert asked, his voice coming out a little rough. Jesse hesitated a moment, then smiled.

"Sure. You prepare it this time."

CHAPTER 13

They were dragged out of their little, peaceful haven when Hugo stormed into camp like a hurricane, cursing a blue streak that could probably be heard for miles. He had found the piece, although it had taken him far longer than expected and a couple of bribes, so he went straight to Herbert and set to work, banishing all intruders to the canteen. No distractions allowed.

The rest of the troupe was awake now, so Gilbert and Jesse joined them at the table where they waited in nervous silence for Hugo to finish his work.

Gilbert rested his chin on his hand, eyes on Jesse—he should be thinking about the act he needed to come up with, but he could only think of Jesse's lips. His mind replayed how enchanting Jesse had looked in the light of the flames. Jesse's hand was right there on the table, too, and he was wondering whether he should touch it—moving his own just an inch would be enough—when a horrible roar sounded. They all nearly jumped out of their skins.

"Was that . . . Mildred?" Constance asked, eyes wide.

"It's coming from outside the gate," Jesse said, calmly.

Clown scoffed. "Are we even sure it's our—"

A very human voice screamed in the distance, as if someone were being eviscerated.

In an instant, they were all up and running. They saw her right away, a few yards from the gate—Mildred, with her teeth bared, waving her claws as she towered over a man who was kicking and screaming for help, trying to scoot away in the grass.

"What the hell?" Gilbert muttered. They were truly in the middle of nowhere. Nobody had any reason to be out there. Maybe a farmer? A lone vagrant who'd stumbled across the camp and was looking for a meal? Or . . .

"Easy now, Mildred. Back off," Jesse cajoled, and the bear begrudgingly obeyed, shooting one last threatening glance at the man before moving away.

The man, who was sprawled and gasping in the grass, didn't look hurt—just scratched up and frightened half to death, his clothes ruined and ripped, either from Mildred or from his thrashing on the ground. *That is no vagrant*, Gilbert realized, frowning. Those were fancy clothes, an expensive black suit with a squashed bowler hat and . . .

A purple silk band on his arm.

Gilbert's heart nearly stopped, but the surprise was swiftly swallowed by a raging wave of anger. How the hell had the guy *found him*? A hundred possibilities flashed in his mind as he strode forward, kicking the man in the shin to attract his attention. How could he have followed them from the pub the night before? It was impossible. It would be inhuman.

"You. How the fuck did you find me?" he roared, blood rushing in his ears. He was seeing red, and it didn't help that the man stared at him with questioning, empty eyes, apparently determined to play dumb.

The performers had surrounded him: Constance and her mountain of muscles, Clown baring his teeth with that mad expression on his painted face, and Todd with his frightening red eyes. The man crossed himself with a trembling hand, breathing fast. They looked terrifying in the mist among the dead trees, cruel and otherworldly in a way they never had around Gilbert before.

"I, sir, I don't know what you're—"

Gilbert grabbed the guy by the collar and yanked him forward, Mildred growling behind him. "Are you alone? What do you want from me? The truth, asshole! You see that guy over there?" He pointed at Humphreys, who was absolutely blood chilling, his tentacles hovering in the air, his black eyes cold and impossibly large, like a deep-sea nightmare.

"See him? He can get inside your fucking head, you hear me, and if you even *think* of lying, he will tell me. And I won't be happy, and you know what I will do then?"

A cluster of fat mushrooms clung to the roots of a tree nearby, and with a flick of his hand, they exploded, spraying the terrified man with their sticky remnants.

"I will blow your fucking head off," Gilbert growled, and the man yelped, growing deathly pale in his grip.

"I-I'm alone, I swear to God! Please, I was . . . I was just scouting the area, I . . ." He hesitated. Gilbert tightened his hold. "I was supposed to scout the area. *Please*! God, I just had to find your location and report back."

"How did you find me? What does Reuben want from *me*?" This was nothing short of ridiculous. Gilbert's body shook, furious. Reuben had *spies* scouring the country looking for *him*? All this for a handful of coins? It made no sense. "How did you know where I was? Answer me!"

He caught a questioning look from Constance—surely all the others must be wondering what the hell was going on, what he was on about. But there would be time for questions later. For now, they leaned in, looming over the man, who was now torn between terrified and uncertain.

"I . . . I don't know what you're talking ab— No, no, *please* don't. It's the truth, I swear!" He scrambled back into the dirt when Gilbert raised his hand. "I don't know who you are! I was following the circus, that's all. Been following it for days. I'm supposed to report back your position and . . ." He paused, sheer terror flashing in his eyes. Looked like betraying Reuben still scared him more than the monsters in the woods. Well, that could be fixed.

Gilbert spread his hands, and the dead leaves the man was lying in suddenly came to life in a tangle of thick, black snakes, hissing and crawling all over the man. He screamed, writhing on the ground, batting at the gleaming serpents.

"No, please! Tonight! They're coming tonight, to . . . to take you away. It's tonight!"

Gilbert pulled him forward by the collar as a snake slithered around his elbow, his arm, and raised its head, fangs bared, to hiss an inch away from the man's colorless face. "Take us *where*?"

"Please, *please*." The man was gasping now and seemed on the verge of passing out. "We have orders to take you all back to Shadowsea. That's all I know, please."

"All right. That's enough, Gilbert. Step back. Let me," Jesse interjected, quietly.

Gilbert took a deep breath and then acquiesced. There wasn't much else to be obtained this way, except maybe to give the man a heart attack. With a last sneer, he shoved the man back down. He landed in a heap of leaves, and the snakes vanished as suddenly as they'd appeared. Gilbert moved away and let Jesse take his place. He crouched down in front of the shaking man and waited in silence until he'd calmed down a little.

"Let's start over. You. What's your name?"

The guy swallowed desperately. "L-Lester."

"All right then, Lester." Jesse's voice was calm, but it had steel in it. "What does your boss want with my circus?"

They guy clung to Jesse's sleeve, looking immensely grateful for how normal and nice Jesse was being compared to everyone else. "I . . . Please. If I tell you, he will kill me."

"And how will he ever find out? We're not going to go tell him, now are we?" When the man didn't reply, Jesse sighed. "But if you don't tell me, Lester, *we* will kill you, here and now. Your choice."

With a last desperate glance, the man broke down. "The count . . . he's been sending men all over the country. Looking for—" He swallowed. "Looking for freaks. Magicians. Illusionists. Circuses, freak shows—anything we can find."

In the sudden silence, Gilbert and the others exchanged glances. A sinister weight had lodged itself in his stomach. *What the hell is going on here?*

"And when you find them? What then?" Jesse prodded, calm and icy.

"We report back with . . . information. What they do and where they are, and if the count is interested . . . then we take them. Kidnap them and bring them back to Shadowsea."

"And what happens when they get there?"

Lester looked at Jesse with imploring eyes. "That's all I know, I swear. That's all anybody knows! The count won't tell *anyone* what he's doing with them. We bring them to the station, and he comes to collect them, just him and his personal guards. That's all I know. Please, I'm begging you . . ."

"Shut up," Gilbert barked. His mind was whirring, and nausea stewed in his belly. He didn't understand what was going on yet, but whatever it was, it couldn't be good. "You want me to make him talk? If this little shit is lying to us . . ."

But Gilbert had spent his life reading people in order to survive, so even as he spoke, he already knew: Lester was telling the truth. Whatever Reuben was up to, this man couldn't tell them any more.

Jesse stood up, his frown like a storm brewing on his face. "Damn it."

"So what do we do with this guy?" Gilbert asked. "We can't let him go. He's going to run back to Reuben and blow the whistle on us. You know that."

Deaf to Lester's insistent begging and promises of eternal allegiance, Jesse dismissed him with a wave. "Don't worry. He won't be able to say a word."

"No, no please!" Lester yelled, his voice unbearably shrill. Jesse looked at him, disgusted, and Gilbert felt a shiver crawl down his back. This was the coldest and most merciless he'd ever seen the ringmaster. It was strangely fascinating.

"Quiet, we're not going to kill you. Constance, grab this idiot and bring him to Dora. She'll wipe his mind clear of ever hearing about the Circus of the Damned in the first place. Then knock him out, take him somewhere far away from here, and dump him there." Jesse turned around, rattling off orders in a steely voice. "Humphreys, go find out if Hugo's done with Herbert. We have to leave, *right now*. He might not be the only one on our trail. And in the meantime, you"—he nodded toward Gilbert—"will tell me all you know about this Reuben. I want to know *everything*."

They traveled all day and deep into the night, not stopping or slowing down for a second. Gilbert sat next to Jesse, who was driving a few wagons chained together with a grim expression on his face. *Damn it.* As if they hadn't had enough to worry about already.

"So you're telling me this Reuben guy had never branched out of Shadowsea until now," Jesse said, still frowning. Gilbert could practically see the wheels turning in his head as he tried to piece it all together.

"Not that I know of. And I have pretty reliable sources." Gilbert shook his head. No, if Reuben had been spreading outside the city limits, Andrea would have been griping about it to no end. "That city is his kingdom, and I've never seen a single one of his men even on the outskirts of town, let alone as far from it as we are now."

"And yet you saw Reuben's men last night . . ."

Despite everything, a shiver of desire ran down Gilbert's back when Jesse mentioned the previous night. Was he even thinking about that kiss at all? Did he regret it, did he want to pretend it never happened, or . . .? *This is not the time*, Gilbert reprimanded himself, shaking his head. He needed to clear his brain and focus, damn it.

"Yes. I saw them, and I thought— After they chased me out of the pub the night you guys picked me up, I figured they might keep looking for me around town for a while and then drop it. Bash my skull in if I ever tried to get near one of Reuben's pubs again anytime soon, but that was about it." He raked his hand through his hair. "I never thought they'd come this far to look for me. I mean, come on, I haven't done anything *that* bad. It doesn't make any sense."

"And you're *sure* they were looking for you?" Jesse asked. "This guy, Lester . . . It seemed like he really had no idea who you were."

"I don't know. I had my doubts, but I figured, hell, they started popping up all over the place after I'd escaped, and you know . . ." Gilbert groaned. "But after what this guy said . . . Maybe there's something else going on and it's really just a big coincidence."

Jesse mulled it over for a moment. "Whatever the reason, they're on our trail now. Maybe not us specifically—maybe it is really about all *freaks*, but even so. We're not exactly being subtle, are we? We've left a trail of posters a mile long. It's our fucking *job* to attract crowds."

"So we can't have shows for a while." Gilbert swallowed as the reality of the situation sank like a stone in his stomach. "Certainly not one as big as this carnival, right? You said it will bring in a huge audience. It will leave us completely exposed."

"It's a secret show, Gilbert. We're not going to do any advertising for it; those people already know." Jesse shook his head. "We cannot miss the Carnival of Hallows. There's too much at stake."

"Jesse, it's not safe! We're in danger, and we should lay low. Look, even Dora said there was danger coming. She saw it," Gilbert insisted. This was madness. Every one of his instincts was commanding him to scuttle off and hide somewhere until it all blew over, the way he'd been doing his entire life whenever trouble came. "We should be hiding now, not putting on the biggest show of the year. It's suicide!"

Jesse's expression was grim when he replied. "We don't have a choice."

When they finally parted, wishing each other good night, the words knotted up in Gilbert's throat, refusing to come out. He wanted to ask Jesse to go with him, to spend the night together. So much had been going on, and now he was the one in need of comfort, even though he would never admit it aloud. And yet, he didn't dare ask. Despite the memory of what they'd done the night before burning in his mind like a torch, he just couldn't bring himself to ask. He stood there, hovering alone and undecided for a pathetic length of time, and finally walked to his wagon alone, cursing himself in colorful ways. He slammed the door shut and yanked off his jacket and shirt, tossing them angrily on the floor.

God damn it. If only I wasn't such a damn coward.

He'd just kicked his boots off when there was a knock at the door, and Gilbert's heart jumped in his chest.

Jesse stood in the doorway, hesitant.

Gilbert's gaze lingered on his neck, on the purplish marks he could see peeking out of Jesse's starched collar—marks that he hadn't even known he'd left. He shook himself mentally, realizing they were still standing in silence at the door, and—if only to avoid the whole circus seeing them—Gilbert stepped aside and gestured for him to enter. "Uh, please, come in."

Jesse stepped over the threshold, shooting him a skittish smile. "Thank you," he said softly. Then he seemed to lose his nerve, because he cast a quick glance toward the closed door, murmuring, "You know, maybe I should go. In case you want to get some, um, rest."

No. *Hell no.* Jesse had made the first move, had come knocking on his door. It was Gilbert's turn not to be a coward.

"What I want," he said, voice rumbling in his chest as he grabbed Jesse and almost slammed him up against the door, "is to have you right here."

Jesse gasped, tilting his head back, so Gilbert dove in. He put his mouth on those purple marks and sucked, grazing the skin with his teeth, soothing it with his tongue, tasting the salt of Jesse's skin and the faint smokiness that always followed him. Jesse clung to his arms, his clothes, holding on.

Without looking, he fumbled with one hand, nearly ripping the laces off Jesse's trousers in his haste. When he shoved his hand inside, he was rewarded by Jesse's breathless gasp, the greatest invitation to go on. He wrapped his fingers around Jesse's cock, finding him already hard, and that ravenous hunger stirred again inside him as he pumped slow and steady, from root to tip, not wasting any time.

"I want to taste you," he growled and fell to his knees.

He took Jesse in his mouth and sucked, grasping the base, licking the few drops of pre-cum already gathered on the tip. Jesse's left hand fisted in his hair, the other clutching his shoulder as he spread his legs to let Gilbert crouch between them. Here he was, shirtless and barefoot, cock already aching in his trousers, holding a fully dressed Jesse against the door of his wagon. Jesse's jacket was askew, his red hair falling all over his flushed face, his lips parted in the most delicious moans as he came undone in Gilbert's mouth.

Gilbert kept him pinned to the door as he licked a slow line along the underside of Jesse's cock, then circled the tip with his tongue— broad, slow swipes that had Jesse's hand shaking in Gilbert's hair. Gilbert made it good and wet, and then coated two of his own fingers with saliva. He brought his hand back, gently grazing Jesse's balls before slipping between his cheeks. He took Jesse into his mouth as far as he could while he circled the puckered hole with his fingers. It seemed to set Jesse on fire. Jesse's head thumped back against the door, and when Gilbert finally breached him, he choked out a curse, fisting his hand in Gilbert's hair, so hard it almost hurt. Gilbert pushed up inside him, the tight ring of muscle giving easily as he slowly thrust his fingers in and out, matching his rhythm on Jesse's cock. A constant stream of gasps and broken curses was escaping Jesse's lips. Gilbert was driving him wild, that much was clear.

For an instant, Gilbert wondered if anyone passing by outside would hear, and he secretly hoped so. He wanted the whole damn circus to gather and listen because *he* was the one doing this to Jesse, taking him to the brink with his fingers and his mouth, and he wanted the whole fucking world to know.

Jesse's legs were shaking, his hips hitching in small, irregular thrusts, and Gilbert wanted to make him come right now, wanted him to cry out even louder, to spill down his throat. He twisted his fingers just so, pressing knuckle-deep inside Jesse as he teased the tip of Jesse's cock with his tongue. He was rewarded by a long, deep moan as Jesse's cock throbbed in his mouth, spouting hot, salty liquid. Gilbert drank it down, greedy, sucking Jesse through his orgasm, loving how he trembled, how that tight ass clenched around his fingers.

Finally, he pulled back and stood up. Jesse leaned heavily against the door, damp locks clinging to his face, his parted lips. He was gorgeous beyond words, and Gilbert was abruptly reminded that his own cock was still hard and aching for attention, trapped in his trousers. He leaned in close, nipping at Jesse's ear, at the corner of his jaw, giving him time to catch his breath.

But Jesse was already moving, shrugging out of his jacket, letting it crumple to the floor before kicking off his boots, his trousers. Gilbert waited, a couple of steps away, admiring every inch of skin that Jesse revealed. His body was muscular, marked by countless tattoos. The lines of black ink were crisscrossed by the occasional scars of cuts and burns, the traces of two hundred years spent on Earth. He ached to learn every inch of Jesse's body by heart, know the story behind every single tattoo, every single mark, but not now. If he had his way, he would have the rest of his life to do it.

With a wicked smile, Jesse sidestepped him and bent over the small table, leaning heavily on his arms, parting his legs to expose his muscular thighs and buttocks to Gilbert's hungry gaze. *Fuck.* His cock was so achingly hard, he wouldn't last long. He grabbed Jesse's hips, loving how they felt under his hands, and slowly rubbed his cock between Jesse's cheeks, smearing pre-cum on his skin, on the puckered ring of muscle. Jesse shivered, arching the black tree branches inked on his back like fingers spreading on his skin. Mesmerized, Gilbert ran his hands over them, following them with his fingertips. "If you . . . if you don't want—"

"Take me," Jesse whispered, craning his head to look at him, coy green eyes peeking out from under his messy hair, and *God*, this was going to be over embarrassingly fast. "C'mon. Spread me open. Fuck me, Gilbert."

No breathing human could have said no to *that*. With a groan, Gilbert parted Jesse's buttocks and guided his cock to the small opening slick with spit and pre-cum. As he sank in, slow and steady, Jesse clung to the table, gasping, head hanging low as he took it all. When he bottomed out, Gilbert had to stop, fighting for his breath. He didn't want to come yet. He kneaded Jesse's muscular buttocks, then grabbed on to his hips, fighting the urge to just pound into him. Jesse's back was beaded with sweat, his red hair spilling in unruly curls over his tattoos. Gilbert felt him slowly relax under his touch, and he moved then, hips stuttering in small, tentative thrusts, before daring to go deeper. Jesse arched his back, thrusting his ass back to meet him, his tight opening relaxing as he adjusted to Gilbert's girth.

With a shudder, Gilbert wondered how long it had been since Jesse had done this, how long since someone had taken him this way, owned him so completely. Gilbert lost control at the thought that Jesse was his right then. His hips snapped faster, shoving Jesse against the table, which wobbled and creaked as Jesse's moans grew louder. He was so goddamn tight . . .

"Fuck, you feel so good," Gilbert gasped, moaning loudly as he sank in until his balls were pressed against Jesse's hot skin. "Next time I'm going to make it last." He panted out the words, barely aware of what he was saying, fucking deeper into Jesse's willing body. "Want to fuck you long and slow, feel you come around me."

Jesse craned his head to look at him, sultry and thoroughly debauched, with parted lips and hooded green eyes, and Gilbert's last coherent thought was that he was beautiful, more so than anyone he'd ever laid eyes on in his life. Then he couldn't think anymore as shuddering white-hot pleasure ran down his spine and straight to his cock, and he spilled himself deep inside Jesse.

The silence afterward was broken only by their panting. It took a lot—more than he'd have liked to admit—to ease back, pull free of Jesse's body. Jesse turned to face him and wrapped Gilbert in his arms. He leaned in and gave Gilbert a slow, languid kiss. They collapsed into bed, naked and damp with sweat, still catching their breaths, trading lazy, delicious kisses. Gilbert savored Jesse's mouth. He already loved to nibble at his lips, to feel his tongue twining with his own.

"I'm glad you decided to stay, Gilbert," Jesse murmured, snuggling close to him.

Gilbert was somewhat taken aback. After all, it wasn't for lack of trying. He'd attempted to escape for weeks. "It's not like I had much choice," he pointed out, caressing Jesse's hair with a little smile on his face.

"That's not true," Jesse said, eyes closed, resting his head on Gilbert's shoulder. "Some people kill themselves."

Oh. In all this time, that particular option hadn't even crossed Gilbert's mind. The circus wasn't *that* bad. "Well, in that case," he murmured, closing his eyes and settling comfortably next to Jesse, "I'm glad I decided to stay too."

Gilbert's eyes shot open in the dark. He clawed his way out from the remains of his dream and emerged with desperate breaths, like a man about to drown. He was covered in sweat, his heart hammering madly in his chest. It took him a couple of seconds to remember where he was, his mind still frozen in terror of that round, blinding light, that piercing whistle, as the train sped toward him.

Oh right. He was where he was going to wake up for the rest of his life—a rickety caravan in a circus that owned his soul. He wiped an unsteady hand over his face. Maybe his dream was accurate, except the light was hellfire and he was the one hurled inexorably toward it, where he was going to spend the rest of eternity.

Man, what cheerful thoughts. This wasn't how he wanted to wake up after the best fuck of his life, with Jesse right beside him, warm and naked in his bed. Trust his goddamn dreams to ruin this for him too, choking him with fear, causing his heart to hammer in his chest. *Damn it.* He needed to get up and get some air. He needed to breathe.

He tried to move as quietly as possible, to not disturb Jesse. But those green eyes were already wide-open, looking inquisitively at him. "Nightmare," he explained, voice rough from sleep. Without adding anything else, he got up and slipped on a pair of trousers. He sat on the edge of the bed, head hanging low, and raked his fingers through his messy hair, feeling Jesse's gaze bore into his back. "You go back to sleep. It's still early."

But Jesse was already sitting, stretching languidly in the pale light. Gilbert doubted the sun was up yet; there was just a mist spreading everywhere, bright enough to see a world painted in shades of gray. He wondered if that was what dawn always looked like or if it was just a thing of damned circuses. He couldn't for the life of him remember; he'd never paid attention.

Jesse pushed his red hair back from his face and lazily gathered it in a ponytail. "Might as well get up. We have to get going as soon as possible, anyway."

Gilbert nodded, then went outside to stand on the first step, leaving the door barely ajar behind him. He closed his eyes, filling his lungs with deep breaths of cold air, reveling in the silence that surrounded him. No thundering train approaching, no shrill whistle piercing his eardrums. He wasn't in a dark, claustrophobic train station, blinded by the headlight of a locomotive. Under his bare feet, he could feel old, ruined wood, not the unforgiving iron of the tracks.

Goose bumps covered his skin as the cold breeze brushed his bare arms. He sat down on the creaking step, letting the wind wash away the remains of the nightmare that still clung like driftwood to his brain. It should be creepy, the dead-looking circus camp, with its ragged tent and mostly broken lights strung around like the net of a drunken spider, all wrapped in that gray, misty light. And yet, somehow, he found it comforting. He was enjoying the quiet, listening to Jesse padding about in the caravan behind him—the creaking floorboards, the clinking of a spoon in an enamel cup, the popping fire in the stove, the pot beginning to gurgle as the strong scent of coffee wafted toward him. Before long, Jesse joined him, and Gilbert nodded, thankful, as he was handed a steaming cup of black coffee.

He held it in his hands, warming his fingers as he waited for it to be not quite so boiling. Jesse sat down beside him, stretching his legs out on the steps. He was already fully dressed, but the first few buttons of his shirt were undone, the sleeves rolled up to expose the tattoos on his forearms. They sat in silence for a while, perfectly at ease, as Gilbert enjoyed the scent of coffee and the faint smell of fuel and smoke that always permeated Jesse's clothes.

"So," Jesse said, eventually. "Would you like to talk about that nightmare?"

Nobody had ever asked that before. Probably because nobody had ever even *known* about it before, but still. He'd never told anyone because there had been nobody to tell. It was odd to have someone who cared, and he was surprised to discover that actually he did want that very much.

"It's stupid, really." He groped around for a starting point. "It's always the same. Not even that long. There's a train, and I'm on the rails. The train is coming right at me. I see it coming, this big—" He paused for a moment because, God, it was so stupid, but just recalling it was making his chest a little tight. "—this big yellow light, growing bigger and brighter. And I *know*, I know I can't get away."

Jesse listened to him with his head cocked to the side, cheek resting on his hand. When Gilbert stopped, grasping for words again, Jesse prodded gently, "And then it hits you?"

"No. Then I wake up. Every time. I wouldn't even know how— I mean, I've never been hit by a train. Obviously. I suppose I don't really want to think too hard about what would happen if I was."

Jesse thought about that for a moment. "But you were *almost* hit by one?"

"Yeah. When I was little," he said, curtly. There wasn't much more to tell. He remembered that fleeting glimpse of his mother's face, and then utter, crushing terror, knowing there was absolutely nothing he could do, knowing he would be mauled to death. A moment of such absolute, chilling terror that— Well, here he was, more than thirty years old still dreaming about it and waking up in a cold sweat.

He felt ridiculous.

"And what happened?" Jesse placed a hand on his wrist, a gentle, reassuring smile on his lips. Strange, how just talking about it with Jesse was helping to lift the weight crushing Gilbert's chest.

"I was dragged off the tracks. That's all I can remember." He considered telling Jesse about what he thought he remembered—the face of his mother, the woman who had left him to die on the tracks—but he didn't want to be the one to wipe the smile off Jesse's lips. No, there would be time to talk about that later. It wouldn't be the last time he had that nightmare, anyway. "Some kids rescued me just before the train arrived. And that's all there is, really."

"So this is why you're afraid of trains." Jesse took a slow sip of his coffee. The sky was growing lighter by the minute. Somebody shut a door somewhere, and Mildred started grunting in the distance. It was pleasant to sit and watch the circus slowly stir awake, the first birds calling from the skeletal trees outside the gates.

"I'm *fine* with trains. You've seen it yourself." Gilbert finished his coffee and played with the still-warm enamel cup. "It's the tracks I don't like. I prefer to keep my distance. But it doesn't bother me as much as the stupid dreams."

"Well, you can rest easy here. No train tracks anywhere." Jesse grinned, and Gilbert kicked him in the shin with his bare foot. He was pretty sure Jesse was about to kiss him when a loud trumpeting yawn came from Herbert's pen, then somebody cursed loudly, and with a thump and a crash, the entire circus was awake. They were on their way.

CHAPTER 14

The night of the carnival, the Circus of the Damned came to life like it was magic.

An endless stream of black carriages arrived, lit by lanterns, led by silent drivers dressed in black, and pulled by black horses adorned with plumes. Gilbert watched as hundreds of people trickled in, getting off their carriages in expensive clothes—silks and velvets of black and red and silver—and walking under the arch above the entrance. The attending ladies wore broad gowns and black gloves, and everyone's face was half-hidden by a black mask—from a simple strip of fabric around the eyes to extravagantly adorned ones in leather and gemstones.

They walked arm in arm toward the tent, conversing in hushed tones, ecstatic expressions on the bits of faces that showed. Gilbert caught snippets of conversation about how they could feel the spirits filling them, and he wondered if any of it was true or if they were just bored rich people with too much money to spend and an interest in the occult.

The tent itself was decked out in ghostly, ice-blue lights and so were the branches of the dead trees all around. The lights trembled in the wind, flickering like so many will-o'-the-wisps. The silence was eerie, the air so cold it seemed the spirits themselves were breathing it from the otherworld. They had been growing stronger every day, and by sunset on Hallows' Eve, the spirits were so powerful that Gilbert could almost feel the black wagon pulsing, like the circus's very own beating heart.

It had come so soon. The troupe had made it just in time. They'd driven to the brink of exhaustion for the few days they were traveling. Gilbert had spent the nights working on his routine in his cramped wagon while everyone slept. Then he'd spent half the day dozing on Jesse's shoulder as he drove, before waking up to take over for a few hours. Jesse didn't rest at all, almost as nervous as Humphreys with his pocket watch, even when it had become clear they would make it in time. He was always on the alert for glimpses of purple, and so was Gilbert.

They hadn't seen any so far. And as far as Gilbert could tell, none of Reuben's men were stalking the entrance tonight. They eyed every spectator like a falcon, but any number of spies could so easily sneak in disguised. Hell, Reuben himself could even hide behind one of those goddamn masks, and they would be none the wiser. They were just letting all these people into their home. It went against every single one of Gilbert's instincts, making him nervous and restless, unable to focus, as he paced back and forth like a caged animal. He felt too exposed.

Hugo was on a podium at the entrance of the tent, where the curtain flap was artfully draped aside and held by a black rope, selling tickets by the dozen. He wasn't part of the act; he'd be hovering around, keeping an eye on the audience, making sure nobody tried to sneak in to the black wagon. Nonetheless, he was dressed as lavishly as everyone else, with a ruffled black-and-red suit and an impressively tall top hat. He'd painted his face in white and black, vaguely resembling Clown and his grimace, and he was busy bowing and greeting and stuffing handfuls of money in a locked box.

The crowd was growing thicker, and Gilbert navigated it with unease, bumping into people left and right. He was about to go look inside the tent in search of that telltale purple band, of anyone behaving suspiciously, when he heard his name being called. With a last tense glance around, he turned his back on the crowd and strode backstage, where the performers were putting the finishing touches to their outfits.

Everyone seemed ready, not really scared or nervous—vibrating with a low, simmering energy. They had been doing this for so long, they seemed remarkably indifferent to the threat posed by Reuben. They didn't know the man, they didn't *realize* just how much danger they were in. Gilbert was a goddamn wreck, though, itchy and restless in his costume, sweating under his top hat. He kept nervously clearing his throat as Miriam passed by, carrying two lacquered red stilts, wearing a skintight costume covered in red and silver sequins, her inky-black hair pulled up in a bun. Her face was painted too, in blinding white, the center of her lips blood red.

Constance dragged in an armful of weights, her muscular arms and legs revealed by an elegant, black ruffled bathing suit. Two long plumes topped off her hat, and they trembled with every step she took. When she saw Gilbert staring, she fussed with the hat, making sure it was still securely pinned to her curls.

"Do you need anything?"

"No, I . . . I think someone called me? I was wondering if there's anything I could help with." *Or if there's any way I can get some sense into you all before we're royally screwed.*

She winked at him and shook her feathers. "No, we got it. It's your first time. You just worry about keeping your lunch where it belongs."

Jesse came in then, all decked out in his ringmaster regalia—a decorated red jacket with polished brass buttons and fringes, black riding boots, and a black top hat with a red silk band. He was carrying a red-and-gold whip, and he somehow managed to be even more handsome than usual. His eyes seemed greener and more piercing, and when Gilbert leaned forward, he noticed they were circled in black kohl.

"Gilbert! There you are, I was just looking for— What is it? Are you all right?" Jesse gave him a concerned glance, placing a hand on his shoulder. Gilbert figured he probably did look kind of stupid, staring at him like a gaping fish.

"No, I'm fine. More or less." He took a deep breath. "Listen, Jesse, I'm just worried about . . . all those people. We don't know who's getting inside the tent, *anyone* could wear a mask and— I know we've talked about this before, but—"

"We've talked about this *to death*, Gilbert. Will you let it go already?"

"But come on, this is insane! Where would we go if we were attacked in the tent?" he insisted, although he'd already posed the same questions to Jesse over and over again. "Do you even have *any* idea who these people are, where they come from? Reuben himself could sneak in and we wouldn't even know it. He could recognize me and—"

"All right, all right. Calm down, will you? Nobody is going to attack us, and even if they do, we're not exactly defenseless, now are we?" Jesse placed his hands on Gilbert's shoulders and looked him straight in the eye. "Stop thinking of your men in purple and try to focus on not botching your performance. And if you're so worried about being recognized, come with me a moment. I'll take care of it."

He followed Jesse through a curtain into a smaller room with three mismatched mirrors hanging above a narrow wooden counter cluttered with bottles and small boxes. Ethel and Bobbie were sitting in front of one of the mirrors, their dresses like matching explosions of ruffles and lace in black-and-white stripes. They were braiding their hair with blood-red ribbons.

"Why, ladies, how beautiful you are tonight," Jesse said with a gallant bow, and the twins giggled. Then he gestured toward a stool and looked at Gilbert. "Take a seat, and face me."

Gilbert obeyed, restless, as Jesse took off his hat and began rummaging through the jars on the table. "What exactly are you doing?"

"Trust me on this. Close your eyes, and keep still."

Something wet and thick was spread on his face with a brush, and Gilbert grimaced. It felt like cold mud being smeared on him, and Jesse covered his whole face with it. When he was done, Gilbert pried one eye open, wary of the sticky substance all over his skin. Jesse picked up a small jar and brandished a black-stained brush.

"Eyes closed, Gilbert. Come on, I'll just be another minute."

He considered protesting, but really, he didn't see the point. Something cold and wet touched his eyebrow, moving slowly in a straight line down his eyelid and onto his cheekbone. It came back, dabbing over and around his eyelid, then the whole process was repeated on the other eye. There was a soft puff of air as Jesse gently blew over his eyelids. "Open up."

Gilbert did and found himself looking right at Jesse, who was peering intently at him from barely a couple of inches away. He brushed his thumb under one of Gilbert's eyebrows, then turned once again to rummage on the table.

"Just one more thing."

He tried to steal a glance into the mirror, but before he could, Jesse grabbed his chin and gently tilted his head up. He carefully dabbed the black brush over Gilbert's lips, then continued, painting a line halfway up his cheek. He did the same on the other side, and when he pulled back, Gilbert tentatively pursed his lips. They felt a little odd with the greasy substance on them, but it had a nice smell—sweet like sugar. He kind of wanted to taste it, but he didn't want to ruin whatever Jesse had done.

"Want to take a look?"

Hesitantly, Gilbert turned to stare in the mirror. His face was covered in thick white greasepaint that was already dry and now pulling at his skin. His lips were painted black, and the color curved up into a somewhat-creepy smile along his cheeks. His eyes were smudged black, with two vertical black slits going from his eyebrows to his cheekbones. He tried parting his lips in a smirk. The face in the mirror looked like a stranger, eerie and mysterious. Like a spirit himself, right at home in the Circus of the Damned.

"I . . . I like it," he said, tearing his eyes away from his reflection to smile at Jesse. "Thank you. I feel much better."

Jesse walked him back to the main backstage area where, judging by the filtering light and noise, only one curtain separated him from the ring, from the audience. Gilbert couldn't resist the temptation, so he tiptoed to the parting in the middle of the curtain and brought his eye to it, squinting. All he could see were rows upon rows of tiered seats—filled with people. Dozens, maybe hundreds, with rows and rows of black masks highlighting the whites of their eyes.

And soon, they would all be looking at *him*.

The thought hit him like an elbow to the stomach. Suddenly, what little he'd eaten during the day morphed into a ball of lead, and he was swept by a wave of nausea, nearly wobbling under it. But he also couldn't tear his gaze away from—God, all those *people*, with all those *eyes. And Reuben could be—*

"Whoa. No, Gilbert, you're not supposed to look! Oh, here we go," Jesse muttered fondly, and suddenly there was a warm hand at the small of Gilbert's back and another on his arm, guiding him away from the curtain. "I shouldn't have let you do that. Just breathe, Gilbert. You're going to do great."

Gilbert tried to swallow, but his throat was parchment dry. He shook his head, his voice strangled when he said, "That's a lot of people."

Jesse patted him on the back. "You know what, maybe it's better if you come out in public a little before your routine. Give you some time to get over the fright before you go on. How does that sound?"

Gilbert nodded, grateful. "Thank you. That sounds wonderful." He swallowed. "Could I watch the others perform? I've never seen their acts before, and I'd really like to. If possible."

And this way I'll be able to keep an eye on the audience. If anyone seemed suspicious, or tried to attack the performers, he'd be able to catch them unawares, maybe knock them out with his magic before they could harm anyone.

"Why, certainly. Just go take a seat at the back. We'll come get you before you have to go on."

Jesse gave him a quick kiss, and on rubbery, surprised legs, Gilbert walked back around the tent before slipping in through the main entrance. The river of people coming in was now but a trickle, and almost everyone was seated. *Not many empty seats left.* Hopefully that would mean enough money to make it through the winter, to stay away from places Reuben's men could find them.

He found an empty seat in the very last row, not too far from the entrance, and sat down, trying not to attract any attention, placing his hat under the seat. He was a little concerned that someone would notice he was the only one not wearing a mask, but as soon as he was settled, the lamps in the tent abruptly went off and bright lanterns lit up the ring, attracting everyone's attention. A buzz spread through the crowd, and even Gilbert felt a frisson of anticipation run down his spine.

The noise faded when the striped curtain parted and Jesse stepped on stage, looking mysterious and dashing in his ringmaster costume. He bowed, tipping his hat to the crowd, then spread his arms to ask for attention.

"Ladies and gentlemen, on this mystical night, it's my honor and privilege to welcome you!" he announced. "Here you will witness incredible feats of magic, and for a few moments, reach through to the otherworld and the spirits that inhabit it. We will guide you past the limitations of this Earth and into terror, wonder, and amazement such as you have never felt in your life. Behold, the Circus of the Damned!"

He bowed out, and a dark, soulful tune began to play. It was the twins, standing off to the side, surrounded by an assortment of instruments. They nodded their heads to the rhythm as they played in perfect harmony. They were nothing short of excellent. Gilbert couldn't imagine a better duo of musicians.

He observed, spellbound, as the performers appeared in the ring, bewitching the audience with their incredible acts. Miriam, bending and knotting her body in ways not humanly possible, as if her bones were made of snakes. She turned her head a sharp 180 degrees, her nape now facing the crowd where her face should have been, and her body followed suit, down to the waist. She walked around the ring like a broken doll, her poorly reattached legs pointing one direction while her torso and head faced another. Ramona entered, in a dark-red velvet gown, riding Herbert like a princess, her white hair falling in ripples down her back. It was Constance and Mildred next, dancing around each other in the perfect simulation of a fight to the death, until Constance revealed her inhuman strength by bodily lifting the bear.

The crowd fell silent during Clown and Todd's performance. People shifted uncomfortably in their seats, and yet they couldn't tear their eyes away, morbidly fascinated. Gilbert had to admit that, disturbing as they might be, the two inhuman creatures had talent nonetheless, performing a dark parody of a clown's usual bumbling routine. Clown couldn't get his puppet to obey, then was persecuted by it—the gags as he got scared and then hurt might have been silly and amusing in a different setting, but laughing at this made Gilbert feel uneasy. In the end, Clown was "dead" and Todd was now using his corpse as a ventriloquist's puppet. The applause was slow and uncertain. Even Gilbert clapped somewhat hesitantly. He had liked it, but he knew he probably shouldn't have, and he wasn't sure he liked what that said about him as a person. Judging from the expressions of the people around him, they didn't feel much different.

They were so focused that they were completely blindsided by Humphreys's appearance. Constance wheeled in a big, rectangular box covered by a rich damask drape as Jesse announced the next number. "In the depth of the most mysterious abyss, among the everlasting ice of the remote North Sea, a creature was found that no man had ever seen before. The only one in existence, the very last of its kind left on this Earth . . ."

As he listened, Gilbert wondered how much of it was true, realizing with some guilt that he'd never asked Humphreys about his life.

Jesse yanked away the damask drape, revealing a huge open-topped glass tank filled with water. Humphreys floated inside it, his long tentacles contracting gracefully to propel him forward. God, how different Humphreys looked in his natural element. Divested of his human costume, he was truly otherworldly, a creature from ancient legends, even more so in the atmospheric light of the lamps.

The music had changed to a solitary violin, played by Ethel, with trembling, drawn-out notes that managed to convey an unbearable loneliness. The melancholic tune sent shivers down Gilbert's back. Did Humphreys miss the sea, his home, Gilbert wondered, captured by the music, by the hypnotic movements of Humphreys's tentacles. Was he really the last of his kind? The octopus man stopped, staring straight at the audience from behind the glass, with his impossibly deep, black, slanted eyes. Slowly, he reached up over the rim of the tank with one tentacle, and then he began to climb out.

There were screams and tussles as some spectators tried to flee in panic, but most remained seated, inexorably spellbound just as Gilbert was. Humphreys touched the sand, and Jesse and Constance swiftly placed a damask screen around him, hiding him from sight as the violin hitched in a suspense-filled, high-pitched tune while Bobbie began keeping the tempo with a large vertical drum. The crescendo reached the breaking point and Constance yanked away the screen, revealing Humphreys in a black damask suit, complete with ruffled shirt, top hat, and his inseparable pocket watch.

As he was welcomed with a delighted applause, Gilbert finally understood why the members of the troupe were all so grateful to the circus: nowhere else could someone like Humphreys be the object of such unfettered adoration. Chances were that someone like him wouldn't last a day on the streets. The circus tent, that patched-up piece of striped fabric, cast a magic more powerful than any Gilbert could ever hope to achieve.

He was leaning forward, fascinated as two trapezes were lowered from the ceiling—Constance sitting on one, Miriam on the other—when someone tapped him on the shoulder. It was Ramona, wrapped in a dark cloak.

"Gilbert, you need to come. Jesse's act is next."

He nodded, albeit a little reluctantly, and followed her out and around the tent to the backstage area. It was difficult to feel nervous or anxious now; he hadn't seen a single glimpse of purple and was hyped up on the wonderful performances he'd just seen. He'd never thought he'd feel right at home in a circus, but now? He couldn't wait to be a part of this.

"Are you ready?" Ramona asked as they walked along. "We're all eager to see your act. Jesse, especially, keeps going on about it. I haven't seen him so excited in a long time, you know."

Really? Jesse had been talking to people about him? That stirred something warm and pleasant in his chest.

The backstage was even more chaotic than before, albeit a quiet chaos, so as not to bother the performers on stage. Gilbert could clearly tell the difference, now that almost everyone was done for the night: the nervous, thrumming energy of earlier had become an overwhelming, satisfied relief. Judging from their faces, it was such an absolute bliss that he couldn't wait to find out what it felt like.

Jesse jogged to him, positively vibrating. "So are you ready?"

Gilbert wasn't sure, but there was no way he could back down now, not when Jesse was looking at him so expectantly, his eyes gleaming with such anticipation. And truth be told, with Jesse by his side, Gilbert was *almost* certain he could do this. So he nodded, feeling a slightly dazed smile blossom on his lips.

"Wonderful. Come out with Ramona then, help her with the props, and . . . hang around. Get used to being on the other side of the barrier, all right? I'll need you in the very last part of the act. I'll come get you," he explained, already heading toward the main entrance onto the stage, dragging Gilbert along.

Gilbert's eyes widened. "What? What do you mean, you will *need* me?"

Jesse stopped, looked at the panic on Gilbert's face, and burst out laughing. "Oh, Gilbert, don't worry! I won't have you juggle fire torches, you can rest easy. You'll just need to stand still and look pretty. Sounds good?"

Gilbert nodded, a little distracted now because the music inside the tent had stopped, and Constance was announcing Jesse's act in a loud and clear voice. "Our fearless ringmaster himself, the master of fire!"

Jesse gently put a hand on his face, making him turn, and looked him right in the eye. "You'll be fine, Gilbert. Trust me, all right? I've got you."

Gilbert swallowed and nodded again, his stomach in knots. Forget about butterflies—there was a whole stampede going on in there. Jesse smiled and gave him a long, chaste kiss. "Then let's go."

Behind the curtain, Jesse closed his eyes for a moment, taking a deep breath. He brushed down his jacket one last time and fixed the hat on his head, seeming to listen intently to the crowd clamoring outside. And while that sound was making Gilbert queasy, for Jesse it seemed to be the most beautiful melody on Earth. He breathed in, puffed out his chest, his face lighting up in sheer, pure enthusiasm.

"All these years," he murmured, opening his eyes, a smile blooming on his lips. "All these years, and the show still makes my blood burn like the first time."

The curtain went up, and Gilbert caught a last glimpse of Herbert pulling the rope with his trunk before being struck blind by the bright limelight.

CHAPTER 15

Jesse strode out into the eerie ring, arms spread, collecting a round of applause from his masked audience as Gilbert awkwardly shielded his eyes with his hand. Ramona came to the rescue, taking his elbow and guiding him to the side, near the trunk holding Jesse's props.

"Just keep smiling," she whispered. "They're not even looking at us. He's the star."

"I can't even see where I'm going," Gilbert muttered, squinting. He couldn't distinguish the faces in the crowd anymore, could barely see them at all, even though they were only a few feet away.

"Exactly why do you think the lights are set up like that?" Ramona kept smiling as she gracefully pulled out the six torches from the trunk. "It helps if you can't see them. Believe me."

But the thing that truly helped was watching Jesse perform. He was even more beautiful than he'd been when they'd been alone, if possible, absolutely enchanting as he performed his flawless routine under hundreds of gazes. The flames made his eyes gleam, his red hair spilled down his back, and he moved without missing a single beat, his undivided attention focused on the flames, on his show. God, he was *gorgeous*, and for a moment, Gilbert forgot everything about the crowd, the fear, the clapping and the yelling, the possibility of his impending failure. There was just Jesse, more handsome than ever, caught in this perfect dance of fire.

Gilbert knew what it felt like to be on the receiving end of that attention, to have Jesse entirely focused on him, with such intensity he thought he might explode at any moment. The memory of those green eyes on him as they'd fucked sent another shiver down his back. God, he would never stop looking at Jesse, if he could. He was stunning in every moment, and he was so dedicated and so passionate, always burning hot, like the fire that lived inside him.

Gilbert wasn't as nervous, now, after nobody had attempted to take their lives during the show, and he was reasonably sure they would be safe. He'd been in crowded rooms plenty of times before, often with all eyes pointed at him. And on more than a few occasions, those people had ended up trying to kill him. At least here, his failure couldn't end in a painful death, just in complete shame and humiliation. But he could live with that.

That was when he realized exactly *why* he was so utterly petrified by the whole situation. Yes, he wouldn't enjoy making an ass out of himself in front of a few hundred people, but it wouldn't be the first time. If he was perfectly honest with himself, it was about Jesse. He didn't want to disappoint him, didn't want to look like a failure in front of those green eyes. But most importantly, this was Jesse's show. And if Gilbert ruined it, if Gilbert messed it up for him, for the whole troupe . . . He couldn't bear the thought of disappointing them all.

He had to do this right. He *had* to.

"Gilbert! Are you listening? It's time for you to step in." Ramona was gently shaking his shoulder, and Gilbert snapped out of his reverie. He was back in the ring, as the crowd cheered wildly for whatever Jesse had just done. Constance was pushing a broad, round wooden plank on stage. It was propped up vertically, taller than she was. She set it in the middle of the ring while Ramona dug a sash out of the trunk that held . . .

"Are those *knives*?" Gilbert asked, too late, as she stepped into the ring to put them in place.

"Oh, indeed. What, you only like them with caramel apples stuck on top?" Jesse teased in a low whisper. Before Gilbert could answer, or protest in any way, Jesse took him by the elbow and led him into the ring. His stuffy brain finally caught on when Jesse gently pushed him in front of the wooden board, painted in concentric circles. *Oh God, it's a bloody target.*

After a couple of attempts, he managed to croak, "Well, you did say I'd just have to stand still."

"And as you can see, I meant *very* still." Jesse smirked, making sure he was standing in the center, then guiding him to spread his arms open. "Don't worry. I've been doing this for longer than you've been alive, and I haven't killed anyone. Not lately, anyway."

Gilbert almost choked on his own tongue as Jesse stepped back and took his place a few yards ahead—where his knives were now laid out—and Gilbert found himself alone under several hundred pairs of eyes, and in front of a goddamn bull's-eye at that. Jesse *really* wanted to make sure he got over his fear, didn't he?

Among the gasps of the crowd, the knife in Jesse's hand started burning at the hilt, and Gilbert's eyes widened. So, Jesse was going to not only throw knives at him, but those knives would be *on fire*. That was reassuring.

Thunk.

Gilbert flicked his gaze toward the sound and found himself starting at very bright, hot flames burning two inches from his stomach. His wide eyes zipped to Jesse, who stood with four burning knives fanned out in one hand, the fifth already poised to throw. With a swift, exact movement of his arm, the orange flames rushed toward him before the knife struck the board, blade jammed halfway in the wood.

He dropped his head back against the board, his heart racing, and looked at Jesse again. The ringmaster smirked, and all Gilbert could think about was how beautiful Jesse was, owning the ring, the entire tent, him. He was utterly, completely at Jesse's mercy. A reckless thrill shot down his spine at the thought.

He *liked* this, he realized, being spread open and powerless before this man. Jesse's piercing green eyes captivated him, much more than the hundreds of strangers' eyes all around him. Jesse, who stood before him with a burning knife in each hand and mouthed something at him. *Don't move.*

The twin blades slammed on each side of Gilbert's head, pinning him in place, and a roaring applause filled the tent. He looked straight ahead as Jesse received his well-deserved applause, bowing with one hand over his heart. Gilbert wondered if he should bow too, but he wasn't going to move a single inch until someone came and took the burning knives away.

It was Ramona who came to the rescue, swiftly putting out the torches with a wet towel before plucking them out. Gilbert sighed in relief, as she patted him on the arm. "Good job, Gilbert. Ready for your turn?"

Gilbert tested his unsteady legs, taking a step forward. Constance was wheeling away the target, pausing long enough to give Gilbert such a slap on the back that he nearly went sprawling facedown in the sand. "I guess? Yes, I think I am just about re—"

"Oh, shhh! Jesse's talking about you. Time to go!"

Ramona darted away, and Gilbert turned in time to see Jesse point at him with his extended arm, announcing dramatically, "For the very first time ever, on this mystical night, I give you an exclusive performance that no others have been privileged enough to admire. I give you, the Amazing Gilbert Blake!"

And with that, Gilbert was left standing alone in the middle of the ring, with everyone's eyes pointed right at him.

Oh crap . . .

A low whistle attracted his attention, and Gilbert glanced to the side to see Jesse looking at him with a bright, encouraging smile on his face. He was sitting on the barrier beside Ramona, hat on the floor, and mouthed one single word at him: *go*. There was nothing but trust and excited anticipation on his face, as if he simply couldn't *wait* to see what Gilbert would do. And Gilbert remembered why he was doing this, whom he was doing it for. It wasn't for all the strangers sitting in the audience. It was for his troupe, his . . . *friends*. It was for himself and, most of all, for Jesse.

He started with the bats, since they had proved so popular at the pub. He took off his hat and pulled one out, releasing it with a flourish. He gave the animal a few moments to attract everyone's attention as it flew in a slow spiral above him before he materialized a handful of shiny black gemstones and tossed them high in the air. They became a cloud of bats too, flapping frantically, speeding toward the crowd. People yelled, somebody even dove to the floor, but Gilbert clapped his hands, and the bats exploded into hundreds and hundreds of black moths. They flew slowly, filling the tent with the soft whoosh of small wings. As Gilbert guided them back to the heart of the tent, the moths slowly faded to gray, shrunk and shriveled, until they were nothing but flakes of ash floating over the ring. They fluttered slowly down, coating the sand like a melancholic snow, settling on Gilbert's black coat and hat.

And under the falling ashes, the puppets marched in.

They emerged from the curtain, suspended in midair, their mended strings and wooden crosses manipulated by invisible hands. They walked with irregular, jerky movements, as if yanked about by a careless master, and formed a circle above the ring where they danced, a slow, unsettling, painful dance to the morbid tune of Ethel's violin.

The marionettes' dance grew frenzied as Gilbert commanded them with his hands, as if maneuvering the invisible strings himself, and the violin followed suit with discordant, jarring notes. Soon the puppets were contorting wildly—the joker and the bird-faced doctor, the straw-haired witch and the devil, a dozen pale faces, their piercing eyes glinting with life—all caught in a feverish, mad dance, until they stopped, abruptly, as the music too snapped to an end. A tense, unbearable stillness swept through the audience, and the marionettes slumped, collapsing to the ground in twisted heaps of fabric and limbs.

And now for his grand finale, the most difficult trick he'd prepared, rehearsed a hundred times. He spread his hands and smoke started pouring out. Thick, black smoke that rose above his head and began to take a definite shape. Within moments, the round face of an enormous pocket watch emerged, its second hand ticking loudly, echoing through the tent. Gilbert closed his eyes, took a deep breath, and stepped back. And when he opened them again he was gone, cloaked in invisibility, just like that night with Jesse in the alley. In his place, standing under a hundred gazes, he'd left an illusion, a projection of himself, that Gilbert could command as he pleased. He guided the illusion to lift its hat, to extend its hand toward the crowd.

It seemed to be working perfectly, and when Gilbert glanced aside, he saw that even Jesse's eyes were fixed on the illusion. He hadn't noticed a thing and, if he hadn't, Gilbert was confident that nobody else could have.

It started discreetly enough: the illusion's eyelids growing heavier, its hair growing thinner, the wrinkles around its mouth deeper. But soon, illusion Gilbert was aging at a mad pace, years running across his face in seconds. The skin turned to sagging, dry parchment; the wrinkles growing deeper as if etched with a knife; its blue eyes now reddened and buried by drooping eyelids. Its hair turned gray, then white, and then it was falling out by the handful, revealing a wrinkled scalp, stained with age. Its clothes, too, grew worn and discolored.

Its hands turned thin and gnarled like claws, extended toward the stunned-silent crowd as if begging for mercy, all under the inexorable, ominous ticking of the smoke clock.

The twins were silent now, letting the silence echo every single stroke of the clock's hand. It made the scene all the more haunting in the pool of cold light at the heart of the dark tent.

Jesse sat, covering his mouth with his hands, seeming torn between a stunned incredulity, sadness, and horror. And only then did Gilbert realize how this must strike Jesse. Because this had already happened to him: he'd seen friends grow old, seemingly at the speed of light, crumble and die while the years refused to pass for him, leaving him forever young and unchanged. And it would happen again. It would happen with Gilbert too. With a sinking feeling, Gilbert knew that Jesse wasn't just seeing his past in that illusion; he was seeing his future, the punishment for his blasphemous deal, playing out right there before his eyes.

As Ethel picked up her violin and started a slow, subdued tune, the illusion's skin dried up like leather and then started to crumble, faster and faster still, as its clothes vanished, eroded by time. An old skeleton remained standing, then its bones cracked and shattered, dissolving into a silent rain of dust, until all that was left was a mound of gray ashes.

The silence in the tent was eerie as the clock itself vanished, turning back into smoke and disappearing completely. It seemed as if everyone had even stopped breathing. Gilbert counted the seconds, gauging for how long he could maintain the tension, how close he could bring them to the breaking point before it became too much.

Bang! With an explosion of sparks and black smoke, Gilbert reappeared in the middle of the ring, his arms spread to the sky, offering himself to the crowd.

The thunder of applause was deafening as the audience jumped to their feet, rising like a wave. Gilbert looked around, struggling to hold back a smile of sheer joy. He'd done it. He'd played them like an instrument and now they all stared at him with that unfettered adoration, crying out for him. God, it felt *amazing*—the release of all that pent-up tension, the sheer relief.

Jesse was also standing, clapping harder than anyone, a proud smile on his lips even though his cheeks were wet. A solemn tune began to play as the twins picked up their full assortments of instruments, and black confetti began slowly falling from above in a silent, dark rain. The curtain at the back parted, and the entire troupe walked out in silence, going to stand in line in the middle of the ring with Herbert solemnly closing the procession.

They bowed this way and that, collecting the last round of applause, as more and more people in the audience began to stand up and make their way to the exit. Gilbert was drunk on the relief and the excitement, the intoxicating burst of energy released by the audience and performers alike.

God, this feels wonderful, he thought as they retreated to the backstage. Jesse pulled him aside to steal a long, messy kiss. Gilbert wanted to do this again and again. He would be happy to remain in the circus for the rest of his life if he could only have more of this. For the first time that he could remember, Gilbert Blake was actually happy.

And, with a sinking feeling, he couldn't help but wonder how long it would be before this too was taken away.

CHAPTER 16

Gilbert woke to Jesse gasping beside him in bed, clutching at his chest.

It was dark as pitch, the only light coming from a faint lantern. Gilbert's mind and heart raced. "Jesse? What's wrong? Are you sick? Do you need—"

Jesse brusquely shook his head no, even as he folded over himself, still scrabbling at his chest. He sounded as if he couldn't breathe, as if somebody was ripping the lungs out of him. He was shaking, every muscle tense, his naked skin damp with sweat. Gilbert knelt beside him, reaching out for him. He didn't know what to do, so he just rested his hand on Jesse's back and rubbed. He started to struggle for breath himself, the terror pulsing through him. This had to be the most terrifying awakening of his life.

"Dead," Jesse managed to gasp. Gilbert's hand stilled. "Someone's dead. In the circus."

"What? How?" Gilbert brushed Jesse's hair away from his face. It looked like Jesse's pain was fading; he could breathe easier, but when he tilted his head up, he was pale and tense, as if he'd aged ten years. His lips were ashen, and his green eyes dark and sunken. "How can you tell? What's that to do with . . ." He gestured vaguely toward him. He meant all of it—his pain, his agonized gasping, as if *he* were the one dying.

When Jesse spoke, strands of his sweat-soaked hair clung to his lips. "I can feel it. It's like . . . she's been torn from me. I . . ." He paused to gasp, struggling to take a deep breath. For a moment, he looked as though he was about to throw up. "My life and the circus are . . . the same. And they all are the circus. Each time . . . each time one of them dies . . ."

So this had happened before. The stupid, goddamn devil was doing this, somehow. Jesse's body seemed to unclench, and he straightened carefully, wincing. He successfully took a deep breath.

"Damn," he said, trying to stretch his lips in a reassuring smile. But he was too shaky and upset, and Gilbert could see right through it. "You'd think I'd get used to it after a while. It's happened . . . fuck. Too many times already."

Before Gilbert could reply, Jesse shoved the blankets aside and swung his legs off the bed, wobbling dangerously when he got up. He grasped the edge of the counter and held himself up, seeming on the verge of collapse.

"Wait, what are you doing?" Gilbert followed suit, ready to catch him should he fall. "Sit back down, you're in no shape to—"

"Did you not *hear* me?" Jesse interrupted, not curt or angry, but simply defeated. "Somebody's dead. I need to go out there."

"Right." Gilbert wanted to smack himself. Of course. He was so worried about Jesse that he hadn't even thought of that. This tunnel vision he got when it came to Jesse should probably have worried him. "Right, I'll come with you. Here." He grabbed their clothes from where they were scattered on the floor and handed Jesse his shirt and trousers. "I'll help you out. We need to find out who—"

"No," Jesse said, shrugging on his shirt. He moved carefully, as if he'd just taken the beating of his life. "I already know who."

"Oh." Gilbert stopped, the laces of one boot half-tied. He swallowed. "Then . . . then who?"

Jesse stared at him with tired eyes. "Dora."

By dawn, the whole troupe was awake and waiting under the gray, cloud-heavy sky, huddling in their coats against the cold, damp wind. The lights and noise and magic of the night before had vanished, seeming impossibly far away, and all that was left was a thick mist. They stood quiet and still, holding a vigil under the looming tent, their pain clearly visible on their faces. She had been there longer than them all; after their ringmaster, she was their touchstone. Gilbert knew what it was like when something you thought you could rely on was yanked away, leaving you lost and reeling. It was why he made a point to never rely on anything.

Jesse was still in Dora's wagon—he'd been there for a while now—and Gilbert wondered whether he should go knock but decided against it. Jesse needed time to say good-bye. He'd known her for almost a century, from childhood to old age, and now he was left to bury her.

It was ugly and complicated and just this side of unbearable. Gilbert didn't want to intrude. So he stood back, head respectfully lowered as they all mourned in silence. Only Mildred was grumbling comfortingly where she sat beside the twins. Ethel had her arm around the bear, face buried in the thick fur as she cried.

They started moving again when Jesse at last came out, every single one of his two hundred-plus years weighing on him visibly. He softly shut the door behind himself, and Gilbert could only wonder what he had whispered to his old friend as a final good-bye as he sat at her bedside, holding her wrinkled, small hands in strong, tattooed ones. Maybe he'd apologized for getting her stuck into this deal to begin with. Maybe he'd asked for forgiveness because he was still young and strong at the price of their souls. Maybe he'd assured her they would meet again someday; they were all headed to the same place eventually. She would just have to wait for a while.

A drizzling rain was starting to fall as the troupe converged toward Jesse, toward Dora's caravan, murmuring among themselves. Gilbert couldn't make out what they were saying; he saw them huddle closer, looking miserable. Jesse bent down to hug the twins. Mildred whined, and Miriam petted her head, seeming to find comfort herself in the gesture. Ramona and Hugo were holding hands. Even Todd and Clown managed to seem mournful.

Gilbert stood back, trying not to listen, not to intrude. It was Humphreys that went to him, standing quietly by his side. He was holding his hat in a tentacle, his head also respectfully bowed. Gilbert wondered if there were tears on his face amid the rain, if those slanted, all-black eyes could cry at all.

"What a dreadful tragedy." Humphreys clutched his hat to his chest. "She was a kind, wissse woman and a loyal and beloved friend. She will be sssorely misssssed."

Gilbert nodded, eyes still on the little group seeking comfort and support in one another. Somehow, he understood why Humphreys would rather keep aside and face his grief alone.

"What a strange coincidence," Gilbert said. "She lived so long, but then on very night of the Carnival of Hallows . . ."

"Ah, but I believe it wasss no coincidence at all, Mr. Blake." Humphreys shook his head. "She was merely waiting for the one day when her spiritual companionsss would be able to come and escort her from thissss world and into theirsss."

It might be true, or it might just be wishful thinking on Humphreys's part. Surely she would have said good-bye if she had known in advance. Or maybe Jesse had found a note, a letter, inside the wagon . . .

"So," Gilbert began, clearing his throat, "now what? Will there be some sort of funeral, a ceremony?"

"No. There is no time for that. We only have twenty-four hours to find a replacement, and the clock is already ticking. All of our lives are at stake." Humphreys's voice grew hollow, as cold and gray as the sky above. "Now, Mr. Blake, the hunt begins."

CHAPTER 17

They rode in silence, packed in the small, traveling wagon, headed to the nearest town, whichever it might be. Hugo and Constance kept each other company sitting at the front, driving the machine hunched under the gray rain, cold and quiet and miserable.

In the back, nobody felt like talking either. Humphreys was toying with his pocket watch; Jesse sat with his hands in his lap, looking out of the small window. He still seemed pretty shaken, pale. Gilbert hadn't ever seen the man this way since they'd met. He was already teetering on the brink, with everything that he'd been dealing with, and Gilbert was afraid this last straw might have finally broken him.

As for Gilbert, he'd offered to go along, and Jesse hadn't really said yes, but he hadn't said no, either, so he'd taken what he could get. Jesse had just stood to the side, hands in his pockets, as Humphreys and Constance prepared the wagon. Even now, it seemed as though his heart wasn't really in it, as if he wasn't so sure they should be on this mission at all. Gilbert wanted to go sit by him, try talking to him, but decided against it and remained next to Humphreys, instead, who was, as always, in the mood for conversation.

"I cannot believe we already find ourselves in thisss predicament again." He sighed as he kept opening and closing the watch. *Click. Click.* "It ssseems like yesterday that we were running ourselvesss ragged looking for Antoine's replacement."

"When you found me," Gilbert murmured. It didn't seem long at all. In fact, it had only been a few weeks. And yet it felt much longer, half a lifetime at least. He was surprised to realize he could scarcely remember what his life was like before he came across all of this, all of them.

"And what a fine acquisition that was," Humphreys replied with that expression Gilbert had learned to recognize as a smile.

He nodded his head, grateful. "Humphreys, if I may ask . . . what *exactly* happens if you—if *we*—don't find someone in time?"

The octopus man stared at him for a moment, his ink-black eyes unreadable. "Jesse hasn't explained it to you?"

Gilbert bit his lip, feeling a little awkward, as if he were going behind the ringmaster's back. But really, Jesse was sitting right there. Even though he was still looking outside, chin on his hand, giving no indication he was paying any attention.

"Yes, yes he has," Gilbert began. "And I understand; it's just that he wasn't too clear on the, um, details. And the mechanics of exactly how . . . you know."

Humphreys sighed. "Well, then you know as much as I do. If we fail to abide by the rulesss to keep the circus sssupplied with a full ssssstaff of performers, the deal is considered broken, and we are all forfeit."

"So the circus would be destroyed and all of us along with it? We would all be killed . . . But how?" Gilbert pressed on.

Humphreys seemed to struggle to answer. "The truth—"

"The truth is that we don't know," Jesse interrupted. He still had his back to them, eyes fixed on the sky outside the window. "We don't know exactly how it would happen. Farfarello never mentioned any specifics, and I didn't particularly care to ask."

Gilbert sat back then, rubbing his beard. Before he could speak, though, the wagon jolted abruptly once more, nearly tossing him off the bench, then stopped. After a bit of noise, the back door was yanked open.

"We're in town. Get out. It's time to find a fellow freak," Hugo called.

Obediently, they all got up and climbed out of the wagon. Gilbert dropped his questioning. He wasn't sure he wanted to know, either.

The town seemed especially poor and dirty. The four of them walked through the cold rain, navigating the narrow alleys, the wooden paving uneven and strewn with rotting leftovers. There were folks shouting from second-story windows, drunkards wobbling by, a man with a crooked stovepipe hat with a dozen pans clanging on a stick over his shoulders. A train passed on the overhead railway, spraying dirty water on the people below.

"So how do we find someone? How do we even start?" Gilbert nearly shouted to make himself heard over the noise of the train.

"First, we check the bills," Jesse replied, pointing to one of the wet posters glued on the walls under the railway. "Sometimes we're not the only freak show in town. We look for acrobats, illusionists, mind readers, all sorts. Sometimes, we find someone who's performing alone and struggling to make ends meet. They're usually pretty happy to join the circus."

"I certainly was," Constance said, hands buried in her pockets.

The posters were old and faded, none more recent than a few months ago. No luck there. Looked like this town wasn't very popular with performers, not that Gilbert could really blame them.

"What now?" he asked.

"Now, we move to bribery," Hugo said. He patted the revealing bulge under his coat. "We find a lodging house or some street kids and tip them to find out if there's anyone weird passing through town. Like a strongman or someone with trained animals."

"Or a gambler that wins too much," Gilbert added.

"Yeah, well. Sometimes, if we're lucky, we find one of those drunk and bleeding in the street, just in time to swoop in and save them from a beatdown." Constance made a valiant attempt at humor and actually managed to make them all chuckle, despite being cold and wet and miserable.

Jesse squinted, nodding toward a guy hovering by a corner. "For example, that fellow over there . . . Sir! You with the goat!"

The man, in tattered clothes and no shoes, looked around, perplexed. He obviously wasn't used to being addressed as "sir." He held a leash, connected to a wet, skinny goat that chewed on some rubbish, and both man and animal stared at them with wary eyes as they approached. Humphreys wisely waited behind, hiding near a corner.

"Greetings, good sir! We have just arrived in this town and are looking for some entertainment," Hugo began, with a bright smile and a shiny coin in his hand. "Are there any performers passing through town? A conjuror, perhaps, or an acrobat . . ."

The man's eyes were now fixed on the coin. "Why, yessir, you're in luck. There's this girl, arrived a couple of days ago. With a monkey . . ."

Hugo waved the coin, which glinted invitingly. "Interesting, indeed. What does this girl do? Is she traveling alone?"

"Yessir. Spent the first night on the street, and now she's allowed to sleep at the inn, in exchange for her show. She's in there all day—I seen her." The man nodded vigorously, eyes still following the money. "It's like she has no weight, sir—an acrobat. Like it's magic or something. Certainly suitable for gentlemen such as yourselves, and the lady, too . . ."

Hugo tossed him the coin and, as the man greedily clutched it in both hands, pulled out another, just as shiny. Gilbert was content with hanging back and listening attentively. This seemed promising. "Sounds like what we're looking for, indeed. And where might we find this acrobat?"

"At the Hangman's, sir, the only inn in this part of town." The man pointed down the street as the goat started munching on his ragged trousers. He didn't seem to notice. "That way, sir. You can't miss it. Follow the trail of drunkards and vomit."

"Thank you, good sir. You've been extremely helpful. We shall be on our way, then." Hugo handed him the other coin and started to leave. But the man walked after him, like a puppy hoping to receive another bite.

"Yes, sir. Thank you, sir. But surely that other gentleman has found her already."

Gilbert stopped in his tracks and so did the others. They all knew they weren't the only one on the hunt for freaks. Could it be that they were too late?

"What other gentleman?" Gilbert asked, no longer content with standing idly by.

The man turned to look at him with the same hopeful expression, hand already extended. "This big fellow. Such expensive clothes and he wouldn't even give me a penny. The tosser shook me up pretty good instead. Unlike your generous selves . . ."

Gilbert's stomach was knotting painfully when he asked, "Did this man have a purple stripe on his sleeve?"

"Why, he sure did, sir. How did you—"

Gilbert was running before the man even finished his sentence.

Following the streak of passed-out drunkards through the alleys worked like a charm and led them straight to the small ramshackle pub. They could spot it from a distance; it was the only establishment with gas lamps along the entire street, possibly in the whole neighborhood. A little crowd was gathered outside, the usual motley crew of petty criminals, plus a handful of guys who'd probably been thrown out and were beating each other up.

The troupe gathered in a shadowed corner. Jesse's face was pale and drawn. "All right. We don't know how many there are or if they're still in there and haven't taken her yet. Let's go in and assess the situation. Humphreys"—he placed his hand on the octopus man's shoulder—"you wait outside in case they come out. Don't let them out of your sight. We'll be right after them."

Humphreys nodded and flattened himself against the dark corner at the mouth of the alleyway as the others set off. When Gilbert glanced back, he had trouble pinpointing the octopus man, as if he was melting into the wall, altering the color of his skin to blend in to his surroundings. Nice trick.

The pub was crowded, hot and loud, full of people trying to escape the rain by ordering the bare minimum and hanging around the fireplace for as long as possible. Just the kind of hole where Gilbert would be able to score nicely on a night like this, when the patrons were drunk enough not to notice, then he'd disappear out the door before they could catch on. But that wasn't going to happen tonight, of course.

As he shook off the rain, Gilbert quickly took stock of the place, looking for the man in purple—or more than one—and locating all possible escape routes. He didn't spot any of Reuben's crew, and he frowned. *God damn it. Maybe we're too late.*

He was turning around to talk to Jesse when he realized that his companions were all staring in the same direction, completely absorbed. So were several of the inn's customers. Gilbert shouldered his way into the crowd, craning his head this way and that to see, and—for a moment—he forgot all about the danger they were in.

A young, olive-skinned girl with a ragged black dress and a spray of black hair under her bowler hat was standing on tiptoe on the mouth of a wine bottle. A dozen more empty bottles were arranged around her and, graceful as a ballerina, she tiptoed from one to the other, remaining in perfect equilibrium. She moved in a delicate dance to the tune she was playing on a little flute, and a small monkey in baggy red clothes was cartwheeling around her. The bottles weren't shattering under her weight, weren't toppling over as she hopped from one to the next, as if she weighed nothing, as if she wasn't even touching them.

Gilbert felt a familiar energy prickle just under his skin, making his fingertips itch. It resonated with the magic nestled inside his chest, a familiar chord being struck. There was a peculiar vibration in the air, and it prickled down his back like an icy-cold spider. And judging from the expression on Jesse's face, he felt it too. It was tapping into their magic, creating some sort of connection the girl might not even be aware of.

Gilbert cast a glance toward Jesse, who returned it and nodded. "She's one of us," he whispered.

Gilbert didn't need to ask in order to know what he meant. *One of us freaks.*

In silent agreement, Gilbert and the others inched closer, fanning out and observing in silence as she played a note on the flute and the monkey took off and started dancing among the crowd—hopping onto a table, jumping on the knees of a guy passed out in his chair, then clinging to the gas lamp, swinging to grab the hat of a tall stranger. Gilbert's breath caught. There was a broad, purple silk band carefully tied around that hat.

Fuck. He'd been so enamored with the girl's act that for a moment he'd forgotten why they were there. He inched closer to Jesse, Hugo, and Constance and quietly directed their attention toward the ribbon.

He let his gaze linger on the man as he snatched the hat back and shoved it on his head. Beneath the ill-fitting though clearly expensive suit, Gilbert could see the physique of a rough fighter with bulging arms and shovel-sized hands. The man seemed tipsy, his huge frame wobbling as he halfheartedly kept an eye on the girl. He looked bored out of his mind, and he was holding a freshly refilled glass in his hand. Didn't seem particularly keen on this mission of his at all. Perhaps his boss's freak collection seemed like a ridiculous eccentricity to him. Or maybe he was too focused on the bottle to really think about much of anything.

"We need to get rid of that fellow while we talk to the girl," Gilbert murmured. "Maybe I can draw him out, get him into a fight or something."

"I really don't think that's a good idea. We don't want to end up running for our lives again. We need something more subtle," Jesse replied. Constance smiled, then she patted her curls, straightened her shoulders, and pushed her remarkable bosom forward.

"Excuse me, gentlemen. I can provide an excellent distraction with minimal fuss. I promise you his eyes will be *anywhere* but on that girl."

Gilbert stared, his mouth hanging open, as Constance smoothly approached the guy and, after a few murmured words and a coquettish smile, swooped him off to one of the tables at the back. She sat him in such a way that he wouldn't be able to see the rest of the room, but that might not even be necessary from the way he was eagerly leaning forward. Constance was much more interesting to him than everything else he was supposed to be doing.

He was brought back to task when the girl's monkey suddenly leaped down from the chandelier right above him, landing on Jesse's shoulder. It ran down his back and then hopped along, continuing its buffoon act among the crowd. It took a little while for Gilbert to notice that the monkey was following short, quick commands that the girl played on her flute.

He narrowed his eyes. She looked young and innocent, but he could see right through her act. Her quick, calculating eyes gave her away, revealing all the maturity of a child used to making a living on the street. In some ways, she was older than many adults in the room, and Gilbert recognized it because he'd been there. He'd been that child, and he remembered how it felt. It would be damn hard to forget.

They'd stumbled right onto the perfect candidate. And at the right time too, if the options were going with them or ending up in the hands of Reuben's men. He had to face it: whatever the count was doing with the folks he captured couldn't possibly be good. Gilbert didn't want to imagine the ways in which that man could exploit people like Gilbert and Jesse and all the others.

A roof over her head, regular meals, a place to sleep, and decent folks around—life in the circus would be a blessing in comparison to the streets. She was thin, too thin, her face and clothes stained and worn. But in her dirty face, her eyes gleamed with intelligence. She was a survivor, and that was what marked her as one of their kind even more than her powers. She might be glad to accept.

The girl ended her number with a flourish on the flute and a deep bow, mimicked by the monkey, not that the drunkards were paying attention anymore. They were already back to their drinks. As the little crowd returned to their tables or went to the counter for another pint, she hopped off the bottles, not even rattling them. Gilbert cast a quick glance to the back of the room. The guy in purple was completely oblivious, still drooling over Constance as she tickled his nose with a feather and threw her head back laughing. They had to act now, before he noticed the show was over and that somebody else had gotten to his quarry first.

But as the three of them got closer, the girl was already retreating to the exit, drawing in on herself like a cat ready to bolt. In fact, Gilbert was pretty sure she'd seen the only sober strangers spreading out and discreetly surrounding her a while ago. He certainly would have, back in the day.

Jesse just had to spread his hand and Gilbert and Hugo stopped. Gilbert was more or less standing between the girl and the door, and he supposed that was an important strategic position. He'd noticed it and *she'd* noticed it, because every street brat worth his salt never lost track of the available escape routes. Gilbert didn't think he'd have the heart to grab for her should she make a run for it.

He hoped it wouldn't come to that.

Jesse crouched in front of her as she clutched her flute with one hand like a weapon and weighed him with sharp eyes. The monkey was quietly bristling and seemed ready to attack at her command. "So," Jesse said, an honest smile on his face. "It would seem that my coin purse accidentally ended up in your monkey's trousers."

The girl widened her eyes, giving her well-rehearsed acting routine a try, even though she must have known it wouldn't work. Habit, probably—keep denying the obvious in the face of damning evidence and attempt escape.

She was already backing away as she replied. "Good sir, I don't know what you're talking about. I'm a poor, wretched soul trying to earn an honest living with—" There was a lilting accent to her words, the way she stressed her vowels. Gilbert couldn't quite put his finger on it. Italian, maybe.

"You can spare that, miss. I'm a better thief than your little friend will ever be," Jesse interrupted, but he spoke gently, matter-of-factly. Before she could react and run, he added, in the same quiet tone, "Don't worry, I'm not going to tell on you. And you can keep the money if you'll agree to talk, just for a moment. We don't have much time."

Gilbert glanced nervously at the tables. The man still had his back to them, Constance now sitting on his lap with the purple-banded hat on her head, laughing delightedly at whatever the fellow had just said.

Hurry, Jesse. They needed to get out of there as soon as possible.

Jesse shifted his crouch so he could look her straight in the eye. "What is your name? And your friend's?"

The girl shuffled her feet and glanced again at the door, but then said in a low voice, "Olivia. And . . . this is Vito."

"Olivia, my name is Jesse, and I work in a circus with these gentlemen. A member of our troupe passed away, and we need someone to take her place in the show. I was wondering whether you might be interested in—"

"I'm not going nowhere with you," she said. "And I'm not joining no circus. I know how it works: people take all your money and treat you like a servant. I will have no master. I'm my master."

"I respect that. But I want you to know we're not like any other circus. We are . . . like you." Jesse cupped his hand, hunching forward to hide it from everyone else in the room. His eyes seemed to sparkle red, and that prickly feeling shot through Gilbert again as a tongue of fire appeared in Jesse's palm, orange and bright.

The girl couldn't hide her surprise. He nodded toward his hand, answering her mute question, and she reached out with hesitant fingers to brush the flame, then jerked her arm back. As she blew on her fingertips, Jesse closed his hand into a fist and the flame vanished. "We don't have any acrobats in the circus at the moment, but we have trapezes and a lot of props you could use if you'd like. We travel, too, so you wouldn't be stuck in one place, and we have two girls just around your age who would love to meet you. You and Vito could keep performing together . . . and a lot of people come to see our shows."

Gilbert kept quiet and observed. This all sounded sincere enough, but it was starting to make him a little uneasy. How could you ask a young girl to sign her soul over forever, to make a choice that would affect the rest of her life? But if the choice was between ending up in Reuben's hands and the circus, between ending up neck-deep in whatever twisted plan the count had concocted and spending the rest of her life performing with them . . . It had to be the lesser evil by a long stretch.

But it looked like Olivia had made her decision. When Gilbert tuned back in to the conversation, she was resolutely shaking her head. "No. I don't want to go anywhere. Thank you, but I've got to leave now."

She hoisted up her flute and turned her back to them, heading for the door. Not that Gilbert expected any other outcome. She was too scared to trust anyone, let alone three strange men promising something that seemed too good to be true. Probably thought she'd find herself chained in some basement. But she was in danger, and she needed to know that, whatever she chose to do.

"Olivia, wait." Gilbert knelt down as she retreated, skittish, eyeing the door. "Listen, this is going to sound mad, and completely out of the blue, but you should know that there are men looking for you. They want to take you and other people like you, like us. They'll try to get you to go with them, or they might even just grab you. You need to be careful."

She blinked. "Yes. I know there are."

Gilbert was taken aback. "You know?"

She simply nodded toward him. "Sure. I'm looking at one right now."

Ah. Touché. It was true: in her eyes, there was no difference between them and Reuben's men, and there was nothing to be done. They had no way to prove they were telling the truth and meant her no harm. He had to try to convince her, though.

"You don't have to come with us, but Olivia, these are dangerous men. Do you understand? Very dangerous. You need to run, now. And be careful."

She definitely did not seem impressed, staring at him with an arched eyebrow. Suddenly, Gilbert realized how useless his advice sounded. She was a street kid; she didn't need to be told. If she'd survived this long, clearly she knew how to be careful already. And if she was anything like Gilbert had been at her age, she thought herself infallible too, and smarter than anyone else.

Without another word, Olivia turned on her heel and ran out the door.

Hugo made to sprint after her, but Jesse's voice stopped him cold.

"Let her go." He was still crouching, eyes on the ground, back to the serious, thoughtful air he'd had in the wagon. The warmth and smiles he'd reserved for the girl vanished, just like the flame had disappeared in his palm.

"What are you doing? Jesse, come on!" Hugo seemed frantic. "We have to take her!"

"She said no! You heard her. We're not bringing her back to the circus if she doesn't want to. Her soul . . ."

Gilbert shook his head. "So you'd rather let Reuben's watchdogs take her? You have no idea what that man is capable of!"

Jesse stood up then, a cold twist to his lips. Something had snapped inside him, and he looked hard and distant. "Are you saying he's worse than the devil? Because I seriously doubt that's possible."

"No, I'm just saying—" He stopped because he actually didn't know exactly what he was trying to say. Both options were unfair, but at least taking her would keep her safe for now, and for the rest of her life. They could give her sixty years, while with Reuben . . . Gilbert shuddered.

He started to look back for Constance but was nearly knocked over as Reuben's man stumbled drunkenly past him, careering toward the door, something like terror on his face. He must have realized his prey had vanished, and the prospect of Reuben's punishment clearly wasn't too appealing. A few seconds later, Constance joined them, adjusting her hat on her curls, frowning.

"Did you— Did she *leave*?" she asked, in patent disbelief.

Jesse nodded, straightening his jacket. "Yes. We're not taking her. Please, go tell Humphreys to let her go and not follow."

Constance shot them a dark, uncertain glance but complied nonetheless.

"So we're really going to let her go? Joining us is for her own good, you know that as well as I do," Hugo insisted, wringing his hands. "Are we just going to let that other guy grab her instead?"

"She'll take care of herself. She's been warned; she'll keep hidden." Jesse shook his head. "Look, it's too late now anyway. She's gone already."

"Or already in their hands," Gilbert muttered, grim.

"Give her some credit. You were a street kid too, once. Would you have let yourself be caught by a moron like that?"

Gilbert paused. He wanted to say, *No, of course I never would have*, but then he'd always thought himself invincible, so much smarter than anyone else, and if recent events had taught him anything, it was that maybe that idea wasn't so true after all.

"I think it's too dangerous, is all. And I know you don't want to have it on your conscience any more than I do if something happens to her," Gilbert said, eventually. He sighed, knowing there was nothing more to argue. "So we keep looking? We have a few hours left, and maybe there's someone else around here that we could . . ." He trailed off. There was a long moment of silence as Hugo wringed his hands some more and Jesse stood stock-still.

It was unnerving: the ringmaster was never that quiet, that serious. His emotions were always strong and impetuous like the fire he commanded, and yet, something inside him seemed to have been put out.

Finally, Jesse took a deep breath and closed his eyes. "No. We go home."

Hugo gasped audibly. "Jesse . . . you can't be serious. We're just going to give up?"

"Yeah." Jesse raised his head, and Gilbert could see a storm brewing in his eyes. "No more dragging people to the circus to satisfy this deal. No more doing the devil's dirty work, damning souls for him. I should never have started all this in the first place."

Hugo's mouth fell open. "Are you mad? Why, all of a sudden—"

"It's taken me centuries, but I finally understand. It could never end any differently." Jesse sounded so torn and raw it made Gilbert ache. "Even if we carry on this time, and the next, and the next, I *will* crumble someday. It was foolish to ever believe I could carry on, for what, forever? I'm not strong enough! It's time I put an end to this before even more people have to suffer the consequences."

Hugo was speechless, his face red, conflicting emotions battling on his features. Gilbert swallowed. "So, what's going to happen to us then? Are we going to be damned now?"

"Nothing's going to happen to you." Jesse was almost shaking, but his voice was steady. "I will take the fall for this. The devil will listen to me, and he will accept my offer. I know he will. I'm the one who started this, and I will be the one to pay the price."

CHAPTER 18

B y the time they got back to camp, it had stopped raining. Everyone was still up, holding a silent vigil around the canteen table. Even the animals seemed to be taking part in the general sorrow and worry: Mildred was huddled next to Ramona's leg, and Herbert stood to the side, hat respectfully held in his trunk. It didn't take long to share the news, and the discussion quickly grew heated. Hugo went over to Ramona, clearly afraid something would happen to her and having second thoughts about going along with Jesse's plan. Miriam was also decidedly unhappy, and Clown . . . Clown was furious, as far as any normal emotion could be read on his face.

"I get that you're upset about Dora. We all are, and you've known her for longer than any of us. I respect that," Miriam said, trying to keep her voice down since the twins were asleep with their heads on the table. "But you can't just act out of impulse when all of our lives are at stake. You're putting us all in danger."

Jesse was pale. "This deal and this decision, they're on me. And I will be the one to pay the price. Nothing is going to happen to any of you, I promise you that."

"And how do you know that? Are you so damn certain that you're willing to bet our lives on it? A little selfish, don't you think?" Clown pressed. He turned to Hugo with an angry gesture; his eyes looked even less human under the smeared make up. "And you, I can't believe you're going along with this madness. You're truly willing to risk Ramona's life because he's suddenly decided to grow a conscience?"

Hugo lowered his eyes. Clown knew very well how to aim at weak spots.

Miriam tried a nicer approach, placing her hand on Jesse's arm. "Look, all these years you've told us that our lives would be forfeit if we broke the deal. And now you want us to believe that you can change the rules just like that, that you can fight off the devil alone? Can you really guarantee we'll be safe?"

Jesse's hands were unsteady. "Yes. Yes, I can. I know him, I can convince him—"

"Bollocks. He doesn't know squat or he would have thought of this a long time ago." Clown turned to point a pale finger at Jesse. "You think you own us, that you can play with our lives as you please? Damn it, Jesse, you have condemned us all without even the decency of talking to us about it first—"

Jesse interrupted him. "I'm telling you I can convince him. I know him. He's not in this for the souls. It was never about the goddamn souls. I know what he really wants."

"And what, pray tell, is this thing the devil wants so much, to the point of letting—"

"He wants *me*!" Jesse snapped. There was instant silence. "All right? It's me he wants. What he's wanted from the start."

It sliced through Gilbert in a flash then, Jesse's words echoing the one thing Dora had said that he hadn't paid attention to until now. And in that moment, it burned through his brain, leaving him struggling for breath. *The devil in love . . . Why do you think he stayed?*

"So this is what will happen. I will give myself over to the devil," Jesse said, calmly. The expression on his face was painful to watch. "Not just my soul. Myself. My heart, my . . . everything. And believe me when I say I *will* convince him to let you all go free in exchange. I know I can."

The stunned silence was simmering with anger and fear and too many questions.

"Now take some time and start figuring out what you will do once the Circus of the Damned is no more. With Count Reuben and his men on the hunt, you must find somewhere to hide for a while." Jesse got up, head lowered. "I am sorry that I won't be around to help you through this."

He strode off, his movements stiff, leaving all the performers stunned around the table. All except Gilbert, whose astonishment was turning to jealousy, then to unfettered fury, making him see red. So, that was it? That was how this ended? Just that simple, and he didn't even get a say? *Hell no.* Jesse didn't get to drag him into the circus forever, make him like it, make him fucking *love* it, and then tear everything from him and walk away like that.

Gilbert was up and striding after the ringmaster as thunder rolled above, much like the anger mounting inside him. He caught up to Jesse when he'd almost reached his wagon, well out of sight from the others.

"Stop. Jesse, *stop!*" He grabbed Jesse's arm, forcing him to turn around. "What the hell do you think you're doing? What are you *thinking?*"

"I can't bear this anymore!" Jesse turned toward him like an animal in pain, eyes raw. "I can't keep watching friends die for all eternity. I can't! I *am* going to break down sooner or later. So I might as well give up now. Not get anyone else into this, save all the souls I would have condemned before I crumble anyway . . ."

"And you couldn't think of this before you dragged *me* into it?" Gilbert was furious, and he wasn't even sure why. It felt like Jesse hadn't just given up on the circus, but on Gilbert too. As if what they had—what they could have—suddenly wasn't good enough. And it was ridiculous, part of him knew. They barely had *anything* to begin with.

Didn't stop him from being angry, though.

"Don't you understand that I can't *do this* anymore?" Jesse yelled, his voice rough. His eyes were filling with tears. "I'm tired of watching people die! How many more centuries do I have to take, how many more friends do I have to bury? That little girl? Hugo? Constance?"

"So what, you're just going to whore yourself out to the devil, hoping he will do what you ask, is that the plan?" Gilbert snapped. He immediately regretted it when Jesse's eyes grew wide and stunned, as if he'd been slapped. Perhaps Gilbert should be more understanding. Jesse was in pain, exhausted and scared, and was doing the best he could to buy a way out for the rest of them. And yet . . .

"Can't be any worse than what I've been doing all these years," Jesse said, voice low. He seemed to be fighting not to lower his eyes, not to yank back the arm still in Gilbert's grasp. "At least I'm not condemning anyone to Hell. Not anymore."

That did nothing to quell Gilbert's anger. "That's a load of bullshit. You don't even know if this reckless plan of yours is going to work!"

"And what would you have me do?" Jesse yelled back. "I'm supposed to stand by and watch as you grow old and die too? Is that what you want me to do?"

"I want you to fight!" Gilbert's words echoed in the silent clearing. As the sound faded, so did his anger. It vanished in a puff of smoke, leaving him tired and aching. Swallowing, he let go of Jesse's arm and looked him in the eye. "So you're just going to . . . to give yourself to Farfarello, and that's it?" The thought was like driving nails into his stomach. It meant losing Jesse forever. "And I'm supposed to stand by and *watch*."

Jesse lowered his gaze, murmuring. "Who cares, if it will save you all?"

"*I* care!" The hurt in his voice surprised even Gilbert. "What's the point of being left here alone if you— I just— I don't want to lose you, Jesse."

But Jesse shook his head. He'd made up his mind, and nothing Gilbert could say would be enough to change it. When he spoke, his words were final.

"Tomorrow, it will all be over." He turned and left.

It was a long night.

They held a small, quiet ceremony for Dora, and Jesse placed her ashes in a black urn that joined the others in the black wagon. Afterward, some chose to stay at the table, comforting each other, talking, finding comfort in company. Others retreated to their trailers, in anger or fear. Ramona prayed. Herbert stood on guard at the gate, blocking the entrance with his body. Mildred went to sit by him, and Gertrude followed too, and the three animals sat side by side, keeping watch over the narrow, winding path that led to the circus. A strange team of guardians, indeed.

Gilbert was sitting at the very corner of the bench, feeding Emilia crumbs, and shooting glances at Jesse's wagon when Hugo came up to him. "So, how do you think the devil kills people?" he asked out of the blue.

Taken aback, Gilbert faltered and looked at him. Hugo continued. "Maybe with illness. Like cholera or the plague? Could take down entire cities in a matter of days. Make people suffer a lot too."

Gilbert was at a loss. "Why, are you . . .? Are you feeling unwell?"

"No. I'm just saying." Hugo shrugged. "Or maybe they send winged demons to tear people apart and drag their souls down into the fires of Hell. That would be quite a spectacle. Quite befitting for a circus troupe, I'd say."

Gilbert shook his head. He wanted to laugh it off, but the truth was, the general uneasiness was catching on, and he'd started feeling more than a little concerned himself. "Say, Hugo, I had no idea you were so morbid."

When he retreated to his wagon to attempt sleep, he ended up tossing and turning most of the night. He kept imagining Jesse with the handsome Farfarello. Farfarello's hands all over him, Farfarello's mouth . . . Maybe the devil would come for him during the night, and Gilbert would never see Jesse again. The thought carved an emptiness into his stomach he'd never imagined possible.

Damn it. That was what he got for breaking his own rules, for lulling himself into this feeling of family, home, love. He gritted his teeth. Despite his best intentions, he'd allowed himself to care, and once again, he was paying for it. Would he never learn?

By dawn, they were all sitting silently at the canteen table, including Jesse. Ramona and Humphreys were quietly working the stove. The twenty-four–hour mark had passed: they were officially in violation of the deal, and they were collectively holding their breath, waiting for something terrible to happen.

Gilbert himself had woken up feeling like a heavy cloak was pressing down on his chest, and it hadn't vanished yet. Something was clogging his throat, making it difficult to swallow. The sky, with its low-hanging dark clouds, only added to the feeling of suffocation. He pulled at the neck of his shirt, seeking relief. He hadn't even worn his scarf, and Emilia sat disgruntled on the table, nibbling at a bit of Ramona's potato omelet.

"You don't like the omelet?" Ramona asked him, head tilted to the side. Gilbert realized he'd been poking at the food on his plate but had barely managed a few bites.

"No, I mean, yes, it's delicious," he reassured her, still rubbing at his neckline. "Sorry. It's just, my throat is bothering me. I don't really feel like eating."

He didn't feel much like talking, either, really. The oppressive feeling had crept to his head, and it was beginning to hurt, like it was pressing down on his brain. He squinted as he looked up at the heavy sky. Something didn't feel quite right, and he didn't like it one bit.

Then, the birds came.

He saw them coming from afar. At first they were a heavy, black cloud swelling at the horizon and rushing closer, faster than any wind. Only when they were closer did Gilbert see that the moving, living, *breathing* cloud rising and crashing forward like a never-ending wave was made of birds—hundreds and hundreds of crows. The flapping of their wings created a strange, hollow sound as the wind swept the encampment.

A cold sweat broke over his entire body as he grabbed Emilia, yanking her away from her food, and shoved her in the open window of the canteen wagon. The black wave was descending upon them, roaring above their heads, and for a maddening moment, Gilbert wondered whether the birds were about to plummet down and devour them. Pick them apart with their sharp beaks, tear at their eyes and flesh until there was nothing left but blood and bones. Maybe these were the winged demons Hugo had been talking about.

Jesse stood next to Gilbert, eyes narrowed against the wind, a look of dread on his face. His plans and promises were going up in smoke. There was no bargaining with this: no negotiations, no deals to make, no begging. Just death, right fucking now.

From the corner of his eye, Gilbert saw Constance ushering the twins toward one of the caravans; everyone else stood out in the open, all eyes fixed on the sky. They knew it was useless to hide. Herbert walked back and forth, waving his tusk in frustration, because this enemy, he didn't know how to stop. He didn't know how to protect his circus from this.

Gilbert had to shout to make himself heard over the loud cawing of the birds and the whooshing of thousands of wings. "What the hell is this?"

Jesse never looked away, shielding his eyes with a hand. "It's *him*," he shouted back. "He's coming."

Before Gilbert could ask more, the crows started falling.

When the first one struck his arm, Gilbert thought the attack had begun. "Take cover!" he yelled, even though it was useless. The birds were already pelting down, a black deluge of heavy, feathered hailstones upturning plates, smashing pots and glasses, breaking windows. One fell on Gilbert's shoulder, one on the ground at his feet, and the next one landed in his plate, spraying food everywhere. Then all hell broke loose.

The performers ran to find shelter, hiding under the rims of the caravans. Herbert and Mildred tried valiantly to fight back, growling and batting at the falling crows in vain. There were too many, and they kept coming. The noise was deafening, sickening smacks and slaps as black-feathered bodies thumped by the dozen on the ground, on the roofs of the wagons. Gilbert shielded his head with his arm and grabbed Jesse's jacket, yanking him under the protruding roof of a wagon, looking around for a weapon to fend the damned birds off. But they were not getting back up; the birds weren't even attacking people on purpose. They were dropping to the ground and staying there. *What the hell...*

Time seemed to drag endlessly as the black cloud came apart and collapsed to Earth. When it stopped, there was an inky carpet of dead bodies on the ground, the tables, the roofs, and the steps of the caravans. Hundreds of feathers still floated in the air, funereal snow fluttering in the eerie silence. Gilbert doubted he could take a single step without walking on the birds; there wasn't a patch of ground left clear.

He glanced at Jesse, whose lips were tight, his gaze hollow as he inspected the massacre. A black feather was caught in his red hair.

Hugo's and Ramona's heads poked out from inside the canteen wagon. She was holding Emilia to her chest with both hands. "What the hell just happened?" Hugo hollered. "The devil is pelting us with dead birds?"

Despite it all, Gilbert had to laugh. God, this was absurd. He couldn't help but wonder what kind of strange devil Jesse had made his sodding deal with.

They spent the rest of the day shoveling bird carcasses.

They took turns, improvising shovels and carts. Herbert and Mildred helped drag the bodies away. They got a huge bonfire roaring in the clearing by the gate, pouring out a thick column of smoke, the bright-orange flames reaching higher than any man—a funeral pyre of sorts. There were so many birds, hundreds upon hundreds—Gilbert had given up trying to keep count—that burning them was the only solution.

The troupe rolled up their shirtsleeves, each member drenched in sweat from the exertion and the heat of the fire. Humphreys was uncharacteristically informal—shirtless, working with all his upper tentacles at the same time. He was doing the work of four men, each tentacle moving independently, grabbing dead crows and tossing them into the cart with such exact aim he didn't even need to look.

Just what was Farfarello playing at?

Nobody spoke much. They didn't have much breath to spare, for one, and they all wore scarves tied over their mouths and noses to keep out the smoke and sickening stench of burning feathers and flesh. Gilbert had a feeling that nobody would have dinner that night, and no one would eat chicken for a very long time. He shoveled a last heap of birds onto the nearest cart, which was now full, and paused to wipe his brow. Sweat and soot were trickling in his eyes, causing them to burn and water, which made it easier to not look at the little bodies consumed by fire. Everyone's face was blackened with soot, hair smeared gray with sweat and ash.

At dusk, the devil himself walked through the gate.

One moment, Mildred was fiddling with a cart and the next she was growling, baring her teeth at the entrance. Still high-strung, Gilbert jerked around and froze in place. The high flames flickered blue as the man approached, announced by a cold wind that swept through the camp and made the crows' feathers flutter and their eyes gleam, as if a last breath of life was brushing over them. Gilbert lifted his head. That wind was calling to him, somehow, like faraway screams, like the wails of the dead and dying, the echo of a battlefield. He wasn't the only one being affected, either. Everyone around him had stopped and was looking with glazed eyes at the advancing man.

Farfarello was as handsome as Gilbert remembered, tall and lean, walking slowly and confidently with something royal in his step, as if the entire world was at his command. He wore an elegant dark suit, an immaculate white shirt peeking out from under the expensive jacket. His steps were marked by the *thump, thump* of the walking stick, and the silver knob at the top reflected the fire so brightly it was unnatural.

"You," Gilbert whispered, then dropped the shovel and strode forward to meet him. Hugo tugged on his sleeve, stopping him.

"You know that guy?"

Oh, right. They'd never seen him before. Gilbert was the only one to have had that dubious honor.

"It's him," he said, voice low. "That's the devil coming."

Constance and Humphreys came closer too, automatically forming a barrier before the man, a thin defense between him and the circus. Constance had her hand on Mildred's broad head. Everyone else was resting after taking his or her turn shoveling, and Gilbert was almost grateful that nobody else had to experience this little run-in.

Farfarello stopped in front of them, both hands neatly folded on his walking stick, and observed them with a pleasant smile.

"Good afternoon, everyone. Mr. Blake, how nice to meet you again. I see you've made yourself quite at home here. I'm glad you listened to my advice."

Gilbert wanted to ask him why—why follow him on that train, why address him now, why *him* and not anyone else—but he didn't want to do it in front of everyone. It wasn't the time. So, instead, he yanked down the scarf from his mouth and asked curtly, "Looking for something?"

Farfarello answered his rude manners with the utmost courtesy. "Actually, no. I am looking for someone. But don't worry. He's expecting me. Has been for quite some time, I believe."

Gilbert and the others exchanged glances. Humphreys, standing straight and pristine even without his shirt, adjusted his monocle to take a better look. "I assume you're referring to Jesse?" he inquired.

"Why, indeed, the one and only. I'm afraid we have some rather urgent business to discuss, so if you don't mind . . ." He lifted his hat to bid them farewell and started toward Jesse's caravan.

Instinctively, Gilbert stepped forward, shoulders back, standing tall. "Hey, where do you think you're—"

He was locked in place then. It coursed through him, shocking him—that same blinding, overwhelming power he'd gotten a glimpse of on the train. It took over him like it was nothing, looming over him, making him feel like a roach about to be crushed. The man turned to look at him, nothing harsh in his eyes, as if he were gently reprimanding a child. "Thank you, Mr. Blake, but I do not need your assistance. I know the way."

Nobody else tried to stop him. They watched in silence as he walked to Jesse's caravan and up its red steps. He rapped on the door, then opened it and stepped in, closing it softly behind himself.

That was when the power released its hold over Gilbert. He nearly collapsed, knees sagging under him, but caught himself at the last moment.

"We can't let this happen," Constance hissed, looking furious and scared, pointing at the caravan. "He's going to take Jesse. We have to stop him! Let's go and—"

"Believe me when I say you don't want to do that." Gilbert wiped an unsteady hand over his mouth. "Anything he doesn't want us to do, we won't be able to. He's powerful, Constance, so much that I can't even . . . I can't even *comprehend it.*"

Gilbert pressed his fingertips to his temples, trying to drown out the insistent, panicky whispers of the others. The fire was still roaring beside them, surrounded by little mountains of dead birds. The smoke was making him dizzy, or maybe it was the lingering aftershock from having all that power in his body.

Constance was almost shaking with anger. "So what, we're just going to stand here while the devil kills him?"

No. No, they most definitely wouldn't. And really, there was only one thing to be done. When he walked away, everyone turned to look at him.

"What are you doing?" Hugo asked.

Gilbert didn't even look back. "I'm going to find out what the hell is going on."

CHAPTER 19

Gilbert snuck behind the wagon as quietly as he could, focusing like never before to make sure his magic shielded him completely. He found a little hole in the old wall, and brought his eye to it. He wasn't at all sure it would work. Could he *be* more pathetic, trying to spy on a possibly omnipotent devil when he was protected by nothing but a flimsy layer of magic? Really, if Farfarello cracked Gilbert's head open in retaliation, he supposed he kind of deserved it.

But he might have been in luck. The two men inside were in the throes of a violent argument, not paying attention to anything but each other.

"After *two hundred years* you have the goddamn *nerve* to just show up and knock on my door and act as if nothing has happened? How dare you— What the fuck are you smiling at?"

Jesse was pacing; everything about his body language screamed *furious*. Even Gilbert could see his eyes flashing red.

"Nothing. It's just— It's so good to see you again. You haven't changed a bit."

Jesse stared at Farfarello with such anger that Gilbert thought the devil himself might burst into flames. "I have changed *plenty*. A lot of things have changed. Just because this . . . this body still looks the same, it doesn't mean everything's the same, that no time has passed."

Farfarello seemed taken aback, like a scolded puppy. "It hasn't been *that* long," he said, but he didn't sound so sure, almost like he was seeking confirmation. And Jesse seemed on the verge of exploding. But instead, he deflated. The roaring fire in his eyes dimmed and faded until they went back to their usual green, and he just seemed weary and sad.

"Two centuries, Farfarello. Maybe that's not long for you and your . . . kind. But it is long for *me*." With that, he turned his back to Farfarello, who suddenly looked extremely uncertain. As if he didn't know how to handle this situation, as if it was something entirely new for him.

"Would you like me to . . . apologize?" he asked, hesitant.

Lord, he was so different from the cocky, powerful being Gilbert had met on that train that he almost had trouble believing it was the same person. Devil. Whatever.

"Would that make you feel better?"

Jesse covered his eyes with his hand for a moment. Then he sighed and sat down heavily on the side of the bed, gesturing for Farfarello to take the chair. "After all these years, you still don't get it, do you?" He shook his head. He looked *done*. "Never mind. I would just like to talk about why you're here, so we can finish this already."

Farfarello seemed to be on more solid ground now. He sat with his back straight and primly folded his hands on the silver knob of his cane. "You know why." He almost didn't seem real, so beautiful and captivating with his handsome face, his dark skin almost glowing, his black eyes. "I had to come. You are violating the deal, Jesse."

"Of course you *had* to come. Now that there's something you *want*," Jesse ground out. His pain was so clear under his anger that Gilbert was taken aback. There was something deeply personal at stake, some still-open wound gnawing at Jesse. It was the only explanation.

"Do you think this is what I wanted? You think I'm happy with this?" Farfarello seemed upset, his lips tight, his hand clenching on the cane. "It was supposed to be so simple: strike the deal, pop by every now and then, come back someday to collect. And yet, somehow, I screwed it up. Two centuries later, I sit here and I look at you and—" He swallowed. He couldn't take his eyes off Jesse. "And I'm still as powerless as I was all those years ago."

"It couldn't have worked, back then," Jesse replied, leaning heavily with his back against the wall. "For a long time I was so angry at you, Farfarello. I thought you had led me on, I thought you'd been mocking me. I kept waiting, waiting for you to come back, for so long."

Gilbert's heart stopped in his chest as he began to piece it all together. The devil had been staying with Jesse, or at least had been seeing him—dating him?—after they had made the deal? There was no rational reason why he would do that.

But an irrational one, such as love . . .

"It could never be, Jesse." Farfarello's eyes seemed pained, something Gilbert would never have imagined seeing on a devil's face. "I thought if I stayed away from you long enough, it would all go away."

Jesse knelt before Farfarello, who was sitting on the armchair. He rested his hands on the devil's thighs, looking up at him, begging. "But it didn't, did it? Farfarello, please. If you still want me, if you ever cared about me at all, just take me. Leave them be, I beg of you."

He reached up to take Farfarello's face in his hands, and the devil looked torn as he whispered, "Jesse, I . . ."

"Just take me. I am yours, in any way you want me. Take me to Hell right this moment, do with me whatever you please," Jesse whispered, lips so close to the devil's, seductive, impossible to resist. Gilbert wanted to scream. "I have learned my lesson. I was an arrogant fool. Please, don't punish anyone else for my mistakes. Please . . ."

"Jesse, don't. You know I can't do that." Farfarello grabbed Jesse's wrists and gently moved his hands away. Gilbert had no doubt the man was hurting, devil or not. "You know the deal, and you know damn well that there is nothing I can do to change it. You know you're condemning everybody if you insist on breaking it. You know they'll all die."

Jesse lowered his eyes. "I'm sure you can't wait," he whispered bitterly.

Farfarello bared his teeth. "I fucking *wish*. I *wish* I could be the heartless bastard you believe I am. And you know what? With anyone else, I could be. With anyone but you." He snapped his mouth shut, looking torn between pain and anger. "It would be so much easier."

"Then do it! Just do it, god damn it! Drag me to Hell right now!" Jesse tore his shirt open to expose the left side of his chest. "Here. Send one of your poisonous spiders. Come on."

"Oh, for fuck's sake, Jesse." It was Farfarello's turn to snap, and Gilbert's eyes widened. He didn't expect the devil to lose his composure. Farfarello dropped his hat on the table, put down the stick, and rubbed his hands over his smooth head, his handsome features drawn in something like worry. "You know that even if I wanted— You know this isn't just about you. You know that everyone's life, everyone's *soul* is at stake here. What are you going to do? Offer me their lives just as easily? You want me to believe you'd be fine with the idea of my spider pumping the heart of your new beau full of poison, with me dragging his soul down to Hell right this moment?"

Jesse's bravado vanished, like the flame of a torch stamped out in the dirt. He looked at Farfarello with something like horror on his pale face. "No," he rasped. "And don't talk about him."

"Oh, Jesse." Farfarello took a step, then another, coming to stand a hairbreadth from Jesse's body. He closed his eyes and brushed Jesse's head with his, breathing him in, looking like he was using all his willpower not to touch him. "I want to say yes. I want to accept your offer with everything I've got. I made a mistake, in leaving, I . . ."

Jesse took a deep breath and looked up at Farfarello. "Then help me find a way out of this. If you ever cared about me at all, you will grant me this. You won't lay a hand on the others. Just take me. I'll be yours, forever. All forgotten, these two hundred years. I'll be yours. don't let anyone else pay." Then he added, low, *"Please."*

"There is nothing I can do. You already know that," Farfarello murmured, sweeping Jesse's hair away from his face. "I cannot cancel the deal. Once it's sealed, it's out of my hands. Even if I promised salvation for your men, I cannot stop another devil from coming to collect once they find out what's happened. And believe me, one of them will, and they will not be kind. I don't know what you thought would happen when you had this bright idea to rebel, but this can only end in one way." He stared straight at Jesse with his impossibly deep, black eyes. *"You all die.* You might hold power over me, but there's no bargaining with the forces of Hell. So you have to find someone else to join the circus. And fast. I've managed to keep your transgression under wraps until now, but I don't know how much longer I can give you."

Jesse took a deep breath, then nodded. "All right, then." He covered his eyes with his hands, his shoulders slumped. "If that's what you can do, then, give me what time you can. And we . . . we will find someone."

"Good." Farfarello briefly lowered his head, still standing before Jesse. Gilbert could imagine how it must burn—just a few inches separating them and yet they might as well be miles apart. He was familiar with the sensation. For a wild, irrational moment, he feared that they would kiss, and something like that just might kill him. But the devil straightened his back, collected his hat and cane, and walked to the door.

He stopped with his hand on the knob. "I can't do much if I don't want to attract any attention your way. But I will try to help you, if I can."

Jesse nodded, but his mind seemed to be elsewhere. He braced his hands on the table, head down. "Farfarello, I . . . You don't know how much I wish I'd never made that deal."

"Everyone always does." Farfarello paused. "But for once, I wish I hadn't either."

Gilbert slumped against the wagon wall, taking a deep breath as the door opened and then clicked shut. Damn. He was utterly screwed. And he wasn't thinking about the very real possibility of ending up in Hell in the foreseeable future. He had been convincing himself that there was something blossoming between him and Jesse, but that fantasy seemed to grow dimmer by the minute. Because two hundred years may have passed, but whatever had happened between those two was by no means over. It couldn't be, if it was still painfully close to the surface after all that time. Jesse's soul literally belonged to Farfarello, and it looked like his heart might as well. He squeezed his eyes shut. The thought was nothing short of terrifying. How the fuck was Gilbert supposed to compete with something like that?

When he opened his eyes, Farfarello was right in front of him.

Gilbert's mouth fell open, and he barely held back a cry, feeling as though his racing heart were about to jump right out as his invisibility was wiped away like a fragile spiderweb. He floundered for something clever to say, or possibly his last words. He wished his magic was powerful enough to make the earth crack open and swallow him whole, so he could get far, far away from Farfarello's reproachful black eyes.

The devil tapped him on the head with the silver knob at the end of his cane. "It's rude to spy on other people's conversations, you know."

Gilbert swallowed. This man—no, this devil—standing before him in his pressed suit and bowler hat could crush him like an ant. So he croaked, "Sorry," because really, he didn't know what else to say.

Farfarello's eyebrows arched, then he burst into a deep, hearty laugh. "Oh, Gilbert. You really are a hoot." With that, he patted Gilbert on the cheek and set off toward the gate. "Just . . . be kind to Jesse. Don't make me come back for you."

Gilbert let his head fall back against the wagon with a *thud* and tried to calm his pounding heart.

CHAPTER 20

G ilbert walked back to the canteen table and looked at the rest of the troupe.

Everyone was frayed—exhausted from the show, the grief, the lack of sleep, and stressed out of their minds. Miriam was dozing off at the table; Hugo was holding his eyes open by sheer force of will. It was a sad parade of bloodshot, red-rimmed eyes and worn-out faces.

This is no good. Jesse was a wreck, the performers were a wreck, and this was going to end in disaster. Someone needed to take charge of the situation and start making decisions.

So Gilbert took a deep breath and stepped up.

He told them only the bare minimum, enough to calm their nerves and reassure them that Jesse was definitely alive and nobody was getting killed yet, that they had more time to find Dora's replacement. It was the best he could do. Jesse would explain more in the morning.

"In the morning? We have to get going, right the fuck now," Clown said, his red eyes making him even more frightening than usual. "If we have to find someone, we've got to move."

"No. What you've got to do is go to your wagons and get some sleep." Hugo started to protest, but Gilbert wouldn't have any of it. "Hey. We've barely slept all week, and we haven't rested a moment in the last two days. We're no good for anything right now, let alone convincing somebody to join the circus. We'll just scare them away . . . or fall asleep on them. Go rest. All of you. Tomorrow morning we'll get going. A few hours won't change anything."

Or at least I really hope not. Who knew how much time they had before some other infernal minion discovered what was going on and decided to pick up Farfarello's slack and slaughter them all . . . But there was really nothing they could do about it in these conditions. They didn't have a choice.

And yet, instead of taking his own advice and retreating to his wagon, Gilbert found himself standing at Jesse's door.

The encampment was silent in the soft light of the lamps. The bonfire had been reduced to embers, and there were still piles of crows gathered here and there. Everything was coated in ashes, soot, and black feathers.

It would be useless to go to bed now. He had to sort things out with Jesse first. He would just spend the night torturing himself, replaying that conversation in his head over and over again, obsessing over the devil—over how he'd been looking at Jesse, how Jesse had been looking at *him*, how close they'd stood, how just an inch more and their lips would have been touching.

No. He had to at least try. He'd be damned if he'd let a two-centuries-old ghost get in his way. That may be Jesse's past, but the present was still up for grabs, and Gilbert was determined to fight.

With a deep breath, he knocked, and when Jesse didn't answer, he knocked again. Hunching his shoulders against the cool wind, he called out, "I'm going to keep knocking, so you might as well open."

Silence. Then the creaking of the wooden floor, and the door clicked open. Jesse let him in, looking pale and worn out. There was an empty teacup on the table.

Gilbert stood awkwardly, hands stuffed in his pockets. He'd come here without knowing what he would say. Maybe he should come clean and tell Jesse he'd heard the conversation. But the whole thing was obviously so deep and personal that suddenly, Gilbert felt guilty for having intruded at all. He cared for Jesse, he wanted him—and he desperately, foolishly wanted Jesse to want *him*—but that hadn't given him the right to intrude on Jesse's past, especially something that was evidently still raw and painful. It was an old wound Gilbert had no business poking.

Jesse swallowed, his voice rough when he spoke. "How are the others?"

"Better. More or less. I ordered them to go get some sleep for tonight. I told them—" Gilbert rubbed a hand on his chin. "Look, Jesse, I have a confession to make. I . . . may have eavesdropped on you. Before. When the devil was here. I just wanted— I *needed* to know. I understand it was wrong of me, and I don't know how to apolo—"

Jesse shut him up with a kiss, crashing into him so hard that Gilbert was slammed against the door. He responded in kind, sinking his fingers in Jesse's hair, holding him close as Jesse grabbed at his clothes, his face.

When he pulled back, they were both breathing heavily, bodies pressed one against the other. Jesse was only an inch away, so close their lips were brushing. God, his taste was so addictive, the best high Gilbert had ever felt, so much better than magic. That devil was an idiot to ever let this man go.

"I don't want to talk," Jesse whispered, hoarse. "I need . . . need you to . . . Please, Gilbert, just . . ." He looked Gilbert in the eye with such hunger. He couldn't say what he needed, but it was clear what he wanted, so much so that it was consuming him, burning him alive.

Gilbert's heart skipped a beat. He hadn't realized how much he'd needed this, to know that Jesse was truly with him, that Gilbert wasn't just filling in for that devil, that he wasn't just a replacement.

"All right. Shh. All right, I've got you, darling," he murmured, brushing a strand of red hair from Jesse's face.

He couldn't stop thinking about how many times Farfarello had touched Jesse, how many kisses they'd shared, how many nights they'd spent making love. It made him want to scream. It burned through his brain, a poisonous fire that almost blinded him. It twisted his stomach in the ugly throes of jealousy. But he was here *now*. He was the one who got to hold Jesse, kiss him, touch him, make him gasp and moan in pleasure, make him come. He was the one Jesse was looking at with those beautiful green eyes, begging him. It was Gilbert that Jesse trusted to give him what he needed, and no one else.

And Gilbert had every intention of burning the devil's memory right out of Jesse's head, at least for tonight. Kiss every inch of his skin, make him forget all about Farfarello. Jesse wanted Gilbert to drive him out of his mind that night, and he had a few aces up his sleeve for that.

He captured Jesse's mouth in a deep, passionate kiss. When he pulled back, licking his lips, Jesse looked flustered, needy and aroused, and so, so delectable. And Gilbert was hungry.

"I want you to stand back. Go by your bed and undress. Slowly," he ordered, his voice rough.

Gilbert dragged over the velvet armchair from where it had been tucked in a corner and sprawled comfortably on it, legs spread, his cock already half-hard in his trousers. He tossed his coat aside. He wanted to watch and enjoy.

Jesse slowly unbuttoned his shirt and let it slip off his shoulders. His trousers followed suit, pooling on the ground. Gilbert loved the way the light from the oil lamp fell on Jesse's perfect body, the shadows playing on his muscles, loved to see all of his tattoos at once, the composition of shapes and lines on the smooth canvas of his skin. A gun was inked low on his abdomen, the muzzle following the line between his thigh and groin, and Gilbert ached with the need to follow it with his tongue. Not yet, though.

Jesse stood naked in front of him, completely exposed, his cock hardening under Gilbert's gaze. His eyes were heated, burning with arousal, not a trace of shame or shyness on his features. It turned Gilbert on so much, he had to fight to remain seated. *Just a little patience.*

He lifted his hand and let his power flow out of him, reaching for Jesse like a gentle caress. Jesse was startled by the first invisible touch, and Gilbert couldn't hold back a smirk. He'd been practicing it for a few days, mostly to manipulate the marionettes, never precisely like this, trying to give his magic the weight of a real, physical touch. He shifted his hand and felt his magic follow, slowly brushing down Jesse's chest. Oh, Jesse could feel it all right; he gasped, leaning into the touch, a shiver visibly running through him. Not being able to see Gilbert's magic, not knowing where he would be touched next, it all seemed to excite him more, make him more receptive to that touch.

Gilbert wondered what it felt like. Was it sleek like glass or soft like velvet? Warm like skin or cool like something else entirely, something alien? He wasn't able to control any of that, all his effort focused on keeping the touch steady, keeping his magic from dispersing in the air. Gilbert moved lower then, brushing Jesse's hip—goose bumps broke out on Jesse's skin, and he shivered—and continued ever so slowly to his thigh, carefully avoiding his now fully hard cock. Jesse gasped, his whole body quivering.

Gilbert smirked again, more than a little pleased with himself, and narrowed his eyes. A surprised moan escaped Jesse's lips when the second touch came, this time on his back. It was harder to handle two separate strands of magic, but their goal was the same: to worship Jesse's body, to tease him. That made it easier.

After a moment of faltering, Gilbert could guide his magic in smooth, fluid movements, following the contours of Jesse's body, drawing sensual patterns on his skin. Without moving a finger, just with his mind and his magic, he caressed Jesse's abdomen, brushed his neck, teased his nipples. When he finally, finally moved lower, slowly slipping between Jesse's legs, Jesse was already flushed, his body coated in a sheen of sweat. It was so erotic, watching him quiver in arousal. Gilbert loved how he could enjoy the sight, drinking it in at his leisure, Jesse's gorgeous body fully exposed to his hungry gaze.

He let his magic slide to Jesse's thighs, and Jesse moaned loudly, spreading his legs in clear invitation. Jesse had to brace himself on the counter now, head thrown back, eyes half-lidded and unfocused. He was completely at Gilbert's mercy. So he let his magic softly brush Jesse's balls, seep around them, tugging ever so gently. Jesse groaned, and Gilbert only wanted more. He inched forward, stroking the underside of Jesse's cock, slowly moving all the way to the tip, making him tremble. A flick of his fingers and the other strand inched back, teasing the soft skin behind Jesse's balls, the touch delicate like a tongue.

"Oh, *fuck*." Jesse was almost incoherent, leaning heavily on his shaking arms, hips hitching in small thrusts as he tried to get more of that delicious stimulation. Gilbert let his magic wrap around Jesse's cock then, stroking him slowly from root to tip, as the second strand brushed against Jesse's opening. Gilbert couldn't see it, but he could guide his magic by touch; if he focused, he could almost feel the tight ring of muscle under his fingertips. So he played with it, around it, until Jesse was a writhing mess, barely holding himself up. And then Gilbert let the magic breach him, just an inch. Jesse's knees almost gave out as he gasped, and it was time to move to a more comfortable position.

"On the bed. Now," Gilbert whispered, hoarse. Jesse complied, his legs unsteady, kneeling obediently on the blankets. The smallest pressure on his back was enough, and he promptly leaned on his hands, on all fours under Gilbert's greedy gaze. God, he was so gorgeous, flushed and trembling, his cock hard, the tip wet as he panted and gasped, naked, his legs parted wantonly, without anyone even touching him. All Gilbert could see, if he really focused, were faint smoky traces of the magic he commanded with his mind.

Gilbert opened his trousers, relieving the pressure on his hard cock as he drew more delightful moans out of Jesse. He wrapped the magic around Jesse's engorged cock, pumping him slowly, drawing out the pleasant torture, while another strand caressed Jesse's back until it reached his neck, slowly trailing up his throat, wrapping around it, just tight enough for him to feel its strength, to know who was in charge. Jesse leaned into it, abandoning himself to the stimulation, gasping desperately as his hips shuddered, pushing his cock into the invisible grip, fucking into thin air.

With a flick of Gilbert's fingers, the tip of the magic around Jesse's neck slid up to his mouth, teasing his plump lower lip, rubbing across it and then slipping inside. Jesse opened his mouth greedily, and Gilbert wondered what it tasted like, whether it prickled like live energy, whether it was at all painful. He pushed in more, then retreated, and Jesse obediently started sucking and licking at the hazy magic, spit trickling down the corner of his lips as Gilbert fucked his mouth.

Fuck, Jesse was thoroughly enjoying this, his eyes fixed on Gilbert as he obscenely sucked on almost nothing, mouth wide open. Gilbert moaned, spreading his legs as he slipped further down the armchair. He started stroking himself in time with Jesse's sucking, grip slow and steady. He would love to stop everything and get that mouth on his cock right the fuck now, but God, Jesse looked too good to stop. Time to add a little something, see how far he could get before Jesse broke.

Gilbert narrowed his eyes and the gray smoke trailed lower, rubbing a slow line between Jesse's buttocks and teasing his opening, over and over. He could make it as wet and slippery as he pleased, and he did, fucking his own fist as he breached Jesse's body, and damn, if this wasn't almost as hot as fucking him. Gilbert had fucked plenty of people in his life but never, *never* like this. He was owning Jesse like he'd never owned anyone before, a connection he wouldn't even *want* with anyone else in the world.

He let some of the magic evaporate, freeing Jesse's mouth to hear his dirty moans again. He adored lavishing his attention on Jesse, playing him like an instrument, drawing the most delicious gasps and moans from him as he lazily stroked himself, enjoying the show. Fuck, he thought this would be torture, but it was anything but. His whole body shivered in pleasure. And while he was burning to get over there and take Jesse, claim him, part of him just wanted to watch Jesse come undone, watch him spread open and be fucked through the goddamn mattress by sheer magic, to enjoy the view as long as possible.

Jesse fell to the sheets then, rolling on his back, panting. He spread his legs on the bed, touching himself, and Gilbert let his magic retreat as he watched Jesse pleasure himself. He was spellbound by the beautiful body, naked and willing before his eyes, flushed and lost in the throes of pleasure. It might easily end like this. He could keep teasing Jesse until he lost it, and Gilbert wouldn't be far behind. But then Jesse opened his green eyes and stared at him, that sharp gaze piercing the fog of desire clouding his brain.

"Come here. God, Gilbert, come fuck me already."

He couldn't have resisted for anything, and with a snap, his magic was gone and Gilbert went to him, abandoning his clothes on the floor, and lay between Jesse's spread legs, hitched high over his hips. He fit against Jesse's body so well, pinning him to the mattress, and for a moment, they looked at each other, an instant of tenderness as Jesse reached to push back a strand of hair from Gilbert's face and drew him down for a kiss. With a growl, Gilbert clutched Jesse's thighs and pushed inside him, and Jesse cried into his mouth, arching back, grabbing at Gilbert's hips, pulling him in, asking for more. Gilbert groaned as he sunk inside Jesse, finding him stretched and wet from the magic, pleasure sizzling through his body. He wanted to mark Jesse, to leave some visible signs, to bite purple bruises on his pale skin, between the black lines of his tattoos.

"Look at me. Fuck, Jesse." He gasped into Jesse's neck as he thrust into him. "Hold on to me. Oh *fuck*, I'm gonna come inside you now, make you fucking mine."

Had he *done this?* Gilbert thought feverishly, sucking a bruise on the tender skin of Jesse's neck. How many times had the devil taken Jesse like this—marked him, fucked him, driven him to a breathless orgasm? Rage and jealousy mounted inside him like a storm, and he bit Jesse's neck, gave in to the urge to mark him and fucked him hard and fast until he came, gasping wildly, blinded by the need to mark and take and own. He was only vaguely aware of Jesse's now desperate moans and gasps.

When he came down and somewhat recovered the ability to think, he realized just how tightly he was still holding Jesse's thighs and let go, lifting himself up on his elbows. There was hot wetness between their bodies, and Jesse was flushed and panting in the wake of his orgasm. He looked utterly wrecked—stomach covered in cum, legs tight around Gilbert's hips, his fiery hair a mess on the sheets. God, he looked breathtaking. Gilbert would never get enough of this. He pulled out with a groan and dropped beside Jesse, instantly reaching for him and holding him close.

The light of dawn began to seep in through the window, lighting Jesse's body as he lay on his back, naked, a crushed cigarette between his lips.

"So, don't you want to know?"

Gilbert, sprawled on his stomach, let the silence stretch, considering the question. There were many things he wanted to know but just as many he didn't. For one, he didn't want to know exactly what had existed, or *still* existed, between Jesse and Farfarello. His imagination was already supplying him with more than enough material, and it really needed no further kindling. He decided to clarify before possibly stepping into something he would regret.

"Know about what?"

Jesse took a deep drag, his eyes on the slow smoke spirals above him. "About why I made that deal."

Gilbert wasn't sure, so he kept quiet, wondering why the hell his brain got so muddled up with Jesse naked next to him.

Jesse turned on his side, resting his head on his hand, and looked straight at him. "Don't you want to know what I wanted to get out of all this? What I asked for?" His voice was hoarse. "You know the price to be paid; don't you want to know what it's for?"

Gilbert cleared his throat, lifting himself onto his elbows. "I don't need to know," he replied, very carefully weighing his words, "if you don't want to tell. But if you do . . ." He trailed off. He wasn't good at this. His words got tangled in his mouth; he lost his train of thought halfway through.

"It's only fair. After all, it's because of my foolishness that you're stuck in this." Jesse flopped back down. "You must have heard the tales of those fools who gamble away their souls in exchange for fame and riches. And then see the light and come to regret it, realizing they've made a tragic mistake." His lips twisted into a little, self-deprecating smile. "Well, I wish I could say I wasn't one of those fools."

Gilbert smirked, poking Jesse's shoulder. "Oh sure. I can see all the fame and riches you've got here. In fact, I'm almost blinded by all the gold and gemstones." He cast a meaningful glance around the dingy, cluttered wagon. Nothing there was shining. Granted, it wasn't as badly off as Gilbert's—he might consider cleaning his own sometime, actually—but it was still a rather lousy abode.

Jesse laughed. "Yeah, well. It wasn't precisely in those terms." He stubbed out the cigarette on the bed frame. "I wanted the best, the greatest circus of all time. I wanted it to draw crowds from all over the land. I wanted kings and queens to come and marvel at our incredible shows. I was a young, arrogant idiot."

"And I have a feeling Farfarello really enjoys those." Gilbert sighed. What seemed like a lifetime ago, on that train, the devil had promised to teach him a lesson in humility. It looked like he made a habit of going after arrogant assholes. "I don't mean to offend you, but I don't exactly see that happening for the circus, either. I'm not saying that the show isn't good. It's wonderful, it's amazing, the best thing I've ever seen," he hurried to add. "It's just that I haven't seen many kings and queens around. If the devil isn't holding up his side of the deal, then why should you?"

"But he is. My life will not end as long as the circus lives on, which would give me plenty of time to shoot for those riches and fame. But . . . after two hundred years, my priorities have changed." Jesse's lips stretched in a mirthless smile. "I was so foolish, chasing after gold and glory. Living with the circus, it's become about something else entirely. This place gives a home to people who have been cast out from the rest of the world. Gives them peace, gives them a family to replace the ones they lost or the ones that shunned them after learning who they were."

Gilbert tightened his lips. That one hit home.

"I figured this was a more worthy cause to carry on. Doing the devil's dirty work, the pain of watching friends die, it might all be worth it if I could help them scrape together a few years of peace on this Earth." Jesse swallowed. "I imagined it would get hard, at some point. That I would crumble, that I would fail them. But I thought I'd make it a while longer."

Quietly, Gilbert pressed his lips to Jesse's warm shoulder. "So, if you were to give up now, would you be fine with the thought of condemning all the souls that belong to the circus to eternal damnation?"

"No. No, I'm not," Jesse said. He didn't sound defensive, just very tired. "You know, at first I thought I would only ever take in those who were already damned anyway, who would end up down there no matter what. It wouldn't make a difference, that way. But then . . . then it got more complicated."

Gilbert nodded. "The twins."

"The twins, and Ramona. And Dora, and so many others. They came here in search of a home, and often they had already lived through hell on this Earth. I couldn't turn them away, and yet, if there is any justice at all, they don't deserve to be damned."

"And as long as the circus lives, they won't be." Gilbert swallowed. They would live on in the black wagon, haunting the circus. But with Dora gone, there was nobody left who could speak with them, hear what they had to say.

"That's right." Jesse took a deep breath. "Losing Dora . . . I fell apart. I honestly believed I had nothing left to give, and I wanted it all to end. But I know I can't give up just yet. I can't fail them. I started all of this, and it's the least I can do to keep this deal going for as long as I can. I've made it this far, right?"

Gilbert reached for Jesse's hand and held it as a comfortable silence spread around them. Jesse lay on his back, a new determined expression on his face, and Gilbert just kept looking at Jesse, at the way his hair fell in unruly strands around his face, on his shoulders, his chest; at the shape of his nose; and at the pale patches of skin still visible under the intricate tattoos.

He wanted to tell Jesse that he would be there to help him shoulder the burden, that he wouldn't have to bear it all on his own, to pay the penance for his arrogance by himself for all eternity. But he couldn't. Because he too would grow old under Jesse's eyes, and he too would die, leaving Jesse with another loss to mourn. There was nothing Gilbert could promise that would change that.

So he rolled on his side and passed his arm over Jesse's chest, holding him close, savoring the warm, naked skin against his. Jesse placed a hand on his wrist, gently caressing it with his thumb, and they just lay there together.

"So, we are going to find someone new," Gilbert murmured, eventually.

Jesse sighed. "I . . . Yes. I think that we should. But this time, I won't be the one to make that decision." Jesse squeezed Gilbert's hand. "I will gather everyone, and we'll talk about it. This time, we'll decide together."

CHAPTER 21

When dawn shifted to morning, it began to rain.

Jesse and Gilbert went 'round to the wagons, wet and cold, and gathered everyone in the big striped tent. That place was the pulsing heart of the circus; it only felt right to make such an important decision there. Gilbert had only been inside the tent a few times, but even he could feel the significance of that sandy arena. It was what they all worked so hard for, what they had devoted their lives to. It was where they came together to bring their show to life, to create something wonderful for their audience.

The lamps were on, even though the tent flaps were tied open and the pale, gray light seeped in from outside, accompanied by the sound of the pouring rain, sometimes a roll of thunder. Gilbert sat away from the rest of the troupe, behind them and off to the side. He knew everything already, anyway, and he was more interested in observing everyone's reactions. Emilia, who had been hogging Ramona's pillow for the night, had joined him as he'd grabbed a mug of watery coffee from the canteen, and was now quietly perched on his shoulder.

All eyes were on Jesse, who stood in the arena, a few steps behind the barrier.

"So," he began, hands in his pockets. "As you know, the devil came to see me yesterday."

"We know, indeed. In fact, we were quite pleased when he didn't burn you to a cinder—or usss, for that matter," Humphreys politely commented, drawing nervous laughter from the others. Even Jesse cracked a little smile.

"Yes, well. He just wanted to talk."

"So did you manage to strike a bargain or not?" Clown asked abruptly. Truth be told, it was probably the question burning in everyone's mind. It was almost a good thing that there was someone brutal enough to just say it.

"Sort of. But not the bargain I was planning." Jesse sighed deeply. "The bottom line is, once a deal is made, it cannot be altered. Farfarello is one devil among many, and not all of them are so . . . accommodating. So far, he has managed to keep our transgression quiet and is granting us a little more time, but it would appear that our best option is to reconsider our position and find someone who will join us."

The performers looked at each other in perplexed silence.

"I thought we had decided we wouldn't do that anymore," Ramona cautiously said.

"No, *we* hadn't decided. *I* had," Jesse replied. "I acted too rashly. Dora's passing . . . It affected me more than I wanted to admit, and I spoke hastily, out of grief. Now, I believe I was mistaken and selfish. Making sure that you all are safe is what's most important to me. So I encourage you to accept the devil's offer and carry on as we have been. But it's your decision, and I will respect it, whatever your choice."

Gilbert craned his head to look at the performers' faces. He read various emotions there—exasperation, doubt, unease—but mostly relief. And really, he felt the same. Like all of them, he had accepted Jesse's decision because there wasn't much else they could do, because he was their leader and it felt like the right thing in a way. But it was clear that this made them all feel like they were back on solid ground.

"I'm glad you came back to your senses," Clown grumbled. "It's decided, then. I don't see what there is to discuss."

Humphreys cleared his throat. "Ssso, the devil refusssed your offer to hand yourself over in lieu of all of usss?"

"Yes, he did. I think he would have accepted, if he could, but I'm afraid I overestimated the degree of authority Farfarello has over this deal."

There was a collective release of tension in the tent. Truth be told, no one in the circus wanted Jesse to sacrifice himself for their sake. Nobody wanted to see him dead.

Humphreys was silent for a moment. "Then I believe I ssspeak for all of usss when I sssay that indeed we should continue to uphold our end of the deal."

"Does everyone agree with that?" Jesse said to the group.

There was a general murmuring of agreement, including from Bobbie, who was nodding in all seriousness, sitting straight-backed with her hands in her lap. Only Ethel seemed indifferent to the conversation, toying with a string.

Jesse nodded, visibly relieved. "Then we are decided."

"That's wonderful, hooray, hooray," Clown deadpanned. "Now can we *please* get a move on and find somebody to join this freak show before the devil changes his mind and we become food for crows?"

"How dreadfully distasteful. I assure you, Mr. Clown, that I am far more classy than you give me credit for."

That voice. Gilbert froze for a moment before turning abruptly. Farfarello stood in the doorway, hands resting on his cane. His tall, slender figure stood out against the gray sky, and the pouring rain went up in steam before it touched his clothes, surrounding him with mist.

Gilbert had to hand it to him: the man knew how to make an entrance.

Humphreys, Constance, and Clown stood up, and so did Herbert and Mildred, who growled. Farfarello raised his hand, and Gilbert wondered whether he was paralyzing them in place, as he'd done to Gilbert on his last visit.

"Oh, no need for that. Please do settle down. I didn't mean any harm yesterday, and I promise you I haven't changed my mind."

Jesse stood up, clearly surprised. Gilbert hated to see Jesse's gaze on the devil again. "Then what are you doing here?"

The devil walked in, calmly heading for the arena. "I have some information you might want to hear. About that girl you spoke with yesterday . . . Olivia."

"Yes, because trusting a devil is such a brilliant idea," Clown hissed, his cruel, pointy teeth bared.

Farfarello looked piqued. "I may be many things, but I'm no liar. I've always been perfectly straightforward with Jesse, and *I'm* not the one who tried to weasel out of his part of the deal. Now, who are the ones who cannot be trusted?"

The silence was awkward. *The guy has a point.*

Jesse cleared his throat. "So what about her?"

"She's been taken. Some men captured her less than an hour ago. They were sent by a certain Count Reuben, with orders to take her with them back to Shadowsea at once."

"What? How do you even know that?" Jesse asked.

"I did promise I would help you search, didn't I? Well, I wasn't able to find any suitable candidates within *miles*. Reuben's men have grabbed them all, and she was the only one left so I was keeping an eye on her," Farfarello replied.

Clown shrugged. "So we will find someone else."

Farfarello tilted his head to the side, regarding Clown with a small, twisted smile. "Well, first of all, I thought you might bother to care a tad about this girl's fate. My mistake."

"We've got enough issues of our own, thank you. We don't need to start ministering to every bum that crosses our path." Clown's face was expressionless as always. Not for the first time, Gilbert wondered if they should be afraid of him. "And excuse me if I don't feel like being lectured in compassion by a devil straight from the depths of Hell. So unless this has something to do with us—"

"*Clown*," Jesse reprimanded. As heartless and inhumane as Clown might be, somebody had to keep him in check before he pissed off one of Satan's minions, who happened to hold all their lives in his hand, at that. But Farfarello waved it off.

"It concerns you because I just told you that you won't be able to find anyone else with supernatural abilities—or anyone who might fit into the circus because of skills or birth—anywhere around." His words fell like stones. "Reuben's men have been scouting the country for weeks, and now the mass abduction has begun. They move much faster than you do. By the time you get your ass in gear, there will be no one left."

In the silence that followed, Gilbert could hear blood rushing in his ears. *Fuck.*

"Do you have any idea *why* this Reuben guy is doing it? How much danger are we in?" Jesse asked.

"When he discovered that people with *abilities* existed, he immediately saw the potential in that, of course. Imagine—if he could build himself an army of supernatural soldiers, if he could exploit their magic for his own interests . . ." Farfarello shook his head.

Gilbert's eyes widened. "He could take over Shadowsea . . . And he probably wouldn't stop there, either. No army would be able to hold him back."

"Okay, so we'll never go near Shadowsea again. There's still plenty of towns for us to travel to." Clown wasn't the least bit bothered by the reproachful glances coming his way. "What? I'm sure it's all very sad, but really, it's none of our business. We've never taken an interest in the politics of cities before. Why start now? This has nothing to do with us!"

"Except it does," Jesse said. "Haven't you been listening? He's been abducting freaks from all over the country. Have you *seen* us? We don't exactly keep a low profile being a *circus* and all. How long do you think it will be before he sends another spy after us, and another, and another? How long before he gets us too?"

The tent filled with tense silence as the realization sunk in.

"Damn," Constance muttered, clenching her fists. "Just . . . damn."

Damn, indeed. Possibilities and plans were whirring in Gilbert's head in search of a way out, any way out. But he discarded one after the other. They were tied to their wagons by the curse; it wouldn't matter if they were captured, no shackles or chains would prevent them from waking up back in the circus anyway. But where would they go after that? The traveling caravan wouldn't go unnoticed. And sooner or later, Reuben's men would figure out how it worked, or maybe get tired and kill them all. Or maybe they wouldn't even make it to that point. If Reuben's plan prevented them from finding someone who would join, the devils would handle that for them.

So, basically they were fucked.

"Damn it. This is an unmitigated disaster." Hugo shook his head, muttering. "How did that Reuben guy even find out about us freaks in the first place? We've been living among people for, well, forever, I'd imagine, and no one caught on until now."

Farfarello's smile was grim. "Oh, I believe he can answer that."

Gilbert lifted his head, realizing that the devil's gaze was on him. He widened his eyes. "I . . . What?"

"Yes, you. You know exactly how he found out." Farfarello waited patiently, head tilted to the side. "Think, Mr. Blake, of the last time you saw Reuben. Of what you did then."

It hit him like a hammer to the chest, knocking the wind out of him. The tent seemed to fall away around him, his head was buzzing so loudly. He couldn't catch his breath. He remembered, all right. He remembered that Reuben was there when he had . . .

"Oh God," he rasped. "God damn it, I can't believe . . . This is all happening because of *me*?"

Come on, it had just been a stupid stunt. A little, drunken bout of idiocy. And wasn't he already paying for it? It had gotten him trapped for life in the circus, caught in this infernal deal, condemned his soul to Hell—wasn't that enough? Did he have to bear the responsibility for whatever Reuben was doing to Olivia, to all the freaks he'd captured?

Gilbert's head was spinning. What if the man succeeded in creating his army, what then? There was no telling what kind of magic he might get his hands on, in what terrible way he'd be able to employ it. First, he would probably wage a war against Andrea and her men, and he would crush them. Kill them. Maybe some would trade their lives for their loyalty, but Andrea . . . She was as good as dead already. And after that, if Reuben really wanted to conquer the city, to create a wretched kingdom for himself . . . *God*.

And it was all because of Gilbert's stupid *hen*?

"I'm going." It came out of his mouth before he could even think about it. He stood, hands shaking. A chorus of surprised cries rose from the others. Jesse stepped toward him, reaching to touch his arm.

"Gilbert, what are you—"

"It's my fault this is happening. I can't just sit here and do nothing."

"This is absurd. *How* can it be your fault?"

"He *saw* me," Gilbert snapped. "All right? He was there, the night you found me. He saw what I did to that guy, saw that stupid hen crawl out of his mouth. He must have understood. Figured out it was more than a freakish trick. God *damn it*."

Jesse looked at him in silence, mouth parted. "Even so . . . It's ridiculous. What are you going to do? And alone?"

"I don't know. Save this girl, for one." Gilbert yanked on his jacket. His head ached, too many thoughts flying by too fast. He had no idea what would come next. He'd figure something out. "I know some people there. I'll tell them, maybe they can stop Reuben before he can put his plan into action. I don't know."

"Then I'm coming with you," Jesse said in a tone that brooked no argument.

"And so am I," Constance added, standing up. Humphreys followed suit and stood beside her in silence, his intentions clear.

Gilbert shook his head. "I don't—"

"Shut up." Jesse raised his hand. "We need to bring this Reuben down if we don't want to end up in a goddamn dungeon somewhere being poked and prodded by some crazy quack. And if we don't want to go to Hell, we have no time to waste. So save your breath."

Gilbert fell silent. There was something in the way Jesse had said it, something in the way some of the others had haunted looks on their faces now. Ethel had gone visibly pale. All of a sudden, he realized that he had been very, very lucky. Some of them had already been in that position—tied down and tortured by sadistic so-called doctors. And with a sinking feeling, he realized that they might decide to take desperate measures to avoid ending up there again.

So he turned to Farfarello and said, "You. You seem to know everything. Where is she, where is he taking her? Can you find out?"

Farfarello smiled at him, a sharp-toothed smirk. Gilbert couldn't tell if the devil was proud of him or just satisfied because Gilbert was being a good pawn. He wasn't sure which idea frightened him the most.

"As a matter of fact, yes, I do. But if you want to catch up with them, you have to move fast. They're taking her to Shadowsea by train. They will leave shortly. You need to get to her before they reach Reuben's stronghold in the city. It would be impossible for you to get in there."

"Can we stop them from getting on that train?"

Farfarello's eyes flashed red. "No," he said, voice rough and deep, as if it were coming from afar. "They already left. Their train departed a few minutes ago."

"Damn it. There's no way we'll catch up with them then." This whole conversation was pointless then. The asshole . . . "And you couldn't have come sooner? Or better yet, stopped them *yourself*? You are truly a devil, aren't you?" he spat.

"Be thankful I came at all. I shouldn't even be here. Believe me when I say you don't want me to attract any attention to the circus." Farfarello shot him a cold look. "Alicante from the Malebranche has been sniffing around, and you *do not* want him to find out what's going on and decide to take this deal into his own hands. *Trust me, you do not. Nor do I.*"

Gilbert sighed. "Sorry," he grumbled. They needed this devil on their side, no matter how much he hated it.

Farfarello waved him off. "They are on a passenger train scheduled to make several stops along the way, to take the scenic route, if you will. It will take the whole day to reach the city. But in two hours, there's a weekly freight train leaving. It heads for Shadowsea, as well, but along the commercial route. No stops. It will get you there in time to welcome Reuben's men when they arrive."

The four exchanged glances, nodding. Jesse turned to Constance. "Get the travel wagon ready. If we head out at full speed, we'll reach town in time to catch that train."

She nodded and dashed out, followed by Humphreys. Everyone else shuffled after them, murmuring nervously, Farfarello walking beside Jesse. They gathered by the gate just as Constance arrived, driving the huffing wagon.

Hugo stepped forward, making to get on, but Jesse stopped him. "No, you stay here. Somebody's got to watch over Ramona and the others in case Reuben's men have already been alerted of our presence here."

That was bollocks. Had Reuben located the circus, his men would have been there by now, instead of on a train headed to Shadowsea. What Jesse really meant was in case they all died in the city.

There wasn't time for good-byes or last words. *Better this way*, Gilbert thought. He wasn't any good at them anyway. And to him, they were bad luck.

"The last carriage will be half-empty. Hide in there. You'll find no guards," Farfarello said, barely brushing Jesse's shoulder with his hand. "I have to go now. Good luck."

Jesse nodded. "Thank you." His voice was solemn, and for a moment, he looked like he might return the touch. But he just turned and climbed onto the wagon.

As they headed at full throttle toward the station of a town whose name Gilbert didn't even know, jostling on the uneven road, and accompanied by the deafening hiss of steam, Gilbert wondered what would happen to the deal, to the circus, if Jesse were to be killed. Was that even possible? Did Jesse even know?

Whatever the answer, Gilbert realized with a heavy heart that it wouldn't matter. He had to make sure Jesse survived. That was all there was to it.

CHAPTER 22

They leaped out of the train as soon as it reached Grand Saudade Station, and Gilbert ran straight to Filmore.

"My, my, Boss! It's surely been a while. Glad to have you back in town. And with some most unusual comp—"

"Filmore, I need your help," Gilbert dropped to his knees beside him. There was no time for pleasantries. "Listen. There should be a train arriving soon, a passenger ride coming from, what's the name . . . the same place where the freight train that just arrived came from? You know which one?"

"Why, indeed. There's only one passenger train coming in at this time anyway: the sleeper train going all the way to the coast," Filmore answered promptly. "It should be arriving in about an hour."

"Which platform?"

"Funny you should ask . . . I heard it's been moved. It was supposed to arrive on One or Two, the fancy ones. But I have been reliably informed that it's been diverted to Thirteen Below." He looked at Gilbert, squinting his watery eyes. "What an odd choice for such a pricey ride. You wouldn't happen to know anything about that?"

"Long story. I promise I'll tell you everything, my man, but it's an emergency." Gilbert placed his hand on Filmore's shoulder. "I need you to do everything in your power to slow that train down. Sabotage the exchanges, block the rails with rats, whatever you can think of. I need to go speak to Andrea, and I need all the time you can give me."

Filmore nodded, no questions asked. Gilbert figured his expression was enough to drive home just how serious the situation was. "Consider it done. An hour of delay, easy. I cannot guarantee any more than that."

"That's great. Thank you, Filmore. And . . . be careful. If you see trouble coming, get out of here. All right?"

Filmore barely had the time to promise he would before Gilbert dashed out, his companions on his heels.

They ran through the streets of Shadowsea, slipping on the wet cobblestones.

Gilbert cursed, leaping out of the way as he was almost run over by an omnibus. Jesse, Constance, and Humphreys—completely hidden under a black cloak—were on his heels, determined looks on their faces. They weren't many, but they were strong and powerful. And besides, they had allies in the city. If they could get to Andrea without being killed by the Devil's Acre's guards.

He stopped abruptly when they reached the edge of the Acre. The change from the casual bustling noise of the rest of the city to the eerie quiet of the Acre was almost palpable. There wasn't a signpost, a fence, or even a fucking line drawn on the ground, and yet Gilbert could tell with exact precision where Andrea's kingdom began. Everyone in the city could.

Jesse, completely oblivious, was about to stride right inside when Gilbert stopped him, lifting his arm.

"What? Are you lost?" Jesse asked.

"No. No, I'm definitely not."

Still, he hesitated.

Jesse looked at him, confused. "Then let's go. What are we waiting for?"

"It's dangerous, here. Strangers aren't welcome. The guards could react very badly." Damn it. His internal clock was ticking so loud, he could barely hear himself think. They were wasting time they didn't have.

They had to risk it. And hope that whoever was on patrol would remember him and wouldn't be trigger-happy.

"All right. Uncover your faces, push down the scarves. Yes, Humphreys, you too," Gilbert said, straightening his shoulders. "Don't try to hide. Hands open, arms by your sides. Walk slowly, and follow me."

He took the first step past that imaginary line, and a burning sensation overcame him. Whatever he was concerned about, he didn't drop dead as soon as he set foot in Andrea's realm, so he walked on, slowly but determined, heading for the Duck.

The others followed him, but he could practically feel their collective tension. They all recognized the chilling feeling—there were eyes on them, tracking their every move, deciding on their life. A sizzling current prickled Gilbert's skin, his fingertips turning to ice. He hoped this was the right decision. The others were trusting him with their lives.

How ridiculous it would be to be shot down by the only allies he had in this city.

When the whistling came from the rooftops above, it sounded . . . different. Wrong. A shiver crawled down Gilbert's back as he broke into a cold sweat. He prayed they would recognize him—he'd been in the Acre dozens of times—but every corner he turned, he expected a bullet to slam into his back. So he called out, "I am Gilbert Blake, a friend and ally to Miss Andrea. I come with urgent news about Count Reuben. He is plotting an attack and must be stopped. You are all in danger!"

His words drowned in the narrow alley. Silence.

Jesse glanced at him, uneasy. "I thought you said this Andrea was a friend," he asked, frowning. Gilbert nodded with a grim, little smile.

"She is. I just can't vouch for all of her guards to know that."

Nothing happened. But they were all still standing, and he supposed it was as good a sign as they were going to get. Gilbert walked on. And sure enough, as soon as he turned the next corner, he almost walked face-first into a group of thugs lying in wait.

He threw his hands up. "Please, give me a moment to exp—" Then he recognized the face above the broad chest he'd almost walked into. "Bartholomew! Thank *God*. I'm Gilbert, Gilbert Blake. I vanished from a room you were guarding a few weeks ago. Do you remember?"

The man's brown eyes widened in recognition. "The magician! For fuck's sake, man, where did you disappear to? We've been running ourselves ragged trying to figure out what the hell happened to you that night."

They clasped hands in greeting, Gilbert's head nearly spinning with relief. He was so grateful to see a familiar face. Diana was there too, hands on her hips, frowning.

"Did you play a trick on us, magician? How did you do it?" she asked.

"No trick. I was kidnapped, sort of. I'll explain later, I promise you." He had to focus on Reuben. "I found out that Count Reuben's planning something—an attack using a secret weapon of sorts. If he has his way, he could take over the whole city. We don't have much time, so we have to act fast. Please, take me to Andrea right now."

Bartholomew and Diana exchanged glances, then nodded. "All right. Just because she trusts you, magician. You, or your comrades here, better not try anything funny."

Gilbert nodded, breathless with relief, and followed them as the guards turned on their heels and marched right into the heart of the Acre.

Gilbert honestly thought he would have to do a lot more to convince her. But Andrea took the news in stride, and didn't second-guess him for an instant. Maybe she despised Reuben so much there was nothing she put past him. Or maybe she was just waiting for the perfect excuse to finally break their supposed truce, the chance to strike out and crush Reuben.

This excuse was all she needed.

"So his men will arrive at the station within the hour, bringing this girl of yours. And you say they've been after you, as well?"

Andrea was sitting at a large, messy table, surrounded by her lieutenants, whom she'd gathered at once. Diana and Bartholomew stood at her right side, eyes gleaming. Maybe she wasn't the only one looking forward to finally ending this once and for all.

"Yes. As they keep hunting for new . . . *freaks* to kidnap, they started sniffing around our circus. We got rid of one spy so far, but I don't know how much longer we can hide." Gilbert paused, and Jesse took the chance to speak.

"Miss Andrea, we have women and children at the circus, at this very moment. Without protection. And I don't know how much longer they will be safe. It is imperative that Count Reuben's mad plan be stopped as soon as possible."

"And by Jove, it will be." Andrea, smoking ferociously, slammed her fist on the table. She'd already burned through a handful of cigarettes. "Bartholomew, you go with them to the station to rescue this girl, then bring them back here. Everyone else, I want you out in the streets, and I want to know the exact location of this laboratory within the next *hour*. Understood? Bribe, threaten, maim, I don't care how you do it. Just find it."

Shouts and slamming doors followed, and the entire Duck seemed to shake as Andrea's whole kingdom woke up and rushed into action. No effort would be spared; this was the final battle for dominance over the city. One way or the other, one of the two underground kingdoms of Shadowsea would fall. And tonight.

As Gilbert grabbed Jesse's arm and led him out of the room, Bartholomew shouted for a carriage. Gilbert tried to stifle the roiling anxiety in his stomach. Andrea was powerful. She would defeat Reuben. She had to.

All of their lives hung in the balance.

Gilbert was lying in wait on platform Thirteen Below when a loud whistle and a rumble that shook the whole platform announced that the train was pulling in. It appeared in a cloud of smoke. He cast a quick look around, seeking the spots where Bartholomew, Jesse, and Constance were hidden. He could barely see them. As for Humphreys, he was out of sight completely.

The train's windows were shut and covered by dark curtains. A door opened at the very end of the train, and their target came out— three large men in dark suits, all sporting noticeable purple bands on their hats and biceps. One was gracelessly dragging Olivia, who looked angry and scared, albeit doing her best to cover it up. She was wrapped in a cloak, but Gilbert could glimpse the heavy iron manacles that fastened her hands together. The second bloke carried a bundle wrapped in fabric that shrieked and thrashed about; a long, brown tail escaped from the blanket and whipped madly around. The third man, broad like a wardrobe, had a thick club slung over his shoulder.

Gilbert counted silently in his head as the men approached his hiding place. They were almost in position. Just one more step . . .

Humphreys launched himself from the ceiling, a nightmare of whirling tentacles coming out of the dark. The men barely had the time to scream before he brought two of them down, leaving the third one frozen, still clinging to Olivia.

That distraction was all they needed. Constance emerged from a corner, swinging a makeshift bat at the man's head, knocking him down in an instant, while Bartholomew and Jesse dove in the chaos of kicking legs and twitching tentacles to help Humphreys. As Olivia's captor wobbled and turned to try to fight back, only to be knocked unconscious to the ground by Constance, the girl wriggled free and sprinted in a blind panic, just trying to get away. Gilbert caught her with ease, riding out her instinctive kicking and screaming.

"Olivia! Olivia, it's me. The magician. Calm down, we're here to help. You're safe now. You're safe."

She looked up at him with wide eyes, breathing fast from the sheer burst of adrenaline. Recognition sparked, and she stopped fighting, almost sagging in Gilbert's arms from the relief. He smiled at her, doing his best to be comforting. From the corner of his eye, he saw Constance roll the man into a corner, while Humphreys held the other two, now unconscious, up by their necks, looking for a place to stash them.

"I told you to be careful," he reproached gently.

She clung to him with her manacled hands, scowling fiercely. "I'd almost made it. No, I had, really," she insisted, piqued. "But then they got Vito . . ."

Almost on cue, the brown monkey tore its way out of its blanket and leaped onto Gilbert's shoulder, clinging to him for dear life. Before he could reply, though, Bartholomew snapped his fingers. "All right. Let's get out of here, right now. Back to the Duck. Let's move—"

"Why, if it isn't Andrea's prized lapdog himself. Bartholomew, what an unpleasant surprise."

Fuck. Gilbert knew that voice.

He turned around, and there he was—Reuben himself, in his expensive purple suit, emerging from the tunnel surrounded by a team of armed guards. So the man had arranged a welcoming committee for Olivia.

The words of Lester, the spy, suddenly flashed in his mind. Among his ramblings, he'd mentioned something about Reuben showing up in person for his victims. God damn it.

"Reuben," Gilbert growled, brain whirring fast, sizing up Reuben's guards. Their chances of making it out with minimal fuss had just dropped to zero. From the corner of his eye, he could see his companions preparing for a fight. "Didn't think you had to get your hands dirty running your errands in person. You must not be quite as powerful as people say."

"It's *Count* Reuben. And if I were you, I would shut up, you little—" He paused, narrowing his eyes. Then a delighted smile spread on his features. "My, Gilbert Blake himself! Patron saint of hens, the man who started it all. I never thought I would see you back in this city." He snickered when Gilbert failed to hide his surprise. "Of course I know your name, magician. Do you think I'm an idiot? I did a little research after witnessing that performance of yours in my venue. Very impressive."

He waved his walking stick toward Humphreys and the others. "So, I suppose these guys are fellow freaks of yours. My, look at that creature—truly remarkable. I suppose I should thank you. Not only have you shown me this utterly fascinating new side of the world, opening countless doors to me—due to my superior intellect, of course—but you've also brought me a most fascinating specimen. I cannot wait to examine your friends and discover what powers they hide. It is a most rewarding process, I assure you, although sometimes I need to be a little . . . *persuasive* to get them to cooperate."

Jesse snarled. The thought of being experimented on had raised everyone's hackles, and Gilbert could practically feel the hatred radiating from them. "You're welcome to try."

"Oh, I fully intend to." Reuben turned to Jesse with a cold smile on his face. Then he snapped his fingers and barked: "Take them alive . . . if you can."

CHAPTER 23

E veryone lashed out at once, and Gilbert barely had time to push Olivia back before facing the first guard, parrying a clumsy punch before landing a blow to the man's nose. He staggered back, hands on his face, as Gilbert caught a glimpse of a swirling tentacle, a tangle of bodies, a bright bout of flames—Jesse.

Beside him, Olivia was yanking frantically at the manacles. "Off! Get me out, take them off!"

Gilbert covered the cuffs with his hand and let his magic pour out, knowing he could snap them open in an instant. Yet, nothing happened. His magic vanished, absorbed by the shackles like water poured on sand. Gilbert's eyes widened. *Of course. Iron.*

Another flare of flames attracted his attention; Jesse's fire had reached the hole-in-the-wall pub and whatever cheap liquor they were hiding was exploding like a grenade. As he watched, Jesse raised his arm, fire bursting to life in his palm, before throwing it forward, aiming at the closest man. But the flames fizzled before even brushing him, and the man launched himself at Jesse, snarling.

What the—

Gilbert's thoughts were interrupted when another man charged him. He was swift to avoid him, and as the man stumbled, Gilbert kicked him in the legs, sending him tumbling head-on into the flames. He went up like a torch, screaming, as the fire rapidly spread to the wooden beams supporting the walls and the roof.

Humphreys was hanging up there, holding two men by their necks in midair, strangling them with his strong tentacles. In the flickering firelight he looked fucking terrifying, a deadly nightmare that had crawled out from the deepest abyss. A third man was slashing at him with an ax from below, and thick, inky blood dripped from Humphreys's wounds as he let out an inhuman howl.

Bartholomew was surrounded, backed in a corner, his teeth bared as he fought four assailants at once. But he was the one they didn't care about taking alive, and under Gilbert's horrified gaze, one of the men lifted a rifle and shot him, point-blank. Before Gilbert even had time to scream, Bartholomew fell, slumped against the wall, blood pouring out of his chest.

Gilbert saw only red. He whipped his head around, easily dodging a kick, until he found Reuben. The bastard was standing in a corner, watching the fight unfold as if he were in one of his goddamned clubs. Without a second thought, Gilbert ran. Oh, he was going to make something much worse than a hen crawl out of that bastard's throat, and he'd leave it stuck in there, choke him to death . . .

Nothing happened. Gilbert's brain was burning, power pouring out of him, flowing through his arm and shooting out of his spread hand, but then it ended, crumbling into nothing, dissolving in the air, leaving him empty and gasping. The feeling of powerlessness was devastating, as if something was sucking the very life out of him, ripping the air from his lungs. Gilbert stumbled, his vision going blurry, and fell on his knees, still too far away from Reuben.

The man tutted, winked at him, then parted his coat. An iron horseshoe, encrusted in shimmering amethyst, dangled from a chain fastened around his neck. *Damn*, Gilbert cursed, trying to stop his spinning head. Reuben had built himself a talisman against magic.

"You think I'm an idiot, son? Your freak tricks don't work on me or on my boys."

Gilbert wanted to scream. *Of course* Reuben had found a way to protect himself, or he wouldn't have gotten far—one of the people he'd kidnapped would have brought him down, eventually. Now he understood why the men weren't rolling on the floor screaming, devoured by the flames, why Jesse was aiming his blasts at the drapes and the wooden supports on the walls, at anything that would burn.

A blinding pain smashed in his nape—a club, a baton—and Gilbert found himself on the ground, confused. Too much movement and fighting continued all around him, yells and thuds and growls and the scorching hotness of the fire, the platform now surrounded by tall flames. He could see Jesse. He'd ripped a wooden pole from God knows where, both ends burning bright like torches, and swung it around, smacking a man in the knees hard enough to knock him down. His trousers caught on fire, and Jesse brought the pole up and around, landing a second blow to the guy's neck, sending him sprawling facedown. His hair was on fire now, his coat, and he rolled on the floor, kicking, trying to get rid of his clothes but achieving nothing except to spread the fire even further.

It was everywhere, now. The smoke was filling the platform, becoming too thick, and Gilbert coughed, his eyes burning. This might not have been such a brilliant move after all. If they ended up trapped in the station as the fire spread . . . Damn, they might be trapped already. He could no longer see the exit, didn't even know if it was still open or if the fire had blocked the way. And it could already be spreading to the rest of the station.

Fuck it. All that mattered was that Reuben not get out of there alive. At least that goddamn plan of his would go up in smoke along with him, and the others at the circus would be safe. If that was the best they could do, so be it.

Because, despite everything, they were losing. Gilbert swallowed, pulling himself up on his knees. It just took a glance to take in the situation and realize it: Bartholomew was dead. Constance was fighting off four armed opponents, but even she wasn't that strong. He couldn't see Humphreys in the smoke—he might be lost already—Gilbert himself was in no shape to keep fighting, and Jesse alone couldn't make up the difference. The fire roared all around them, and Reuben was standing there with his purple top hat and that goddamn smirk on his face.

It hit Gilbert, then. He was bringing that man down with him, if it was the last thing he did.

"Olivia!" he yelled, hoarse, chest racked by his coughing, and she materialized by his side within moments. The smoke was so thick he couldn't even tell where she'd come from.

"What?" she asked, eyes on the fight going on around them, a grim expression on her soot-stained face. Gilbert could tell she was calculating their odds, and they didn't look good to her either.

"Can your monkey get the pendant off Reuben's neck? The man in purple," Gilbert gasped.

Olivia didn't question him, just nodded and called out, "Vito!" then stuck two fingers in her mouth and whistled a short command. A brown flash leaped out of the smoke, clinging to one of the few remaining roof beams.

Gilbert was about to throw himself at Reuben when he heard a familiar voice cry out, the sound freezing the blood in his veins. He turned in time to see Jesse fly through the air and crash down onto the tracks. He remained crumpled there, unmoving.

"Jesse!" Gilbert screamed. He wanted to drop everything and go to him, but he could already see Vito hopping along toward Reuben. And really, the quickest way to bring this fight to an end was to bring down that man. His lapdogs would run like scared puppies once their boss was down. He had to do this. It hurt to turn his back on Jesse and run at Reuben, shouting as loud as possible as he brandished his knife. Useless, he knew, but as long as it kept Reuben's gaze away from the monkey approaching him, it didn't matter.

With a condescending sneer, Reuben lifted his arm, pointing a gun right at him. Gilbert stopped, so close to him now—just a few more steps. God, if only he could use his magic. It was boiling inside him, roaring in waves that his body could barely contain, like a river pressing against too weak a dam, a turmoil so intense Gilbert thought he could feel the ground shaking under his boots.

"Drop that pathetic little knife, Gilbert. This is useless. *You* are useless without your magic." Reuben shook his head. "I was going to give you a place in my army, you know? I really wanted you there. The man who started it all! But now, I see you would be of no use to me. A soldier who can't obey is nothing but a liability."

Talk, Gilbert prayed silently. *Keep talking. I know you like that. Go on. A little longer.* He needed Reuben to be distracted for a few more seconds.

The ground shook harder, and a cold wind blew from the tunnel, fanning the rising flames and pushing Gilbert's hair into his face. What it meant, what that wind truly was, hit him like a punch to the chest.

Something in his face must have revealed his shock because Reuben smiled, delighted, eyes widened in mock surprise. "Hear, hear, the train is coming!" he said, clearly enjoying this supremely. "Why, I was going to shoot you, but now I think I'll wait a minute. Let you watch your friend be squashed to a pulp by the train. How does that sound?"

Hurry, monkey. Where are you? God, it was taking too long. There was a train coming—*a train coming, damn it*—and there should be no fucking train, not when Jesse was passed out on the tracks.

Gilbert bit the inside of his cheek hard enough to taste blood, trying to keep silent, keep focused. He forced his eyes to stay fixed on Reuben's face, even though, from the corner of his eye, he could glimpse little furry arms reaching down from above just behind the man's back, aiming for the clasp of his necklace. Gilbert held his breath and drew on all his experience as a cheater, because this was the most important bluff of his life, and if he glanced at that monkey, even for a second, if Reuben caught on, it would be over. Jesse would die under that train. Gilbert with a bullet between the eyes. Everybody dead.

Reuben must have felt something—the click of the clasp or maybe Vito's hand had brushed him—because his eyes went wide, and he jerked his arm back to grab at whatever he'd felt. Too late. Vito launched himself back up to the beams with his powerful legs, yanking the chain and pendant up with him. Reuben barely had time to grimace in horror before Gilbert raised his hand and closed his fingers, feeling his magic sink into Reuben's chest, clenching around his heart like claws.

The man went still, face twisted in pain, his hoarse cry cut short when Gilbert squeezed harder. He'd never caused someone's heart to burst inside their chest before, but this time, he thought wildly, feeling the thirst for blood consume his brain like the hot flames roaring all around him, this time he was going to, and he was going to fucking enjoy it.

"Screw you, Reuben—"

"No! Wait, I'm . . . I'll make you captain, give you money. Power! Everything!" Reuben begged, his voice strangled, caught in the brutal hold of Gilbert's magic. "Join me, Gilbert, and I . . . will give you everything you've always . . . dreamed of. You deserve better. You're . . . not like them, not . . . a freak."

It was true. Gilbert had dreamed of money and power and a hundred different lives other than the one he was leading now. But just because he'd wanted it didn't mean that it was truly what he needed. He understood it in that split second, and he saw it all with a clarity that left him breathless. He'd never thought he'd end up in an old circus with a ragtag gang of misfits, but it was where he belonged, and he wasn't afraid to admit it anymore.

"That's where you're mistaken," he said, and smiled. "I *am* a goddamn freak."

He clenched his fist, and Reuben's heart exploded inside his chest. The man went down without a scream, eyes wide and glassy, but Gilbert didn't stick around to look. He threw himself across the platform, leaping down onto the tracks as the train's headlight emerged from the tunnel. The wheels were already screeching on the rails, but the locomotive hurtled forward too fast, and Jesse was right behind him, still slumped on the tracks. There was no time.

For a moment, the world went silent. It was right there—his nightmare, the big, round, yellow eye of the train coming toward him, sending a paralyzing fear shooting down his spine, freezing his brain.

And then Gilbert snapped out of it, because Jesse's life was on the line. He planted his feet on the shaking tracks, set his shoulders, and spread his hands, blasting his magic at it. If it was the last thing he did in his life, he was *stopping that goddamn train*. He was vaguely aware of Jesse stirring behind him, against his legs, and then there was only the wave of power surging up inside him and pouring out, *out*, draining him, hurting him, as though it were tearing out his insides. Gilbert gritted his teeth and squeezed his eyes shut as he was blinded—by the train light or by his own, burning power, he couldn't even tell. His arms and shoulders throbbed. His muscles were on fire. It was just too much, and Gilbert had to scream, a desperate roar that ravaged his throat until he ran out of air.

Then it was over. The blinding light had dimmed, and Gilbert opened his eyes. His head hurt, his hands pressed against the warm metal of the locomotive that had stopped, huffing and wheezing, mere inches from his face. He gasped as his knees nearly gave out, and he had to lean into it, the yellow light now faded above his head. He felt empty and nauseated, and he would have keeled over to throw up if it wasn't for the fact that he had nothing left to give. He was utterly, completely empty, and the ridiculous thing was, he didn't even know if he had helped at all, if he had been the one to stop it, because he'd felt something bigger, stronger, a somewhat familiar power accompanying his, entwining with it. He knew that power, but he couldn't place it. It hadn't belonged there, and his head, his head was spinning so badly.

It was Jesse's touch, then Jesse's voice behind him, muffled as if his head were underwater, and then gentle hands pressed on his shoulders, guiding him as he turned and staggered to the edge of the platform.

"Are you all right? Gilbert, can you hear me?"

He looked at Jesse, dizzy, head buzzing loudly. Really, he was the one who should be asking that question, because there was a streak of blood down Jesse's face from a gash on his head, and he'd been passed out on the floor just a minute ago. He tried to speak, but a cough racked his chest.

The flames had now surrounded the platform, having taken over the roof, and *God* he'd somehow managed, in his blind frenzy to save Jesse, to completely ignore that there was still a fight raging on. "I'm fine. We have to help the others," he rasped, staggering toward the platform. As he'd predicted, Reuben's men had faltered once their chief had fallen, and the circus folks were pressing on, gaining the upper hand.

With a deafening screech, all the train's doors were yanked open at the same instant, and a black sea came pouring out in a rumbling, living wave. Hundreds and hundreds of roaches coated everything like spilled ink—the pavement, the walls, Reuben's men, Reuben's own body on the ground. The only spots of color left were the circus performers and their comrades, all of them, miraculously spared. The roaches parted around them, as if repulsed by a magnetic force. Gilbert couldn't look away, stunned and horrified. The desperate screams of Reuben's men were quickly cut off as the roaches devoured the flesh off their bodies.

A loud whistle caught his attention, and he turned back to see a handsome face poking out the locomotive's window. "All aboard!" Farfarello called with a wink. "The station's burning down, and this is the only way out!"

Gilbert nodded, breathless and half-choked. "You heard the man. Everyone on the train! Move!"

He helped a still-stunned Jesse into one of the now-empty train carriages, then got back off to help the others just as Constance wobbled along, pressed against Humphreys, who was painfully shuffling on his wounded tentacles. Olivia stood still, looking with a mix of horror and fascination at the roaches crawling on an almost-clean skeleton, so Gilbert snatched her up and balanced her on his hip as he reached out to help Humphreys. The roaches parted for them like the Red Sea, easily avoiding their steps and closing instantly behind them, black waters falling back into place.

"Can you make it?" Gilbert rasped, and Humphreys just nodded his head, sliding painfully toward the open door. He was leaving traces of thick, inky blood behind, and a couple of tentacles had been chopped off altogether.

"Don't worry," Humphreys wheezed, barely understandable. He was as far from human as Gilbert had ever seen him, a giant purple mound crawling forward on the floor among a flowing river of roaches. "They . . . grow back."

Gilbert pushed him onto the train with his free hand as Constance and Jesse pulled from inside, until the giant octopus was on board. As Gilbert followed suit, something hard landed on his back, clutching little arms around his neck and holding on fiercely. Vito.

As soon as he set foot in the carriage, the train shook and rumbled and started rolling forward, just as the wooden roof above the platform creaked ominously. Holding on to the open door, with Olivia still clinging to him, Gilbert saw the sea of roaches stop at once—unreal, as if they were all listening—and in an instant, the black cover coating the platform melted away as they streamed into every nook and cranny, vanishing too fast for Gilbert to keep track. The last thing he saw before the carriage disappeared into the dark tunnel ahead was the wooden beams collapse in a bout of raging flames, crushing the blood-red bones abandoned on the now-deserted platform.

Gilbert felt the train speed up and listened to the rhythmic huffing and clanking of the machine, and to the irregular breaths of the people surrounding him. In the darkness, a tentative hand found his and twined their fingers together. Gilbert blindly reached out to wrap his free arm around Jesse's shoulders, and he pulled him against his side, holding as tight as he could. He felt Jesse sigh against him and leaned his head to the side, resting his cheek on Jesse's hair, which was singed and soaked with smoke. The monkey on his back was poking its wet nose in his ear.

Gilbert closed his eyes and wondered if it would be too blasphemous to thank the devil for this.

CHAPTER 24

The train slid to a stop, and the door clanged open. Gilbert expected to find himself somewhere outside the tunnels, but they had stopped at a quiet, empty underground station he was certain he'd never seen before. And he knew every station in Shadowsea by heart. He'd slept in all of them at some point, too. But here, everything was coated in inches of dust, except a well-traveled path in the middle. Barred doors, faded posters, the gas lamps covered in cobwebs and replaced by lanterns. A ghost station, Gilbert realized, one of the many scattered around the underground, forgotten by everyone. The tunnels connecting them to the surface were said to be sealed. Why had Farfarello stopped here?

Gilbert poked his head out the door. The torches were lit, spreading the thick smell of fuel. Somebody had fixed the place up, and among all the worn-out, termite-eaten wood, there was a visibly brand-new, iron door. It was solidly encased in an iron doorframe with a big iron lock.

Hang on a second . . .

He looked around again to find there was brand-new iron all over the place. Bars crisscrossing on the floor, the walls, the ceiling. Iron lanterns. Iron locks and bolts and handles. The mere thought of stepping out there was already robbing him of his breath. He could feel the iron's pull, an emptiness growing in his chest as his magic was slowly drawn out of him.

Oh God. Farfarello had led them right into Reuben's lair.

Of course, once the count had discovered the power iron held over magic, he'd used it to magic-proof his prison, or laboratory, or whatever the hell it was, so that his prisoners—his freak prisoners—wouldn't be able to fight back with their powers.

Still, Farfarello had no reason to bring them there. They were already hurt and exhausted and half-choked to death, and they would be utterly and completely powerless as soon as they set foot on that platform.

"Magician, is that you? What the hell happened to you?"

Looking for the source of the hurried whisper, Gilbert turned to see a familiar face poking out of a narrow tunnel, its ruined wooden door removed from its hinges. A crowd of armed people filled the narrow tunnel to the brink.

So, Andrea had found the laboratory after all.

After a quick glance, she rushed to the train and took cover as her men quickly spread to occupy every strategic corner of the platform, keeping an eye on the massive bolted door. As secure as Reuben felt down there, it was unlikely he wouldn't have any guards at all, and someone must have noticed a train had just stopped there for no reason. Surely guards were gathering inside, frantic about what to do since their boss wasn't there.

"What the hell is going on?" Andrea quickly inspected the inside of the carriage, and her eyes turned sorrowful and angry. "Where's Bartholomew?"

Gilbert swallowed. "Reuben and his personal guards showed up at the station. They attacked us, and . . . I'm so sorry, Andrea. Bartholomew . . ."

"*Reuben*. God damn your filthy soul to hell," Andrea growled, slamming her fist against the wall. Then she straightened her shoulders, her eyes like sharpened blades. "Tell me that son of a bitch is dead."

"He is. I killed him myself," Gilbert assured her.

"Good. And now we'll bring down this wretched laboratory of his, if we have to tear it apart brick by brick, if we have to slaughter everyone inside." Hatred gleamed in her gaze, but Gilbert didn't think that was the best solution. It would just mean more fighting, more bloodshed. And he'd had enough for one day.

"Listen, Andrea, what if . . . if we were able to prove to them that Reuben is dead. Maybe they'll surrender, some of them at least. Might make things easier."

Andrea bared her teeth. "Right, because they're going to take my word for it. Or did you bring his head back as a souvenir?"

"We have something that could work, perhaps," Olivia's voice piped up. Gilbert turned to where she stood, her soot-stained face pale but determined. Vito was on her shoulder and was holding the iron horseshoe encrusted in shining purple amethyst. "If you show them this, maybe they'll believe."

Andrea considered it for a moment. "Maybe they will. Come on then, let's go find out."

She was already stepping off the carriage when Gilbert shook his head. "You have to take it yourself, Andrea. We can't step off the train."

She frowned. "What? Why?"

Gilbert swallowed. "The . . . all the iron. It hurts people of magic, people like us. We won't be good for anything if we touch it."

Andrea arched her brows but took it in stride. "Whatever. You're not too good now anyway, all banged up as you are. Stay hidden in here. We'll take care of it."

They did, and it didn't even take long. Once Andrea and her men broke through the door and let the henchmen inside know their boss was dead, chaos ensued. Only a few stubborn ones tried to resist and were mercilessly cut down; everyone else surrendered. They were mercenaries, after all: Reuben's men had no loyalty to the count. It wasn't worth dying for, not when they could just join another boss right away.

Andrea took over the place, ordering people around and making decisions like a captain sorting out her ship. Her men made short work of Reuben's guards, leading them away in chains and manacles—some of them already bargaining to be hired—then began the patient work of freeing the poor folks that Reuben had already trapped in there. Gilbert only had the chance to see the first few they brought out on makeshift stretchers, looking hollow and withered, moaning in pain as the iron kept pulling out whatever little magic they had left. It must have been unbearable to be in that place for days, maybe weeks. It had been less than an hour and Gilbert was already beginning to feel the ache, and so were the others huddled in the carriage with him.

Then the train door shut on its own, and the machine slowly huffed out of the ghost station.

Gilbert stood outside in the cool air, tired and banged up, as dawn came over the city, and a crowd of people gathered around the burned remains of the station. Filmore had rolled himself out at the first signs of trouble and was now grousing in a corner, offended because his kingdom had been burned down.

As for Andrea, she had a lot to do: she had Reuben's many enterprises to take over, and she was receiving an endless stream of associates who meekly pled allegiance to her. Gilbert was ready to bet none of them cared about Reuben at all; they just wanted to make sure whoever was in charge was going to continue business with them. And while Andrea may be no saint, she was better than Reuben by a long stretch. Case and point, she'd ordered the victims of Reuben's experiments transported to the Rotten Duck, and she sent for her personal physicians to assist them.

Gilbert was standing at the back of the crowd with Jesse and the others—slightly unsteady on their feet but valiantly keeping their eyes open—when Andrea jogged over to them, bright-eyed and energetic as ever. The woman did not need sleep.

"Magician! I want to thank you for killing that asshole and for warning me about his plan in the first place. I would have been in serious trouble otherwise, while now . . ." She slung her arm over his shoulder, a most satisfied expression on her face. This was the night of her triumph, when she'd finally trumped her nemesis once and for all. "You will always be welcome and protected in this town as long as I have a say. Is there anything I can do to repay you? All of you? Just name it, and it's yours."

Gilbert glanced at where Constance, Humphreys, and Olivia were huddled, exhausted and shivering. Olivia had dozed off in Constance's arms, the monkey sprawled on Humphreys's shoulder. Jesse stood beside him, shoulder to shoulder, tired but focused and proud.

There was so much Gilbert could ask for, but really, as he looked at them, there was only one thing he wanted.

"I would like a steady place for the circus in this town. A theater, maybe." He heard Jesse's breath catch. "It's hard to travel around, especially in winter. They . . . *We* need a home. A base. Somewhere we can work on our performances in peace, without worrying about how we'll survive the next month, without constantly wandering from town to town. Could you grant us that?"

Andrea laughed and clapped him hard on the shoulder. "I thought you were going to ask for much more! Consider it done, magician. I will make you the greatest act in the city, so damn popular you won't even know where to stash the money. Why, I could start a whole new line of entertainment, employ more performers. Rich people are bored, Gilbert. They always need new ways to spend their money!"

Gilbert tried to hold back a smile. "So it's settled?"

"Absolutely. Go get the rest of your troupe and come back. By the time you reach Shadowsea, the theater will be furnished and waiting for you."

Gilbert didn't have time to reply before Jesse threw himself into his arms and kissed him breathless. Andrea guffawed and returned to her business. By the time Jesse stepped back to smile at him, bright and joyous—there it was again, the wonder on his face that Gilbert would never tire of seeing—they were swept off their feet by Constance and Humphreys, who drew them in a bear hug with his tentacles.

"This is wonderful!" Constance exclaimed, squeezing Gilbert's shoulder. "It will be such a relief, not having to worry about making ends meet during the winter."

"And sssome of the folksss this Reuben had already gathered might be interested in working with usss," Humphreys added. He still sounded wheezy but stronger, like all the new prospects were giving him fresh energy. "I understand there were a few dozen already. We could have a much bigger show, with many different actsss. The possibilities are endlessss."

Gilbert slung his arm around Jesse's shoulders and squeezed him, smiling. "Who knows, this might just be the starting point to those fame and riches we spoke about."

"And what about the devil? What did he do next?"

Bobbie and Ethel were resting their chins on their hands, listening with rapt expressions on their faces. Gilbert spread his arms as Emilia, happily nestled back in his scarf, nosed at his neck.

"Nothing. That was it. He drove off on the train at full throttle, singing at the top of his voice about how he was on a railway to Hell or some such."

There had been just one stolen moment, that Gilbert was certainly not going to share with the twins, where Farfarello had leaned from the window, looking at Jesse with a sweet sadness in his eyes and a smile on his lips. Jesse had lifted his hand, and the devil had clasped it for an instant, as they smiled quietly at each other.

It had been surprisingly easy to watch. In fact, it had made something inside Gilbert feel stupidly good. As much as he hated to admit it, the devil had grown on him, and those two deserved to say their good-byes. And Gilbert was glad that they had parted on good terms. He'd seen the raw pain that their unfinished business had caused Jesse, and he didn't want to see that expression on his lover's face ever again.

Gilbert smiled and looked around. He and the others were gathered around the canteen table in the first warm afternoon of sunshine that Gilbert could remember spending with the circus. They'd all slept in the carriages, provided by Andrea, that were taking them to the Rotten Duck, and had woken up back in the circus way after lunchtime—including Olivia, who had decided to join them.

The news of their future in Shadowsea had been welcomed with unfettered joy, and everyone was serene and hopeful, already fussing around the costumes wagon to prepare for their trip to the city. They all wanted to look their best, like "proper city toffs," Hugo had said.

Olivia yawned loudly. "Humph. I know the story already! I'm bored," she complained, swinging her legs from the bench. Then she turned to the twins. "Do you want to go play?"

"Of course!" Bobbie replied enthusiastically. "Come on, we have to show you everything before we leave!" The three girls left the table, already deep in conversation, and within a few minutes they were running around, caught up in the new game.

"It was about time we had someone around their age in the circus," Constance commented, finishing her cup of coffee. "And this change will be good for them too. Growing up with a more stable home, with more folks around besides a handful of old freaks, will do wonders for them. For all of us, I think. After everything we've been through, lately..."

Everyone just nodded, in silence, the excitement vibrating in the air, the energy almost palpable. She was absolutely right: it was only fair that they should finally catch a break. And as Gilbert looked at the faces of his friends—hopeful, relieved, full of anticipation—he thought that maybe this new beginning, so full of unexplored possibilities, was exactly what they had earned.

The warm afternoon turned to dusk, and Gilbert sat on his wagon's steps, eyes closed, determined to enjoy it until the very last ray of sunshine. It was doing wonders for his stiff, aching muscles, and he couldn't remember the last time he'd felt so good, as if the sun was thawing ice that had been clinging to his very bones.

Laughter and yells came from behind the tent, and Gilbert cracked one eye open to see Olivia and the twins run by, closely followed by a monkey, a hen, a brown bear in a feathered headpiece, and a colossal clockwork elephant with a stovepipe hat. He chuckled at the strange procession as Emilia wiggled in his scarf, poking curiously out.

"Looks like they're having fun," a familiar voice said softly.

Gilbert squinted. Jesse was standing beside the wagon with his hands in his pockets, the same small smile on his lips that had been there the whole day. Gilbert liked it. It suited him. So different from the permanent frown Jesse had sported when they'd first met.

"Looks like everybody is," Gilbert said, pointing to where Hugo had emerged from between the caravans, wearing a shimmering sapphire suit and a plumed hat almost as tall as he was. He twirled and walked back to where he'd come from, welcomed by the whistles and shouts of the others. Gilbert patted the steps. "What about you?"

Jesse sat down, snuggling against his side. Whatever had made him reluctant to show his affection previously seemed to be gone, left to burn to ashes in that station. Or maybe, it had been left on that train along with Farfarello. Gilbert rested his arm on Jesse's shoulder and gently caressed his head, fingers combing through the singed red hair.

"I'm . . . relieved. I guess that's the only way I can explain it." Jesse leaned into Gilbert's touch like a cat. "I can't remember the last time I felt so free. So confident about all this. About the future."

Gilbert turned to brush a kiss against Jesse's hair as they watched the girls run back and forth, chasing after Mildred, who was now perched on her unicycle. "Things are going to be different from now on. Maybe we can finally stop hiding."

Jesse's eyes went wide. Something told Gilbert that he hadn't quite realized what moving to the city would entail. "Stop hiding," he repeated slowly, as if he was savoring the words. After being shut inside the circus for almost two centuries, it must be difficult to imagine stepping out again. Well, Gilbert was from the outside, and he was more than willing to hold Jesse's hands as he timidly poked his head back out into the world.

"I know this place is a refuge for many of us." Almost holding his breath, Gilbert reached over to gently take one of Jesse's hands in his. His skin was warm, and Gilbert rubbed it in gentle circles with his thumb. "But maybe, maybe we are just about ready, just about healed enough to try to be part of the world. We'll do it together. All right?"

Jesse looked him in the eye, seeming full of questions, and Gilbert held his gaze with determination. He was there, and he would help. There was nothing to be afraid of. Then Jesse's lips stretched into an almost dreamy smile, and there it was again—the sheer wonder.

"Yes," he whispered, barely louder than a breath. He clutched Gilbert's hand. "Together. I would love that."

And in that moment, Gilbert knew what he had to do.

That night, he untangled himself from Jesse's embrace and snuck over to the black wagon. The door creaked open, and it was dark inside, except for the cool light cast by the lamps. The flames were blue and dancing, will-o'-the-wisps floating in that small traveling cemetery of theirs. Gilbert stepped between the wooden shelves bolted to the walls, lined with dusty, black urns that were tied in place with ropes. That was all the wagon held: the ghastly lamps, two rows of shelves, a handful of urns, and a lone, moth-eaten black velvet armchair at the far end.

Gilbert wasn't sure what he was doing made sense, it just felt right to go there. It had to be the right place. And as he stepped inside, he thought he felt something so warm and comforting that it didn't seem real float up from the urns like steam from warm water, enveloping him. He closed his eyes and felt Dora's calming presence and a multitude of others he didn't recognize. But, whoever they were, they surrounded him with nothing but benevolence. As if assuring him that he was making the right choice.

When he opened his eyes again, Farfarello was sitting on the velvet armchair, cane resting in his lap.

The will-o'-the-wisp lamps cast a cold reflection on his polished skin, giving his beauty an even more supernatural quality. The light glinted off the knob on his cane, and it looked like the spider was dancing, its little legs spinning around and around. Farfarello waved his hand, and a seat materialized for Gilbert, and he accepted it with a nod. He leaned forward, his stomach in knots, his hands folded.

Sitting opposite a silent devil, between rows of ashes, the silence seemed eternal.

Finally, he cleared his throat. "I wasn't sure if I would find 'you here."

Farfarello shrugged. "Well, I had a feeling you might want to see me."

Gilbert's throat closed up with sudden nervousness, and he realized he hadn't planned anything to say. He knew—he just *knew*—that this was the last time Farfarello would come, and there was so much he wanted to ask, wanted to know. About Jesse all those years ago, young and reckless, about how it had happened, that something that had been born between them. About Hell and what he should expect once he got there. About Farfarello himself, what he wanted, who he really was. But somehow, none of those questions made it past the lump in his throat.

"I never thought devils could be sad," he blurted out instead. That caught Farfarello by surprise, it seemed. Well, Gilbert too. "I thought you were supposed to be, I don't know, without emotion. Maybe angry and evil and . . . you know." He waved his hand, pointlessly. "It's just . . . you *look* sad."

Farfarello's lips curled in a smile. Not the constant, mocking smile Gilbert had come to expect from him, but something more genuine. Certainly not what he'd expect to see on the face of any devil. "I suppose I am, yes. A little sad." He tapped his fingers on his cane, and the spider ran up his hand, a silver gleam on that mahogany skin. "But it's long past time I let go of this particular folly. I'm not the one who can make him happy. I trust you will do a better job of it."

Gilbert kept his mouth shut, barely. *Oh.* He was not expecting that, either.

"But you're not here to discuss my hopes and dreams, now, are you, Gilbert?" Farfarello stared knowingly at him. Something told Gilbert the devil knew exactly what he was doing there. So he cleared his throat and said it.

"I want in. I want in on Jesse's part of the deal. I know he has to be alive for a long time, maybe forever, and I . . ." He swallowed, looking Farfarello in the eye, and tried to keep his voice steady. "I don't want him to go through it alone."

Farfarello's expression was unreadable. He tapped his cane on his hand. "And I assume you've thought about the consequences, yes? You will be trapped in the circus for as long as it will live—not just in spirit, but alive, like Jesse. You've heard how hard it can get. Jesse told you. Forever is a hell of a commitment to make without even asking the person you're making it for."

Gilbert's face heated. Damn. Farfarello always *had* to know everything, didn't he? It was starting to get annoying.

"I know. That's fine." Gilbert straightened up. "Look, I know you must think I'm some sort of idiot. But . . . I just . . . I want in. That's all. I want to be here with Jesse, for Jesse, through all of this. I want to help him make this circus a home for others like us."

"Other *freaks*?" Farfarello's smile was faint. Gilbert nodded, though. The word didn't burn anymore.

"Yes. Freaks like us, like me." He swallowed. "I am not afraid anymore."

"Well, magician, it would seem you have learned your lesson." Farfarello tilted his head to the side. "And if someone is allowed a little idiocy, it's a human in love."

"So you will do it? Even though you already own my soul? I know there's nothing else I can give you, but—"

"Yes, Gilbert, I will. Gladly." He paused as something trembled on his lips—a smile so gentle and nostalgic that Gilbert could hardly believe he was seeing it on a devil's face. "Being loved by him was . . . Well, you will find out yourself, Gilbert. And trust me when I say—and I never thought I would say this to a human—you are so *damn* lucky. Don't make the same mistakes I did."

Gilbert was left breathless, utterly crushed under the magnitude of the connection they shared in that one moment. "I will do my best. Thank you."

"Good." Farfarello rubbed his hands, something sparking to life within him, as the odd vulnerability vanished from his features, replaced by his trademark cocky grin. It was time for business. "Now, let's seal this deal, shall we? Give me your hand. Don't worry, it won't hurt a bit."

The knots in his stomach melted into a quiver of excitement, and Gilbert extended his hand. God, he was really doing this. It was so huge, he should have been terrified, and yet, he just felt elated. The silver spider crawled onto his palm, his wrist. Gilbert could feel Farfarello's eyes on him, and every little pinprick of those eight silver legs on his skin.

It was still dark when he went back to the wagon. God, the most important decision of his life—the second one of those he'd made within a few months, at least—and it had taken, again, just a handful of minutes. It seemed to have become a habit of his.

Emilia was dozing on top of the armchair, and Jesse was still asleep in bed, buried under a mound of blankets. The flickering light of one single lamp made the red furniture, the quilted fabrics, seem even warmer and cozier. Gilbert was starting to like this whole having-a-home thing. He could really get used to it.

He rubbed Emilia's head with one finger, then quickly took off his clothes and slipped back under the covers. Jesse mumbled and nuzzled close to him, placing a light kiss on his shoulder. Gilbert loved having that warm body pressed against his, loved Jesse's beautiful sleepy face, his red hair spilling on the pillow. He loved everything about this man, and he would get around to telling him, one of these days.

"You're cold," Jesse murmured with a yawn. "Where did you go?"

"Nowhere, darling. Go back to sleep." Gilbert pressed a kiss to Jesse's hair as he sleepily tucked his head under Gilbert's chin, and he wrapped his arm around Jesse, reveling in his warmth. He closed his eyes and murmured, "I'm not going anywhere anytime soon."

And he had never meant anything more in his life.

Explore the rest of the *Deal with a Devil* series:
riptidepublishing.com/titles/devil-crossroads

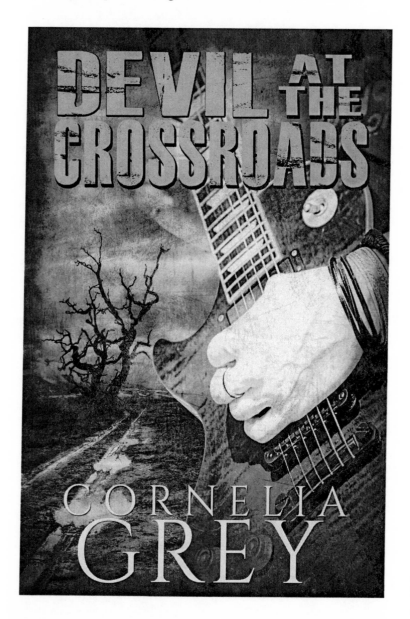

Dear Reader,

Thank you for reading Cornelia Grey's *The Circus of the Damned*!

We know your time is precious and you have many, many entertainment options, so it means a lot that you've chosen to spend your time reading. We really hope you enjoyed it.

We'd be honored if you'd consider posting a review—good or bad—on sites like **Amazon, Barnes & Noble, Kobo, Goodreads, Twitter, Facebook, Tumblr,** and your blog or website. We'd also be honored if you told your friends and family about this book. Word of mouth is a book's lifeblood!

For more information on upcoming releases, author interviews, blog tours, contests, giveaways, and more, please sign up for our weekly, spam-free newsletter and visit us around the web:

Newsletter: tinyurl.com/RiptideSignup
Twitter: twitter.com/RiptideBooks
Facebook: facebook.com/RiptidePublishing
Goodreads: tinyurl.com/RiptideOnGoodreads
Tumblr: riptidepublishing.tumblr.com

Thank you so much for Reading the Rainbow!

RiptidePublishing.com

ACKNOWLEDGMENTS

I'd like to thank my wonderful editor, Danielle Poiesz, who stuck by me with endless patience, whipped this novel into shape, and supported me through a very difficult time.

Thank you to my dearest friend Seraf, who let me ramble on about devils and circuses over countless cups of tea and pushed me to believe in myself when I couldn't.

And thank you to the folks at Riptide Publishing, who were amazing and patient, and always helped me out whenever I needed.

ALSO BY
CORNELIA GREY

ABOUT THE AUTHOR

Cornelia Grey is a creative writing student fresh out of university, with a penchant for fine arts and the blues. Born and raised in the hills of Northern Italy, where she collected her share of poetry and narrative prizes, Cornelia moved to London to pursue her studies.

After graduating with top grades, she is now busy with internships: literary agencies, publishing houses, and creative departments handling book series, among others. She also works as a freelance translator.

She likes cats, knitting, performing in theater, going to museums, collecting mugs, and hanging out with her grandma. When writing, she favors curious, surreal stories, steampunk, and mixed-genre fiction. Her heroes are always underdogs, and she loves them for it.

Connect with Cornelia:
Website: corneliagrey.com
Blog: corneliagrey.blogspot.com
LiveJournal: corneliagrey.livejournal.com
Twitter: @corneliagrey
Facebook: facebook.com/corneliagrey
Goodreads: goodreads.com/Cornelia_Grey

Enjoy this book?
Find more fantasy romance at
RiptidePublishing.com!

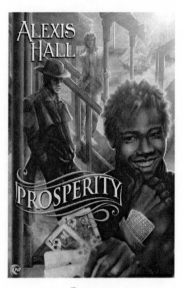

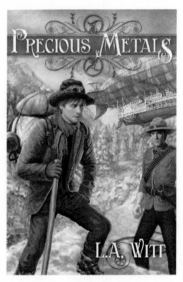

Prosperity
ISBN: 978-1-62649-177-9

Precious Metals
ISBN: 978-1-62649-175-5

Earn Bonus Bucks!

Earn 1 Bonus Buck for each dollar you spend. Find out how at
RiptidePublishing.com/news/bonus-bucks.

Win Free Ebooks for a Year!

Pre-order coming soon titles directly through our site and you'll
receive one entry into a drawing to win free books for a year! Get
the details at RiptidePublishing.com/contests.

CPSIA information can be obtained at www.ICGtesting.com
Printed in the USA
LVOW08s1604101114

412895LV00006B/745/P

9 781626 491663